ADAM PALMER

The Moses Legacy

AVON

AVON

A division of HarperCollins*Publishers*
77–85 Fulham Palace Road,
London W6 8JB

www.harpercollins.co.uk

A Paperback Original 2011
1

Copyright © Adam Palmer 2011

Adam Palmer asserts the moral right to
be identified as the author of this work

A catalogue record for this book is
available from the British Library

ISBN-13: 978-1-84756-184-8

Set in Minion by Palimpsest Book Production Limited,
Falkirk, Stirlingshire

Printed and bound in Great Britain by
Clays Ltd, St Ives plc

Mixed Sources
Product group from well-managed
forests and other controlled sources
www.fsc.org   Cert no. SW-COC-001806
© 1996 Forest Stewardship Council

FSC is a non-profit international organisation established
to promote the responsible management of the world's forests.
Products carrying the FSC label are independently certified
to assure consumers that they come from forests that are managed
to meet the social, economic and ecological needs
of present and future generations.

Find out more about HarperCollins and the environment at
www.harpercollins.co.uk/green

THE MOSES LEGACY

Adam Palmer is a polymath – well-read in many fields and disciplines. He has studied across a number of subjects ranging from the Sciences to Ancient History. His work experience includes everything from computer software to private investigation. He is British but has lived abroad extensively.

For my cousin Avi, fellow writer and most generous source of encouragement, and to Ira who first put me on to this theme by introducing me to Freud's theory on Moses and Akhenaten.

But mostly for my father.

Family tree of the Pharaohs – the later part of the Eighteenth Dynasty (circa 1427 BC to 1292 BC)

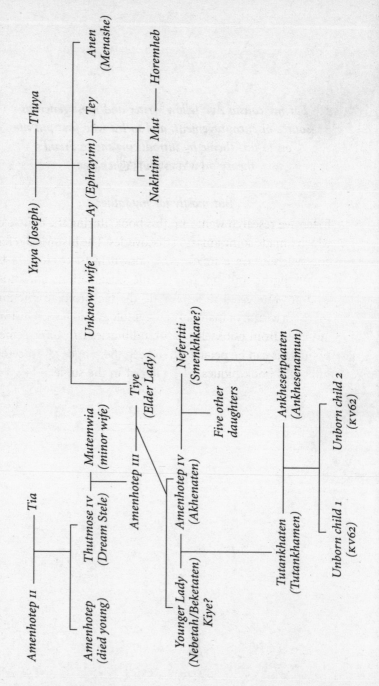

Foreword

Extensive research went into this book, during the course of which I made some amazing discoveries. The historical references herein are a mixture of known facts, conjecture by Egyptologists and my own fertile imagination. For those who are interested in separating the fact from the fiction, there is a wealth of material on Egyptology and Jewish history available from booksellers and in libraries (if our esteemed politicians can be persuaded to keep them open). I sincerely hope this book piques your interest in the subject.

Prologue

'Joshua, my time is coming and the mantle of leadership will pass to you.'

The white-haired man was lying down in the cave on a bed of hay, looking at the one whom he had chosen as his successor. The younger man, a dark-haired forty-year-old, had torn his robes in mourning, while the older man yet lived. There were tears of grief in his eyes.

'I will not leave your side, my teacher.'

Joshua had long known that this day would come, that one day the man who had led the Israelites out of slavery in Egypt would be taken to God's bosom and that he, the loyal disciple, would take over the mantle of leadership from the man to whom he owed so much. Yet he still felt ill-prepared for the duties that would fall upon him. It wasn't just the fact that this once vibrant man was now reduced to the frail figure before him. It was also the terrifying sight of the red lesions on his mentor's flesh that looked like fiery snakes.

'I am not long for this earth, Joshua. When I die, you must bury me here and leave this place forever.'

From the valley below the sound of the murmuring of the people, as they awaited news of their leader, billowed up to the cave on the desert wind.

'But why must we leave?' asked Joshua. 'Why can we not stay here and make peace with the Snake God?'

'Because the Snake God is false!' The old man's voice resonated once again with the strength of his youth. The harsh tone instilled his disciple with fear and joy in equal measure. Despite his age and the ravages of disease, his vitality had not yet deserted him. 'That is why Jehovah has punished us. It was for our appeasement of the Snake God that we were chastised with disease. Jehovah commanded us to have no other gods before him and yet we built that . . .' he waved his arm towards the cave entrance, '. . . that monstrous *idol* to the Snake God.'

'Then I shall tear down the monument and show the Snake God that we are loyal only to Jehovah,' the younger man replied earnestly.

'That is not enough. This place is cursed. You must lead the people across the river into the Promised Land, the land flowing with milk and honey. Jehovah your God will go with you.'

'But we are weak. We cannot fight the Canaanites. They are giants and we were like grasshoppers in their eyes.'

A blazing fire lit up the old man's eyes. '*Enough!* Do you really believe those foolish rantings? Did not Caleb tell us that Jehovah will give us strength to conquer them?'

'But they are more numerous than we.'

The old man's voice mellowed again, as if he had spent himself with his wrath and had no more fight left in him. 'Then live in the hills not in the valleys, and leave them alone until you are ready. Bide your time, Joshua, just as I bided my time.'

Joshua nodded. But the teacher was not finished. Through his frailty, the old man raised his head and shoulders to speak one more time. Joshua leaned forward to place his ear next to the mouth of Moses.

'Be strong and courageous. Because you will lead the people into the land which Jehovah promised their fathers . . . and you will make it their legacy.'

Chapter 1

Khamsin – the hot slow dry wind that blows in from the west.

Derived from the Arabic word for 'fifty' because according to Arab tradition, it is supposed to blow for fifty days during the course of the year.

The lean nineteen-year-old from West London was sweltering, unaccustomed to these desert conditions. At least the heat was *dry*, he thought; that made it just about bearable. All he had to do was remember to drink plenty of water. Having holidayed once in Sharm el-Sheikh, he was grateful that it wasn't humid here like it was on the coast. But even so, it was weather for relaxing by a hotel swimming pool, not for working on an archaeological dig.

Now, in the heat of a morning in late March, over a dozen fit young students worked in their designated areas under the watchful eyes of Egyptian soldiers. Dressed in t-shirts and Bermuda shorts (referred to locally as 'Islamic shorts' because of their relative modesty), these enthusiastic volunteers came from all over the world: Egypt, Europe, South America, even Australia and New Zealand. Each volunteer was assigned an area of one metre square, marked out on a grid with flags stating their co-ordinates.

It was painstaking work. Armed with a metal trowel,

4

plastic scoop and small-headed brush for cleaning larger finds, the youth dug out to a depth of six inches below the previous level, put the contents into his bucket and took it over to the two volunteers who operated the sieve screens. The pair were known as JJ because of their initials: Joel and Jane. Though similar in age – he at the end of his teens, she barely out of hers – they were an unlikely team: the wiry, ginger-haired nerd and the bottle blonde with a cheerleader body. But they had been thrown together by chance and now the two of them were inextricably linked by this coincidence of nomenclature.

Joel had been assigned to this relatively simple job because of his lack of experience, but it was a role that carried its fair share of responsibility. And as the volunteer from London turned up at his shoulder with a bucketful of sand and pebbles, Joel sighed – he wasn't expecting anything to break the monotony of the day.

From a corner of the dig site, the work was being overseen by a blonde woman with a commanding presence and an almost Nordic appearance. She preferred to watch from a distance, because whenever she wandered around the site, people stopped their work to look at her, especially the men.

It was an understandable reaction – she was not a woman whom it was easy to ignore. Her back was both broad and straight, and her well-toned thighs and arms subtly muscular. But her torso was by no means devoid of body fat. In a woman of average height, this combination of muscle and fat would have made her look rather squat, but at five foot eleven she towered over most other women and was perfectly proportioned, especially in the eyes of men.

She was Gabrielle Gusack, a young Viennese archaeologist, and she was looking at the work with a mixture of exhaustion and pride. It had taken a lot of determination and a healthy dose of diplomacy to get this dig approved. The site was in a restricted military area at the foot of Mount Hashem el-Tarif, closely guarded by the Egyptian army due to its proximity to the Israeli border, and for this reason had never been subjected to proper archaeological excavation, despite hints and signs that it might be of historical significance.

After some delicate lobbying, the authorities gave the dig an official green light, albeit with some stringent security conditions attached; no mobile phones or cameras were to be brought to the site and only an official cameraman working for the Supreme Council of Antiquities would be allowed to take pictures. Thus the Egyptian authorities could control the flow of information that came out of the dig.

It was the SCA and its head, Akil Mansoor, that had proved to be the lynchpin of this whole project. Mansoor was not only an enthusiastic supporter of the project, but also Gabrielle's mentor – she had done her PhD under him at the University of Cairo, and their friendship had proved enduring, if somewhat volatile at times. He was also a friend of her uncle, the much respected British biblical historian, Harrison Carmichael. Perhaps most important of all, he was the Vice Minister of Culture.

But not even he could override security considerations or the wishes of the Egyptian military, and he had been forced to engage in a certain amount of horse-trading as he gingerly tiptoed around the objections and won over the key decision-makers in the political and military hierarchy.

And now with the job of brokering the deal accomplished, he stayed away from the site and let the enthusiastic kids rise to the challenge of 'painting the fence' – with his young, attractive protégée playing the role of Tom Sawyer. Of course, if they found anything exciting, he would lose no time in going out there to make the official announcement in front of the cameras.

The volunteer who had just emptied his bucket into the sieve screen that Joel was operating didn't wait to see the results, he simply returned to his digging. The screen consisted of a four-sided wooden box with a quarter-inch metal mesh 'floor' and a pair of handles that could be used to shake it.

Joel shook the screen now to begin the separation process, and as the sand fell away through the mesh, a large number of stone fragments remained. Normally the residue proved to be nothing but desert pebbles, but this time something caught his eye. Mindful of Gabrielle's instruction to observe the residue before bagging it up, he looked more closely, blinked and then looked again.

It wasn't that the stones were of any radically different material – quite the contrary: they were typical of the local stone – nor were they any larger than usual. And they certainly didn't have the glint of noble metals or the crystalline glow of precious stones. No, it was just that these stones, or rather fragments of stone, seemed to have markings on them.

Joel picked one up and held it closer to get a better look. Turning it this way and that, he noticed that on one side it seemed to have some engraved shapes. The shapes were too simple to be hieroglyphics and they looked too unfamiliar to be any alphabet that he knew. But they did look like writing, not merely random markings.

He picked up another and looked at it, then another and then yet another. He noticed some repetition of the symbols, which confirmed his suspicion that there was nothing random about these engravings. They had been made purposively, by a human hand. And that made this a *find*!

He could just bag it up and mark it, leaving the others to figure out its significance in due course, but something about this discovery appealed to his ego. He wanted some small share of the kudos, even if someone else had dug it up, and someone more knowledgeable than himself would interpret it. And in any case, if it was something important, they would surely want to know about it *now*.

Joel realized that he had been daydreaming and Jane had noticed that something was up.

'What?' she asked, in that ever cheerful way of hers.

He held out one of the stone fragments and let her look at it, making sure that she didn't actually get her hands on it.

'Oh . . . my . . . *God*!' she blurted out.

Fearing that others people would hear and start gathering round before he had had a chance to claim his glory, he threw the fragments into a plastic bag and raced over to Professor Gusack, suppressing the urge to cry out aloud like Archimedes on his homeward sprint from the public bath house.

While Joel was racing off to claim his share of the glory, Jane felt her breath constricting. Unlike Joel, she understood the full significance of what she had just seen. And she had to do something about it.

Mumbling some excuse about a stomach bug, she raced off to the latrines, which were little more than holes in the ground with individual booths around each drop. She closed and bolted the door behind her and whipped out her slender mobile phone from the pocket of her combat trousers. She was supposed to have handed it in to the security people at the entrance to the camp, but she had been forewarned of this in advance, so she had made sure she had two mobiles. The large flashy one she had handed over meekly with a look of

8

disappointment. But this small thin one with its limited features, she had retained. She knew that the male soldiers wouldn't frisk a woman, and they had no female soldiers at hand to do the job. So her secret was safe.

Safely ensconced in the latrine, she frantically keyed in a message and hit the 'Send' button. A minute later her message appeared on another phone six thousand miles away. It said: *They found the stones.*

Chapter 2

'I got the message at two in the morning,' said Arthur Morris.

They were seated round an oval cherrywood table in a small meeting room; two men in their fifties and a woman in her early forties. Morris was practically bald, except for two small, neatly combed patches on either side of the crown that were silver, but with some slight remnant of the brown that it had once been. His eyes were also brown and held just a hint of menace, warning friend and foe alike that he was a man not to be denied his wishes.

Behind him, a 555-foot obelisk glinted in the morning sun, forming a backdrop to their tense gathering.

'Would they have had time to figure it out yet?' asked the second man.

He was slightly older than Morris, with a short, neatly-trimmed beard. He was also taller and thinner. But the main contrast between them was the informality of his attire. A pair of light summer trousers and a beige sweater with the word 'Georgetown' written across it. Arthur Morris, on the other hand, was impeccably clad in a dark-blue suit. He favoured blue over grey and solid over pinstripe because he had read somewhere that they were signs of political conservatism.

'She had to be brief in her text message, Professor. But

the fact that she sent the message with no qualifications or reservations suggests that they probably did. And even if they didn't, it won't take them long. They're not stupid and we must assume that things will start moving quickly from here on in.'

'I don't know how you can use Jane like that,' said the woman uneasily. 'She's just a child.'

Morris thought for a moment before answering slowly and deliberately. 'She doesn't need to understand the whys and wherefores.'

'But if she doesn't even understand our cause, then how can she support it?'

The woman – Audrey Milne – had once been a trophy wife. Though she had long ceased to be the spring chicken who had once attracted her husband via his libido, she had retained her position in his heart and home by good grooming, a rigorous fitness regime, an adroit and skilful manner in the salon, and most important of all, a readiness to accept her husband's serial infidelity with stoic equanimity.

Her husband had always known that she would never embarrass him professionally or personally and she knew how to host a dinner party and say the right things to the right people at the right time. With those social skills and her selective blindness to her husband's extra-curricular activities, there was no need for him to cut her loose. And for her part, she had no reason to *break* loose. In their relationship, the whole was greater than the sum of the parts.

She was, however, no longer a trophy wife. She was now a trophy widow.

'Jane understands family loyalty,' said Morris. 'That means she's loyal to *me*. That's all that matters.'

'Carmichael might be a problem,' said the professor. 'Once the shit hits the fan.'

'Why?' asked Audrey Milne defensively. 'A befuddled old man suffering from dementia . . .'

The professor looked at her irritably. He had never really liked her and the only reason she was even at this meeting was because she had inherited proprietorship of a chain of fifteen newspapers from her husband. He had served the cause well, but had died towards the end of the previous year. So now, if their work was to continue unhindered, they needed his widow on-board, or at least access to her newspapers.

The Internet was fine for creating publicity, but what it couldn't do was create credibility. A prestigious newspaper, on the other hand, lent the imprimatur of its authority to any story that went out under its masthead. That made Audrey Milne a powerful ally in their cause.

'He's already getting agitated over the fact that his paper still hasn't been published.'

'But the journal is only published once a year.'

'He *knows* that, Audrey. But he's angry that we missed the deadline for the last edition.'

'So tell him that it took a few months to do a proper peer review. He's an academic. He'll understand.'

'I *did* that!' the professor snapped. 'But he's still upset about it. At one point he even threatened to pull the plug and send it to another journal.'

Ignoring their bickering, Arthur Morris played with the handle of his walking stick. It was an elaborate, overly ornate affair made of lacquered mahogany topped with a bronze snake head.

'But if they've found the stone fragments,' said Audrey, 'then doesn't that make it irrelevant what Carmichael does?'

Morris looked at Audrey as if trying to weigh up the subtext to what she was saying.

'Whatever comes out of Egypt, we can control. It may even lead us to solve the questions posed by Carmichael's research. But Carmichael himself is a problem. He isn't one of us and he would resent any attempt to recruit him.'

'He probably wouldn't even understand it,' said Audrey, 'in his mental state.'

'We can't take a chance,' said the professor.

'I agree.' This was Morris. And his word on the issue was final.

'So what are you going to do?' asked Audrey.

'We need to send someone to deal with the problem.'

Morris's mobile beeped. He took it out and cast a quick glance at the message.

Foreign Aid Bill vote 20 mins.

'Sorry,' said Senator Morris, 'we'll have to cut this short.'

'Who are you going to send?' asked Audrey hesitantly.

'Someone whose loyalty is unwavering and whose talent for doing the work is unequalled.'

Audrey closed her eyes as she uttered the next word. 'Goliath?'

Chapter 3

'It's a pity you didn't find the rest,' said Akil Mansoor in a quiet monotone.

'Assuming there is a "rest",' Gabrielle replied.

'Of course there's a rest!'

They were in the lab at the University of Cairo that the Supreme Council of Antiquities used for examining ancient Egyptian artefacts. Mansoor was somewhat shorter than Gabrielle and was showing signs of a middle-aged paunch. But his white hair gave him a kind of patrician gravitas that made others around him instantly recognize his academic authority.

'We branched out radially from the square where it was found,' Gabrielle explained, 'stopping at forty-nine square metres.'

The air conditioning had failed again and so Mansoor left three buttons undone on his check shirt and used a handkerchief to wipe the area between his chin and neck. The assembled fragments of stone looked like an incomplete jigsaw puzzle. Mansoor moved to his left, as if to get a better view of the engraved characters on the surface, brushing against Gabrielle in the process. She didn't say anything, but moved away quietly to the other side of the workbench to give him room to view the stone fragments.

Temporarily distracted from the arrangement of stones, he watched her athletic body, more with a sense of curiosity than outright lust. He remembered that she had been a competitive swimmer, winning a silver medal for Austria in the European Student Games. Even now, in her tight-fitting T-shirt and dark blue jeans, she cut a striking figure.

'The distribution of fragments was like a V formation from the main group.' Her words snapped him out of his thoughts. 'That would suggest that the stones had been dropped or thrown from a certain position and smashed outwardly in the same direction. So working outward radially any further made no sense.'

'You could have excavated another line of squares on the far side, to follow up your V distribution theory.' His tone was impatient.

'We *did*. And we found another two pieces. But they were both quite small, without any engravings. The only reason we think it might have formed part of the stone or stones is because of the shape. One of the students on the dig is a physics graduate and he said they looked like break lines. He also told us that lighter pieces travel further when they bounce.'

'And?' Mansoor prompted.

'Well, he also said that with stone lighter means smaller, and that meant that if we found any more fragments, they'd be too small to physically handle to put them together.'

Mansoor shook his head. 'We've got people who can do that with tweezers and glue. Besides, nowadays we scan them in 3-D and then examine them on a computer screen. I'm surprised your physics student didn't tell you that.'

There was more than a hint of mockery in his tone.

'I thought it was more important to bring back what we already found.'

'I figured as much when you phoned me on your mad dash to Sharm el-Sheikh Airport.'

'Well, it's not as if the remaining stones are going to get up and walk away.'

Mansoor frowned at Gabrielle's levity. She should have remembered that he was an utterly humourless man, and proud of the fact.

'We can carry on today. I put the team on standby, waiting for your decision. I'd already pulled them off their regular duties to concentrate on this find. I didn't want to put them back on the areas they were digging because they're all too excited about—'

'*You told them your theory?*' he blurted out in a mixture of shock and fear.

'I didn't *tell* them,' replied Gabrielle. Then after a few seconds she added, 'But it must have been fairly obvious.'

'To an overenthusiastic kid, perhaps. Not to a serious scholar.'

'I think a credible case can be made out.' Her tone was defensive. She knew that Mansoor was always sceptical about Big Theories.

'Let's keep some sense of proportion. So far all we can say is that we have fragments of two stone tablets with an old, somewhat simple linear script with repeated characters engraved on them.'

'But it is definitely *two* stones?' she asked cautiously.

'We have seven corner pieces. That suggests *at least* two separate stones.'

'What's your assessment of the writing?'

Mansoor peered at it carefully. 'Well, the style is a bit like hieroglyphics, but only the simplest hieroglyphics. In fact, some of the symbols are quite recognizable – if we can find the right light to view them in.'

16

'So it can't be a diplomatic document or treaty.'

'If it was, it would be written in Akkadian cuneiform.'

'And that also rules out Hittite and Sumerian.'

'Exactly,' Mansoor confirmed.

'I'm wondering if this could be our Knossos.'

'This isn't Mycenaean or Minoan, Professor Gusack; I can assure you of that!'

'I didn't mean that,' replied Gabrielle irritably. 'I mean another syllable alphabet, like Linear A or Linear B.'

'And I suppose you were hoping to be the next Michael Ventris.'

'Well, it would be nice to follow in the footsteps of the man who rewrote ancient Greek history.'

'Nice, perhaps. Likely, no.'

'What makes you so sure?'

Mansoor's voice took on a dour tone. 'Well, as far as I can tell, there aren't enough unique characters for a syllable alphabet.'

'So it's . . . what? A phonetic alphabet?'

'Precisely. More specifically, an *abjad*. No vowels – just consonants.'

'Aramaic? Phoenician?' She didn't bother to include Hebrew or Arabic in her question, because both were familiar to her and she could tell immediately that it wasn't either.

'It doesn't look all that much like Aramaic. It might bear some vague comparison to Phoenician.'

'Vague comparison?' Gabrielle echoed.

'It's hard to tell until we can look at them under the right lighting conditions. I'll get one of the photo experts to take some pictures and play around with the contrast then we'll take another look.'

'But what's your gut instinct?'

Mansoor looked at Gabrielle with mild irritation. She was

being pushy. He decided nevertheless to hazard a preliminary speculation.

'It reminds me of the Serabit el-Khadim inscriptions.'

'Proto-Sinaitic?'

'Yes.'

Proto-Sinaitic was one of the oldest phonetic alphabets ever used – if not *the* oldest – dating back nearly 4,000 years. The name was derived from the Greek 'proto' meaning first and the place where the writings in the alphabet were initially discovered: Sinai. Some thirty engravings of the script had been found in Sinai at the turquoise mines at Serabit el-Khadim, once used as a penal colony by ancient Egypt.

'Can you translate it?'

Mansoor was amused by Gabrielle's eagerness.

'Well, assuming I'm right, we know how it sounds, but not what it means.'

The letters of the Proto-Sinaitic alphabet had been matched to their equivalent letters in all the other main consonant alphabets – like Hebrew and Arabic – so the pronunciation was reasonably certain. But the underlying language was unknown. Was it an ancient form of Hebrew even older than the Bible itself? Some generic Semitic language that later split up into several different languages? Or was the same alphabet used for a whole variety of languages that were already different, and spoken all around the Middle East?

'Maybe this could be our Rosetta Stone.'

The Rosetta Stone; written in three languages – hieroglyphs, Egyptian demotic script and ancient Greek – had facilitated the deciphering of hieroglyphics by enabling scholars to compare the Greek, which was already understood, to the unknown hieroglyphics and demotics.

'The problem is that the writing on these fragments

18

appears to be all one language, or at least one alphabet. In order to use it like the Rosetta Stone, we'd need a suitable candidate text in another language to compare it to.'

'Well, if *I'm* right, then we already have one.'

Mansoor noticed the look on Gabrielle's face and realized that she wasn't backing down.

'That's a bit of a quantum leap in logic, Professor Gusack.'

'Is it really? The site where we found it is a very good candidate for the real Mount Sinai—'

'In the opinion of *some* people.'

'According to the Bible, Moses smashed the original tablets of stone—'

'If you take the Bible literally.'

'And now we've found fragments of stone with ancient writing on them that appear to have been smashed, quite possibly deliberately.'

'Well, even if you're right, my biblical Hebrew isn't that good. And neither is yours.'

'Then maybe we should call in someone who has specialized knowledge of biblical languages.'

'I'm not going to call in anyone from Israel,' said Mansoor. 'At least not at this stage. It would just be too controversial.'

'I wasn't thinking of an Israeli. The man I have in mind is British.'

'Who?'

'Daniel Klein.'

'Klein?' said Mansoor, not recognizing the name. 'That sounds like a . . .'

'He was my uncle's star pupil,' said Gabrielle. 'Just like I was *yours*,' she added with a twinkle in her eye.

Mansoor was silent for a moment. After a while, he nodded reluctantly. 'Well, I guess if this Daniel Klein was Harrison Carmichael's star pupil, then that's good enough for me.'

'Shall I call him?' asked Gabrielle. 'He knows me.'

'Okay, you call him and introduce me and then put me on.' Sensing her excitement, Mansoor added, 'But let's not tell him at this stage that we think we've found the original Ten Commandments.'

Chapter 4

'This is the bread of affliction that our ancestors ate in the land of Egypt,' Nathan Greenberg solemnly intoned.

In a house in Golders Green, Nathan Greenberg, father of three, was holding up a plate of three matzos, reciting a paragraph attesting to its significance. Nathan's own parents and siblings lived in America, but he and his glamorous wife Julia had invited some of Julia's extended family for the Passover *seider*.

The *seider* is a quasi-religious service performed at the dinner table before the festive meal marking the beginning of Passover in which Jewish families retell the story of the Exodus of the Israelite slaves from Egypt. 'Bread of affliction' was perhaps a misnomer, because it wasn't the bread the Israelites ate when they were slaves in Egypt, but rather the bread prepared in haste when they were allowed to leave by the Egyptian Pharaoh whose will had been broken by the Ten Plagues.

But Nathan's six-year-old daughter May and her twin sister Shari were not looking at the plate with the matzos. Their big, wide eyes were focused squarely on the area of the tablecloth just to the left of their father, under which he had placed half of the middle matzo that he had broken off and wrapped in a serviette less than a minute before. This was the *afikoman* – from the Greek meaning 'leave it till later' – so called because it was to be put aside and eaten at the end of the meal. According to a long-standing tradition, the children are supposed to 'steal' the *afikoman* and use it to bargain for presents and gifts from their beleaguered parents.

However, the twins were sitting too far away from their daddy to get their little hands on the prize, and any attempt to get up from their seats now would merely alert their father to the fact that juvenile intrigue was afoot. This was where Uncle Danny came in.

Daniel Klein, who had recently celebrated his fortieth birthday, was sitting to his brother-in-law's immediate left. In addition to his ideal position, Daniel also had a background as an amateur magician, so it was only natural that the twins should enlist his aid in this conspiracy to commit grand larceny. However, he set a high price for putting his reputation on the line in such a criminal enterprise.

'You must ask for a present for your little sister Romy, as well as your own presents.'

Little Romy was less than three and a half, and although she could stick up for herself, she couldn't always explain what she wanted with quite the same clarity as her older siblings.

'But she likes different things,' said May.

'And what if she wants something that costs too much money,' said Shari, demonstrating her eminently practical side.

'Well, why don't you ask for a toy you can all play with?' suggested Danny.

The twins rose to the occasion and after putting their heads together for half a minute, came up with the ideal solution.

'We'll ask for the play house,' Shari announced.

The 'play house' in question was a colourful, flat-packed, plastic kit that they had seen on a previous visit to a toy shop and it was just the right size for all three of them to play in.

There was no time to waste now because Nathan had come to the end of his recital and was putting down the plate with the matzos, and this was the cue for the twins' turn in the spotlight. According to an old tradition, the youngest person present at the *seider* asks the 'Four Questions' that kick-start the process of reciting the story of the Exodus. However, Romy was too young to read and so it fell on the twins to sing it as a duet. After a few nervous coughs, a shy exchange of eye contact and a little musical prompting from their mother, the twins started singing in perfect unison.

By the time they had got to the end, Daniel Klein had availed himself of the distraction to draw on his sleight-of-hand skills and take possession of the *afikoman* on behalf of his nieces. Oblivious to the theft that had taken place under his nose, Nathan graciously responded to his daughters' ceremonial questions by reciting the reply.

'We were slaves to Pharaoh in Egypt . . .'

The twins, who neither understood Aramaic nor cared for anything other than toys and getting to the food, cast a hopeful glance at Uncle Danny. He responded with a wink, prompting a smile from May and an unsuccessful attempt to wink back by Shari.

'*Al Matzot u'Morerim Yoch-lu-hu!*'

They all shouted the last word of the pre-dinner service together because it meant 'They shall eat.' It was a desperate cry from a hungry family, anxious to get to the food after the long, drawn-out ceremony that preceded it.

Daniel Klein was starting the meal in the traditional way: dipping an egg in saltwater. The egg, like its Easter counterpart, signified rebirth and renewal – the hallmark of all religious-inspired spring festivals, whether Judeo-Christian or pagan. The saltwater symbolized the tears of the Israelite slaves.

By his own admission, Daniel was a bit of a geek, combining intellect and maturity with a childlike sense of fun. He still had the same curly brown hair that he had had as a kid and had always wanted to straighten. He was of an average height and build, and had recently started working out in the local gym to counter the first onset of middle-aged weight gain. Although he sometimes went abseiling and white-water rafting with his teenage nephews, he spent too long at the writing desk or in the lecture hall, and by his own strict standards and keen eye, his waistline was just beginning to suffer in consequence. Hence his decision – albeit at the suggestion of one of his nephews – to go on a diet and start working out. So far it was having a good effect. After an initial week of aching muscles, he was now starting to feel the benefit.

'So why were they slaves?' asked May, tugging at Uncle Danny's sleeve.

Daniel swallowed and put the egg down before answering. 'Well, it all started with Joseph's brothers. You remember Joseph, the son of Jacob – the boy with eleven brothers.'

May nodded.

'Didn't he have a coat of many colours?' asked Shari.

'That's right. His daddy gave him a coat of many colours, but that made all his brothers jealous. And also he told them about his dreams that they were all bowing down to him and that made them even more jealous and angry.'

'So what did they do?'

'Well, they were so mad with him that one day they sold him to some people as a slave. And then those people sold him to some Egyptians and then he ended up in prison in Egypt.'

'So did he get out of the prison?' asked Shari.

'Well, hold on. Not so fast. When he was in the prison, two of the other prisoners had dreams. And they told Joseph about them and he told them what the dreams meant.'

'What *did* they mean?' Shari pressed him.

'They predicted the future. He told one of them that he'd be let out of prison and would get his old job back – working as a servant for the pharaoh. *And it came true.*'

'What about the other one?' asked May.

'Oh, I don't remember. It's not important.' He didn't want to upset them with the gory details about the baker being hanged and the birds pecking at his flesh.

His sister Julia and mother Helen were bringing in the boiled and fried fishcakes – Danny's contribution to the meal. Realizing that the Passover *seider* is not the ideal time for sticking to a diet, Danny took one of each, embellishing the flavour with the horseradish and beetroot sauce that was the traditional accompaniment to the dish. The twins decided to steer clear of the boiled ones altogether and to give the hot sauce a miss. Instead they picked up the fishcakes in their fingers and ate them the way children do.

'You didn't tell us how Joseph got out of prison,' said May.

No peace for the wicked, thought Danny.

'Ah yes, of course. Well, one day the pharaoh had a dream and in his dream there were seven fat cows and seven thin cows, and the seven thin cows ate the seven fat cows . . .'

The twins started laughing.

'It was just a dream,' Daniel explained to this young pair of sceptics. 'Anyway, after eating the fat cows, the thin cows didn't get fat. They stayed just as thin as they were before.'

'But how could they eat the fat cows and not get fat?' Shari asked.

Daniel smiled wryly. If he knew the answer to that one, he'd be a billionaire.

'That's exactly what the pharaoh wanted to know. So he asked all his advisers what the dream meant and none of them knew. Then the servant who had been in jail told him that there was a man in prison who could interpret dreams. So Pharaoh had Joseph brought to him and Joseph told him what the dream meant.'

'And what did it mean?' Shari asked impatiently.

'It meant that for seven years there would be lots of food. All the crops would grow and they would have more food than they knew what to do with.'

'Why didn't they sell it to other people?' Shari probed.

'Because they would *all* have too much food. It wasn't just in Egypt. All the other countries would have lots of food. But then, Joseph said, after the first seven years there would be another seven years in which there wasn't enough food. There would be famine and the people would starve.'

'So why didn't they save some of the food?' Shari said.

'That's exactly what they did. And that was because Joseph told Pharaoh to do that. He said they should build storehouses for the grain and save it. Then, at the end of the seven years, they would have enough grain not only to feed themselves but also to sell to the people in other countries. And the king was so pleased with Joseph that he made him prime minister.'

The twins started laughing again. Their mirth gave Daniel a chance to tuck into the chicken soup with matzoball dumplings that his sister had just placed before him.

'And what about his brothers?' asked May, who was very finicky about details and didn't like loose ends.

'Well, when the famine started, they also needed food. So they went down to Egypt to buy grain . . . I mean, food.'

'And did Joseph catch them?'

'Sort of. He saw them and decided to play a trick on them.'

'What sort of trick?'

'He sold them the grain and then he put the money back in the sacks with the food.'

'But *why*?' asked May.

'He was playing a joke on them.'

'That's silly,' said Shari.

May got irritated at this. 'You mustn't say that. It's the Bible.'

'I can say what I like. It's a free country.'

'Shush. There's no need to fight. Yes, you can say what you like. But don't fight.'

Shari looked down guiltily. May pressed on with her questions. 'But you still haven't told us how the Israelites became slaves.'

'Okay, let's move on,' said Danny. 'Because of the famine, Joseph's brothers and their wives and children all came down to Egypt to live as there was more food there. And as time went by they had children and grandchildren and there were more and more of them. But then one day the pharaoh died and a new pharaoh came along. But he didn't remember Joseph and all the good things he'd done for them. He only saw that there were lots of these Israelites and he was afraid of them because he thought there were too many of them and they were getting too powerful. So he made them slaves.'

'And then he tried to drown the babies,' said May.

'Only the boy babies,' Danny explained. 'He said that all new boy babies would be drowned, but not the girls.'

'But why?' asked May.

'Because he thought there were too many of them.'

'But why not the girls?'

Danny shrugged; he wasn't sure how to explain a patriarchal society to a six-year-old. 'Anyway, when Moses was born, his mother wanted to save him. So she put the baby in a basket and hid him in the bulrushes on the River Nile.'

'What's bulrushes?' asked Shari.

'Just something that grows by the river. Anyway, Pharaoh's daughter found the basket with the baby in it and she was nice. She didn't want anyone to kill the baby so she took it home and asked her father if she could adopt it and he said yes. So she adopted the baby and brought him up as an Egyptian prince. In fact she was the one who called him Moses.'

The girls were looking at him in awe, hanging on to every word and desperate to hear more about this fascinating story. But he paused to take a generous helping of roast chicken and potatoes and served the twins who were shy about taking food for themselves. Once the twins started tucking into their food, it gave Danny a chance to enjoy his own, at least for a while.

'Tell us some more,' said Shari.

'Okay, where was I?'

'You said that Moses was an Egyptian prince.'

'Oh, yes. Well now, this is where the story gets interesting. One day, when he was grown-up, Moses saw an Egyptian slave master beating an Israelite slave. And he was so angry that he killed the Egyptian slave master. Then, after that, he saw two Israelites having a fight with each other and he stopped them fighting and told them not to fight.'

'Like you told *us*,' said May.

'Exactly. But when he told them not to fight, one of them

got angry and said to him, "Are you going to kill us like you killed that Egyptian?" And when he said that, Moses realized that someone had seen him. And if they'd seen him, then maybe *someone else* had also seen him, so he was afraid. So he ran away because he knew that the pharaoh would be angry. And then he came to the burning bush.'

'What's that?' asked Shari.

'It was a bush that was on fire. It was burning and burning, but it didn't get burned up, it just carried on burning. And then God started talking to him from the bush.'

'What did he say?' asked May.

'He told Moses that he was really an Israelite not an Egyptian and he must become the leader of the Israelites and tell Pharaoh to let them go. So he went to Pharaoh and said to him, "Let my people go." But Pharaoh said no. So God sent the first plague.'

'What was the first plague?' asked May.

'It was *blood*,' said Daniel in his most theatrical tone, causing the girls to giggle. 'God turned the River Nile into blood, so they couldn't drink the water. And then when Pharaoh still refused to let the Israelites go free, God sent a plague of frogs. Can you imagine that? Frogs running around all over the place?'

He created a pair of imaginary frogs with his hands and showed them jumping all over the table. As the twins giggled, Daniel and his sister exchanged a smile. It was her quiet way of thanking him for keeping the little ones entertained.

By the time he'd got to the Egyptian army drowning in the Red Sea, Shari had gone off to the couch and fallen asleep and May was finding it hard to keep her eyes open. Julia came over and asked her if she wanted to go to bed. May nodded, gave Daniel a hug and then went off to her room with her mother.

29

Amidst all the noise and clatter in the room. Daniel almost missed the sound of his mobile phone ringing.

'Hallo,' he said, moving to the hallway so that he could conduct a proper conversation without having to strain to hear the other end of the line.

'Hallo Danny,' said a woman's voice faintly.

'Yes?'

'It's Gaby. Gaby Gusack.' She didn't normally call herself Gaby. But she made an exception for Danny – sometimes.

'Oh, hi Gaby.'

Two memories swept over him in quick succession: the almost-forgotten fifteen-year-old girl with a crush on him from his days as a PhD student and the tall, supremely self-confident woman that he had worked with on a recent archaeological dig in Jerusalem.

'Listen, I'm calling from the University of Cairo. I'm with Professor Akil Mansoor.'

'The head of the Egyptian Antiquities Authority?'

'That's right. He'd like to speak to you.'

Daniel was familiar with some of Mansoor's statements, as well as his deeds, and he hadn't exactly warmed to him. But if Mansoor wanted to speak to him, then evidently there must be some matter of mutual interest, and Daniel had no desire to seem rude to anyone, let alone a fellow academic.

There was some movement at the other end and then a man's voice came down the line.

'This is Akil Mansoor. The reason I'm calling you is that we have found something out here that may be of interest to you and we'd like to fly you out here to take a look at it. It will all be at our expense of course, and first class, naturally.'

Daniel smiled at the attempt to bribe him with first-class travel. But he was intrigued and wanted to know more.

'Can you give me some idea of what this is about?'

'I would prefer to tell you when you get here. But I can promise you that it will be of considerable interest to you.'

Daniel felt awkward. 'The problem is I have several lectures to give here and I also promised my nieces that I'd take them to Stonehenge as their birthday treat.'

'It needn't be a long visit. Possibly even just a day or two. We would be ready to reward you handsomely.'

'It's not a matter of money. It's a matter of time. I mean, I can come, it's just that it would be a lot easier if it were in a couple of weeks' time.'

'Unfortunately, time is of the essence. Besides, I think this is something you'd really be excited about if you saw it. I'd rather not say what it is over the phone, but I can tell you that it appears to be an artefact of considerable interest to Jewish history.'

Daniel sensed the excitement in Mansoor's tone and he knew that this was a man who wouldn't take no for an answer. The words could have been hyperbole, but the fact that a man of Mansoor's position and prestige had called him out of the blue and extended such an invitation was telling in the extreme. And the invitation also had the imprimatur of Gaby behind it. That was the tie-breaker.

'Okay,' he said, intrigued.

Chapter 5

'How many years has it been?' asked Harrison Carmichael as they stood surrounded by the shrubs and flowers in the back garden of the seven-room detached house in Hertfordshire. He had been shown here by Roksana, the young Polish maid who had opened the door for him. The garden was Carmichael's favourite part of the house. With its tall, leafy trees, it offered privacy. You could sit here in the shade, reading a book and just forget about the world.

'It's been longer than it should have been,' said Daniel, shaking his professor's hand warmly. 'And it's my fault.'

It had in fact only been a few months. He had been to Agatha's funeral and come back to the house afterwards. That was why Roksana knew him well enough to let him in.

'Nonsense, old chap. I shouldn't be such an old stick-in-the-mud. I should get out more.' His voice became softer. 'Instead of letting myself turn into an old recluse, like one of those characters you read about in those books by . . .'

He trailed off.

Daniel avoided his eyes. Harrison Carmichael was still intellectually vibrant, but he had lost a tiny bit of that spark that Daniel remembered from his own PhD student days, when Carmichael was his supervisor. He didn't like to think that maybe Carmichael was in the first stages of Alzheimer's or some other form of dementia, but it was a possibility that he could not deny. He knew that Carmichael had been shattered when Agatha died. It was that recent bereavement that may have taken the spark out of him.

Daniel just hoped he would get the care that he needed when he needed it. He had the money, but he didn't have that one special person watching over him to make the decisions for him when they needed to be made. He had a day maid to clean the house and he was still capable of cooking for himself – something that he enjoyed as a hobby, not resented as a chore. But there was no one there to watch out for those tell-tale signs when he might need the help of a trained carer. It pained Daniel to think that he could say nothing on the subject to Professor Carmichael and had no one else to talk to about it.

'I'll get Roksana to make some tea.' He turned to the French doors where Roksana was standing.

'The kettle is on,' she shouted. 'I'll bring it out to you.'

He nodded to thank her and then indicated to Daniel to sit.

'Now tell me what all this is about.'

Daniel told him about the phone call from Gabrielle yesterday evening, Akil Mansoor's cryptic invitation and his decision to accept.

'I would be very careful about going there if I were you, Daniel.'

'Careful? Why?'

'Well, you wouldn't want to get the plague.'

Daniel felt a flush of embarrassment. It wasn't like Harrison to make puerile jokes. Daniel wondered idly if this was a symptom of the creeping dementia.

'I know what you're thinking. You're thinking that I'm just a silly old fool.'

'I could *never* think that, Professor.'

'I wrote a paper about it you know,' said Carmichael. 'Based on my translation of an old manuscript in Proto-Sinaitic script. But they're refusing to publish it.'

'Who?'

'The Americans. In *The Journal*. They say it's still being peer reviewed, but I know what they're up to. They're going to rewrite the article in someone else's name and claim the credit.'

Plagiarism in the academic world was hardly unknown, but once a paper was submitted to an academic journal, plagiarism became *less* likely. It would require the co-operation of too many people.

'Did you make a copy?'

'Oh yes. Roksana typed it for me on my computer.'

'So you've got proof of authorship. You could have a copy witnessed by a solicitor.'

'Yes, but I want them to *publish* it. People need to know. The plague could come back.'

'*Which* plague?'

'The sixth.'

Daniel did a quick flick through the reference pages of his mind. He realized that the professor must be referring to one of the infamous biblical plagues of Egypt.

'Boils?'

'Yes.'

'But why would that plague in particular come back?'

'Because it can lie dormant for centuries. It had already made a comeback when they were camped outside of Canaan.' The voice was becoming agitated. 'That's what the story with the fiery snakes was all about – the one where Moses put the snake on the pole.'

Harrison was rambling now and Daniel was desperately

34

trying to think of something to distract his mentor from the convoluted thoughts that were tormenting him.

'Here's the tea,' said Roksana, appearing from the house with a tray in her hands.

It was about half an hour later that Harrison Carmichael was trudging back to the house alone. He had insisted on seeing Daniel to the driveway, despite Daniel's own insistence that it was unnecessary. He watched as Daniel drove away and at the same time saw another car pulled up nearby. As Carmichael turned towards the house, a very tall, powerfully built man got out of the car and approached.

'Professor Carmichael,' the man called out, with a quiet sense of urgency in his voice.

'Yes?'

'I have to talk to you on a matter of grave importance . . . about your paper . . . to *The Journal*.'

A sense of realization returned to Carmichael and he smiled at the gushing enthusiasm of this man, whose words seemed to convey so much respect for him.

'You'd better come in.'

The professor led the man inside and asked Roksana to make some more tea as he led his new guest through to the garden. Roksana looked nervous at the presence of this powerfully built stranger, but the professor appeared to know what he wanted.

'Now, tell me what it is that you wanted to tell me about my paper,' said the professor.

'Well, I was wondering if you had a copy of it.'

'You mean the one I sent to the *American Journal of Egyptology*?'

'Yes. Do you have a copy of it? Is it on your computer?'

'Yes, in my office upstairs. Would you like me to ask Roksana to get you a copy?'

'Yes. Let's do that now.'

'Why don't we wait for the tea—'

'I said, let's do it *now*!' shouted the visitor, rising to his feet and yanking Carmichael out of the chair.

The professor looked at him, terrified. This man was a student of his, or so he had said, yet now all he could see was a giant of a man towering over him and being rough and aggressive.

'Okay,' said Carmichael meekly. He shuffled along nervously with the tall man walking behind him, giving him a couple of shoves and pushes in the back to assert his control.

When they arrived in the house, Roksana looked confused. 'I was going to bring the tea out,' she said.

'No need,' the tall man replied. 'I'm not staying for tea. I just need to know where the office is.'

'I don't understand.'

'You don't need to understand, bitch! Just show me where it is.'

In that moment Roksana understood, or at least thought she did. 'There's nothing valuable there. Just a computer and some books.'

'It's the computer that I'm interested in. That and its content!'

Roksana had enough of a grasp of the situation to realize that this man had come here to take something and he was not looking to leave any witnesses. She made her decision in a flash.

A fraction of a second later, a pot of scalding hot tea was flying at the big man. He was too big and his feet planted too firmly on the floor to dodge it, but a lightning-fast movement of his arm deflected it. After an initial moment of numbness, a searing hot pain shot up his left forearm.

But he was a man who could handle pain, and he had no intention of being stopped by a woman. As she made her desperate dash to the door, he closed the distance between them in three quick strides. She tried to scream, knowing that it was her last chance for survival, despite the isolation of the house. But the intruder clamped a giant hand over her mouth as his other arm encircled her neck from behind. With a powerful motion, he snapped her neck and let her lifeless body slump to the ground.

Carmichael looked on in terror, knowing that there was nowhere to run.

'The office!' the giant commanded.

He shuffled along meekly while the man pushed and shoved him from behind. Once in the office, Carmichael turned round hesitantly with tears of terror and confusion in his eyes. The tall man noticed, with relish, that the front of Carmichael's trousers was wet.

'Do you keep hard copies?' asked the intruder.

'What?'

'*Hard copies!*' He slapped Carmichael viciously across the face.

'No. I mean . . . I don't know. I leave all that to Roksana.'

The big man looked at the computer and knew that he had a decision to make. He recognized that the confused Harrison Carmichael had told him all he knew, so he decided to dispense with him now. Picking up a paperweight from the desk, he smashed it down on Carmichael's head. The old man slumped to the ground, without a sound. But he was not yet dead. The big man crouched down and struck the old man with the paperweight again. And again . . . and again . . . and again.

He dropped the paperweight and placed a hand on the professor's neck, looking for any sign of a pulse. He felt none. Satisfied that the old man was dead, he proceeded to do what he had come here for.

Switching on the computer, he went into set-up and changed the boot order so that it would boot from the CD drive first. He then inserted a bootable CD which contained a utility program called *Darik's Boot and Nuke* that would automatically destroy the entire contents of the hard disk. Then he rebooted the computer and let it do its work.

However, this was only the first stage. He was sure that Roksana would have made at least one hard copy as well as backups on a CD or memory stick, but he had no intention of spending any more time looking for them. It could take ages and he couldn't be sure of finding them all. He knew that Carmichael probably wouldn't have been able to tell him and he had been a little too quick dispensing with Roksana.

So while *Darik's Boot and Nuke* did its work, he went to his car and siphoned off some petrol. He poured it on to the floor in the office and carefully placed a lighted candle there, making sure there was no draught that could extinguish the flame. There was no more to be done.

Half an hour later, the big man was well on the way to Heathrow Airport and Harrison Carmichael's house was well and truly ablaze.

Chapter 6

Akil Mansoor had been true to his word about providing first-class service to bring Daniel over to Egypt. As an internationally acclaimed scholar, Daniel was accustomed to flying. But he wasn't used to changing his plans at short notice.

So now, Daniel was trying to relax in the First Class lounge of Terminal 5 at Heathrow Airport. Bedazzled by its gold leaf adornments, he considered trying the aromatherapy treatment or shiatsu massage in the travel spa. But there wasn't going to be enough time before boarding. His normal remedy for stress was a single glass of wine taken slowly and savoured, but he didn't like drinking before a flight, so he stuck to mango juice.

The boarding call came quite soon after that. He followed the other priority passengers feeling somewhat calmer than he had been when he first arrived at the airport.

He didn't know why now of all times, he should think of his ex-wife Charlotte. Perhaps because travelling by air reminded him of their near-constant travel between the two worlds of New York and London, bringing back a flood of memories and endless speculations about maybes and might-have-beens.

Once airborne, he decided that he wasn't really interested

in the in-flight entertainment. He always found it hard to follow the plotline of a movie on an aeroplane, but the one thing he could always do on a flight was read. So he took out his widescreen smartphone and carried on reading a legal thriller that he had started a few days ago, set in California but written by his favourite British author.

'Is that the new one?' asked the huge, muscular man in the seat next to him. He had piercing eyes that looked at Daniel in a way that was neither hostile nor friendly, but was certainly unwavering. He was going bald, but did not look more than about forty.

'What, the book?' asked Daniel, seeking to clarify the man's question.

'The reader.'

'Er, yes,' said Daniel, hoping to get back to the novel. 'It's like a smartphone, only better.'

'Is it any good?'

'I've only had it a couple of weeks. But it seems okay so far. It's one of the new 3G ones. You can order the books direct to the reader in over a hundred countries.'

'I was thinking of getting one myself. Not that I read much of the commercial trash that they're spewing out these days. I'm more into academic books.'

Daniel wasn't really interested in prolonging the conversation, but it would have been rude to seem too aloof. 'What's your field?'

'Oh, I don't really have a field as such. A jack of all trades but a master of none. I'm what would have been called a dilettante in the old days. Anything from the anthropology of the Balinese to Egyptology and ancient hieroglyphics. That's why I'm off to Egypt, you know. A spot of amateur research. Not for any academic purpose, you understand. Just for fun. A cruise down the Nile, a visit to the Valley of the Kings and all that. I inherited a spot of money from my late aunt and that rather lets me indulge my passion. What about you?'

'I'm a professor of ancient Semitic languages.'

'Oh gosh, now I feel awfully embarrassed. Here I am, an enthusiastic amateur and you're one of the intellectual giants of our time. You must seriously look down on people like me. A little learning is a dangerous thing and all that. The name's Carter, Wally Carter. Pleased to meet such an eminent scholar.'

Daniel smiled. 'Daniel Klein. And there's nothing wrong with being an enthusiastic amateur.'

'Could I have a look at that phone? Like I said, I'm thinking of getting one.'

Daniel hesitated a moment and then, realizing that this man could hardly run off with it, handed it over. The man appeared to press a few buttons and Daniel was about to say something when the man handed it back.

'It looks pretty good. How's the battery life?'

'Reasonable.'

'Listen, I know this is very cheeky but do you think I might take your number? I'd love to keep in touch.'

Daniel wasn't keen but obliged, not wanting to be rude.

'Well, I should stop bothering you and let you get back to your book.'

Daniel smiled with relief as he took his phone back and turned away. What he didn't know was that with a few swift movements, the big man had downloaded an application that would enable him to track the phone – and Daniel with it.

Chapter 7

Joel awoke in the men's communal tent, sweating heavily. He knew that at this time of year even the nights could get hot, but not like this. He was sweltering and itching.

What was it?

His arms, his legs, his torso. He hadn't felt like this since he had chickenpox as a child. Except that this time it wasn't just a scratching itch, it was a burning sensation.

He tried to look at his arm, to see what was causing the itch, but it was too dark. He had a torch by his bed, though he wasn't sure if he should turn it on – it might disturb the others. But he had to know. Finally, plucking up the courage, he switched on the touch and shone it at his forearm.

And when he did so he got the shock of his life!

His arm was covered with boils. But these were not normal round boils. They were long, elongated trails of fiery red-orange on his skin, almost snake-like in appearance. And they were accompanied by a burning sensation. Joel realized that something was seriously amiss. The boils alone were frightening enough, but his head was also aching and his eyes watering. He realized that the sweat was not from the external heat and it was actually rather cool outside. The sweat came from his own body. He was going down with a fever.

He knew that there was a medical officer in the sick bay next to the soldiers' hut and he decided to go there. Staggering out of bed, he threw on some clothes and began walking. But as he got to the entrance to the tent he fainted, emitting a cry that woke several of the others and raised the alarm.

An hour later, a helicopter arrived to take Joel to a hospital in Cairo. There was talk about a scorpion sting which the commanding officer tried to play down. He told them that according to the medic, Joel had chickenpox and it was more serious because he was an adult. However, he added, if they had already had it as children or been vaccinated against it, they had nothing to worry about.

Jane took advantage of the situation to make another visit to the latrine with her concealed mobile phone. However, instead of texting Senator Morris, this time she decided to call him and tell him what had happened.

'Okay, now listen carefully,' said the senator. 'This is what I want you to do: you need to get a sample of his clothes—'

'But they've flown him out to Cairo,' Jane rasped into the phone.

'Did they take all his things with him?'

'Probably not.'

'So most of his clothes are still in the tent.'

'I guess.'

'Okay. We only need a sample. Preferably something that he wore recently. Put it in a plastic bag and pack it with your things. I'll give you instructions on how to get it out.'

'Okay, Dad.'

She put the phone away before stepping out of the latrine . . . where she was confronted by a soldier.

'Who were you talking to?' he demanded.

Jane gasped in fright, fumbling mentally to find the right words to placate his suspicions. Then she noticed the red marks on his cheeks . . . and the sight made her realize that her own torso was itching.

Chapter 8

'It's definitely Proto-Sinaitic,' said Daniel, struggling to contain his excitement.

Mansoor had pulled out all the stops to make sure that Daniel got the VIP treatment when he arrived at Cairo International Airport. He was fast-tracked through border control and customs at breakneck speed and brought to a luxury Cairo hotel in a stretch limousine. Now, after a good night's sleep and a Mediterranean breakfast, Daniel was studying the carefully arranged fragments of stone as well as the pictures of them in various lighting conditions.

'The strange thing, in my opinion, is that these stone fragments have smooth flat backs as well as flat fronts. And the overall thickness is no more than two inches. That suggests that they were small, portable stones and not just broken fragments of a large monument. This is the first time I've seen Proto-Sinaitic script on tablets like this. It's usually found carved on local rocks in short one-line inscriptions, obviously designed to be seen by anyone who passes by. It's basically a sort of simple graffiti by the untutored and uneducated.'

He looked up at Mansoor. Despite their mutual reservations, they had taken an instant liking to one another. It had been the firmness of the handshake by both men that had cemented the bond of trust between them.

'Did you find this anywhere near the turquoise mines at Serabit el-Khadim?'

He noticed the fleeting eye contact between Mansoor and Gabrielle.

'Where the original inscriptions were found, you mean? No. They were found about 130 kilometres east of that.'

'So that also makes it pretty far from the Temple of Hathor.'

'Hathor?' said Gabrielle excitedly. 'The Egyptian cow goddess? Why do you ask?'

'I was just thinking about the story of the Golden Calf,' said Daniel. 'You know . . . when Moses went up Mount Sinai and the Israelites got restless and built a golden calf and started worshipping it.'

He noticed that Gabrielle's excitement was growing. At first he thought she was just happy to be working with him again, but he sensed that there was more to it than that.

'We were wondering,' Mansoor asked gingerly, 'if there was any possibility that this could be an early version of a known Hebrew text.'

Daniel spoke his next words very slowly, sensing what was coming. '*Which* known text?'

There was a long pause before Mansoor replied. 'The Ten Commandments.'

In the silence that followed, a hundred emotions swept through Daniel's head. It was as if they were waiting for him to laugh. But laughter was the last thing on his mind. He chose his next words carefully.

'I noticed the word *El* several times – that's the Hebrew word for God. And I also noticed a few instances of the word *Yahowa* or *Yehova* – which is now usually read as Jehovah, the sacred name of God in Judeo-Christian religion.'

'And?'

'Well, that at least opens the possibility that it's a text of the early Israelites,' Daniel concluded.

'There's no evidence that the early Israelites worshipped Jehovah,' said Mansoor. 'The only ancient group known to worship a god called Jehovah were a nomadic group called the Shasu of Yahowa.'

'But there is evidence that the Israelites were descended from a larger group called the Habiru,' said Gabrielle. 'From whom we get the name *Hebrews*. And they could be the same people as the Shasu of Yahowa.'

'The Habiru was a term used for roving bandits,' said Mansoor. 'The Shasu were shepherds.'

'Some people think the names may have been used interchangeably,' Gabrielle pressed on.

'But we have graphic depictions of both people,' Mansoor replied firmly, 'and they wore different styles of clothes.'

'That still doesn't answer the question of whether this could be the Ten Commandments,' said Daniel, trying to get the discussion back on track. 'And to answer that I'd need to compare it to the text in a Hebrew copy of the Bible.'

They made their way to the university library where Daniel lost no time in studying a photo of the assembled stones side by side with the Ten Commandments, looking for any signs of the recognizable words *El* and *Jehovah* with similar spacings. After a few minutes he looked up, disappointed.

'I can't find any sign of a match,' he said. 'Although the words *El* and *Jehovah* appear in both, they don't appear in the same places. That proves that the text on the stones is something other than the Ten Commandments.'

He noticed that Gabrielle's mood mirrored his own. Mansoor on the other hand appeared to take it more philosophically.

'Oh, well. Back to the drawing board.'

'Could I ask why you thought it was the Ten Commandments? I mean apart from the fact that it's fragments from two tablets and they were broken.'

'Because of—' Gabrielle started. But she broke off in response to a look from Mansoor. 'Because of where it was found.'

Daniel was about to ask Gabrielle to explain when Mansoor got a call which interrupted their conversation.

'Yes? . . . A mobile phone? . . . But how did she? . . . You were supposed to have searched them . . . No, we don't want any trouble with the Americans . . . How many of them? . . . *And* the soldiers? . . . And what does the doctor say? . . . Quarantine? On whose decision?'

Chapter 9

'First of all, I have some good news. Carmichael is no longer a problem.'

Senator Morris was addressing the professor and Audrey Milne in their regular meeting room in the Capitol Building.

'How sure can we be that a copy of his manuscript won't pop up somewhere down the line?'

'Goliath didn't just dispose of Carmichael and the woman, he—'

'Woman?' echoed Audrey nervously.

'He has a maid – *had* a maid – who apparently doubled as his secretary.'

'And he killed her too?'

There was a sharp edge in Audrey's tone. The senator wasn't sure if it was chiding or fearful. Either way he didn't like it, but he wanted to keep her onside.

'She was there at the time. Apparently she was his de facto carer. Also, as I said, she was his secretary. That is, she typed the paper for him. That means she knew about it.'

'But what about copies?' the professor reminded him.

'He wiped the computer and burnt down the house. Unless they sent a copy somewhere else, the only copies left are the ones with you.'

'But how is this going to help us end the vile dominion of the Semitic interlopers?' asked the professor.

'Carmichael's paper can't. But what it revealed certainly can. It appears that he was right: the sixth plague can make a resurgence.'

'What do you mean?'

He told them what Jane had told him about Joel and about his instructions to her to get a sample of his clothes.

'You don't really think . . .' The professor trailed off.

'It was an article of faith among the Israelites that they were spared from the plagues,' said the senator. 'But after this young man on the dig has become ill, it looks like Carmichael was right. The Israelites were stricken by the plagues too. And we can use that to our advantage.'

Audrey sat there in silence. It wasn't until the meeting had ended that she made her way to her car and drove safely out of the area before making a phone call. There were three or four rings before it was picked up at the other end.

'Israeli Embassy.'

Chapter 10

'We're here,' said Mansoor.

They got out near what seemed like an army camp in the middle of nowhere. Daniel looked around. He wasn't exactly in awe of this environment – he had seen sights far more spectacular than this, both in Egypt and elsewhere. But in the dry desert heat and with the desolate expanses around him, he felt the sense of humility that a harsh or hostile environment can induce in a man.

'Where are we?' asked Daniel.

'We're at a mountain called Hashem el-Tarif.'

'Which some people believe to be the real Mount Sinai,' said Daniel, to show his understanding.

'Exactly,' Mansoor confirmed.

They had flown into Sharm el-Sheikh from Cairo International Airport and driven north to this spot near the Israeli border. Now Daniel was looking in the direction of the cordoned-off dig site.

'And that's where they found the fragments?'

'Yes,' Gabrielle and Mansoor replied in unison.

Gabrielle pointed to the mountain.

'There's a cleft over there from which a man's voice can carry to this whole area – it's a natural amphitheatre. You could have a group of people down here and a man could speak in a moderately raised voice from up there and be heard by everyone.'

Daniel looked around, trying to imagine the Israelites gathered here, listening to their teacher.

'And there's *no* possibility of being allowed to take a look at the dig site itself?' asked Daniel.

'We're lucky that we can even come here at all.' Mansoor's tone had taken on an irascible edge. 'I had to move heaven and earth to get the Minister of Defence to allow the dig in the first place and then when the food poisoning broke out, the Minister of Health was informed before I was. He contacted the Defence Minister and between them they decided to close it down – at least until we've established the cause.'

Daniel wasn't sure why an outbreak of food poisoning should render the site a no-go area. But he was a guest in this man's country and one of the things he had learned in his field was to respect the laws and customs of one's hosts. It was an honour that they had showed him what they thought to be the original Tablets of Stone on which the Ten Commandments may have been written. Now they were showing him, if not the dig site, then at least the surrounding region.

His reason for wanting to see the site was that he thought that it might give him some clues as to what was on the stones. Even if it wasn't the Ten Commandments, it was the largest single extract of text in the ancient script that he had ever seen. That made it significant *whatever* it was.

'Let's go up the mountain,' Mansoor suggested.

They walked up a slope to a security checkpoint manned by armed soldiers. It was obvious that the soldiers recognized Mansoor and Gabrielle, but they viewed Daniel with caution if not suspicion. After a few words in Arabic from Mansoor,

Daniel was waved through with the others, without so much as a cursory search.

It was a tiring trudge up the mountain, but as they neared the summit, Daniel noticed something else. 'What are those?' he asked, pointing to some pits.

Gabrielle nodded approvingly at Daniel's perspicacity. 'Those are the remnants of ancient open-pit fires. The sort of fires people might have lit to warm themselves on cold desert nights, or to cook their food. There are also a number of ancient graves and shrines on this site.'

Daniel shook his head. 'But according to the biblical narrative, only Moses went up the mountain. The rest stayed at the foot, so you wouldn't expect to find campfires on the mountain, let alone graves and shrines.'

'That's only if you take the Bible literally, Daniel.'

He noticed Gabrielle's cheeky grin when she said this. She'd always had that look when she won a round in their intellectual sparring – even when she was a teenager. And of course she was right. He was supposed to be a serious scholar not a sycophantic follower of religious dogma. Furthermore, the biblical account was certainly confused as to the order of events. In fact . . .

'Daniel?'

Gabrielle's voice cut into his cogitation. There was a note of concern in her tone. He realized that his train of thought had found expression on his face and she was alerted by it.

'I've just had a thought. We may have been looking in the wrong place.'

'Meaning?' Mansoor prompted.

'In the Bible, I mean. About the text on the stones. The story of the Ten Commandments is actually somewhat convoluted. It starts off in Exodus 20 with God giving a series of commandments *orally* to all the Israelites, amidst smoke and thunder. Those commandments are the ones we all learnt as children. You know, thou shalt not kill, thou shalt not steal, etc. You could call them the *official* Ten Commandments. But in fact nowhere in the Bible does it actually say that those *are* the Ten Commandments. Then after that, the Bible continues by stating that the Israelites were so afraid of all that smoke and thunder that they pleaded with Moses to go up to the top of the mountain and get the rest of God's law and bring it down to them. So Moses goes up the mountain and God tells him a whole long list of laws, called the Testament of Moses, which Moses duly writes down on two tablets of stone.'

'So you're saying that the tablets of stone might actually contain this Testament of Moses, not the Ten Commandments?' asked Mansoor.

'That's what it says in the Bible. But, there's a problem with that, because the Testament of Moses is much too long to be written down on a couple of tablets of stone. It would have needed more like a dozen tablets to record that much detail.'

'Then what could it be?' asked Mansoor.

'The clue to that comes from what happened next. According to the Bible, the Israelites were getting restless over the amount of time Moses was spending up the mountain. They thought Jehovah had abandoned them. So they melted down all the gold they had brought with them from Egypt and turned it into the Golden Calf, to worship the cow goddess, a local god of the region. And when Moses finally came down from the mountain, he saw the people worshipping the Golden Calf and blew his top – smashing the tablets in his anger. Then after he calmed down a bit, he got the Israelites to repent for their sins and then he went back up the mountain with another pair of blank stone tablets to get the commandments all over again.'

'But he didn't break the second lot of stone tablets,' said Gabrielle.

'No, those were the ones that ended up in the temple in Jerusalem. But let's get back to what happened at Mount Sinai. When Moses went up the mountain a second time, in Exodus 34, he actually got an *alternative* version of the Ten Commandments. Not completely different: the first and second commandments are the same – and the fourth commandment of the old ones becomes the fifth in the new version. But the others are different.'

'So are you saying that it's those alternative commandments that are the *real* Ten Commandments?' asked Gabrielle.

Daniel's eyes were wide with excitement as he spoke. 'Exactly. The Bible even says that it's the commandments in Exodus 34 that are the Ten Commandments. Whereas the official Ten Commandments from Exodus 20 were never referred to as such. Also, it says that these alternative Ten Commandments were written on tablets of stone. On the other hand, the official Ten Commandments from Exodus 20 were never written in stone. They were merely spoken out loud by God.'

Mansoor was leaning forward keenly. 'But if that is the case, then the Ten Commandments that you tried to compare to the stone fragments back in Cairo were the *wrong ones.*'

'Exactly. What I *should* have compared to the stones was the alternative Ten Commandments – the ones in Exodus 34.'

And with that, Daniel opened his bag and took out the copy of the Hebrew Bible that he had brought with him, as well as a photo of the assembled stone fragments. Finding a perch on a large rock, he sat down and began making a comparison while Mansoor and Gabrielle looked on in silence.

'*Ki loh tisht-hazeh le'El aher ki Yehova Qana shemoh El qana hu.* "For you shall not bow to another God because Jehovah, jealous is his name, a jealous God is he." Now, if we look at the first line on one of the stone tablets, which is just about visible, it has the word *El*, the generic name for God, which we recognize by the symbols for the ox and the shepherd's crook – that is, a silent placeholder for a vowel and the consonant "L". Then a few words later we see God's personal name of Jehovah, shown by the hand symbol, followed by the matchstick man, then the peg symbol, then the matchstick man again. That's like Y-H-V-H. Then a few words later we see the name *El*. And the spacings all correspond neatly to the text in the Hebrew Bible.'

'So it's a perfect match,' said Gabrielle excitedly.

'Let's not jump to conclusions just yet. Let's see if we can find anything else. Again, using the two recognized words of *El* and *Jehovah*, if we look just above the middle of the second tablet, we see the name *Jehovah*, the word *El* and also . . .' His inflection was rising as he felt the growing excitement. '. . . the word *Yisral*, which appears to be an early form of the name Israel.'

By now, even Mansoor's hitherto sceptical eyes were lit up with the fire of enthusiasm. 'Does that mean what I think it means?'

Daniel was pleased to hear emotion in Mansoor's tone for once and he was unable to conceal the passion in his own. 'It means we've gone some way to deciphering Proto-Sinaitic script. But more important than that . . . it means that what you've got back in Cairo are the remnants of the *original Mosaic tablets!*'

Chapter 11

'Look, could you at least give me my phone back so that I can call my folks?'

Jane's tone was like that of a stroppy teenager. She was being held in the isolation wing of a military hospital along with the other volunteers from the dig and also some of the soldiers. They were segregated from each other in order to further reduce the risk of infection.

They had been told very little, beyond the fact that it was a precaution and it was for their own wellbeing.

'We aren't allowing phone calls for the time being,' the man from the Ministry of Health explained to her, in the tone of a kindergarten teacher to a not very bright child.

'Why not?'

'We don't want to start a panic.'

'You're probably starting more of a panic by holding us incommunicado like this.'

The man from the Health Ministry, an alumnus of Harvard, looked impressed by Jane's vocabulary as he thought of her as an empty-headed blonde. She sensed the patronizing attitude from the smile on his face, even though he said nothing.

'My father's a United States senator.'

'I know,' said the official, still smiling. 'And this is against your constitutional rights.'

'Look, it's *not* funny!'

'I'm sorry, I shouldn't laugh. But you have to understand that a panic is the last thing we need. We depend heavily on the tourist industry in this country.'

'Look, I'm not going to start a panic. Besides, my father already knows.'

The official looked at her blankly and then understood.

'Oh yes, aren't you the one who smuggled a phone into the dig?'

She blushed and then smiled, realizing that the look on the health official's face was actually one of approval.

'Okay, yes that was me. Look, I know I shouldn't have done it, but I just didn't want him to worry.'

She gave the official a seductive smile. He looked at her hesitantly.

'Okay, *one* call. And don't mention that anyone else is in quarantine. You can tell him that you're okay – and that you'll be released in two weeks.'

She smiled as he handed his mobile phone through the sliding drawer into the isolation area. Then she took the phone and put in the call.

'Hallo Dad.'

'Jane,' said Senator Morris.

'Listen, I've got some bad news. Because of what happened at the dig with Joel, we've been put into quarantine.'

'What? At the hospital?' The shock was palpable.

'Yes, but a different hospital. They've said they'll release me in two weeks, but I'm not allowed to have my phone with me.'

'Why not?'

She looked at the health official, wondering how much she was free to say.

'Something about contamination.'

'Did you manage to get any of Joel's clothes?'

'No, I didn't have a chance.'

'Okay, well, look . . . don't feel bad. You tried your best.'

She did feel bad though, or at least mildly guilty. 'Thanks, Dad.'

'Oh, just one thing.'

'Yes?'

'You're sure they don't know that I told you to get a sample of Joel's clothes?'

'Absolutely.'

'Okay, that's good.'

They said goodbye and Jane handed the phone back to the official through the sliding drawer. He picked it up with an alcohol wipe and cleaned it all over before putting it in his pocket.

Amused as she was by the official's paranoia, Jane was more concerned by what her father was up to. She could tell from his tone that whatever he was doing, he wasn't finished yet.

Chapter 12

'This is where we keep all the artefacts that aren't on display,' Mansoor was explaining as he led Daniel and Gabrielle through a labyrinth of corridors in the basement of the Museum of Egyptian Antiquities.

Daniel had worked on the details of the translation of the text from the stones on the plane back from Sharm. It was painstaking work, matching the recognized words and then pairing up single words or groups of words from the stones with the counterparts in the Bible. But after a while it had become easier. It was like a crossword puzzle: the more matches he found, the easier it was to find suitable matches for the remainder.

By the time they landed in Cairo, he had finished the translation and created a concordance of some 138 words in the old language and the equivalent in biblical Hebrew.

'I think we need to agree the terms we're working on,' Mansoor had said on the plane. 'Whilst it's your translation, Professor Klein, and Gabrielle was in charge of the dig, I am the senior scholar amongst the three of us and I think it should be my name first when we publish our findings.'

This was more than just a wish. It was a firm decision. He couldn't actually stop Daniel from publishing a paper from memory about the language in abstract, but the finding of the original Mosaic tablets was much bigger news than the mere decipherment of an old script. Mansoor had control over the stone fragments themselves.

Furthermore, as Vice Minister of Culture, he could stop either of them from working in Egypt again. This would have been more of a blow to Gabrielle than to Daniel, but it was Daniel who was the more conciliatory of the two.

'That's fine with me. I don't even mind if my name goes last. I'm just thrilled and honoured to be part of this.'

Mansoor responded to Daniel's pliant reply by offering him a consolation prize.

'You *do* know of course that we have another long document in the ancient script.'

'*What* document?' Gabrielle had asked, taken aback by this revelation.

'Oh, just a papyrus that's been lying around in the archives for some time. It was never really given much thought, but in the current light, I think it's fair to say that it takes on a new importance.'

It was this other document that Mansoor was taking them to see now. He led them into a room full of metal shelves laden with boxes. He went over to a shelf and stood before a brown cardboard box with some Arabic writing on it in thick, black magic marker. Daniel understood the writing, but all it said was 'Papyrus' and 'Clay jar'. Mansoor lifted the box and brought it over to a workbench. He deposited it carefully on one side, while Daniel and Gabrielle stood on the other. Then he opened the box, reached in and produced what looked like a wooden-framed glass box which he also deposited on the table.

Daniel stared at it in awe. What he was looking at, he realized, was a glass-mounted papyrus which contained about fifty lines of writing in Proto-Sinaitic script. Gazing now at the longest piece of text that he had ever seen in this ancient language almost brought tears to his eyes.

The writing was set out horizontally relative to the paper in a single column, running parallel to the shorter side of the papyrus and perpendicular to the longer side. In this respect it differed from, say, a Jewish Torah scroll written in a series of columns, to be unfurled horizontally and read one column at a time.

Daniel stared at it for a long time, taking in the fact that what he had before him was a very ancient papyrus in remarkably good condition. After a while, he looked up at Mansoor. 'What is it?' he asked.

Mansoor frowned. 'That's what you're supposed to tell me.'

'I mean what can you tell me about its provenance?'

'First of all, can you translate it?'

Daniel sat down, took out his one-page concordance and started looking for words in the papyrus that matched. After some considerable time, he looked up, disappointed.

'There aren't enough words matching the concordance. I found nine instances of *Jehovah* and three variants of *El* which I assume is a generic reference to God. But there were no other common words.'

He noticed that Gabrielle looked disappointed. He could always tell her mood from her face, even when she tried to hide it. It was harder to tell with Mansoor; Daniel had not known him long enough.

'But nine instances of *Jehovah*,' said the Egyptian contemplatively. 'What's your general impression? I mean what *sort* of a document do you think it is?'

'Well, my first impression was that it was a proclamation intended to be unfurled vertically and read out loud by a herald to an assembled audience. But then I rejected that because proclamations would more likely be engraved on a stone monument and displayed in public to be seen by one and all.'

'Not if it were a proclamation to a *nomadic* people,' Gabrielle interrupted, picking up the theme of the nomadic Shasu of Yahowa that they had talked about earlier.

Daniel nodded approvingly. 'True. But then I considered the possibility that it might be a letter or missive to a single individual. I also noticed a peculiarity about the way it was set out: every single line is different in length. That is precisely the way that *poetry* would be written.'

'So which is it?' asked Mansoor. 'A proclamation to a nomadic people or an ancient poem?'

'Well, if it weren't for the presence of the name Jehovah, one might speculate that this was copied or plagiarized from an old Egyptian poem. But *Jehovah* precludes that.'

'So it must be a proclamation to the Israelites,' said Gabrielle.

Daniel wanted to proceed more cautiously. He turned to Mansoor. 'I've told you as much as I can based on looking at it. I might be able to tell you more if you can give me some idea about its origins.'

'I can tell you that it's been carbon dated to around 1600 BC,' said Mansoor.

'That makes it older than the Bible.'

'Yes it does. But I can't tell you when or where it was found.'

'Why not?'

'Because I don't know. That is, I can tell you where it was found *latterly*. But I cannot tell you where it was found *originally*.'

'What do you mean?'

'It was found here in one of the storage rooms, when we were in the process of entering all the items in the museum on to our new computer database. But it didn't have any object card with it, so the provenance is completely unknown. All we found was the clay jar with the papyrus.'

'Clay jar?'

'Yes, the papyrus was actually found inside an old clay jar. We only mounted it in glass recently, shortly after finding it. But we haven't been able to trace the origins of either the papyrus or the jar.'

'But aren't they listed in the museum's register?'

'We did a thorough search of the register and haven't found it.'

'Isn't that rather . . . strange?'

'It's not *suspicious*, if that's what you mean. There are quite a few items in the storage rooms that we haven't been able to find listed in the register books.'

'When you say "the register *books*" . . . I mean, aren't the records computerized now?'

'Actually, we're still in the process of creating our computerized database of objects and artefacts – with the help of an American non-profit organization. But you have to understand that until 2006 the registration system was entirely manual. We've got a quarter of a million objects in this museum, only half of which are in the database. It was when this papyrus and its container were due to be entered into the system, that we discovered it was unlisted.'

'But how could something like that happen?' asked Daniel.

'You have to understand,' Mansoor continued sheepishly, 'that due to historic reasons, the manual numbering system is a bit fragmented. We actually have four different numbering systems that developed over time. But unfortunately, different objects were categorized according to the different systems. In fact, some items have numbers in more than one of the numbering systems.'

'But how could you track so many objects with such a fragmented system?'

'We couldn't. It was a real nightmare. And to make matters worse, we didn't even have anyone specifically trained in archive maintenance. In practice, responsibility for keeping the records was divided between the sections. Each section had responsibility for its own objects and artefacts.'

'Okay, may I see the clay jar?'

Mansoor put on a pair of latex gloves, reached into the box, pulled aside some padding and then produced the clay jar, carefully depositing it on the workbench in front of them. Daniel put on a similar pair of gloves and gently turned the jar this way and that to get a better look. The outside of the jar looked quite plain. Then a very faint trace of an engraving on the side caught Daniel's eye.

'Holy shit!'

'What?' asked Mansoor, picking up on Daniel's excitement.

'Take a look at that,' said Daniel, handing the jar over to Mansoor.

The Egyptian held it up to the light and tilted it back and forth to get a better view. His face changed when he saw what Daniel had seen: a barely visible engraving of a serpent coiled around a pole.

'But that looks like . . .'

'The Rod of Asclepius!'

'But that's a *Greek* symbol,' said Mansoor, lowering the jar and meeting Daniel's eyes. 'It didn't exist at the time when Proto-Sinaitic script was used.'

'Not under the *name* Rod of Asclepius,' said Daniel.

'Wasn't Asclepius the Greek god of medicine?' asked Gabrielle.

'Exactly,' said Daniel. 'And the Rod of Asclepius – the rod

with a snake coiled around it – is widely associated with medicine and used by a number of pharmaceutical organizations. Snakes were often associated with medicine as well as illness. Hence snake oil.'

'Also in ancient Egyptian culture,' said Mansoor.

'But not in this specific form,' Daniel cut in. 'The snake coiled around a pole, I mean.'

'That's true, Professor Klein. But then again there's a lot of ancient Egypt that remains undiscovered, even today. And much of what we had was lost to theft – both foreign and domestic.'

Daniel was thinking about something Gabrielle had said about the Greek god of medicine. At the back of his mind he was also remembering what Harrison Carmichael had said about fiery snakes, Moses putting a snake on a pole and the possibility of the sixth plague returning. Now the dig had been closed down because of 'food poisoning' according to Mansoor. He was turning these thoughts over in his mind, uncertain of what to make of it. For a moment he considered asking Mansoor why the dig was *really* closed down, but he sensed that if Mansoor was holding out on him, he was unlikely to be more candid and open if pressed. He was more likely to clam up completely.

Daniel decided to test the waters.

'I wonder if we could get some outside advice on this point. Would it be all right if I called Harrison Carmichael?'

'Okay,' said Mansoor. 'But be discreet.'

Daniel called Carmichael's number on his mobile, but the voice that answered was not that of Professor Carmichael. 'Hallo, could I speak to Harrison Carmichael please . . . Daniel Klein. Yes, he knows me . . . *What?*'

Gabrielle was looking at him, concerned.

'When? . . . How? . . . The *police*?'

'What is it?' asked Gabrielle.

When Daniel looked at Gabrielle next, his face had turned to stone.

'It's Harrison. He's dead.'

Chapter 13

'They're anti-Semitic, anti-American, anti-British and anti-Western. They'd like to wipe us off the face of the earth.'

Sarit Shalev stared at Dov Shamir, trying to gauge how much of his manner was showmanship for her benefit. It was hard to tell with Dov, or 'Dovi' as she called him. Everything about him was uniformly dark – appearance and mood alike – except for the odd flash of excitement. Although he was dressed like a typical casual Israeli in a blue shirt and jeans, he somehow reminded her of Heathcliff – or at least the way she imagined Heathcliff to be when she first read *Wuthering Heights* as a gangly teenager.

Now a compact but kick-ass fit twenty-four-year-old, she was no longer quite so enamoured by characters in fiction, and thinking about Dov's appearance, she realized that perhaps 'dark' was too strong a word. It was true of his eyes and hair, but applying it to his skin tone was stretching it somewhat. His ancestry was central European, and his skin wasn't naturally dark, merely tanned by the Mediterranean sun.

'They sound like the usual crowd of semi-literate rednecks.'

'Except these guys aren't semi-literate, Sarit. These are movers and shakers, people with power and influence. These are the people who *manipulate* the rednecks: the educated people who use pop science to sell people on their crackpot conspiracy theories.'

She was eight years his junior, and in terms of intelligence experience, that difference was vast. But it didn't restrain her feisty, independent spirit when it came to questioning his judgement as he briefed her on the assignment in this windowless room at Mossad's headquarters in the coastal town of Herzliya.

'Why did this Milne woman contact us in the first place?'

'She first approached us a couple of years ago. Technically she's been my asset even before she took her husband's place.'

'But *she* initiated contact, not vice versa?'

'She didn't like what her husband was doing.'

'Can we trust her?'

'Walk-in assets are always potential bait. But we have ways of verifying. Everything she's told us checked out.'

'But if she was your asset, why did she have to go through the embassy?'

'I was treating her as passive. Once we ID'd the key people from her, we maintained silence.'

'So what's changed?'

'*They've* changed. They're becoming more active . . . and more dangerous.'

He told her about the murder of Harrison Carmichael and Roksana.

'Does it check out?'

'According to the British press and the police statements, yes. The fire, the ante-mortem injuries. They're planning to do a report about it on a programme called *Crimewatch*.'

'And have we passed on any of the information that she gave us?'

'Not yet. We're hesitant about passing it on. We don't want to compromise her position at this stage. We may want to use her more actively, either to flush out more of their members or to disseminate misinformation to them.'

'So we're going to let these murders go unpunished?'

'No, but right now the most urgent priority is tracking down this Goliath. We don't actually know his real name. And at the moment, we don't even know where he is.'

'So what *do* we know?'

Sarit and Dov went back together some four years, when she was the eager young twenty-year-old immigrant from Ireland, fresh out of her two-year army service. In those days, she was called Siobhan Stewart. At eighteen, she had left her sheltered middle-class life in Cork and volunteered to work in Israel and ended up staying. The trigger for her decision had been a visit to the Holy Land the previous year with her family during which her brother had been killed in a suicide bombing in Jerusalem along with twenty-one other people. She herself had been one of the 135 wounded, albeit comparatively mildly.

After that she had tried to understand both sides in the conflict and not merely jump to a conclusion based on emotions alone. But what she found particularly galling were the one-sided condemnations when Israel retaliated against the organizers and planners of a whole spate of similar suicide bombings that followed.

So the following year, bypassing the more traditional picking-apples-on-a-kibbutz option, she had volunteered for eight weeks of equally menial duty on an Israeli army base under the auspices of an organization called Sar-El. It was soon discovered that she had a sharp mind and was a fast learner and so she ended up being given duties that a foreign volunteer would not normally be trusted with.

This was followed by her bold decision to apply for

permanent residence and volunteer for a full two years of service in the Israeli army, much to the horror of her parents. After some gruelling interviews to test her sincerity, and in the face of plaintive appeals to come home, she was accepted by the Israeli army and spent the next two years serving in communications. She also changed her name in that time to the more Israeli-sounding Sarit Shalev.

In the course of her two-year stint, she was based at the Urim monitoring unit in the Negev Desert – a vast array of large satellite dishes that picked up information from telecommunications satellites over the region, covering everything from India and China to Europe. This enabled them to monitor not only cell phones but also intercontinental landlines and shipping. Ultra-fast supercomputers and highly sophisticated software analysed the voice and text messages for keywords and particular phone numbers of interest.

Upon leaving the army, she was planning to go to the Hebrew University in Jerusalem to study psychology. But she took the fateful decision of responding to an ad for a job interview involving 'interesting work abroad'. After passing that interview and several more – where they looked at motivation as well as intelligence – she went through a rigorous initial training course, that was itself part of the selection procedure. Only then was she inducted into the Mossad and the real hard work began.

One of the first lessons she learnt was that the hunter can all too easily become the hunted if alertness flags, even for a moment. This was a lesson that she learnt all too well on one of her training exercises, when her designated target turned the tables on her. She had assumed that she had an advantage, because the targets were not told which of the 'hunters' in the exercise had been assigned to them. But he had been alert and set an ingeniously baited trap, making himself look careless so that she made her move with insufficient preparation.

He had punished her for the error by capturing her and then twisted the knife by subjecting her to the embarrassment of being marched hogtied back to the field HQ for the exercise. It was a humiliation that she resolved never to be exposed to again. And she never had. But more than that: it was a humiliation that she was determined to avenge. The problem was, she couldn't just seek revenge willy-nilly. She had to maintain her professional façade in order to avoid failing the final selection process. But she suspected that her instructors were aware of her intentions and used it to their advantage.

So she waited patiently until she got the chance to get back at the trainee who had sandbagged her, and when it was delivered on a plate, she grabbed it. It took a while, because the exercise assignments were random. But she knew that despite her self-restraint, their instructors had evidently picked up on her competitive spirit, because in the very last exercise, they had made her former nemesis *her* designated hunter. And she suspected that this assignment had not been as random as it was supposed to be. However, unlike her arch-enemy, she *did* know who her hunter was, because when he opened the envelope, he had given himself away by the glint in his eye – as powerful a 'tell' as any she had seen.

From there it had been easy. Just like he had done in the first exercise, she had used a subterfuge: making it seem like she thought another of the class was her hunter, a nerdy type, smart but socially awkward. When the *real* hunter closed in for the kill, he avoided the obvious trap that he had set for her – and fell into the subtle one instead.

The trap – the idea for which came from a story she had read – consisted of allowing herself to be captured in her flat. The hunter had persuaded the trainee whom, she

72

appeared to think of as her assigned hunter, to help him. She 'captured' the trainee and then her real hunter captured her – or at least *thought* he had. Certainly he had her tied to a chair, which he meticulously photographed using his still camera and videotaped using hers. But this didn't surprise her. She knew that he wouldn't be able to resist rubbing her nose in defeat in a macho display. But the exercise called for her to be 'delivered' to their field HQ. Until then, it wasn't complete.

However, between the moment she had captured the decoy hunter and the real one captured her, she had taken out a bottle of sparkling wine from the fridge and told the decoy hunter that she was going to drink to celebrate her victory and record it on video. The real hunter had picked the lock and pounced before she could open the bottle. But he made the mistake of assuming that an unopened champagne bottle couldn't be drugged – or more likely he hadn't thought about it at all.

In fact, it is possible to open the bottle, lace it with Rohypnol or GHB and then reseal it. She had not only done this, she had even carefully preserved the foil and re-covered the plastic stopper. And Mr Macho Israeli couldn't resist the urge to drink her sparkling wine before her eyes and then pour some over her, accompanied by the crude words: 'I like you wet.' (He later explained that this was to 'toughen' her up to the real world of espionage and was not in any way a representation of his real self.)

She had wanted to smile, as he had already drunk enough of the drugged sparkling wine. But she held her facial muscles, showing great patience, to maximize her victory. It was only when he held the bottle to her lips and offered her the chance to toast his victory – which she politely declined – that he got his first inkling of what was about to happen.

73

'Why don't you want to be magnanimous in defeat?' he asked mockingly.

'You've got it wrong,' she replied. 'It's magnanimous in victory; *defiant* in defeat. Besides, I want to stay awake.'

That was when he realized. But by then it was too late, he was already feeling the lethargy that precedes unconsciousness. So a few hours later, it was the hunter who was deposited bound and gagged on the floor of the field HQ by a triumphant Sarit. Then, after three days, when his sleeping patterns had returned to normal, she was confronted by her 'victim' again and told the whole story.

She was led into an office – amidst the utmost solemnity – and found herself facing a tribunal. Her first instinct was panic, assuming that it was some sort of disciplinary tribunal. But that assumption was contradicted by the even more terrifying fact that her deadly foe was *on the tribunal*. The chairman of the panel introduced him as 'Dov Shamir' and explained that he was not a trainee but a long-serving intelligence officer and one of the training team. This in itself was none too reassuring, but what did put her at ease was the fact that Dov was smiling, and it was not a gloating smile, although there was perhaps a hint of mockery about it.

The chairman went on to say that they had identified her early on as a promising recruit for training as a *kidon* officer. This meant that her job would be assassinations of Israel's enemies and not merely intelligence gathering like a regular *katsa*.

Dov had been assigned to bring out the best in her, to put her through her paces and test her to the limit. And she had passed with flying colours. He was to give her one-to-one coaching, and after that they had got on like a house on fire. It was obvious that he respected her – especially after she had turned the tables on him. And it was also obvious that he was attracted to her.

'What we know is that he's extremely dangerous,' he said to Sarit.

'But why should that concern us?'

'For several reasons. Apart from anything else, what Daniel Klein is doing involves discovery of old material pertaining to our ancient history and the doctrine that forms our very justification for having a homeland in this part of the world.'

'So what?' said Sarit with a cheeky grin. 'We're going to execute him for challenging biblical dogma?'

'We're not going to execute him at all unless he becomes a threat to us. But you have to understand that we may be facing a much bigger threat here: a threat to our very survival.'

'What threat?' she asked, knowing that Dov was not one for idle talk.

He told her the nature of the threat . . . and she listened with growing alarm.

Chapter 14

'You've got to be kidding!'

'That's what he told me, just before I drove to the airport.'

Daniel and Gabrielle were on a plane back to London. Mansoor hadn't been happy about them flying out like that, when they were supposed to be collaborating on the most important paper of all their careers. But Gabrielle was clearly upset and Daniel had been in shock when he discovered from the police *when* the fire had occurred.

Daniel realized that it was on the same morning that he had visited Carmichael and he had been racking his brain trying to remember if he had seen anyone at the time.

'So let me be clear about this. He said that the plagues could recur?'

'He said the *plague* in the singular. When I pressed him, he specified the sixth plague.'

'Which was?'

'Boils . . . on the flesh.'

'Look, I shouldn't say this about my own uncle, but he was suffering from the early stages of dementia.'

'I know that.'

'Then we shouldn't really be surprised about the fire. It was probably an accident.'

'That wouldn't account for the injuries that the post-mortem revealed.'

Gabrielle looked away, blushing.

'You're right. I shouldn't have said that . . . do the police have any idea who might have done it?'

'If they did, they didn't tell me.'

'Then why are you so sure that his death has anything to do with this nonsense about the sixth plague?'

Daniel thought for a moment.

'Maybe it's just the timing. One minute, he's telling me something that sounds awfully conspiratorial. I dismissed it at the time – for the same reason as you did, because of the dementia. Then, right after that, he dies . . . in a fire . . . after both he and Roksana have been subjected to other physical injuries.'

'Did he say anything else?'

'He mentioned the incident with the fiery snakes and the bronze snake on a pole.'

'What's that?'

'It's a passage from the Bible,' said Daniel, rummaging through the light bag he had taken on as hand luggage. He found his copy of the Bible and thumbed through it. 'Here it is: Numbers 21, verses six to eight.'

And the Lord sent fiery snakes into the people and they bit the people and many of the Israelites died. And the people came to Moses and said 'We have sinned because we spoke against the Lord and you; pray to the Lord and he will take the snakes from us'; and Moses prayed on behalf of the people. And the Lord said to Moses 'Make a burning one and put it on a pole and it shall be that all the bitten ones that see it will live.'

'Burning one?'

'It's widely understood to be a bronze or copper snake.'

'But how does that relate to the plagues suffered by the *Egyptians*? There wasn't a plague of snakes, was there?'

'No. And I wasn't clear what he meant when he mentioned the sixth plague – which was boils – in the same breath. But it wasn't so much the fiery snakes I was thinking about. It was the snake that Moses put on the pole to *save* the Israelites who had been bitten by the snakes. It reminded me of the symbol we saw on that clay jar.'

'The Rod of Asclepius?'

'Yes, or some sort of Egyptian precursor to it. I was wondering if that could be some symbol associated with Moses. I think that the association has been suggested in the past.'

'Maybe it is. But why did Uncle Harrison think the sixth plague could recur?'

'He never really said. I think it may just have been . . .'

He didn't want to say it.

'A symptom of the dementia.'

Daniel avoided Gabrielle's eyes.

'But in that case . . . why are you worried about it?'

Daniel forced himself to meet her eyes and he chose his next words carefully.

'Because now I'm not so sure. I was thinking about what Mansoor said about the food poisoning outbreak. Did *you* see any sign of it when you were there?'

'No, it happened after I left.'

'Because I was just wondering if Mansoor's covering up for something.'

'How do you mean?'

'Well, I can understand them closing down the dig because of food poisoning, but why didn't they allow *us* to go there?'

Now it was Gabrielle's turn to think for a moment.

'You have a point. He did seem a bit cagey.'

A few hours later, when they landed at Heathrow, they found themselves held for a long time while the doors were kept closed and the passengers were told to stay in their seats. Eventually, when they were opened, four uniformed policemen entered the aircraft and made their way straight to Daniel.

'Daniel Klein?' said one of them.

'Yes,' Daniel replied nervously.

'I have a warrant for your arrest.'

Chapter 15

Goliath was lying on the bed in his hotel room, thinking about how he had failed his mentor. Arthur Morris had told him to keep track of Daniel Klein. But he had lost sight of him, quite suddenly, and now he was feeling guilty.

When first given the task, he had asked if he was to kill Klein, but Morris told him not to ask questions. He would be told later if anything more was required of him. Right now all he had to do was keep tabs on Klein and report in regularly to tell Morris where he was.

And Senator Morris had always been good to Goliath – even giving him his nickname which he said was a sign of respect. Goliath was the more worthy opponent, the senator had told him once. In a fair fight he would have won against David. He was the victim of Jewish treachery. And contrary to popular mythology, the Philistines were culturally more developed than the Jews. Indeed, after becoming king, David had chosen a personal bodyguard of Philistines because he didn't trust his own people.

Goliath felt a debt of gratitude towards Senator Morris, because it was Morris who had saved his life – or rather stopped him from taking his own life. In the old days, when Goliath was plain old Wally Carter, his wife had left him for another man and had taken him to the cleaners with the aid of her smooth-talking Jewish shyster. Between them they had played up his size and his occasional tendency to lash out when things did not go the way he wanted. And he had watched as the house was sold from under him and she took most of the money as well as the children. Watching them drive away in the car had been the most painful thing of all.

But when he was about to jump to his death, it was Senator Morris who had stumbled across him by chance and talked to him for three hours, persuading him not to. After he was hospitalized for mental illness, it was Arthur Morris who had provided him with the lawyer and the doctor's reports that secured his release. It had been Morris who had invited him to his home and treated him like a son and told him that God had a plan for him. It had been Morris who had trained him in various social skills that enabled him to get on with people better than he had in the past and without the former awkwardness that had plagued him. It was Morris who had explained that the social conventions and manners of the upper classes were just a form of acting and it could be learnt like any other role.

For that Wally Carter – now Goliath, the man who walked tall and held his head up high – would do anything to serve Arthur Morris, knowing that in so doing, he was serving God.

Yet now he was miserable, for the trace on Daniel's phone wasn't working. It was possible that the phone was switched off or that he was in a tunnel or underground; but whatever the reason, when he logged on to the website and tried to find the phone, it was showing 'no signal'.

It was just then that Morris phoned. Goliath was fearful of the prospect of having to tell his mentor that he had failed. But he never got the chance, because instead of asking him about the whereabouts of Daniel Klein, Morris launched into a set of rapid-fire instructions, telling Goliath that he was to go to the hospital attached to the Theodor Bilharz Research Institute, locate a patient called Joel Hirsch and get some of his clothes. He was to put them in a bag, seal it up to keep it dry and bring it back to the United States.

And he was not to let anyone see him.

Goliath was about to ask why when he remembered that he was not supposed to ask questions: he was just supposed to do what God requires.

Chapter 16

'So you admit that you were at the house that morning?' asked the Detective Chief Inspector.

'*Yes!*' said Daniel for the umpteenth time. 'I went there to speak to him just before I flew off to Egypt.'

'And you flew off to Egypt at short notice, at the invitation of the Vice Minister of Culture.'

'You can call him and verify that yourself.'

'We will. But perhaps in the meantime you can tell us what you talked to Professor Carmichael about?'

'It was just a bit of catching up on old times. Nothing special.'

Daniel was aware of how implausible this sounded.

'You're about to leave the country at short notice, at the request of the Egyptian Vice Minister of Culture, and take a detour from your drive to the airport to stop off at your old professor's house for small talk?'

The DCI shot a sceptical glance at his colleague who shrugged his shoulders as if to express his own disbelief of Daniel's account.

'He was my *mentor*,' Daniel continued. 'I hadn't seen him in a while and I was quite surprised at Mansoor's invitation. So I wanted to ask for his advice.'

'But how could he advise you, if you didn't know why you were being invited to Egypt?'

'That was the point. I figured he might be able to tell me how to play it.'

'And *did* he?'

Daniel looked away awkwardly. He had nothing to hide on this point, but the truth made him feel uncomfortable.

'He was too far gone to help.'

'Too far gone?' the DCI echoed.

'Dementia. I could tell that he wasn't really with me.'

'Is it possible that he had something on his mind? Something that might explain why someone would want to kill him?'

Again Daniel lapsed into thought. On this point he *did* have something to hide. For the next few seconds, he thought carefully about how much he wanted to share with the DCI. Did he want to mention Carmichael's paranoid claims about his unpublished paper? The belief that the plague of boils could make a resurgence? At the time it had seemed preposterous. But Harrison Carmichael was dead and there was no question that he had been murdered. Even if the fire could be dismissed as an accident, the injuries to Roksana and to Carmichael himself could not.

But did he want to share his suspicions with the police? Would they come over as credible? Did he really have anything to tell them? Certainly nothing that Carmichael had told him amounted to solid information. All Daniel had was a nagging suspicion, but what he really wanted was an explanation and he wasn't going to get that from the policeman.

Daniel saw no reason to stick his neck out by offering what might come over as a self-serving explanation. So he decided to hold his peace.

'I can't think of anything.'

'Okay, Professor Klein. Interview suspended at 5.45 p.m.'

'Look, I know you have to investigate thoroughly. But I've told you all I know and I'm a very busy man. Is there any possibility that I could be released on bail?'

'We're awaiting the results from the forensic team. If we can eliminate you – and assuming that we have no other grounds to hold you – you will be released at that time.'

Daniel didn't see how the forensic tests would eliminate him. If he *had* started the fire, he could have taken the clothes he was wearing to Egypt and disposed of them there. They would certainly find his fingerprints and DNA on the garden chair where he had sat and it was unlikely that they would find any of the killer's DNA in the house, because of the fire. Even if the forensic tests came up negative, he knew that a cloud of suspicion would hang over him until the case was solved.

In the meantime he was going right back to the police cells, to await his fate.

Chapter 17

'He was a friend of Lord Byron, you know,' said the curator, a young Indian. 'They met at Cambridge.'

'Yes, he was actually two years ahead of Byron, at Trinity,' said Gabrielle. 'In many ways he was his mentor, until Byron's fame left him behind. But they stayed friends.'

Gabrielle was in an office on the top floor of the British Museum, sitting at a large work table with one of the curators of the Egyptian department. The police had told her that she wouldn't be allowed any contact with Daniel before he was either released or charged. He had chosen not to take a lawyer, so she couldn't even get a message to him indirectly.

She faced a stark choice. She could either sit around doing nothing except brood about her uncle's death and Daniel's fate or she could keep herself occupied, following up on the trail that had started in Egypt. It was ironic that finding the Mosaic tablets had proved to be not the end of the trail, but the start, and had in fact opened the door to other discoveries.

Having her name second or third on a paper about the discovery of the Mosaic tablets was prestigious enough. But after Mansoor had told them about the mysterious papyrus in the Egyptian Museum, it looked like there was a lot more to discover – especially as he had told them that the papyrus was carbon-dated to 1600 BC. That would make it older than the Bible – yet written in the same script as the original Mosaic tablets.

A secret that pre-dated the Bible? And one that must have been *related* to the Bible because it was written in the same ancient script as the original Ten Commandments!

That was a find well worth pursuing. If the credit for finding the Mosaic tablets would be great, the prestige for revealing older documents relating to the Semitic peoples would be enormous.

But of the three of them, only Daniel could decipher the papyrus. He had made it clear that to have any chance of doing so, he needed some idea of its origins. So now Gabrielle was sitting here with the curator talking about William John Bankes, explorer, artist and Egyptologist. Between 1815 and 1819, Bankes travelled throughout Egypt, Nubia, Palestine and Syria, meticulously recording many of the great sites and artefacts with notes and drawings with a skilled and practised hand in the days before photography.

Several huge ledger-sized folders with cardboard 'pages' and heavy covers were stacked up on one side of the table. These were the Bankes archives. Pictures were held between the cardboard sheets, and many had clear plastic or cellophane over them to offer fuller protection of the drawing beneath. Gabrielle turned the pages in awe.

'It's amazing,' she said with a shake of her head, admiring the skill and detail of the drawings.

Through his travels, Bankes had accumulated a substantial portfolio of manuscripts and illustrations of previously unknown historical sites in ancient Egypt and Sudan, preserving the details and imagery of sites that, in some cases, later became lost to vandalism and theft. For while the artefacts plundered by foreign explorers were still extant in Western museums, the spoils taken by local thieves – who were usually looking for gold and didn't always appreciate the priceless value of knowledge – were in many cases gone for good.

'So if I've understood you correctly,' said the curator, 'you don't actually know *where* you're looking, only *what* you're looking for.'

'Exactly,' said Gabrielle. 'We have an ancient Egyptian jar that bears a symbol like the Rod of Asclepius. We think it may have some connection with the ancient Israelites, as well as the Egyptians. So what we're wondering is if there's anything in the Bankes archives that shows such a symbol in ancient Egypt.'

'I do actually remember seeing a drawing with that symbol before, in the Bankes collection,' said the curator. 'Now let me see.'

He selected one of the folders and started flicking through it.

'Oh look,' he said.

He had just stopped at a picture engraved on a rock showing a snake coiled around a pole.

'It's at Deir el-Medina,' said the curator. 'Literally "monastery of the town".'

'The town where the stonemasons, carpenters and scribes who worked on the tombs in the Valley of the Kings lived. Of course in those days, they didn't speak Arabic.'

'That's right,' said the curator. 'They called it Set Maat.'

'"The Place of Truth".'

'Precisely.'

Gabrielle was staring at the picture.

'This would presumably have been *before* the place was excavated.'

'Oh, *long* before,' the curator acknowledged. 'The first archaeological excavation was by an Italian called Ernesto Schiaparelli from 1905 to 1909. The second, between

1922 and 1951, was by French archaeologists under the direction of Bernard Bruyère. That one was somewhat more extensive.'

'That's about a hundred years after Bankes travelled in Egypt and Nubia,' said Gabrielle. 'Why the long wait before they started digging?'

The curator scratched his chin. 'Well, let me just put that into its proper historical context. The site was known about for some considerable time before that. Indeed, a large number of papyri were found there as far back as the 1840s.'

'*Papyri?*'

'Yes.'

'Were any of them in Proto-Sinaitic script?'

'Proto-Sinaitic?' The curator sounded genuinely surprised. 'Not as far as I know. But not all the papyri are extant. Some of them were stolen.'

'And never found?' asked Gabrielle.

'Well, a few of them ended up in the village well. Actually, that's from the second excavation. The Schiaparelli excavation turned up loads of pottery and ostraca but no papyri. The Bruyère excavation, on the other hand, turned up many papyri. But unfortunately it wasn't administered or controlled all that well. Consequently, something like half the papyri were taken without Bruyère's consent or even his knowledge. Those were the ones that got stolen.'

'And do we have any way of knowing how much of it ended up in private collections?' asked Gabrielle.

'Probably not.'

'And by the same token,' she pressed on, 'we have no way of knowing what language or writing system they were written in?'

'Not unless the heirs of those private collectors come forward,' the curator conceded.

Gabrielle's mind was racing ahead.

Could the papyrus Mansoor showed us be one of the missing Deir el-Medina papyri? If so, it could be part of a huge collection – and what a story THEY could tell!

Chapter 18

Goliath hardly noticed the streets of Cairo sweep by as he drove his rented car to the Theodor Bilharz Research Institute Hospital. In his head he was turning over the mantra about doing God's work that gave him solace when times were hard. It was the same thought that had kept him going in prison.

After he had gone to work for Senator Morris, he had been given a difficult assignment. It involved killing a rabbi whom the senator said was part of the Jewish conspiracy to create a New World Order. Goliath had felt uncomfortable about killing. But, as Arthur Morris had told him, it was the will of God.

Only it had gone wrong – horribly wrong. He accomplished the killing all right, but he had got caught. However, Arthur Morris had not abandoned him. He had got him a lawyer who managed to get him off with manslaughter. He learnt an important lesson at the trial, namely that securing the right verdict had less to do with the law or the facts than with getting a sympathetic jury. The lawyer had managed to get the trial relocated to a different venue and had used a lot of so-called 'peremptory challenges' to get undesirables off the jury.

However, the judge was angered by the verdict and sentenced

91

him to seven years in prison, of which he had served three and a half. It was a strange experience. He had always heard that prison was a tough place. But most prisoners stayed away from him, especially after he had killed one who tried to steal money off him. Amazingly, although there were several witnesses, they all told the prison guards that they had seen nothing. He was told by one old prisoner that he should do the same if ever he were asked if he had seen anything.

When he arrived at the hospital, he set about finding the patient, Joel Hirsch. Morris had told him not to draw attention to himself so he couldn't ask at the main desk. Instead, he started walking down the corridor towards the intensive care unit, where Morris had told him Joel would be. He found it by following the path marked on the map at the entrance. When he walked in there was only one nurse on duty. That was good.

'Excuse me,' he said in slow English, to make sure that he was understood. 'I'm looking for a patient called Joel Hirsch.'

The nurse appeared to respond to the name and pointed to a glass-encased unit. Goliath started to walk towards it, but the nurse signalled him to stop with a gesture and the word '*Lah*'.

'No, you don't understand. I'm his uncle.'

She made a sign with her hand and said something in Arabic. Then she reached for the phone.

He knew what was happening. She didn't speak English and she was going to call someone else. If only she had gone to fetch someone, that would have given him time. But instead she was going to stay here and wait until help came. That was no good. He didn't want to be seen.

There was only one thing to do. He reached out and grabbed her, clamping one hand over her mouth to stop her screaming and encircling her neck with the other. And then with that technique that he was so good at, he snapped her neck and let her body slump to the floor.

But now he was in a panic. If this was the intensive care unit then there would normally be several people on duty and that meant that someone could come back at any minute. He knew that he had to find a sample of Joel's clothes, but he didn't know where to look. A patient's clothes would normally be in a cabinet beside the bed, but in this case, the bed was in an isolated unit. And it was probably locked or at least alarmed.

He looked for some sign on a cabinet or unit next to the room that housed the bed, but there was none. They might have destroyed his clothes or taken them for analysis – he simply had no way of knowing. All he knew was that he could hear voices. That meant that people were approaching. He didn't want to fail his mentor, especially after he had lost track of that Daniel Klein character. But what other choice did he have?

It was now too late to go back into the main corridor. Instead, he made his way across the unit to the emergency exit and slipped out just as he heard a woman scream.

They had discovered the body.

He broke into a sweat and started sprinting.

Chapter 19

'Well, I'm pleased to tell you, Professor Klein, that you are free to go. For now. You're being released on bail as we may have some more questions for you. However, one of your bail conditions is that you remain in the country, so we'll be retaining your passport for the time being.'

'Thank you,' said Daniel, not sure what he was thanking the DCI for.

Ten minutes later, back in possession of his other personal items, Gaby was driving him back to his place in North London.

'So let's assume that it was one of the papyri from Deir el-Medina, it could be the key to unlocking a sizeable chunk of Jewish history. I mean, it could open up the whole history of the Israelites in Egypt from the arrival of Joseph to the exodus of Moses.'

'Look, Gaby, I don't mean to be rude, but this isn't really what you want to talk about, is it?'

'What else would I want to talk about?'

'Your uncle.'

'I do *not* want to talk about my uncle!' she snapped. 'And it's *Gabrielle*.'

'Look . . . I'm sorry. I know this is painful—'

'I said I *don't* want to talk about it! My uncle's death is a tragedy, but there's not much we can do about it. Some burglar who doesn't like to leave evidence behind . . . some disgruntled former student . . . some rival academic . . . some local lunatic . . . Whoever it was, we're in no position to catch them. That's the job of the police.'

An uncomfortable few seconds went by. Daniel knew that any further attempts to comfort her would only backfire, that much was certain. So he returned to the subject of the mysterious papyrus and its origins.

'Okay. Well, let's consider your theory, Professor Gusack,' he said with a forced smile. 'The scribes who worked at the necropolis were fully literate in the various writing systems of the day, including hieroglyphics. Indeed, most if not all of the workers there were fully literate.'

'I know. They were skilled workers – *paid* workers, not slaves. In fact, the Deir el-Medina papyri even contain the first known record of a strike, when they downed tools after going unpaid for too long.'

'Which just goes to prove my point. The stonemasons had to be literate in order to carve the hieroglyphic characters into the rock.'

'Your point being?'

'My point being that Proto-Sinaitic script was used by the uneducated. Why would the literate, skilled workers at the necropolis bother with it?'

'Have you got a better theory?'

'Well yes, as a matter of fact I have. Who says the papyrus had to have been found at an *archaeological* dig?'

'What else is there?'

'I was thinking about it while I was cooling my heels in the police cells. I was wondering if it might have been found accidentally during some building project.'

'*Which* building project?'

'Only one of the biggest in the world! The Aswan High Dam.'

'How do you mean?'

'Well, maybe one of the workers was operating a bulldozer? Or clearing out the rubble that the bulldozer had dug up.'

Gaby's mind drifted back.

The bulldozer . . . moving forward . . . forward . . .

Get out of the way!

'Gaby?'

'What?'

'You were miles away.'

'Sorry.'

He wouldn't have been so worried if it wasn't for the fact that it was Gabrielle who was driving.

'I've just thought of something, Daniel. Aswan is just across the river from Elephantine . . .'

'. . . And Elephantine was the site of a huge discovery of papyri, dating from the fifth century BC, connected with the Jewish community that lived in the area when it was under Persian control – the so-called Elephantine papyri.'

'How much do you know about that?' Gabrielle asked.

'Quite a lot, actually,' said Daniel. 'This is right up my street. When the Kingdom of Judah was destroyed by the Babylonians, they brought most of the Jews as captives to Babylon. But when the Babylonians were defeated by the Persians, Cyrus of Persia allowed the Jews to return to Jerusalem, and also tolerated them in other parts of the Persian Empire, including Elephantine, where they grew into a flourishing community.'

'And were any of these Elephantine papyri in Proto-Sinaitic?'

Daniel pursed his lips. 'That's the downer. They were

written in a variety of languages: hieratic and demotic Egyptian, Aramaic, Greek, Latin and Coptic. But *not* Proto-Sinaitic. The majority of those that specifically concerned the Jews were in Aramaic, using the old Aramaic script that developed round about the eighth century BC.'

'Is it possible that they were still using the Proto-Sinaitic in the *fifth* century BC?'

Daniel thought for a moment. The answer, dictated by his scholarship, was not encouraging.

'It's highly unlikely.'

Daniel was disappointed. Gabrielle's question had brought him right back down to earth. They had arrived at his house and Gabrielle parked the rented car in the driveway.

When they got inside, Daniel put his suitcase in the master bedroom while Gabrielle went to the kitchen to put the kettle on. He was about to unpack when he heard a cry from Gabrielle. He raced into the kitchen to see her holding her mobile phone to her ear, listening to something.

'What is it?'

'You've got to hear this!'

She handed him the phone and pointed to the button to play the message again. It was from Mansoor.

'Hallo, Gabrielle, I'm sorry I didn't tell you this before, but there are some things happening here that we need to talk about. I heard about Harrison Carmichael being killed and I understand that Daniel has fallen under some sort of suspicion. I have explained to the British authorities that I invited him here. I do not know if this helps, but in the meantime, I have to tell you that I have not been completely honest with you. There was no food poisoning epidemic at the dig site, but there was some sort of outbreak of disease which we think may have had something to do with the site itself. We are looking into this but in the meantime we have put the volunteers into quarantine. However, the first one to become ill was at another hospital and he has since died. The reason I am calling you is that a nurse in the hospital wing where he was being treated was murdered. It is unclear if the two things are connected, but I just want you to know that we have concerns on a number of fronts. Please call me as soon as you can.'

'You'd better call him,' said Daniel, handing back the phone.

'I don't think you should bother unpacking,' Gabrielle responded.

He looked at her in shock.

'I can't leave now. I'm on bail.'

'I'll talk to Mansoor, but I think we've got more important things to worry about than you being on bail.'

At the back of Daniel's mind, he was thinking about the outbreak at the dig site and remembering Harrison's words about the resurgence of the plague. Harrison had said that he knew the plague could return based on his translation of an old manuscript in Proto-Sinaitic script. Mansoor had shown him such a manuscript. Could that be the one that his mentor had translated?

Yet there was still one obstacle in his way.

'They've got my passport.'

A smile lit Gabrielle's face.

'What about your US passport – the one you had when you were married to Charlotte?'

Chapter 20

Sarit arrived in Cairo from Cyprus, entering the country using her Irish passport under the name Siobhan Stewart, after they had tracked down Goliath via the Urim telecommunications monitoring unit, the same unit where Sarit had served.

The unit functioned like a well-oiled machine. Anything that was flagged by the system as important was then sent for human analysis to 'Unit 8200', the Signals Intelligence centre in Herzliya. Any intercepts that were found to be encrypted were also sent there. From there, the messages were deciphered or simply analysed for relevant content and disseminated to the appropriate department or organization, such as the Mossad – based in the same building – or military intelligence.

In this case, the key word that they had picked up on was the name 'Joel Hirsch' that Audrey Milne had given them. This had given the monitors at Urim both the number of Goliath's cell phone and the means to track him in the future.

But Sarit's initial instructions were to proceed to the hospital and find out what was going on on the ground. When she arrived, she saw several police cars, and police milling about, along with dozens of onlookers both outside the building and in the reception area.

'What happened?' she asked a nurse in Arabic.

'A nurse was killed.'

'How?' She made sure to sound surprised.

'By a madman. A big man. He ran away.'

'How did he kill her?'

'With his bare hands. He broke her neck.'

The nurse seemed to be enjoying herself as she told the story. But at the back of Sarit's mind, a question was nagging away: had he got the sample of Joel's clothes? She went to the reception desk.

'I'm here to find out about a patient called Joel Hirsch.'

The receptionist looked mildly alarmed.

'Are you related to him?'

She had to think carefully. If she said yes and it didn't check out, she'd have some explaining to do. She knew why he had been brought in and she understood the panic. She decided to use it to her advantage.

'No. I'm a journalist. I heard that he was ill. I was just wondering if it was contagious?'

'We have no evidence to suggest he was contagious.'

The receptionist's tone was defensive, and her left hand looked like it was itching to reach for the intercom.

'*Was* contagious?'

'He died last night.'

'From what?'

'I'm afraid we don't know that yet. There'll have to be a post-mortem.'

'Yes, but I mean it was from the illness, right? He wasn't killed or anything?'

The receptionist looked puzzled.

'Why do you ask?'

Sarit knew that there was no backing down now.

'Well, I just heard about a nurse being killed. I was wondering if there's any connection.'

100

'I'll have to refer you to my superiors,' said the receptionist, reaching for the intercom. 'What did you say your name was?'

Sarit turned sharply on her heel and left.

Chapter 21

'I still don't like it,' said Daniel, feeling self-conscious as they walked into Heathrow Airport from the car park.

'Would you prefer that we just sat around doing nothing?'

'I can't help thinking I should be trying to clear my name instead of running off in pursuit of academic glory.'

'And how do you propose to do that? Do you have the investigative resources of a police force? Their authority to arrest people? Access to a forensic lab perhaps? A computer to co-ordinate all the information?'

Daniel sighed. 'No, but I can try and find out what Harrison was talking about . . . about the plague and the fiery snakes and all that.'

'And how are you going to find out? Are you planning on consulting a medium?'

He looked at her in shock. She was being surprisingly cold and heartless considering that it was her uncle who was dead – the uncle with whom she had spent so many summers as a child and later as a teenager. But he sensed that she was using aggression to keep her grief at bay.

'If I leave now I'm breaching my bail conditions. That'll make me a more credible suspect in their eyes.'

Gabrielle was shaking her head.

'I don't think it'll make a difference one way or the other.'

'What if they stop me when I try and pass through to airside?' he asked nervously.

'You think they've got a list of everyone who is out on bail?'

'In this day and age? It wouldn't surprise me.'

'Well, you can quit worrying. They may have a list of people who have *jumped* bail or people who have outstanding warrants against them. But they wouldn't have a list of everyone on bail. If they did that, they wouldn't have needed to hold on to your passport.'

'I hope you're right.'

'I *am* right. Now stop worrying. Let's check in and get airside. Then we can see if we can track down a copy of Uncle Harrison's paper. If he sent it to an American journal, someone must know about it.'

What Daniel didn't realize was that now that he had switched on his mobile phone, it was transmitting his location again. That meant that someone thousands of miles away was tracking him.

Chapter 22

The curator was sweating, but it wasn't just from the heat. It wasn't such a warm day and the air conditioning was on. It was something on the *inside* and he felt like he was going down with flu. And it had started soon after that visit from Gabrielle Gusack.

It must be swine flu. Damn!

He decided to check the symptoms online. Fever, sweating, headache, aching muscles, limb and joint pain, tiredness. On the other hand there was no diarrhoea, no sore throat, no runny nose and no sneezing. And there was something else. He was itching all over his torso, like he had measles or even chickenpox. But he had had both of those as a child.

He opened his shirt and looked at his torso only to be confronted by a frightening sight. His body was covered in red marks – not streaks but more like the elongated letter S or several such letters strung together. He touched one and his mind shrieked with pain, like he was burning. But now he realized that with this fever, his whole body felt like it was burning. The touch only made it worse.

A wave of fear swept over him. His mind panicked as he wondered what it could be. He had come into contact with people from a foreign country where hygiene standards are not so high and now he was going down with something

104

that produced these S-shaped marks and a fiery pain on his flesh.

He felt his legs going weak.

Is that just fear or the disease itself?

Whatever it was, he knew that he had to act quickly. He leaned over to grab the phone and called 999.

'Emergency services, which service do you require?'

'Ambulance,' he rasped as he felt the heat rise up in his stomach. He wanted to say more, but he felt his vision go blurry and could no longer support himself.

The last thing he remembered before passing out was his body slumping to the floor.

Chapter 23

'It couldn't have come from the Aswan High Dam excavations,' said Mansoor.

'Why not?' asked Daniel, defensively.

'Because I've been thinking about why the jar and papyrus are undocumented and I think I know the reason.'

In Mansoor's office at the SCA, Daniel and Gabrielle sat forward.

'Which is?' Daniel prompted.

'The most likely cause of an artefact not getting recorded would be if it were found round about the time when the museum moved to a new location. The museum was built in 1835 and has moved twice, first to the Boulaq district in 1858 and then to its present location at Tahrir Square in 1902. But the High Dam wasn't constructed till the 1960s.'

Daniel thought for a moment about Mansoor's comment. But then a thought came to him.

'What about the old dam?'

'The *Low* Dam?' Mansoor considered this. 'It was initially constructed between 1898 and 1902 and then raised twice after that.'

'So maybe it was found when they were nearing completion . . . in 1902.'

Mansoor was shaking his head.

'They would have been more likely to find an artefact during initial excavations than when they were finishing construction. Besides, the Elephantine papyri date from the fifth century BC. There's no way they'd still be using the script then, when they already used the Aramaic alphabet!'

Daniel felt frustrated. He and Gabrielle had already considered this objection, but hearing it now from Mansoor reminded him how far off the mark that particular theory had been.

'What about Deir el-Medina? Could it have been found there?'

'None of the papyri that survived from there were in Proto-Sinaitic.'

'I guess that puts paid to *both* those theories,' said Daniel with a wry smile.

'I'm sorry to put the dampener on it,' said Mansoor. 'Especially after you came back here to help out.'

'Actually, what really prompted me to come back here was your message about that outbreak of illness.' He preferred not to mention what Harrison Carmichael had said about the plague at this stage. 'Any more news on that front?'

Mansoor looked tense.

'It's not looking good. We've had four more deaths. Most of the rest are on the road to recovery. But we still don't know what caused it and we're having a hard time keeping the lid on it. They *are* foreign citizens after all.'

'Why are you trying so hard to keep it a secret?'

Mansoor looked at Daniel as if he were an idiot.

'My country thrives on the tourist business. Can you imagine what it'll do to the trade if it leaks out?'

'You're right, I'm sorry. I just wish I understood what was causing it.'

'We have our best doctors working on it. They're checking

dust samples from the site. They sent teams there to conduct chemical and radiological analysis, but so far they haven't turned up anything.'

Daniel was on the verge of mentioning Carmichael's cryptic words, when Gabrielle changed the subject again.

'I just had a thought about what you said about the public works projects, Daniel. Could it have been found in some other public project?'

'Like what?' asked Mansoor. 'A road? A bridge?'

'Yes,' said Gabrielle.

'Holy shit!' Daniel blurted out.

'*What?*' asked Mansoor, ignoring the vulgar language and latching on to Daniel's contagious excitement.

'I think Gaby may be on to something – sorry, Gabri*elle*.' He looked at Mansoor. 'When was the Suez Canal constructed?'

'Between 1859 and 1869.'

'And you said the museum moved to Boulaq in 1858?'

'That's right.'

'So the jar and papyrus might have been found during the initial Suez Canal excavations.'

'Quite possibly,' Mansoor replied, approvingly. 'And the chief engineer of the Suez Canal project was Linant de Bellefonds. He was a close friend of William John Bankes. He would have made sure that it was handed over to the authorities!'

'Then we've cracked it!' said Daniel, his voice rising with elation.

'But why is that so exciting?' asked Gabrielle, confused. 'If it was found by workers excavating the Suez Canal?'

'You don't understand, Gaby. If this papyrus *was* found during the Suez Canal construction, then we don't just know where it was found. *I know what it is!*'

'*What?*' Mansoor and Gabrielle said in unison.

'*The Song of the Sea!*'

Chapter 24

'What could it possibly be?' asked the consultant.

'It's nothing I've ever seen before,' the toxicologist replied.

The curator was in an isolation unit at University College Hospital as the experts discussed and debated what he was suffering from. They had ruled out swine flu, bird flu and pretty much any other form of flu. But that didn't tell them what it was.

They were treating him with a cocktail of antibiotics in case it was bacteriological and antipyretics to bring down the fever. They were awaiting the results of toxicology and blood sample tests and they had asked his colleagues what he had eaten and drunk recently and if any of them had experienced similar symptoms.

So far they had drawn a blank on every one of their speculations. They were further hampered by the fact that he alternated between unconsciousness and delirium, making it impossible to glean any useful information from him.

Right now, he was just emerging from unconsciousness and apparently trying to speak. They couldn't enter the isolation chamber because that would be a contagion hazard, but there was a microphone by the bed and they were pointing to it and telling him to speak into it. He half sat up and struggled to move his lips close to it.

'Nehu . . . Nehu . . .'

'What's he saying?' asked one of the doctors.

'It sounds like Nehu.'

'What does that mean?'

'I don't know. Sounds like something in Hindi maybe.'

'Nehushtan!' the curator finally blurted out and then slumped back on to the pillow.

The monitoring equipment let out a high-pitched whine, warning that the patient's vital signs had failed.

'Nehushtan?' one of the doctors echoed.

'It must be a country,' said another.

'Why would he mention a country?' asked the first.

'Or a province?' a nurse suggested.

'You've heard of it?' asked one of the doctors.

'No, but it could be a province or a region instead of a country. Maybe it's where he comes from.'

Meanwhile, down the corridor, a member of the hospital ancillary staff had gone to use a phone.

'Hallo, is that the news desk? I've got a story that might be worth a few quid.'

Chapter 25

'"I will sing to Jehovah for he has . . ." and then the next words in the Hebrew are "*Ga-ah, Ga-ah*" or "*Ga-oh, Ga-oh*." It depends on which vowels you insert and also whether you use the Sephardi or Ashkenazi pronunciations.'

Daniel was reading a biblical passage out loud, anglicizing words like *Jehovah* to make their meaning clear to Gabrielle.

'In the Bible,' Daniel explained, 'when the same word is repeated in immediate succession, it's for emphasis. It's like saying "very" in English. In this case, the word itself means to triumph or achieve victory. So the repetition, "He is triumphant, is triumphant," could be translated as "He is very triumphant," or "He is highly triumphant." It could even be a superlative: "He has triumphed above all." And on the papyrus we see the word *Jehovah* followed by a similar repetition of a word. That's one point of comparison.'

'But what made you think it's this Song of the Sea?' asked Gabrielle.

'It's all a matter of location. Once you suggested that the papyrus was found in the Suez Canal excavations, it all fell into place. You see, in the Bible, the sea that parted to let the Israelites escape from the pharaoh was called *Yam Suph* in Hebrew. That's usually translated as the *Red* Sea, but it actually means the *Reed* Sea or Sea of Reeds and most modern scholars believe that it was a shallow body of water in the place that today is occupied by the Suez Canal.'

'But what exactly *is* the Song of the Sea?' she pressed on.

'Well, according to the Bible, after the Israelites crossed the Sea of Reeds, with the pharaoh's army in hot pursuit, the waters flooded back and the Egyptian soldiers were drowned. When this happened, the Israelites were so delighted that they sang a song celebrating their escape and the destruction of their enemies. It's called the Song of the Sea or the Song of Miriam, after Moses' sister. When the song is described, with Moses singing it, there's a repetition of the first verse sung by Miriam and the women – hence its alternative title. That incidentally is also the reason why Orthodox Jews insist on separating men and women in synagogues: because the women sang *after* the men.'

'But why would the Song of the Sea be written on its own, if it was part of the Bible?' asked Gabrielle. 'And why would this copy of it be at precisely the location of the Sea of Reeds? I mean, presumably the Israelites carried on with their travels. They didn't *remain* on the eastern banks of the Sea of Reeds. According to the Bible, they *moved on*, crossing the Sinai Desert. So why would this manuscript be there?'

'According to modern theories about the Bible, the Song of the Sea was originally a separate work, an old poem that existed before the rest of the narrative. In fact, according to one theory, it's the oldest text in the Bible. And this might be one of several manuscripts of the song that happened to be left at the scene. It probably described some minor event or battle that was then elevated to a greater importance.'

Mansoor picked up on this.

'The idea that it was a separate ancient work that got written into the biblical narrative fits in very neatly with the carbon dating of the papyrus. 1600 BC would put it well before the traditional dating of the Israelite exodus. But more importantly, it would also fit in very neatly with the volcanic eruption of Santorini round about that time.'

'Why would the eruption of Santorini have anything to do with the parting of the waters in Egypt?' asked Daniel.

'Because according to oceanographers, the eruption of Santorini would have produced a tsunami that would have reached the shores of Egypt and would have been especially pronounced in a shallow body of water that had an outlet to the sea. And when a tsunami strikes, because of the way waves move, the first thing that happens is that the water flows *out*, thereby creating a dry area which then becomes flooded when the water rushes back.'

'Of course!' said Daniel. 'And that perfectly fits the biblical account of the parting of the waters, followed by the deluge.'

'Are there any other points of comparison in the text?' Mansoor followed up.

'Well, if we look down to lines five and six in the biblical text, using the common word *El* or God as our point of comparison, we see, "*Zeh Elohi veAnveihu.*" This is my God and I will live with him, or it could be translated as "I will beautify him", depending on how you understand the problematic word *anvei*. Then the next line is "*Elohei avi veAmromemenhu,*" which means: "God of my father and I will exalt him." Now if we turn to lines five and six of the papyrus, again we see the letters for *El* written as the beginning of a longer word, and in *just the right places*, relative to the length and word spacing on the lines.'

He looked over at Mansoor for approval. Mansoor nodded.

'Okay, now if we go down to the next two lines in the biblical passage, we see that they begin with the name Jehovah. And again the same is true of the papyrus.'

'So it's looking like a match,' said Gabrielle.

'It's beginning to,' Daniel confirmed.

'So does that mean,' asked Gabrielle, 'that by comparing the papyrus text to the version of the Song of the Sea in the Bible you can use it like the Rosetta Stone to decipher the ancient language?'

'Basically yes,' said Daniel. But he realized that the downer was that this papyrus could not be the one that Harrison Carmichael had translated – the one about the plague. Assuming that his mentor really had translated a papyrus that made reference to the plague, he still had to find it.

But where?

'I guess all we need are some more samples of the ancient language to translate.'

It was a long shot, but he noticed a flicker in the face of the SCA chief.

'I have some more good news for you,' said Mansoor. 'While you were away, I did some checking in the archives and it appears that there are a few other samples of the ancient script that haven't received all that much publicity.'

Daniel's eyes lit up. Did Mansoor unwittingly have a papyrus that described the plagues?

Chapter 26

Once again, Goliath was afflicted by a feeling of failure. Senator Morris had told him that it was going to be a difficult task, but had been sure that he could pull it off. All he had to do was get the clothes and leave. But instead he had left empty-handed and a nurse dead.

Now, sitting alone in his hotel room, he was turning over the events in his mind, feeling something that he didn't often feel: guilt.

He didn't like killing the innocent, even though he knew that God would take them to his bosom in the next life. It was only the wicked that he enjoyed killing.

He remembered how, after he was released from prison, he had killed the lawyer who had represented him at the murder trial over the killing of the rabbi. He would have liked to have killed the lawyer who represented his wife in the divorce, but he was already dead of natural causes, so he decided to kill the lawyer who had defended him instead.

It wasn't that he blamed the lawyer for his imprisonment. His lawyer had in fact done very well to get him off with manslaughter. But he was Jewish and he was a parasite, making his money off other people's misery. It was only because of money that the lawyer had represented him in the first place.

The lawyer was no different from a hooker: he went with anyone as long as he was paid. Today it might be Goliath, tomorrow it might be some crooked Jewish banker who had embezzled billions of other people's money. To the lawyer, it was all the same.

So Goliath had had no qualms about killing him. He wasn't even troubled by the fact that he had killed him in front of his five-year-old son. The kid would probably grow up just like his father. He had intended to kill the kid too, but the kid had screamed and that alerted other people. He had to flee before any witnesses saw him. Just as he had to flee from the hospital. Witnesses could land him in prison.

His thoughts were interrupted by the phone.

'Hallo.'

It was the senator.

'Can you talk?'

'Yes.'

'I've just heard a news item from England about a curator at the British Museum.'

'What?' asked Goliath, confused.

'Never mind. The point is, it's given me another idea. It still involves getting a sample of clothes, but from Daniel Klein and the Gusack woman.'

He explained the details. When he had finished, Goliath asked a question.

'What should I do with the people, once I've got the clothes?'

'Kill them.'

Chapter 27

'This is the famous Mernepteh stele,' said Mansoor. 'Made of granite, it was by far the largest inscribed stone ever found, not just by Flinders Petrie, but by anyone. The stone was actually stolen by Mernepteh from the mortuary temple of another pharaoh who had already used the other side. But it was the proclamation that Mernepteh inscribed on it that makes it one of the most famous monuments of ancient Egypt.'

Daniel stood there staring at the huge stone monument in awe, flanked by Mansoor and Gabrielle. His lips moved, but no words came out of his mouth. It was as if there *were* no words that could describe the magnificence of what he beheld. Lit by special lighting in an otherwise dark area of the Egyptian Museum of Antiquities, it stood more than ten feet high and five feet wide, dwarfing those who stood in its imposing presence.

Daniel craned his neck to look up to the graphic image at the top. It showed the pharaoh and his consort standing with various others in attendance.

'You feel it, don't you?' said Mansoor.

Daniel saw a mocking smile on the Egyptian's face and he knew exactly what he meant.

'Yes,' said Daniel, subconsciously muting his voice in

token of the humility that he felt before this imposing monument.

'Mernepteh used this stone to proclaim his victories over Libya.'

'Or his father's victories,' Gabrielle added.

'True,' Mansoor confirmed. 'Considering that his father, Ramesses the Second, ruled for sixty-six years and lived for ninety, it's far more likely that the father was the architect of the victories commemorated in this stele than his son, who ruled for no more than ten.'

Mansoor started reading out loud.

'He drove back the Libyans who walked in Egypt,
Fear of Egypt is great in their hearts . . .
Their best fighters were left abandoned,
Their legs made no stand except to flee,
Their bowmen abandoned their bows.'

'I notice it's written right to left,' said Daniel.

The normal way to write hieroglyphics was left to right, but they could be written either way.

'I didn't know you could read them,' said Mansoor.

'I can't. But I can tell from the way the figures are facing.'

Mansoor nodded approvingly. Hieroglyphic animals and human forms always face the beginning of the line.

'And do you attribute any significance to that fact?' asked Mansoor.

'Only that Semitic languages are written right to left. And I understand that this monument contains the first known reference to Israel.'

'That is true.'

'I assume that this has something to do with the reason you're showing it to me.'

'Oh yes,' said Mansoor. 'When this stone was found, Flinders Petrie called in a German linguist and philologist by the name of Wilhelm Spiegelberg to translate it. As Spiegelberg was nearing the end of his translation, he became confused by something he read. In just two lines close to the end, the inscription switches from Mernepteh's military victories against Libya, in the *west*, to his purported triumphs in the *east*. The text goes something like this:

> 'Canaan is captured in misery.
> Ashkelon is defeated, Gezer is taken,
> Yanoam is destroyed;
> Israel is laid waste, nought of seed.'

'Nought of seed?' Daniel echoed.

'It's a standard formula in the context of ancient war,' Mansoor explained. 'You destroy the enemy's grain supply to weaken them economically.'

'And it actually says "Israel"?' asked Daniel.

'The word that Spiegelberg read out phonetically was actually *Isrir*.'

'But there's a problem with that timeframe, isn't there?' said Daniel. 'I mean, the stone dates from 1208 or 1209 BC. And according to the archaeological record, Israelite settlement in Canaan didn't begin until shortly after that.'

'Yes, but nowhere on this stone does it say that Isrir was in Canaan.'

'No, but hold on a minute. All those *other* places were: Ashkelon, Gezer, Yanoam. And Isrir is mentioned right after them, implying that it was in the same general location.'

'Ah, now it's interesting that you mention that,' Mansoor replied, obviously in his element. 'Because the text actually distinguishes between those other places and Isrir. Ashkelon,

Gezer and Yanoam are all followed by a throwstick symbol and three mountains. Those symbols represent a *city state*. In other words, each of those places *was* a city state. But the name Isrir, on the other hand, is followed by a throwstick followed by the figures of a man and a woman. And *those* symbols represent a foreign *people* rather than a city state. So, in effect, the text is telling us that Isrir was a people without a country.'

'But what about the fact that it says they were *destroyed*?' asked Daniel. 'Evidently the Israelites weren't destroyed because they were still around later.'

'No, but you have to understand that mighty though the ancient Egyptians were, they were not averse to a touch of hyberbole. They were politicians after all.'

'You said that a papyrus was found at the same site as this.'

'Yes. It's in the archives.'

Mansoor led them once again to the basement archives and showed Daniel and Gabrielle a papyrus fragment containing ancient script. Daniel sat down and stared at it for a long time, referring to his concordance to check each word.

'Can you translate it?' Mansoor asked encouragingly.

Daniel peered at the papyrus again before struggling with the words out loud. 'He killed the women who drew forth the sons, but spared them the daughters.'

'That doesn't make sense,' said Gabrielle.

'No, of course not,' said Mansoor. 'The women who drew forth the sons – presumably that means the midwives. But they would have had the same midwives for sons and daughters.'

'Wait a minute, I think I can solve it. They're using the causative case. It's not "He killed," it's "He *caused* to kill." In other words, "He caused the women who drew forth the sons to kill them, but made them spare the daughters."'

As soon as the words were out of Daniel's mouth he turned to Gabrielle with a look of amazement on his face.

'The killing of the sons!' they blurted out in unison.

'Are you sure?' asked Mansoor.

'Absolutely,' Daniel followed up. 'In the Bible, it says that Pharaoh decreed that all male babies of the Israelites be thrown into the river – hence Moses being hidden in the bulrushes to save him. And on the Mernepteh stele it says, "Israel is laid waste, *nought of seed*." It couldn't be clearer.'

Daniel had mixed feelings. He was making monumental progress in deciphering ancient texts that played an important part in Jewish history. But he felt like he was treading water when it came to finding the papyrus that Harrison had purportedly translated in his elusive paper.

Chapter 28

Sarit was back in her hotel room in Cairo, waiting for further instructions after sending in her report about what happened at the hospital.

She had prepared the report as a text file and concealed it in a picture, using a technique known as steganography. The idea was based on the fact that a text message consisted of far fewer bytes than a picture. The message was broken down into bits and these bits were distributed over the picture in such a way that their only effect would be to make extremely slight changes to some of the colours of some of the cells. There would be no way that this could be detected by the human eye.

The pictures were purportedly of friends of 'Siobhan Stewart' in places like Switzerland and Australia. After embedding the report into the picture, she had logged on to the Internet via the hotel's broadband, signed in to her social network account and sent it.

Now it was up to Dovi. It was probable that Goliath had failed in his mission, but he was still a threat.

Her phone beeped: *New pics uploaded to your wall.* She knew what this meant: her controller had some information for her.

She logged on and noticed that 'Felicity' – her Canadian

friend – had uploaded a new picture. She downloaded the picture and then logged out and disconnected from the Internet. This would make it harder for anyone to see what she was doing, if indeed she was being watched. She then assembled the improvised aluminium foil screen around her laptop, to stop it from being monitored by way of electromagnetic radiation, and then launched the steganography program (itself cleverly disguised) and typed in her password.

Within seconds, this simple operation yielded the text – shown on screen but not saved to disk.

Goliath is back at Cairo hotel. He has been ordered to get a sample of Klein's and Gusack's clothing and then to kill them. They have booked a flight to Luxor and so has he (following them). He is evidently planning to kill them there, probably in the Valley of the Kings. Follow him and neutralize him.

Chapter 29

Daniel was hit by an unexpected blast of heat as soon as he set foot outside the rented, air-conditioned jeep. They had flown in from Cairo earlier that morning and driven from Luxor Airport.

'It's this way.' Mansoor was leading Daniel and Gabrielle across the sands of the eastern part of the Valley of the Kings – the main valley. The contrast between the lush green valleys of the Nile banks and the dry sands just a couple of kilometres beyond was striking.

They were passing a foothill which was over fifty feet high. People were getting around by open buses that reminded Daniel of the transits at Disneyland. It was the tourist season all year round these days, and visitors were usually advised to beat the midday heat by coming early. Indeed, many were already emerging from the small number of tombs that were open to the public, while others were queuing outside, preparing to enter. Only a small number of tombs were ever open to the public and of those, only a few at any one time.

But Mansoor was taking Daniel and Gabrielle to one that was not open to the public.

'Here we are,' said Mansoor, as the wall of rock to their left was almost in touching distance.

They were eyed from a few yards away by jealous tourists, wondering who these gatecrashers were. Most of their eyes were on Gabrielle, in fact. She had traded in her dark denim jeans for a faded, well-worn pair. They were still tight-fitting, showing every curve of body, but the fact that they had worn thin gave them a flexibility of movement that made them more comfortable when walking and climbing stairs. There was a tear in one of the knees, which gave her a slightly tomboyish look, but with her impressive height and perfectly toned form, she had the aura of a gladiator from ancient Rome.

The guardian at the entrance to the tomb smiled as Mansoor arrived and greeted him with the traditional, 'Ahlan wa-sahlan.' The words – literally meaning 'Family and easy' – could loosely be translated as 'Make yourself at home.'

They exchanged a few more words in Arabic and then Mansoor motioned with his arm to Daniel and Gabrielle, shepherding them towards the entrance.

'This is KV46,' said Mansoor.

'The tomb of Yuya,' Daniel replied, his memory stirring as he joined the Egyptian before the entrance. 'A powerful courtier in ancient Egypt who served both Thutmose the Fourth and his son Amenhotep the Third.'

Mansoor nodded approvingly and entered the tomb ahead of them. The guards had switched on the electric lights that had been installed in the tomb soon after it was first opened, but a few steps down the stairway that was hewn into the rock, they all stopped like a column of cars held up by a red traffic light, to accustom their eyes to the dim light.

At the foot of the stairs, they found themselves walking down a corridor about thirty feet long that led to another staircase. The walls were rough and undecorated, not even smoothed let alone plastered, but they were covered with a meticulous grid of black dots spaced evenly apart both vertically and horizontally, effectively dividing the walls into squares. Daniel stopped to study them, shining a torch on to them to see more clearly. He had noticed the same square pattern of dots on the walls by the stairway. Daniel estimated that they were about sixteen inches apart. That would put them at the lower end of that variable ancient unit of measurement known as a cubit.

Mansoor led them to a second stairway and when they arrived at the bottom, they found themselves in another corridor, shorter than the first. But this one had a rounded ceiling, rather than a flat one. This was consistent with the fact that the ancient Egyptians understood the principle of the arch as far back as 4,500 years ago – a thousand years before this tomb was constructed – even if their public buildings continued to be post and lintel constructions for more than a whole millennium thereafter.

At the end of the corridor, they entered the burial chamber.

'Much has been removed from here,' Mansoor explained. 'It was raided in antiquity, although the robbers took very little, possibly because they were scared off and the tomb resealed. But a number of the larger items remained, such as the sarcophagus and the three coffins, originally placed one inside the other – although they had been disturbed by tomb-raiders. Also, remember that Yuya's wife Thuya was buried here too. And both their mummies were extremely well preserved.'

Daniel looked around in amazement. He knew about this tomb, but he had never dreamt that he would actually be standing here.

'Yuya and Thuya were, if my memory serves me right, probably amongst the few non-royals to have a private tomb in the Valley of the Kings.'

'That's right,' Mansoor confirmed.

'And also in Yuya's case,' Gabrielle added, 'one of the few *foreigners* to reach such a high rank, judging by the physical characteristics of his mummy. He was taller than most Egyptians and he had a beard, which Egyptians tended not to do. Also he had no body piercings.'

'Is there any significance in that?' asked Daniel.

'Well . . . I believe that body piercing is forbidden by Jewish law.'

'And Orthodox Jewish men have beards,' Daniel added.

Ignoring the exchange, Mansoor pointed to some hiero-glyphics on the wall.

'He had an impressive list of titles: "First among the King's Companions", "Deputy of the King's Chariots", "He whom the King made Great and Wise, whom the King has made his Double". And of course "Father of God".'

'What does that mean?' asked Daniel.

'Well, there's a dispute over the meaning of that title. Some say it was a purely priestly title, but others say it was a title reserved for the father-in-law of a pharaoh.'

'And was Yuya the father-in-law of one of the pharaohs?'

'Oh yes,' Mansoor confirmed. 'We know, both from the written record and from DNA evidence, that Yuya and Thuya were the parents of Tiye, the mummy known as the "Elder Lady", found in a tomb called KV35. Tiye was married to Amenhotep the Third and they in turn were the parents of Akhenaten.'

'The monotheistic pharaoh?'

'That's right. The one who ruled from 1351–1334 BC and who decreed that the Aten – the disk representing the sun God – was the one and only true God.'

'The first exponent of the "one god" system of belief,' muttered Gabrielle.

'Not strictly true,' Mansoor corrected. 'Akhenaten never really got rid of all the other Gods. He just declared war on the cult of the Theban God Amun, because the priests in Thebes were getting too powerful.'

'So he didn't get rid of Ra,' said Daniel.

'Not really. Ra was the sun God. The Aten was originally the sun disk – a *manifestation* of Ra. Somewhere along the line, it evolved into a God in its own right.'

Daniel froze, not in response to Mansoor's words, but rather because something had caught his eye. Very low on the wall in front of him, engraved in rather small letters, was some ancient text written in the old script that he had been brought here to decipher.

'Can you translate it?' asked Mansoor.

Daniel stared at it for a long time, squinting in the dim light, before he started. 'God made me the father to the king and all my brothers bowed down to me.'

Mansoor turned to Daniel. Daniel and Gabrielle turned to each other as Daniel uttered one word: 'Joseph.'

Chapter 30

Goliath was looking at the entrance to the tomb that Daniel and the others had entered. He wanted to act now, firmly and decisively, but there were too many people about. It wasn't just the guard outside the tomb, it was also the Egyptian soldiers and the throngs of tourists. There were just too many people.

He had followed them there from Cairo with relative ease. The tracking program that he had smuggled into Daniel's phone had started transmitting regular updates on his position again after the police gave it back to Daniel in London, and Goliath had been tracking him ever since.

Goliath had raced to Cairo airport after him and had seen Daniel, Gabrielle and their Egyptian friend at the desk for an internal flight to Luxor. He guessed that the Valley of the Kings was their destination, so he had simply booked himself on to another flight that was due to land shortly after theirs. From the airport he had taken a taxi to the valley and then made sure to keep them in his sights. He had already been told that they were working with someone important in the Egyptian academic and political hierarchy and so he knew that he would have to tread carefully.

Now it seemed that they could gain access to places that others couldn't. This could be both a help and a hindrance.

He wanted to get them alone, but it didn't help if they were in an area inaccessible to the public, as it was also inaccessible to him. And by the same token, it did him no good being able to keep a close eye on where they were, if others were milling about and able to see precisely the same thing.

He would have to bide his time.

The trouble was that they had hired a jeep while he was relying on a taxi. He had told the driver to wait and paid him handsomely for doing so, but he could hardly leap into the taxi and say 'Follow that jeep' without giving away that he was up to something. And he could hardly expect a local taxi driver to help a foreigner against a powerful public official.

But the very fact that they were visiting places that others couldn't get to was an encouraging sign. He sensed that an opportunity would present itself very soon.

Chapter 31

'The theory that Yuya was Joseph of the Old Testament has been around for donkey's years,' Mansoor acknowledged, still in a state of shock. 'But the academic community never took it seriously. I'd always thought of it as an amateur's theory.'

'But it has quite a lot going for it, even apart from what Daniel's just translated,' said Gabrielle. 'A foreigner who rose to high rank in ancient Egypt. The beard and lack of body piercings. The name itself, which also has elements of Yahowa or Jehovah. The fact that he was the pharaoh's father-in-law. And then there's the Great Harris Papyrus.'

'Oh, you're *not* going to throw that in surely?' Mansoor sneered.

'Why not?'

'Wait a minute,' Daniel interrupted. 'What's the Great Harris Papyrus?'

He looked back and forth between Mansoor and Gabrielle, who were looking at each other. Eventually Gabrielle shrugged and spoke.

'The Great Harris Papyrus was the longest papyrus ever found in ancient Egypt. Named after the collector who acquired it, the Great Harris Papyrus was one of the most important papyri of ancient Egypt. Some 42 metres long, it contained 1,500 lines of text.'

'But what's it got to do with Joseph?'

'In its final section, it refers to someone called "Yarsu", which sounds a bit like Yosef, the Hebrew form of Joseph. The text goes something like "Yarsu, a Syrian was with them as Leader. He made the whole land pay tribute to him; he united his companions and looted their possessions. They made the Gods like men, and no sacrifices were offered in the temples."'

'*Syrian*,' Mansoor echoed for emphasis.

'Yes, but the term Syria was sometimes used to include Canaan, where Joseph originated. And making "the whole land pay tribute to him" sounds like the way Joseph gained effective control of Egypt, by winning the support of the pharaoh.'

Mansoor looked decidedly underwhelmed.

'And what about: "united his companions and looted their possessions"?'

Gabrielle thought about this for a few seconds.

'It could refer either to the act of holding the ordinary Egyptian people to ransom because of the famine and his monopoly over the grain supplies. Or it might refer to the way he played those mind games with his own brothers before revealing himself. But the clincher is: "They made the Gods like men." Who else do we know who made Gods like men? Who believed that man was created *in the image of God*?'

'The Israelites,' Daniel muttered, not quite trusting his voice.

'*Exactly!*' cried Gabrielle triumphantly. 'And it says that no sacrifices were offered in the temples. That must be a reference to the Amarna experiment when Akhenaten not only banned the worship of Amun and decreed the Aten to be the one true God, but even created a new city in his honour and moved his entire court there.'

'But that was a generation later,' said Mansoor. 'Yuya wasn't around by then.'

'Yes, but the papyrus was written over 200 years after *that*, when the time-scale might have got confused.'

Mansoor was shaking his head.

'Most historians believe Yarsu to be another historical figure.'

'But there's no proof that they're right,' Gabrielle declared. 'In any case Yarsu clearly *sounds like* Yosef or Joseph. But more important than that, it means "the self-made man". Who could be more of a self-made man, than a foreigner who rose from humble origins to become the pharaoh's right-hand man – like Joseph?'

Mansoor was not one to admit defeat easily, but he smiled at Gabrielle's arguments, impressed. He turned to Daniel, who seemed to be in a dream world as he stared at a wall.

'Earth to Daniel,' he said, remembering the old taunt that his American students sometimes used.

'What's that?' asked Daniel, pointing to a part of the wall.

'Those are inscriptions from the Book of the Dead. Every tomb has some. Why?'

'Every tomb has the *same* inscriptions?'

'No, every tomb is different. The inscriptions are supposed to relate to the individual.'

'And those illustrations?'

'That's Chapter 148.'

'The cows?'

'The seven celestial cows and a bull. A symbol of fertility. What of it?'

'It's just that it reminded me of . . . the very thing that led to Joseph being appointed Pharaoh's right-hand man: he predicted the seven years of famine to follow the seven years of plenty by his correct interpretation of Pharaoh's dream about the seven fat cows and the seven thin cows.'

Chapter 32

The office was busy when a six-page fax arrived at the Egyptian Ministry of Health. The message was picked up from the machine by a very junior member of staff who, upon recognizing its importance, handed it over to one of his superiors, who in turn handed it over to another. It ended up in the hands of a sixty-three-year-old white-haired wiry man, with a frail body, but a piercing, determined look in his eyes. That man was Farooq Mahdi, the Minister of Health, and he was now studying the document.

The fax described certain events in England and warned of the threat posed by two people: an Englishman called Daniel Klein and an Austrian citizen called Gabrielle Gusack. The document went on to say that both of them were highly respected academics and that they were believed to be travelling in the company of the Vice Minister of Culture, Akil Mansoor.

However, the document took great pains to emphasize that there was no suggestion that Akil Mansoor was in any way, shape or form aware of the threat posed by these two individuals. Indeed, it was because of his ignorance of the danger they posed that he was himself vulnerable to them and it was for this reason all the more imperative that he be warned and that they be apprehended as quickly as possible.

But where was Akil Mansoor now? And where were Daniel Klein and Gabrielle Gusack, for that matter?

A few minutes later, Mahdi's secretary had tracked down the information that Mansoor had flown with Klein and Gusack to Luxor with the intention of visiting the Valley of the Kings. But because the secretary had said it was urgent, Mansoor's office had kindly given his mobile number.

The minister wasn't sure if there was coverage in the area where Mansoor was, but he decided to try. The call went straight to voicemail, and a voice told him that the number could not receive calls for the time being and invited him to leave a message.

The Minister of Health left an urgent message for Mansoor, hoping that he would hear it soon.

Chapter 33

'It's known to the locals as the Valley of the Monkeys and the tomb itself is known as the Tomb of the Baboons, because of the depictions of baboons on one of the walls.'

Mansoor was driving them on a spur road across the hot, dry sands, from the main car park of the Valley of the Kings to the western valley, some three kilometres away.

'Didn't they actually find a cache of mummified baboons in the valley?'

Mansoor glanced at Daniel and smiled. 'They only found one from this western valley. Others were found in various other locations.'

They had arrived at the entrance to the valley. Gabrielle spoke from the back of the jeep.

'You know, the best way to see this valley is on foot. It has some wonderful rock formations around the narrow paths that you can't get to by car.'

'I don't think our friend could take the heat,' Mansoor replied with a mocking smile, applying the brakes.

'Then why are we stopping here?' asked Gabrielle.

'We have to get the guardian to open the tomb,' Mansoor explained. 'Let's hope he's at home.'

The three of them stepped out of the jeep and into the silence of the western Valley of the Kings. But this time, the blast of dry heat that hit Daniel was not quite as oppressive as it had been before. What was disconcerting, however, was the desolate loneliness that hung in the air around them. This, Daniel realized, was the sensation that the old adventurers must have felt in the main valley when they first explored and excavated the area, before it was transformed into the tourist beehive that it had now become.

Mansoor looked around, as if this were new to him also, and then started walking towards the guardian's house at a snail's pace.

'The ancient Egyptians believed that the valley was watched over by Meretseger, a local goddess whose name translated, appropriately enough, as "She who loves silence". But there was a bit of a pun in her name, because the first syllable, *Mer*, was also the first syllable of the word for pyramid and the goddess was said to dwell in the pyramid-shaped mountain that overlooked the valley. To the ancient Egyptians she was perceived as both kind and cruel – the dispenser of both favours and pain.'

'Perhaps the archetype for women ever since,' added Daniel with a teasing smile in Gabrielle's direction. She did not look amused.

Mansoor stopped in front of the door to the old shack and knocked aggressively.

From within the house, Daniel heard a deep baritone voice mumbling in Arabic about the world surely not coming to an end and how the visitor was making enough noise to arouse the pharaohs from their eternal slumber.

The door opened with a clanging of chains and a clacking of bolts, as the gravel-voiced grumbling continued. But it came to an abrupt end when the diminutive, wizened guardian of the tomb came face to face with Mansoor. In the polite Arabic exchange that followed, Mansoor explained without introducing himself that he and his guests had come to see Tomb 23.

The guardian went back into the house and returned seconds later with a huge bunch of oversized keys. When they went back to the car, it was clear from Mansoor's body language that he wanted the guardian of the tomb to sit in the front with him, in deference to his age. So Daniel joined Gabrielle in the back, greeting her with a smile. After holding out for a second or two, she reciprocated. Daniel sensed that her sombre mood was due in no small measure to the way in which she was being squeezed into the background, as Mansoor and Daniel engaged in their detailed discussions, despite the fact that she was academically on a par with them. It was as if all the old Middle Eastern stereotypes about women were coming into play.

Mansoor restarted the jeep and drove slowly along the increasingly narrow and rock-strewn track. Along the way he stopped by an old brick hut, but kept the engine running. The guardian of the tomb got out and went over to the hut, opening it and disappearing inside, mumbling something inaudible in Arabic that could have been a curse, but was more probably just a lament at having his daily routine interrupted. After a few moments, there were clanking noises, as if things were being moved about inside, then silence.

A second or two later, the silence of the valley was broken by the whirring drone of a generator. In an instant, the valley had lost its tranquillity as the incessant rumbling permeated the air around them, not as noise, but as a faint background sound. The guardian emerged, locked up and strolled at a leisurely pace back to the jeep. No matter how much of a hurry the others were in, he was going nowhere fast in this heat.

The drive that followed seemed to last an eternity. Daniel

couldn't imagine what it would have been like to walk it, especially in this midday heat – the worst possible time to be doing this. And when Mansoor finally pulled up and they all got out of the jeep, it was clear that there was still a distance left to walk.

'The tomb we are about to visit,' Mansoor explained, 'is one of only four in this part of the valley. These are all tombs that are in one way or another associated with the Amarna period.'

Mansoor was referring to the brief period between 1341 BC, when Akhenaten moved his court to the purpose-built city, and 1331 BC, when his son, who was then called Tutankhaten, ended the religious reform, restored the cult of Amun and moved the capital back to Thebes. To signify the end of his father's experiment, he changed his name to Tutankhamen and completely abandoned the city of Akhetaten or "Horizon of Aten", which his father had built. It was the modern name of the location – Amarna – which was now used to describe not only the location itself, but also that turbulent period in Egyptian history.

'Which four tombs?' asked Daniel.

'The first two are Akhenaten and his father.'

'I thought Akhenaten's tomb was actually *in* Amarna.'

'It was, although ultimately his mummy ended up in KV55 in the main valley because of vandalism and tomb-raiding by those who sought to wipe out his memory in the counter-revolution against his reforms. But his original tomb was prepared here in the western valley, and in fact it's quite large and complete. But in any case, that tomb is closed, as is his father's and also a third tomb here that appears to have been used as a storage area. However, it is the fourth tomb that we are here to see.'

They walked on a bit until they arrived at the entrance.

'This is the tomb of Ay, son of Yuya. He was the father of Nefertiti, who became one of the wives of Akhenaten. He was also the brother of Tiya, the wife of Amenhotep the Third. Tiya and Amenhotep were the parents of Akhenaten. Therefore Ay, although not of royal blood himself, was a closely related in-law to the royal family of the Eighteenth Dynasty.'

Daniel realized from the way in which both Mansoor and Gabrielle were staring at him that his face must be showing the awestruck feelings that he harboured on the inside. This was one of the great tombs that he had always wanted to see. But Mansoor wasn't a mind reader, and he was not the sort of man to indulge Daniel's wishes for the sake of it. Mansoor had an agenda. And everything that he had shown Daniel so far had something to do with this project.

'Would I be jumping the gun if I were to ask where this tomb fits into the big picture?' Daniel asked, looking from Gabrielle to Mansoor, wondering which one of them was going to speak first.

It was Mansoor. 'They found, in this tomb, a papyrus written in Proto-Sinaitic script. It is kept in the museum archives in Cairo.'

'Then why bring me here?'

'I wanted you to see this tomb first, to get some sense of the importance of it all.'

'And then you want me to translate the papyrus?'

'Yes, although we don't need to go to the museum. I have a copy in my office at the SCA. But we have more to see here first.'

He led them down a long staircase, through an entrance passage with unfinished walls. In the middle of the chamber floor stood Ay's red quartzite sarcophagus. Daniel walked up to it for a closer look and then, gripped by an intense curiosity, proceeded to walk round it, admiring its engraved decorations: winged females, wrapping their wings around the corners.

'It used to be at the antiquities museum,' Mansoor explained, 'but it was returned here a few years ago, after some intensive restoration work.'

'These corners . . .' Daniel trailed off.

'Goddesses,' Mansoor replied. 'Protecting Ay on his journey into the afterlife. Isis, Neith, Nephtys and Selket.'

Daniel looked up and noticed a decorated doorway leading off the main chamber. Above it was a painted illustration of four figures with animal heads, wearing crowns sitting at a table. But these figures were clearly male.

'The four sons of Horus,' said Mansoor, again reading Daniel's mind.

In response to an encouraging nod from Mansoor, Daniel walked into the side chamber, but found it strangely disappointing. Its walls were unadorned and it did not even contain the Canopic jars with Ay's internal organs. Noticing that neither Gabrielle nor Mansoor had followed him, he returned to the main chamber and looked at the painted walls. Before him was a scene showing Ay in a swamp with twelve wild birds, probably ducks, rising out of it. Ay appeared to be hunting and his wife was also present in the scene. Ay's image had been defaced, apparently delicately.

Once again, Mansoor provided the commentary to Daniel's thoughts. 'It is widely believed that this tomb was actually built for Tutankhamen, but that Ay appropriated it and had King Tut buried instead in the small tomb that Howard Carter found. At any rate, there are similarities between the paintings here and those in Tutankhamen's tomb. They were probably the work of the same hand.'

Towards the top of one of the walls were two illustrations

of boats. Daniel looked around at some of the other wall paintings and noticed that parts of the image – presumably Ay himself – had been erased. This was not in itself a surprise to Daniel. He knew that there had been a power struggle between Ay and his successor Horemheb and that the latter had launched a campaign of *damnatio memorae* against several of his predecessors. The 'cartouches' – or royal symbols – had been targeted particularly vigorously as had the image of Ay.

Daniel stopped before the image of the baboons. After a few seconds he noticed Mansoor's presence beside him. And Mansoor was smiling.

'These are the baboons that gave their name to this tomb, and possibly also to the entire valley.'

Daniel nodded, but he was confused. 'The thing that I was most interested in is the Great Hymn to Aten.'

'That's at his old tomb.'

Daniel looked at Mansoor for an explanation.

'Ay originally prepared a tomb for himself at Amarna. But when Amarna was abandoned by Tutankhamen, it became impossible to use that one, so instead he prepared a new tomb for himself here. But it was the tomb in Amarna that had the Great Hymn to Aten.'

'I see,' said Daniel.

He was distracted by the look on Gabrielle's face.

Chapter 34

Goliath had decided not to take the taxi across the spur road to the western valley. That would have created one more witness and thus one more person to kill. Instead he had walked across. This was not something forbidden, or even discouraged. Indeed, tourists were told that it was the best way to enjoy the view. However, they were warned that the walk there and back would take two to three hours and they should only attempt it if they were fit. Most important of all, they should bring plenty of water and drink it regularly.

Goliath knew that he was fit enough to make it easily, and his height and long strides meant that he could do the walk quicker than most. He knew also that Akil Mansoor was a very determined man and there was presumably a lot that he wanted to show Daniel Klein. This offered him a perfect opportunity.

As he approached, he saw an old man in traditional Bedouin costume sitting idly by a hill smoking a hookah pipe.

What on earth . . .?

Then he realized when he saw a jeep parked only a few yards away. The hill wasn't just a hill, it was a cave . . . a tomb. And this man was the guardian of the tomb.

They're in the tomb!

And that meant a perfect target.

As he walked along slowly, the guardian looked up from his pipe. Goliath realized that he might arouse some suspicion, so he waved casually and made his face look confused and uncertain, like a lost tourist. He had every right to be here. The western valley was not out of bounds, even if the tombs were not open.

'Oh, er . . . excuse me,' he said. 'Do you speak English?'

A lot of the Bedouin guides did speak English, making money from the tourist trade, but Goliath wasn't sure if a tomb guardian would. The last thing he wanted was for this man to run off to the tomb calling for Mansoor or the others. But fortunately the old Bedouin smiled.

'Yes . . . a little.'

'I was wondering if you could help me. I'd like to know if any of these tombs are open?'

'Not to the public,' said the guardian as Goliath drew closer. 'But one of them is open at the moment, and some important people are there. I can ask them if they will give you permission to—'

Before he could finish, Goliath took him out with a single chop, just below the ear. As the man fell, Goliath moved round him, grabbed and locked the V formation of his left biceps and forearm under the man's chin and with a crossing-over motion of his right arm, snapped the man's neck.

Goliath didn't even wince at the crunch, he simply dragged the Bedouin to the entrance to the tomb. The door was made of heavy iron and had a key still in the padlock – a thick snap-shut padlock, not one of those cheap jobs that you can pick with a hairpin.

When he reached the doorway, he leaned in to hear what was going on. He heard voices, male and female, engaged in earnest conversation about hymns and psalms. It was, no doubt, all very interesting. But not today. These people were dabbling in affairs that were not of this earth, and soon they too would no longer be on this earth. He threw the guardian's body into the tomb, moved back and slammed the door after him. Then, with a swift movement, he closed the padlock and heard it click.

'Hallo!' a woman's voice rang out from the tomb. 'Who's there?'

He heard a rumbling exchange of voices in English, but it was no longer of interest to him. He had more important things to do.

He didn't know how long it would take them to die, and therein lay the problem. Had they told anyone where they were going? Even if they hadn't said exactly, would their approximate location be enough to find them?

There was still, however, one factor that might give away their location: the jeep. It was big enough to be picked up by a satellite or an aeroplane. But then again, he realized, that wasn't really a problem after all. In fact, it would also provide an easy way of getting a sample of their clothes.

Quick as a flash, he got into the jeep and drove back along the spur road to the main valley.

Chapter 35

Gabrielle had been the first one to hear something going on above them. In fact, she was the only one to realize the significance of it. The others had heard the door slamming, but assumed it was the wind. Her initial inquiry in English had received no response, prompting Mansoor to switch to Arabic.

'Nasir! *aYn a'aNt!*' shouted Mansoor.

Gabrielle and Daniel both understood. 'Nasir, where are you?'

It was not a case of shouting from fear or anger, he had raised his voice simply because he wanted to be heard. But the silence that followed was frightening.

'Nasir? . . . *Hl Huneka* . . . Nasir?'

'*Mā Yhdth,*' Gabrielle shouted in her own flawless Arabic. '*Mā Yhdth.*' She was asking what was happening.

Daniel was wondering that too. He hadn't yet reached the panic stage, but he was concerned.

What *was* happening? Why had they heard the door slam? He could understand an old man like the guardian suffering a stroke or a heart attack. But that wouldn't explain the slamming of the door.

'I think he locked us in,' Daniel proffered.

Mansoor looked at Daniel contemptuously. 'Why would he want to do that?'

'I don't know,' said Daniel, embarrassed at the absurdity of his own suggestion, yet seeing no other answer. 'Islamic fundamentalism, maybe. Anti-Westernism.'

'He's a Bedouin,' Mansoor snapped tersely, as if this alone were sufficient explanation. And with that, Mansoor raced out of the chamber up the first staircase, with the others in hot pursuit.

As he followed, Daniel thought about Mansoor's words. Contrary to popular Western prejudices, Arabs in general were the least likely amongst Muslims to be radicalized. The Bedouin especially tended to be pro-Western and particularly pro-British.

The Bedouin had a strict code of honour and one could get on the wrong side of them if one failed to appreciate this. But neither Daniel nor Gabrielle had done anything to offend Nasir. Indeed, one of the traditions of the Arab code of honour – especially strong amongst the Bedouin – is *Dakheel*, the protection of the stranger who is within one's tent – even at the risk of one's own life.

And tent did not literally mean a tent only, but the area of one's home turf. To a family patriarch, this could be his house and those of his extended family. To a local sheikh or village *mukhtar*, it could mean his village or neighbourhood. In the case of Nasir, it would surely mean the tomb of which he was the appointed guardian. But as Daniel contemplated this, his thoughts were interrupted.

'Oh my God!' screamed Gabrielle as she reached the entrance corridor.

Mansoor was leaning over the dead figure of the guardian of the tomb.

Chapter 36

Sarit had watched Daniel and the others drive across to the western valley, and she had watched Goliath follow them on foot. She waited for Goliath to disappear into the distance and then set off after him.

The killing of Goliath had now been sanctioned by the Israeli Prime Minister and it was up to Sarit to decide how to do it. Normally a *kidon* assassin would work in a team of at least four, but it had taken them time to catch up with Goliath and time was of the essence now that they knew his intentions.

Sarit's original plan had been to run him down on the way there and kill him. But she realized that someone in the main valley might see. Even if she didn't get caught on the spot, she knew her rented car could be identified and traced back to her. So she let him go and then followed, watching him through her binoculars.

But as she drove towards the valley, she saw the jeep that Daniel and the others had been in drive past her in the opposite direction. And it was not Mansoor at the wheel. Indeed, neither Mansoor nor either of the others were in the jeep. It was Goliath – and he was on his own.

In an instant she realized what had happened. She was too late! He must have killed them.

Damn! She had screwed up, big time.

She realized now that she should have gone after him and run him over. Then, instead of worrying about people finding the body and linking it to the rented car of an Irish tourist, she should simply have buried him in the sand. They would never have found him.

Instead, she had given him time – time to do his dirty work. Time to kill three more people and time to get the clothing sample that he had been sent there to find. That was far more serious. Three people dead was bad enough, and that was on top of the other killings: Carmichael, Roksana and the nurse at the hospital. If Goliath was allowed to fulfil Senator Morris's evil scheme it could be the fate of an entire nation.

So she had to stop him – and stop him now.

But then another thought came to her. What if he hadn't killed the people in the tomb? What if he had merely locked them inside? What if they were still alive? Shouldn't she go there to check?

Then she realized why she couldn't do that. First of all, revealing herself to them would compromise her identity and her mission. Secondly, time was of the essence. They could probably survive in the tomb for several days – possibly even weeks if they had enough water. But if Goliath escaped now she might not get a second chance to catch up with him – at least not while it could make a difference.

Even in a worst-case scenario, they could survive for several hours, and she could always put in an anonymous call alerting the authorities to their whereabouts. But she couldn't afford to lose Goliath's trail. He already had a head start, but she was still in contention. Moreover, she had a pretty good idea where he was going.

She swung the car round and headed back along the spur road in pursuit of her quarry.

Chapter 37

'His neck's been broken,' said Mansoor. The sorrow in his voice was genuine; although he did not know the guardian personally, the man had been loyal. And he almost certainly had a family.

'What are we going to do?' asked Gabrielle, her fear growing.

'Let's not panic just yet,' said Mansoor.

'But no one knows we're here!' she replied. 'You never told anybody! You didn't phone in or anything.'

'When we don't make contact tomorrow they'll know something is up. They'll know where to look. They'll see our jeep.'

'If it's still there,' said Gabrielle. 'I heard a car drive off.'

'That must have been the car of whoever did this,' said Daniel. 'Whoever locked us in must have got here somehow – presumably by car – and whatever you heard, it was probably them driving off.'

'Not necessarily,' said Mansoor. 'It's possible to walk across from the main valley.'

'I've got an idea,' said Daniel, taking out his mobile phone.

Almost in unison, the other two whipped out theirs. Daniel pressed the button to illuminate his and noticed that there was no signal. He tried a number, but got nothing. A brief glance at the others confirmed that they had not had better luck. He had hoped that because they were almost at surface level, they would get at least a weak signal – enough to call for help. Then he realized that they were behind an iron door and shielded on all sides by a thick layer of rock. Aside from that, the coverage in this country was none too good at the best of times.

'We're gonna die here!' said Gabrielle, breaking down in tears and gasping for breath. Daniel put a comforting arm round her in the hope of calming her fears. Her sobbing declined in intensity and her breathing became shallower. Meanwhile, Mansoor quietly arranged the guardian's body into some semblance of a dignified position. And then, quite abruptly, a smile graced his lips.

'What?' asked Daniel.

Mansoor reached into the tomb guardian's pockets to produce a giant bunch of keys.

For a second, Daniel too was caught up in the euphoria, but then reality set in. 'What good does that do us? We can't reach the padlock.'

The door was shut not by a lock that could be reached from inside, but rather by a padlock on the outside. The door could only be unlocked from the other side.

Then Daniel saw something. 'Look.'

The others turned in the direction he was pointing. It was a loose, fist-sized piece of rock, embedded in the wall, but with the break lines clearly visible.

'What?' asked Gabrielle in confusion.

Mansoor understood. And as Daniel took out his pocket-knife and opened it to prise the rock out of the wall, Mansoor crouched down to help him. Between them, they managed to free the piece of rock, which was about the size of half a brick and had a nice pointed corner.

With the rock in his hand, Daniel charged at the iron door and began smashing away at a single point on its surface, near where the lock would be. Iron, when smashed repeatedly with the pressure on a single point, can eventually break. By hitting it repeatedly, Daniel was trying to puncture the iron door and then enlarge the hole sufficiently to reach through it. But after many attempts, all he had managed to do was make a dent in the heavy iron. And he had exhausted himself. Over the course of the next hour, Mansoor took over and then Gabrielle. Finally Daniel took the stone back and went at it with a vengeance.

'There's a hole!' he cried with delight, noticing a pinprick of light. It was very small, but it was progress, and it encouraged the others to take over and go at it with similar vigour.

Daniel wondered why no one heard the noise. To him it was deafening. Having heard the silence of the valley, it seemed strange that such a din did not carry. But then again, he realized that in the main valley the clamour made by the throngs of tourists would surely drown out the noise they were making. In any case, the distance was quite great and the fact that the noise of the tourists did not puncture the peace of the western valley testified to just how far apart those two worlds were.

But as they continued with their exhausting efforts, Daniel noticed two things. The first was that the hole was getting bigger and the second was that the light that was coming through the ever increasing gap was ebbing. It was getting on for half past six and the sun was setting.

A renewed sense of urgency set in and it manifested itself in the vigour with which Daniel wielded the stone as he attacked the hole. Finally, he stopped, exhausted. He held out the stone to Gabrielle, but she refused to take it. She was looking straight past him.

'I think it's big enough,' she said.

Daniel turned and looked. It was hard to tell. The poor light inside the tomb and the dimming light outside made it hard to assess the size, and the jagged edges made it uncertain how safe it was to put one's hand through, not to mention one's wrist. Daniel would personally have preferred to enlarge the hole before trying, but he was ready to defer to Gabrielle.

'Do you think you can reach through that?' he asked.

Gabrielle stared at him, not answering.

'No, she can't,' said a voice behind him. 'But I can.'

Daniel turned round to see Mansoor holding the key ready and realized that he was right. Gabrielle, because of her hand size and well-developed wrists, would not be able to reach through and neither could Daniel. But the more slender Mansoor might just be able to.

'Please don't drop it,' said Daniel.

It wasn't intended to sound patronizing, but Mansoor responded with a withering look. Then, very slowly and carefully, he reached through with the key and tried to angle it towards the padlock. The other two saw the pained expression on his face as he rotated his arm in a desperate effort to get the key to where they needed it. And then he felt the key slipping in his sweaty fingers. He tried to pull his arm back in, but in his haste he cut his wrist on the jagged metal. Blood spurted from it and he cried out in pain.

The others watched in horror as they realized that both his hand and the key it was struggling to hold on to were still on the other side of the door, trapped in the jagged-edged hole.

Chapter 38

Driving at night along the Nile Valley was a dangerous business. The main 'highway' was a single lane in which vehicles parked at night with their lights off, and donkey carts with neither lights nor red markings or reflectors to make them visible trundled along invisibly. Added to that, there were also trucks with unsafe loads and long-distance taxis, driven with a brazen disregard not only for the speed limit but even for the laws of physics.

This meant that drivers had to make a hard choice between high speed, to mingle with the flow of local motorized traffic, and low speed to avoid the pitfalls of the stationary vehicles and donkeys. Navigating a middle course between those two perils was difficult.

But Sarit didn't really have a choice.

She had followed Goliath back to Luxor, thinking that he was going to ditch the jeep and either fly back to Cairo or take the overnight train. But instead he proceeded to drive north along the Nile Valley, presumably intending to make it to Cairo by road. This was understandable – the further he took the jeep away from the western valley, the less likely Mansoor and the others were to be found. And this made Sarit more convinced that they were still alive.

Sarit calculated that she had two options – either to press

on and try to catch Goliath, or to turn back to save the people she was supposed to protect. The drive back would take several hours and it was already dark. On the other hand, she had had to stop for petrol and was not sure if she was still in with a chance of catching up with Goliath. He might be driving fast, in excess of the speed limit. Of course she could do the same, but what if she was stopped by the police? The last thing she wanted to do was come to the attention of the authorities.

Finally, she made a decision. She pulled over by the roadside and logged on to the Internet via her mobile phone. Lacking the time for the usual photograph and steganography routine, she put a message on the wall of her social network page that said: *I'm looking for big man.* She just hoped that Dovi or someone at the Mossad would get it and give her a real-time update on his whereabouts.

Right now she didn't have time to wait for an answer. Instead, she restarted the car and drove on, keeping to the main road north. After a while she got a message on her phone that a friend had commented on her wall. She pulled over again, logged on and saw a message that said: *You're only two kilometres away from the man of your dreams. Maybe you'll have to chase him faster, but keep going the way you are and you'll meet him.*

She smiled and realized that Mossad were tracking both her and Goliath via the GPS on their mobile phones. The message implied that a slight acceleration would be all that she needed to catch up with him.

Looking at the terrain, she realized that she might find a quiet spot without witnesses where she could deal with Goliath once and for all. Then she remembered that this was a petrol car, not diesel and that meant she could nip this problem in the bud. Instead of restarting the car immediately, she got out, opened the tank and siphoned off some petrol into the soft drink bottle she had retained from the gas station. Using a rag from the boot of the car, which she soaked in petrol, she created a Molotov cocktail. She got back into the car and shoved it into the door compartment.

Now all she had to do was drive fast, without attracting the attention of the police. She realized that the way others were driving, she might just get away with it.

Chapter 39

Ignoring the blood and struggling desperately not to let the key slip from his fingers, Mansoor made another turn of his hand and just about managed to find the insert point of the padlock. But he still had to twist the key with his fingers to rotate it to the right angle to get it in. For a minute he thought it was going to slip from his sweaty grasp, but then he felt something catch and he realized that the key was in.

Now it was just a matter of turning it . . . turning it some more . . . and some more . . .

Yes!

The padlock was open. He pulled on the heavy lower part to disengage it, then he turned the bottom away ninety degrees. Finally he removed the whole thing and let it drop to the floor.

'Quick! Let's get him out!' Daniel yelled to Gabrielle. Mansoor was hardly able to speak.

They pushed the door open and Daniel rushed round to the other side to help free Mansoor's hand, gently guiding it through so that the sharp metal didn't tear into the flesh any further.

But it was already clear from the blood pouring out that an artery had been opened. Mansoor sat down and lifted his arm above the level of his heart while Daniel applied arterial pressure using his belt to stem the flow of blood.

'I still can't get a signal,' said Gabrielle, frantically moving her mobile phone this way and that in the hope of getting it to work. She tried the same with Daniel's phone, and Mansoor's, but she was unable to get a signal.

'What are we going to do?' she asked.

'You'll have to walk. Go that way,' said Mansoor, pointing west towards the Nile Valley. 'Leave me here and get help.'

'We have to take you with us,' said Daniel, brushing off Mansoor's selflessness.

'We haven't got a stretcher.'

'You can still walk, can't you?'

'I can still walk, but I'd only slow you down.'

Daniel looked at Gabrielle. She had been panicking before when she thought that they were going to spend their last few days dying of starvation in the unused tomb of an ancient pharaoh, but now that her own life was no longer under threat, her concern turned to her former teacher.

'Are you sure you won't be in any danger here?'

He looked around and pointed this way and that contemptuously. 'My dear girl, do you see any predators around here? Any lions or tigers, perhaps? Or maybe a wild camel?'

It was true that male camels could become violent to the point of killing during the mating season, if anything got between them and the fertile females, but aside from that, there was no danger out here in the desert.

'I'm sorry. I was just concerned.'

She was none too bothered by his irascible response. She knew his character very well after all these years.

'I'll be all right, just as long as you get help. Make sure you tell them my exact location.'

'Should we ask them to use a helicopter?' asked Daniel, suddenly feeling unsure.

'They'll know what to do!' snapped Mansoor. 'Just tell them my circumstances. Now go!'

For a split second, Daniel and Gabrielle hesitated, meeting each other's eyes, as if seeking the other's approval for what might seem like a callous act. Then Daniel took the initiative, nodded and set off, followed a second or two later by Gabrielle.

'Wait!' Mansoor cried out.

They froze and turned to see the Egyptian holding out his mobile phone.

'Take my phone. Keep checking it. As soon as you get a signal, call the number I've keyed into it. It's the nearest hospital.'

'We can do that on our phones,' said Daniel. 'Just give us the number.'

'My phone is better in these conditions. Also the pair of you kept checking your e-mail, like little Western nerds. You're probably low on juice.'

'But we can't leave you without a phone,' said Gabrielle, her voice weak with guilt.

'A phone doesn't do me any good without a signal.' He held out the mobile to Daniel. 'Now, get going! And make it quick.'

And with that, they were off. It was one of those walks that seemed to become less tiring as it continued. After the first couple of hundred yards, they already felt sore, perhaps because of muscle cramps. They had spent several hours immobile in the tomb and when they came out into the open, the night air was cooler than they had expected now the sun had gone in. But as they continued and their muscles warmed up, it became easier.

But it was the psychological exhaustion that made it truly

tiring – the thought of how much depended on them getting help in time. Also Daniel felt worn-out at the thought of how long they would have to walk even to get to the edge of the Nile Valley. It was a five-mile walk, but the terrain was rough and Daniel knew that even at their current brisk pace it would take them at least an hour. It wasn't so much the prospect of an hour's walk that worried him: it was concern for what would happen to Mansoor in the meantime.

How long did he have? How rapidly was he losing blood?

Daniel looked over at Gabrielle and saw from the look on her face that she too was concerned. Without any exchange of words, she seemed to pick up on his suggestion and whipped out her phone. The look in her eyes said it all even before she put it away again. He tried to get a signal with his, but had no more luck, and Mansoor's proved no better, despite his confidence.

They carried on more in desperation than hope, Gabrielle taking the lead.

'I wish I'd followed my nephews' advice and got into shape sooner,' said Daniel, trying to make light of the situation.

'You're pretty fit,' said Gabrielle.

'Not like you.'

'Flattery, flattery.'

He quickened his pace and lengthened his stride to catch up with her, just in time to catch the smile on her face before it vanished.

'You know, I always wanted to be like you,' she said.

'What? A *man*?'

'Ha fuckin' ha. No, I mean when I used to visit Uncle Harrison during the summer . . . when you were working on your dissertation.'

'So how come you went into Egyptology instead of Semitic languages?'

160

'That came later. No, at the time, I wanted to be a magician.'

'A magician?'

'Yes. Remember all those tricks you did with cards and coins and all that?'

'Oh, yeah. That was something I did at school. It was the only way I could make friends. I didn't know you were interested in that.'

'Oh God, yes! I used to spend hours practising . . . hoping I could be as good as you.'

'And were you?'

'Did I ever show you my magic skills?'

'Not as far as I recall.'

'Then there's your answer. Rest assured, Daniel, if I'd thought I could have impressed you in those days, I would have done.'

He remembered that she had had a bit of a crush on him in those days. She was fifteen when he first started work on his PhD. He had got into University College London's Department of Hebrew and Jewish Studies at the age of sixteen and graduated with a First in Language and Culture. At twenty he had gone on to do a direct doctorate at Cambridge under Harrison Carmichael. Gabrielle lived in Vienna, but spent her summers in Cambridge with her uncle, while her widowed mother travelled.

Daniel was well aware at the time that Gabrielle had a crush on him. He remembered all too well the constant flirting, the dressing up to look older, the ostentatious way she used to swish past him in a short skirt, desperately trying to catch his attention. He had to admit to himself that at times his eye did rove and his imagination was aroused. But she was a girl on the cusp of womanhood and he was an adult. To take it beyond the occasional acknowledgement of her flirting would have been as improper as it was illegal.

So he had played it cool and somewhere along the line she had grown out of him.

Half an hour into the walk, they tried the mobile phones again. This time, Gabrielle's face lit up, so that even before she made eye contact with Daniel, he knew that the news was good.

She spoke urgently into the phone and when she was finished, she turned to Daniel with a beaming smile on her face.

'They're on their way.'

'I heard. Did they say which hospital they're taking him to?'

'Luxor. But only because it's nearer.'

'Okay, well, let's keep going till we make it to the valley, then see if we can get some sort of transport.'

Gabrielle nodded.

In the quarter of an hour that followed, they heard a helicopter in the distance and glanced at each other for encouragement. Privately, Daniel still had concerns. Would they arrive on time? Was Mansoor still alive?

'What?' asked Gabrielle, seeing the look on his face.

'Nothing.' He had no wish to worry her too, and no reason to share his fears with her either.

After a time, the land beneath their feet turned from sand and rock to lush green grass, and they knew that they had reached the edge of the Nile Valley. Gabrielle took out Mansoor's mobile phone and played with the buttons, looking at the display. Daniel wasn't sure what she was doing, but he decided not to ask until she had finished. In the meantime, he looked around and kept his eyes peeled for a taxi.

A few went past, but they already had fares. Meanwhile,

Gabrielle was using Mansoor's phone to make a call, but Daniel was still too preoccupied with his concerns for Mansoor to ask who she was calling. He hoped that they hadn't got lost or failed to find Mansoor. Gabrielle had told them the exact location, and he would have had no reason to leave the area. In any case, how far could he have gone?

And then another thought struck Daniel – a frightening thought. Someone had tried to kill them before, by locking them in. *What if the killer was still around? What if he was following them?*

Daniel quickly dismissed this thought as nonsense. When they got out of the tomb, their jeep had been missing. Whoever had done it would have no reason to come back. But why had they locked them in to begin with? Who was the intended target? Was it Mansoor? Gabrielle? Daniel himself? All three?

It makes no sense!

And there was one more thing that didn't make sense. Although Gabrielle was holding the phone to her ear, she wasn't speaking. She was *listening* . . . but she wasn't saying a word. And the look on her face concerned Daniel. It was a look of fear.

He was about to ask her what the problem was when a police van appeared in the distance heading towards them on the main road. Daniel started waving his arms in a desperate attempt to flag it down. The police van screeched to a halt and four police officers leapt out. But what happened next took him by surprise: they drew their guns.

Not sure of what was happening, Daniel opted for the common-sense approach and put his hands up.

'British,' he shouted, as if that word conferred some sort

of magical protection. But then something happened that Daniel couldn't believe.

The police started firing!

Instinctively, Daniel hit the ground. Gabrielle did likewise, except that she took half a second longer to react.

Chapter 40

Sarit's training had involved the advanced driving course, including night driving, but she still felt uncomfortable doing it. Along the way she had evaded a donkey cart and two parked cars and nearly been demolished by a heavily loaded truck that shed some of its load in an effort to overtake her.

And now she caught sight of what she thought was the jeep that Goliath had driven away from the tomb, though it was hard to tell in the darkness. She could make out the form, but not the colour, much less the occupant. In any case, there were too many other cars on this stretch of road to be able to do anything. She would have to bide her time.

But she stayed in contact, keeping several car lengths back. The drive back to Cairo would take seven or eight hours all told, and she had barely been driving for two.

It was some three hours later that she finally got her opportunity. The traffic had thinned out considerably because many people did not want to drive that late, and somewhere along the line it got to the point that she was no longer able to keep other vehicles between them because they were on a stretch of road that *had* no other vehicles. That meant that the time to strike was *now*. She opened the driver's window, knowing that she would not be able to reach over to her passenger window whilst controlling the vehicle, but this also meant that she could not throw the Molotov cocktail while overtaking him. Instead, she would have to get him to overtake her.

Steeling herself, she overtook him in a highly aggressive manoeuvre and then slowed down in front of him, just sitting there in the single lane, knowing that he was getting increasingly annoyed. She didn't respond when he hooted and flashed his lights at her. But when he started moving out to overtake, she knew the time had come. Holding the steering wheel with her right hand, she lit the rag with her left, dropped the lighter and took the Molotov cocktail out of the side pocket.

As Goliath pulled up level with her and shouted something out at her, she threw the Molotov cocktail as hard as she could through the open driver's window of her car and the passenger window of his. She had been intending to throw it through the rear window, so that it would shatter on impact and explode. But at the last minute, she realized that she couldn't be sure that it would penetrate. It would depend on how strong or reinforced the windows were. Within seconds, the interior of Goliath's car was ablaze, including his clothes, as he screamed with pain and skidded this way and that.

But Sarit had no time to survey the results of her work. She put her foot down and pulled away quickly, casting a brief glance in her rear-view mirror to satisfy herself that the job was done.

What she didn't see was the old man with the donkey and cart on the side road. But he had seen her and was surprised that she didn't stay to help. It was for that reason that he whipped out a pen and wrote down what he remembered of her registration number on his hand.

Chapter 41

'My name is Daniel Klein!' Daniel shouted. 'I'm a British professor and a friend of Akil Mansoor! This is Gabrielle Gusack! She's also a friend of Professor Mansoor! We're unarmed!'

'I don't think that's going to help,' said Gabrielle.

'Why not?'

'I don't think they're in a mood to listen.'

'But they surely can't think we did anything to harm Mansoor. We were the ones who summoned help, for God's sake!'

'Listen, Daniel, there's no time to explain now, but on the count of three, get up and run to the left. There's some cover there by those trees, and then some buildings. We can make it to a side street and get clear of them; they'll have to drive the long way round.'

'But if we run, it'll just make it look as if we've got something to hide.'

'And if we *don't* run, we'll be the subject of endless discussions and debates on the news and talk radio long after our funerals.'

And with that she started her quiet countdown. 'One, two, *three!*'

She raised herself only as high as she needed to in order

to run and sprinted to the left, just like she had said. Danny barely had time to admire her speed, for – against his better judgement – he found himself running too.

Keeping his head down, he couldn't see the flashes of the guns or the streaks of the bullets. Neither could he see where the shots were landing. It was only when the gunfire subsided and he felt safe enough to slow down, that he saw Gabrielle turning back towards him, almost smiling with exhilaration.

For a moment, Daniel's mind returned to the thought that maybe the police *did* think that they had deliberately harmed Mansoor. But even if so, shooting at them *still* made no sense. Why not simply tell them to put their hands up and surrender?

'I don't understand why they're firing at us,' he said in desperation.

He was about to say more, when he noticed that Gabrielle was bleeding from the shoulder.

'They're afraid of coming into contact with us,' she said, grimacing from the pain.

Chapter 42

The bitch! thought Goliath. *The fucking evil bitch!*

He didn't know who she was. In his agony, with his clothes on fire, all he knew was that she was the enemy.

The searing pain enveloped his body.

Get out! his mind was screaming. *Get out!* But it was easier said than done. To get out he would have had to use his hands and he couldn't even *feel* his hands.

Neither, for that matter, could he see. His eyes were closed and his eyeballs were so hot it was as if they were melting in their sockets.

He heard the door opening and felt hands upon him, under his armpits. The hands were small, yet their grip was surprisingly strong.

'*Wa ismaholiya mousa'a aidatica.*'

He didn't understand the words. But he could tell from the tone that someone was trying to help. He allowed himself to be dragged from the car. Once outside, his instinct was to run, to escape from the flames that engulfed him, but he knew that running would merely fan the flames and feed them with oxygen.

Instead, he allowed the man to push him to the ground and roll him. He continued to roll by himself, sensing that it was working. He felt a soft blow to a wide area of his torso.

Fabric on flesh. The stranger was trying to beat out the flames. Eventually, it became clear that the flames had subsided, but the searing pain on his flesh lingered on. The only thing he knew for sure was that he was alive.

But he felt his consciousness slipping away.

Chapter 43

'It's just a flesh wound,' said Gabrielle with a smile, tying her headscarf around her shoulder.

Harsh as the situation was, Daniel couldn't fail to see the humour in it.

'You've been watching too many Clint Eastwood movies. We've got to get you to a doctor.'

'With those guys trying to kill us? Are you crazy?'

They were moving in the shadows, avoiding the pools of light thrown by the street lamps. They weren't sure if they were still being followed, but it was clear that the cops – if indeed they *were* cops – were in no mood to listen to them.

'So what do you suggest, Gaby? You're bleeding.'

'It's Gabrielle to you.'

'Oh, cut it out! You'll always be Gaby to me.'

'Whatever! Anyway it's not bleeding.'

'So what's that then?'

He pointed to the blood on the scarf.

'It's congealed blood.'

'Covering quite an area. And blood doesn't coagulate that quickly.'

'It was never bleeding in the first place. It was a scraping injury, the bullet just grazed me. There was blood but no bleeding. It's like when you scrape a limb on a rough surface.'

'It must hurt like hell.'

'I'm a woman. We're biologically programmed to pass an infant's fifteen-centimetre cranium through a ten-centimetre passage. Do you think a little scraping on my upper arm is going to bother me?'

'If it was me I wouldn't be so stoic.'

'I guess you're handicapped by what you've got between your legs.'

Daniel smiled. 'I take it back, what I said about Clint Eastwood. It's too many reruns of *Xena: Warrior Princess*.' If she could keep this up, in the face of what must have been at least moderately painful, then at least he didn't have to worry about her any more. 'So what happened to that frightened little girl from the tomb back there?'

'It's not the pain that bothers me. It's not being in control. I guess I can take danger, I just can't take confinement.'

Daniel nodded, approving of the logic. 'The thing I don't understand is why they were shooting at us.' He looked at her expectantly. She said nothing. He had another go. 'You said something about them not wanting to come into contact . . .'

Gabrielle held out Mansoor's phone. 'There's a message. You might like to listen to it.'

He took the phone and held it to his ear.

'Hallo Professor Mansoor, this is the Minister of Health, Farooq Mahdi. We have a little problem on our hands. We understand that you are travelling in the company of a British man called Daniel Klein and a woman called Gabrielle Gusack. Please be very wary of them. There is an arrest warrant out for Daniel Klein after he jumped bail on a murder charge. We believe that he could be very dangerous. There is also evidence that they are both carrying the same contagious disease as the volunteers at the dig. The Gusack woman is known to have been in contact with a curator at the British Museum and he later succumbed to the same disease. Please get away from them as soon as possible and contact us.'

Now he realized why Gabrielle had been so determined to get him to run. As far as the cops were concerned, they were a dangerous health hazard and the police didn't want to go anywhere near them – even if shooting them was the only alternative. The fact that Daniel was also suspected of being a murderer on the run, made it easier for them to take that shoot-first-ask-questions-later approach. Daniel knew that in these circumstances, there was no point trying to reason with them.

But why on earth should anyone think they were carrying a disease? They weren't showing any symptoms themselves. This had to be some sort of mix-up. But there evidently was an outbreak and there had had to be *some* cause.

However, until such time as they could approach the authorities without getting themselves shot, they'd have to keep a low profile. They needed breathing room . . . time to unravel the mystery and work out a plan.

'We've got to get out of here,' said Daniel.

Chapter 44

Sarit arrived in Cairo sometime after four in the morning. She parked her car and took an invigorating shower to rouse herself from the lethargy that was engulfing her.

She put on the white bathrobe supplied by the hotel and made her way to the bed, still feeling an intense desire to sleep. But she had something to do before that: she had to report in. She switched on her computer and uploaded the tourist-style pictures she had taken of her day in the Valley of the Kings. Then she connected the laptop to the hotel's broadband and prepared the message for embedding into one of the pictures:

> *Goliath locked Klein, Gusack and Mansoor in tomb in western valley and stole their jeep. May have killed them, but I suspect not. Arrange for them to be freed. I followed Goliath on road to Cairo and disposed of him with homemade incendiary.*

She embedded the text in the picture, then wiped the text file and uploaded the picture to her social network account for all her 'friends' to see. Then she ran the utility to delete any temporary files and overwrite unused areas of the hard disk.

Then she did what she had wanted to do for hours: crash out on the bed.

Sometime later, she was awakened from her uneasy sleep by an aggressive banging on the door. She barely had time to throw on a robe before the door was flung open and three Egyptian policemen walked in.

'Miss Stewart, you are under arrest for leaving the scene of a motor accident.'

Chapter 45

Daniel had let Gabrielle do the talking. After a sleepless night in the open by the Nile, just outside a small village, they had made their way to the riverbank in search of the means to escape. And they found it in the *feluccas* – the local riverboats that operated on the Nile both as fishing vessels and as cheap tourist rides.

Gabrielle was so much more persuasive than he could have ever been. First of all, it was obvious that Walid, the dark-skinned, southern Egyptian owner of the *felucca*, found Gabrielle very attractive, as did the other two crew members who were there with him – his teenage son Na'if and someone else who was either Walid's younger brother or his cousin. Secondly, they seemed to be impressed by her fluent, almost classical Arabic. Daniel could have spoken Arabic equally well, but somehow hearing it from a pretty blonde foreigner – and a woman too – was considerably more impressive, and they warmed to her immediately.

Gabrielle had warned Daniel that it would be risky to try to join a normal tourist river cruise without arousing suspicion. Not that there would have been any shortage of room on a northbound cruise; holidaymakers tended to prefer the shorter cruises between Aswan and Luxor, and in any case the tourist season was almost over. Joining a cruise without a booking at the last minute, though, might arouse some suspicions. For all they knew, the riverboats and car hire firms might have been alerted to watch out for them.

But travelling by *felucca* was another matter. Those old, narrow, engineless riverboats were used both by fishermen and by canny locals to ferry tourists on short trips.

'We want to get the authentic local experience,' Gabrielle had explained. 'Or rather my husband does.'

She realized, quite spontaneously, that the afterthought was a nice little touch to make it sound convincing. She knew that Walid and his crew could well relate to that. The Western city slicker who wants to get his hands dirty, and the educated, dutiful wife reluctantly going along with her adventurous husband's wishes.

'And you want to go all the way to Cairo?' Walid asked by way of clarification.

'Yes.'

If they could make it to Cairo, they had several options, including going to their respective embassies and asking them to liaise with the Egyptian authorities – even if it meant Daniel being returned to the UK and arrested. But what they really wanted was to have a look at the papyrus from the tomb of Ay that Mansoor had told them about – the one at the Cairo Museum. Daniel was hoping that it was the one that Harrison had mentioned – the one that described the resurgence of the plague. It might hold the key to why Harrison was killed and why someone had locked them in the tomb.

'You know there is no toilet on boat, yes?'

'We understand,' Gabrielle confirmed, giving Daniel a dirty look as if to say: *Why are you forcing me to go through this?*

'Okay, you have American dollars?'

'No, only sterling or Egyptian pounds.'

'Okay, give me twelve hundred pounds.'

He meant Egyptian pounds. But that was still too much – even allowing for the fact that it would take them about five or six days to make it to Cairo.

'I'll give you five hundred,' said Gabrielle.

Daniel smiled; it was obvious that she knew how to haggle a lot better than he.

'Five hundred?!' The mock-indignation in Walid's tone was almost theatrical. 'For *one* person I do for five hundred. Give me thousand, I take you all the way to Cairo.'

'A thousand? Look, we're not first-timers. This is my fifth trip and my husband's third. I'll give you six hundred.'

'Okay, give me eight hundred,' he said with a smile. 'I do for you for eight hundred.'

'Seven hundred,' she replied, matching smile for smile.

'Why you do this to me? Where else you find beautiful boat like mine?'

That was not exactly the way she would have described it; ramshackle old dinghy might have qualified. But she had to be careful not to overplay her hand. Most of the *feluccas* operated south of the Esna lock, between Luxor and Aswan. They wanted to get to Cairo and there were very few *feluccas* trying to compete with the cruise ships on that northern stretch of the Nile. So it was a case of beggars can't be choosers. But the competitive streak in her made her decide to have one last try.

'Seven hundred,' she said firmly.

'Seven fifty.'

'Okay,' she said. If he had stuck at eight hundred, she would have said seven fifty herself. Still, it was better this way. It was always better to let the man name the final figure and then agree to it.

After the money had changed hands, they boarded the

178

boat and within minutes were drifting downriver. Sails were useless in this environment as the prevailing wind was almost always southerly, taking the boats upstream. Hence the rule of the Nile: sails *up*stream, current *down*stream.

All of this made for a very energy-efficient, and gentle mode of transport along the Nile. The vessel had no engine, no 'indoors' and no shower or toilet. It was this, as much as the Western preference for comfort, that made most tourists prefer the luxury cruises on offer from the numerous tourist companies, to the Spartan austerity of a *felucca*.

Walid insisted on making a pot of strong Turkish coffee for them. Having these interesting foreigners on his boat was something of a social occasion, and it was clear that he wanted to get the most out of it. As they drank the coffee, they were content to let Walid tell them about his beautiful fat wife and five wonderful daughters. He was sad that he only had one son, but if that was Allah's will then he must accept it.

Listening to this man, well past his prime, talk with loving affection about his family, Daniel felt safe for the first time in several hours. It was unlikely that a *felucca* owner eking out his living on the Nile would sit with his ears glued to the radio to hear the news. To Walid, the things that mattered most were the weather and the exchange rate.

'So what you do here?' asked Walid in English, addressing Daniel.

'Well, my wife is a professor of Egyptology and she has to come here often because of her work. I'm a businessman myself. I don't really have time for all this academic stuff. I've been here a couple of times before and the first time I saw the pyramids and the Sphinx and the Valley of the Kings. But the second visit, I spent most of the time scuba-diving in Sharm el-Sheikh, so this time the missus here challenged me to see the real Egypt. And I figured if I'm going to see the *real* Egypt, I may as well go the whole way.'

He looked around at the scenery to emphasize the point.

'What business you do?' asked Walid.

'Computer software,' said Daniel. He figured it would sound suitably Western and wouldn't prompt too many questions.

'Ah, Microsoft,' said Walid.

'They're our competitors,' Daniel replied, laughing. 'They're much bigger than us.'

'I have an X-box,' said Na'if, obviously anxious to add something to the conversation.

'This is *goooood*!' said Daniel, as he sampled the lamb stew that Walid had prepared for lunch. Walid looked relieved by his reaction. He had apologized for the fact that it wasn't as good as his wife's lamb stew. He explained that his wife made the best stew in the world and Daniel and his wife should visit them in Cairo sometime and taste it. He also explained that when he wasn't taking people on his boat, he usually existed off fish, caught in the river and grilled over an open flame in the metal bucket and grill rack that doubled as a barbecue.

After lunch, Walid and the crew took a siesta on deck, leaving Daniel in charge of the helm.

'We should have turned ourselves in when we had the chance,' said Daniel. 'We might have been able to sort this out if we hadn't run away.'

Gabrielle's Nordic face held a cold, implacable look. 'You seem to be forgetting one thing: they *didn't* give us the chance. They started shooting before we could say a word.'

'I guess they must have panicked because of that story

180

about us carrying some disease. That message on Mansoor's phone said that you infected that curator at the British Museum.'

'I know, but that doesn't make any sense. I haven't got any symptoms.'

'Maybe it only affects men.'

'But Mansoor said it affected the volunteers.'

'Only a few. They put them all in quarantine, but not all of them were infected – and he didn't say anything about the gender of those who were.'

'And what about you? And Mansoor? Neither of you have shown any symptoms and you've had at least as much exposure as the curator in London.'

'Okay, but some people evidently *are* getting ill. And your uncle did say something about it when I went to see him on the morning I flew out here, just before he was . . .'

'That's the other thing, Daniel. Too many bad things seem to be happening at once. People are getting killed. First Uncle Harrison and the maid. Then the guardian of the tomb. And of course whoever did that also tried to kill *us* – and Mansoor. I'm just wondering if they're connected.'

'We don't actually know *who* they were trying to kill. It might have been any one of us.'

'The question is, Daniel . . . what are we going to do?'

Chapter 46

'Can you hear me?'

The big man on the bed didn't want to hear him. He didn't want to do anything. All he wanted to do was sleep. But he couldn't sleep any longer; the time for sleeping was over.

Goliath opened his eyes. There were maybe half a dozen people in the room. Two of them were nurses. The rest . . .

They were in white.

Doctors? Policemen?

At the back of his mind, he remembered seeing Egyptian policemen in their white summer uniform.

'Mr Carter? Can you talk?'

He felt the bandages upon him. Where was he? Hospital. He remembered what had happened to him. Fire . . . driving . . . woman . . . she threw something . . .

'Yes,' he muttered.

Through blurred vision, he fancied that he saw one of the nurses smiling. Was she happy because he could talk? Or was she cunning and scheming, like most women?

'Do you know what day it is?' asked one of the men in white coats.

What day is it?

He couldn't think. How long had he been here? He had been slipping in and out of consciousness.

'Mr Carter . . .'

Goliath turned his head and tried to sit up, but he couldn't.

'We need to ask you about the car you were driving . . . the car . . . it was destroyed by the fire. But we need to ask where you got it?'

'The woman . . .'

'The woman? The woman gave you the car?'

The man who had asked the question looked at his colleague. The other man shrugged.

'But didn't the woman have another car? Her own car?'

'Petrol bomb . . .'

'What?'

'She threw it into my car . . .'

'The woman threw a gasoline bomb into the car?'

Goliath made a slight nodding motion.

'Did you *know* the woman, Mr Carter?'

Goliath said nothing, just looked at the policeman blankly.

'Mr Carter, we need to know what's going on. That jeep you were in was hired by our Deputy Minister of Culture. Someone tried to lock him in a tomb.'

Something flickered in Goliath's mind when he heard the words '*tried* to lock him' – did that mean that he had failed?

'Was it you, Mr Carter? Was it you who killed the guardian and locked him in the tomb? Or was it the woman?'

'Captain, this man is extremely weak,' said one of the doctors. 'He needs time to recover.'

'I need *answers*!' snapped the captain.

'He isn't going anywhere. You can ask him when he's stronger.'

'I will ask him now!'

'Look, Captain, it's obvious that he isn't fully conscious. At the moment he's in no position to give you any answers. Give me a day or two to get him better and you can have all the answers you want.' The tone was as appeasing as the words.

'All right. You have *one* day.'

And with that the captain turned and left, followed by another man.

Goliath felt an itch on his nose and tried to rub it. It was then that he noticed that his left hand was handcuffed to the iron bed frame.

Chapter 47

On the *felucca*, the rest of the day drifted by uneventfully as Daniel and Gabrielle sat on deck with Walid and his two-man crew, chatting and watching the scenery go by. They even both had a go at smoking through the *narghilla*, which neither of them liked, though Daniel pretended to.

The evening meal was a light affair, after the very filling lunch. As the evening descended upon them, Daniel amused them with his Wild West, cowboy style of harmonica playing. The harmonica belonged to Walid, but he confessed, with some embarrassment, that he had never learnt to play it. But despite the cultural differences, they seemed to enjoy Daniel's rendition of 'Clementine' and 'The Yellow Rose of Texas'.

A few hours later, they were shown to their sleeping quarters – a space on the open deck. Daniel and Gabrielle had the privilege of sleeping in the semi-covered part of the boat, although the cover was little more than a tarpaulin thrown over a metal frame. Walid and his crew slept at the other end of the boat, under the moonlight, affording their Western guests at least a modicum of privacy. But the quilt that Walid had offered them to soften the discomfort of the wooden deck was not the cleanest of items, and it seemed to have lost most of its padding a long time ago.

As he lay there in the darkness, with only the stars, the moon and the lights from the riverbank for company, he saw Gaby as she was now, rather than as the teenage girl that he remembered from his student years. They were lying together like two spoons, him behind her. But even though she was fully clothed, he could see her firm arms and strong shoulders – the powerful build of the swimmer who had won the silver medal in the student games. And he realized how incredibly sexy he found her. Daniel was never one to be drawn to thin, spindly women, but nor was he particularly enamoured of the fat women favoured by some Eastern cultures. He admired fitness and his ideal women were athletes, not sexless supermodels.

And Gabrielle was one such woman. It amazed him to realize now that she had been like this for some time, yet he hadn't realized even when he worked with her on a dig in Jerusalem. Thinking about her as she was now, he wasn't sure if he wanted to make love to her or wrestle with her. And if he did wrestle with her, he was equally unsure if he would want to win or lose. Then again, perhaps it really made no difference.

As if sensing his eyes upon her, she rolled over on to her back and then turned another ninety degrees to face him.

'Have you got something on your mind?' she asked.

He felt embarrassed, almost as if she actually knew what he had just been thinking.

'I was wondering, maybe we should turn ourselves in to our respective embassies when we get to Cairo.'

'I don't think that's a good idea, Daniel.'

'It'll get us out of immediate danger. Maybe we can be tested for whatever they think is causing this illness. If they're still worried that we're infectious they'll let us stay in the embassies or arrange to have us quarantined instead of shot by trigger-happy cops.'

Gabrielle was looking at him with that same implacable look as before. 'That's all right for me, but what about you? That message on Mansoor's phone said there's a warrant out for your arrest in England. Do you want to be extradited back to London to face a murder charge before we can figure this out?'

'I don't think I *will* be facing a murder charge.'

'Then why did they issue a warrant?'

'Probably because I breached my bail conditions. That's an offence in its own right.'

'You may be right, but if they arrest you and send you back, you'll be putting yourself in their hands – and we don't know for how long. In the meantime you'll be treading water, waiting for someone else to solve the mystery. The way I see it, whoever killed Uncle Harrison is probably the same person who locked us in the tomb and we need to find out—'

'We don't *know* that.'

'I think it's a reasonable starting point. And then there's the small matter of these manuscripts that you're supposed to be translating for our joint paper. This could be the biggest thing in our careers. Do you think the British authorities will let you work on academic papers while you're a guest of Her Majesty? I can just see the citation: "Daniel Klein is currently the Professor of Semitic Languages at Wormwood Scrubs. He is sharing a cell with a pyramid salesman who . . ."'

Daniel burst out laughing. If nothing else, Gabrielle's humour had broken some of the tension.

'That's the only thing that's holding me back,' said Daniel.

'What, the prospect of prison?'

'No, the fact that I still want to solve this mystery – well, actually both of these mysteries.'

'How do you mean, *both*?'

'The disease *and* your uncle's missing paper. And I guess

187

also his death and the people trying to kill us. I think you're right: it probably *is* all tied in together. Your uncle said his paper was based on a translation of a manuscript in Proto-Sinaitic. We need to find that manuscript. Maybe it's the one that Mansoor was going to show us.'

Gabrielle thought about this for a moment. 'So let's stick to the original plan. When we get to Cairo we try and get a look at that papyrus that he was going to show us: the one from the tomb of Ay.'

'I wish we could actually phone Mansoor and find out if he's all right. Maybe he could even help us.'

'It's too risky. Even just switching on our phones could give away our position.'

'Okay, but how are we going to get into the museum archives without Mansoor to help us?'

He saw the twinkle in her eye.

'You're forgetting what he said. He has copies in his office at the SCA.'

Daniel waited for the other shoe to drop. After a couple of seconds, he prompted: 'And what do you think we're going to do, Gaby? Just walk in there and take a copy of an ancient papyrus from under the noses of the staff?'

'No, we'll go in after lunch when most of them are out. You're forgetting, Daniel – this is Egypt and we're heading towards summer.'

'So?'

'So, the old ways of the Levant die hard. Between one and four in the afternoon, most of them are away taking a siesta. That'll give us the perfect opportunity.'

'Oh, don't tell me these trusting Levantines leave the door unlocked?'

'Of course not. But a locked door never stopped anyone really determined, especially if they're properly equipped.'

'And I suppose you're also an expert on picking locks?' he asked with a sarcastic smile.

'Oh, do me a favour. This isn't *Charlie's Angels!*'

'Then how are you going to get us past that locked door?'

She reached into one of her pockets, and with a smile and a flourish, pulled out a key.

Chapter 48

'These are very serious charges, Miss Stewart,' the police captain said, leaning forward to emphasize his point. 'This is no longer just a case of leaving the scene of an accident. According to Mr Carter you threw a gasoline bomb through the window of his car. And I have to tell you that despite the fire, we found melted glass fragments in the burnt-out wreckage that supports this claim.'

Sarit knew that she had to think quickly. The story she had told them so far was that she had thought the car was trying to force her off the road and that she had sped on to escape, having heard that women drivers on their own are sometimes vulnerable on these roads at night. However, in the light of this new accusation, she realized that it wouldn't work and she'd have to change her story.

'All right, I'll tell you. I didn't throw a petrol bomb at him – but he tried to throw one at me. We'd had an argument earlier on the road and I drove away ahead of him. Then he caught up with me and I saw him lighting the Molotov cocktail and holding it like he was going to throw it. So I sideswiped his car and he dropped it. Then his car went up in flames.'

'So why did you drive on? Why did you not report the incident immediately?'

'Because I was afraid. A woman alone in a foreign country,

attacked on a lonely stretch of road in the dead of night. What was I to think?'

'And you thought our policemen are corrupt woman-haters who would rape you or beat a confession out of you.'

'I don't know what I thought! Okay, maybe I had that stereotype in the back of my mind. I don't know.'

A man from the Irish Embassy was sitting there, but strangely he was sitting opposite her next to the police captain, rather than at her side. He was not talking; just listening. Occasionally he made a note of something, but not very often. She had been told that she could have a lawyer, but so far none had materialized.

'And this man – the one in the car – did you know him?'

Tread carefully, a little voice inside her head said.

'I'd been at the Valley of the Kings that day. I think I may have seen him there.'

'And the jeep he was driving . . . do you know anything about that?'

Don't let it show on my face, her mind was screaming.

'No. It was just an ordinary jeep. I mean, I didn't really think about it.'

'Why were you driving back to Cairo, Miss Stewart?'

She swallowed nervously. 'I don't understand,' she said, trying to buy time.

'You flew into Luxor Airport from Cairo and then you hired a car to visit the Valley of the Kings. Nothing unusual in that. But then instead of driving back to the airport and taking a plane back to Cairo, you set out on a seven- or eight-hour night-time drive on an unfamiliar stretch of road that you yourself admit is dangerous for women.'

'I didn't have a return ticket. I'd wanted to keep my plans flexible.'

'You could have bought a ticket at the airport.'

'It was late.'

'They have a five to eleven flight. And another at one-twenty in the morning.'

'I didn't know.'

'Well, you could have tried. Or why not stay overnight in a hotel in Luxor? You said yourself your plans were flexible.'

'I'm not exactly rich. I was already paying for a hotel in Cairo. I hadn't checked out. I didn't want to pay twice.'

She realized after she had said it that this was a mistake. The hotel she was staying at, although far from deluxe, was not cheap and she had now drawn attention to this. It was another contradiction, which the police captain would surely flag as another lie – even if it hadn't registered yet.

'Well, why didn't you take the train?'

'That's also seven hours.'

'But at least it's safer than the road.'

'I didn't think about it. I wasn't thinking straight.' And then she suddenly had an idea. 'Look, could I go to the bathroom? I need to . . .' She looked at the man from the embassy. 'It's a woman's thing . . . the time of the month.'

The embassy man blushed and then leaned over to the police captain and whispered a word in his ear. The police captain nodded, though the look on his face remained neutral.

'Very well.'

He called for a female officer to escort her to the bathroom. Only when they got there did Sarit say, 'I haven't got any tampons or sanitary pads.'

The policewoman didn't react.

Not wanting to alert the policewoman to the fact that she spoke fluent Arabic, Sarit spoke hesitantly and falteringly, like she had been taking lessons but lacked confidence.

192

'*Leisal adeiya ay al-fau'ad asahaya.*'

The policewoman reacted to this. '*Sa ahduru lekawa ahad.*' I'll get you one.

And with that she left. Sarit knew that there was no prospect of simply walking out of there. There would be a policeman outside the door. But she had a few minutes to act. There was a window. It was high, but it could open. The problem was how to reach it.

The cubicle on the end was empty. She went in and stood on the toilet. She gripped the ledge of the window and pulled herself up, using all her upper-body strength and the tension of her legs and feet against the sides of the cubicle. With an almighty effort, she found herself perched precariously on top of the cubicle – its door and walls a couple of feet below the ceiling.

She pulled down the latch and opened the long thin window. Then she inserted her head and hands and then arms and began pulling herself through. Now came the tricky bit. She was thin enough to get through, but the problem was landing safely. The building was set over different levels and this window opened out on to a stretch of roof. But it was an eight- or nine-foot drop from the window to the roof.

Falling head first would probably break her neck. Of course if she slid through slowly and lowered herself as she did so, the actual drop would be less than that. And of course, she could also take the fall on her hands, albeit at the risk of a broken wrist or worse. But then she noticed some kind of a utility box against the wall. By putting her hands on this as she hung there, she was able to angle her body, swing her legs round and . . .

Yes!

She landed on her feet, albeit awkwardly, like a springboard diver whose dive had gone horribly wrong. But there were no points to be had here; it was all about escape and survival. Right now she was on a section of the roof. She didn't know how long it had been, but she realized that if her escape hadn't been discovered yet, it pretty soon would be. And escape was perhaps not quite the right word. She had escaped from the toilet, but she had not yet escaped from the building.

She looked for a way down, realizing that if there was a utility box on the roof then there had to be a ladder or some other way of reaching the ground. All large public buildings must have accessible roofs to enable work to be done. The question was where was it? And would it simply take her back into the building, which would almost certainly be locked down before she could affect a complete escape?

Then she saw it: a fire escape, diagonally across the roof from where she was standing. She raced towards it, but as she did she thought she heard someone shouting out to her in Arabic.

Chapter 49

Breakfast on board Walid's boat was *shakshouka* – fried eggs in a thick sauce made from fresh tomatoes, onions and chillies, that he had bought from a riverside vendor. As they ate, they listened to the radio in the background. It was tuned to some local music station, lulling Walid and his crew into a state of restfulness. But it was coming up to the hour and the news came on.

Daniel and Gabrielle both listened out just in case anything was said about the tomb incident. The first two items were about local politics and the third was about the United States. But then another item came on that caught them by surprise.

'Police in Luxor are looking for a Western couple after an attempt was made on the life of Akil Mansoor, the Deputy Minister for Culture and Head of the Supreme Council of Antiquities. Professor Mansoor was locked in a tomb together with the Western couple in an apparent attempt to kill him, but the three of them managed to escape. The couple, however, then abandoned Professor Mansoor and ran away when confronted by the police. Professor Mansoor is now recovering in hospital from the incident.'

Daniel sighed with relief at the news that Mansoor was okay. He exchanged eye contact with Gabrielle and saw that she shared his feelings.

'The couple are Daniel Klein, an Englishman, believed to be an expert on Semitic languages, and Gabrielle Gusack, an Austrian professor of Egyptology. They are also being sought over other matters, concerning a recent death in England. Professor Klein is forty years old, brown haired and of average build. The woman is blonde, thirty-five years old and speaks with a slight Austrian accent.'

Even before they looked up from the radio, Daniel and Gabrielle knew that Walid and the other two were looking straight at them.

Chapter 50

'We thought we should warn you. If she was trying to kill you then she might try again.'

The police captain was talking to Goliath, who had now fully regained consciousness. The doctors were treating his burns and the police were treating him with compassion and humanity. But he remained handcuffed to the bed frame as a precaution.

'Thank you for telling me.'

'You have no need to worry, of course. We will post extra guards outside your room and at the entrances to the hospital. If she *does* try to come here, she will be arrested before she gets anywhere near you. But we thought that you should be informed.'

'Thank you.'

'But having got that out of the way, the best way we can protect you is if you tell us the truth. *Why* did this woman try to kill you? And why were you driving the jeep that was rented by our Deputy Minister of Culture?'

At that moment a man in a suit entered the private hospital room, flanked by a couple of soldiers. The police captain and the uniformed officer by the bed both leapt to their feet in an obvious sign of deference to the visitor.

A vociferous exchange in Arabic followed; the new arrival

appeared to be throwing his weight around and the police captain appeared to be pleading or at least arguing from a position of weakness. Eventually, both men calmed down and the police captain looked – and sounded – beaten.

He took out his evident frustration on a subordinate, barking an order to the unformed policeman, who produced a key and unlocked the handcuffs from Goliath's wrist and the bed frame. Goliath rubbed his wrist while the uniformed policeman put away the handcuffs. The police captain looked embarrassed at his sudden loss of authority.

'I don't understand,' said Goliath.

'It would seem, Mr Carter, that you have friends in high places. I have been ordered to release you. You are, of course, free to go at any time. However I would strongly advise you to stay here in the hospital to continue with the silver nitrate treatment for the burns.'

Chapter 51

'I'm telling you – we didn't have anything to do with it,' Gabrielle was saying in Arabic. 'We were locked in the tomb and stuck there for several hours.'

Walid's brother and son were looking at her like they *wanted* to believe her. But Walid himself was hard to read, like he had been around the block a few times and was a natural sceptic about everything except his religion.

'Then how did you get out?'

'We used a stone to smash a hole in the door. Then we used the key. That's why Mansoor is in hospital. He cut his wrist on the metal of the door.'

'Then why are the police looking for you? And why did you run away?'

'Because the police started shooting at us! They didn't even give us a chance to talk.'

She was worried that he was going to ask why the police would do that. This could be a problem. If she told him that the police thought they were carrying a contagious disease, he would hardly be inclined to carry them further. All she knew was that they hadn't spread this news in the radio reports – presumably because they did not wish to start a panic. In the face of such restraint, it would hardly make sense to share the police's belief with the very person they were still hoping would help them get to Cairo.

'Okay, I know our police can sometimes be a bit . . . overzealous. But I still don't understand why you abandoned Professor Mansoor.'

Daniel finally decided to step in. The reporter had already blown his cover and revealed that the Englishman was an expert on Semitic languages, so there was no reason not to show his fluent command of Arabic.

'We didn't actually abandon him. We left him temporarily because it was a five-kilometre walk to get help and he'd cut his wrist badly. We bandaged it up as best we could and then set off to get help.'

Walid did not seem surprised by the quality of Daniel's Arabic. 'Couldn't you have called for help? Don't you have mobile phones?'

'We tried, but we couldn't get a decent signal. Then when the police saw us – maybe because he wasn't with us – they assumed that we'd done something to him and started firing. But you know he's all right because they said so, and as they pointed out, *we* were locked in the tomb too. Whoever did it might have been trying to kill us.'

'And what about what they said about you being responsible for a death in England?'

Daniel wasn't sure which way the wind was blowing in Walid's mind. He knew that his and Gabrielle's fate lay in his hands. He had to say something more to sway him.

'The man who died was Gabrielle's uncle. He was a great professor. The police think it was a family dispute but we think he was killed by a jealous rival.'

Daniel wanted to convey a sense of aggrieved innocence and he sensed that offering a hint of high intrigue would create the kind of cover story that a man who led a mundane life would *want* to believe. As a former amateur magician he knew that getting the audience to want to believe was half the trick.

'This sounds so . . .'

Daniel wondered if he had *over*-dramatized it, so he was relieved when Walid's face mellowed. 'I believe you. But I have a family to feed. If we get caught then I will be in trouble too . . . and that will hurt my family.'

Daniel sighed. 'You're right, of course. I cannot ask you to put yourself and your family at risk for us – especially after we took advantage of your hospitality and didn't tell you the truth. If you can put us ashore, we will be on our way.'

Walid looked at him, surprised.

Daniel followed up quickly. 'You can keep the money, of course. Consider it as payment for the trouble we've put you through.'

Walid met his eyes. They both knew what the other was thinking, as did Gabrielle. The radio report hadn't said anything about a reward, but at some point a reward might still be offered. Daniel was offering to pay Walid for his silence. Even if a reward was offered that dwarfed the money already paid him, Walid would consider it dishonourable to betray them after accepting their money.

'I cannot do that,' said Walid quietly.

'You don't understand,' said Daniel. 'I *want* you to keep the money. I have put you to so much trouble already . . . and you have a family to feed.'

'No, it is *you* who do not understand,' said Walid firmly. 'I *will* take you to Cairo.'

Chapter 52

Sarit was in the Wekalat Al-Balah Bazaar, wearing a *jilbab* that she had just bought to cover her body, and *khimar* to cover her hair. By dressing modestly she knew that men were less likely to bother her, and she also reduced the likelihood of being recognized. But at one point she would have to take a risk.

What she was looking out for were Western women – specifically Western women with large shoulder bags in which they carried everything under the sun. In some Muslim countries, women tended to be more careless than they would be in a Western street market, because they knew that the draconian laws made theft less likely. However, here the laws were not quite so severe and so the women were more careful.

Eventually, she found what she was looking for: a young, obviously Western woman who had a bag with some other items already and who was interested in trying on one of the colourful dresses. Even better, when the woman spoke, it was with a Liverpool accent. Sarit could do American accents if she had to but RP was a lot easier. And of course the passport wouldn't say 'Liverpool', it would state 'United Kingdom'.

Sarit had already bought several items and had them in

a collection of bags, to create her cover, so now she was ready to pounce. She sidled up to the woman and started looking at the dresses. By giving the impression that she was not sure, she drew the attention of the merchant to her. He was not going to let her slip away if he could persuade her to stay and make a purchase.

'Would you like to come in? We have many more dresses inside. Very nice dresses for the pretty lady.' He pointed to the inside of the shop.

'Oh, I like this one,' she said, holding up a particularly gaudy, colourful embroidered dress from the rack. 'But I was wondering if it's too big for me. Do you have somewhere I could try it on?'

'Yes, I have a changing room inside.'

Again, he pointed. Sarit looked down at her bag full of other purchases.

'You can take it ins—'

She didn't let the man finish. She half-turned to the woman who had been looking at the same colourful collection and addressed her quickly.

'Excuse me, would you mind keeping an eye on my bag for two minutes? I just want to try this on.'

The woman looked hesitant.

'I'll only be two minutes. I just want to see how it looks.'

'Okay,' said the other woman.

And with that, Sarit went inside, leaving not only the big bag containing the items she had bought earlier, but also her shoulder bag – as if to imply that it was unsafe to take it into the shop. The reality was the exact opposite. The shopkeepers here would guard it with their lives sooner than let anyone take it, whereas outside there was a chance that someone might steal it.

Two minutes later, Sarit emerged a happy, satisfied

customer, reclaimed her possessions and after a bit of skilful haggling, bought the gaudy embroidered dress. Meanwhile the woman who had guarded her possessions appeared to have made up her mind, at least to the point of narrowing down her choices.

'Listen,' she said, 'could you keep an eye on my stuff? I'm going to go in and try these on too.'

'Sure,' said Sarit.

The girl went in, with the shopkeeper in tow. Without lowering her eyes from the merchandise in which she was feigning continued interest, Sarit opened the shoulder bag and groped around inside. Working more by feel than by look, she found the passport and quickly pulled it out and dropped it into one of her shopping bags.

Then she found the purse and moved it to the top of the shoulder bag, so that the girl would be able to get to it easily. The girl may or may not remember the purse being lower down in the shoulder bag, but this way she was less likely to notice the missing passport. In any case, if she was suspicious, it was more likely to be over the purse with money and credit cards than the passport.

Seven or eight minutes later, the girl came out and bought a couple of the dresses, oblivious to the theft of her passport.

Chapter 53

Six days after they had set out, Daniel and Gabrielle arrived on the outskirts of Cairo.

Gabrielle had taken to life on the *felucca* a lot better than Daniel had expected, but Daniel had surprised himself by finding it enjoyable too – especially considering how heavily dependent he usually was on his urban comforts.

He realized that as an archaeologist, accustomed to roughing it in some pretty exotic locations, it wasn't such an unusual experience for Gabrielle. But for a North Londoner who was used to clean hotel suites, business-class airline seating and deferential waiters, it was something of a culture shock. He wondered what Charlotte would have made of it – genteel Charlotte, whose world was that of crisp starched linen and manicured nails.

He wondered if it was *because of* rather than merely despite the danger that he had found himself enjoying this adventure. It was as if this was the part of his life that had always been waiting for him. It reminded him of that famous line in Henry David Thoreau's *Walden* about 'when I came to die, discovered that I had not lived'.

They bid their goodbyes to Walid and his crew, wished Allah's blessings on his family and then set off for Cairo's Zamalek District.

Zamalek was an island in the Nile, connected to the rest of Cairo by bridges – a sort of Manhattan in North Africa. Heavily developed and built-up, the area was home to several luxury hotels as well as quite a few foreign embassies. It was, all in all, quite an upmarket area. But there was only one thing in the Zamalek District that interested Daniel and Gabrielle: the Supreme Council of Antiquities.

Daniel knew that there was a risk of being recognized, but was relieved that their most distinguishing feature had now been negated. There were lots of dark-haired Western men in Cairo and none of them would get a second glance. But Gabrielle's blonde hair was quite striking, and if the police or anyone else was on the lookout for a tall blonde woman, Gabrielle's hair would have been more than enough to guarantee that they would get a second glance.

They had considered hiding it under a headscarf, but that was not a sure-fire way of avoiding attention. Her height and Western looks might be enough to make it clear that she was trying to hide her hair. Then the game would be up. So instead she had played the adventurous tourist card and persuaded one of the women in the villages along the Nile to dye her hair with henna.

'It's something I've always wanted to try,' she had explained with almost schoolgirlish excitement.

She had considered using henna to darken her skin too, but it was more usually used for tattoos. In any case, she was now covering herself up with a robe, showing very little of her flesh. There was nothing she could do about her height, but now, instead of appearing as a tall blonde, she came over as a tall redhead who could pass for a local. And that was not what the police were looking for.

They hailed a taxi in the street and took the short ride across the city to the Supreme Council of Antiquities. The driver dropped them off at the front of the building, which had been given a modern glass entrance and a silver, metallic grey façade with the words 'Supreme Council of Antiquities' emblazoned across the portals in huge Arabic letters as well as somewhat smaller in English. Daniel noted, with silent amusement, that the letter *f* in the word *of* had become loose and fallen into a diagonal posture.

He let Gabrielle lead the way up the wide steps to this grand entrance. She introduced Daniel as an Australian professor, hoping that the nationality would throw the guard off if he had heard anything about an Englishman being wanted by the police – which was unlikely. The guard had smiled and said a tentatively English 'hallo' – prompting Daniel to respond with his best Aussie 'g'day'.

And with that, they were inside.

As Gabrielle had predicted, the building was surprisingly empty, even allowing for the fact that this was siesta time. They made their way quickly to Mansoor's office, which Gabrielle promptly opened with her key. Once inside, they went to work rapidly on the oak desk and the grey metal filing cabinets, taking advantage of the fact that the drawers of the desk were unlocked and the filing cabinets had their keys still in them.

For a while it looked like they weren't going to find anything and then that old cliché about 'the last place you look' kicked in.

'Found it!' shrieked Gabrielle, louder than she had intended.

It was actually in the very first drawer that Daniel had searched. Somehow he had managed to miss it, probably because he was grabbing whole wads of paper and not going through the pages individually.

She handed the papers to Daniel who started looking through them. In his mind, he started deciphering one marked 'Tomb of Ay', testing his memory of the language and script.

'Interesting.'

Gabrielle picked up on Daniel's tone. 'What?'

'It says here something about "the Sibolet stores built by my father".'

'*Si*bolet?'

'Yes. I think it's a variation of *Shi*bolet. The Hebrew word for grain or at least the grain-bearing part of wheat or corn.'

'Presumably it's a reference to the grain houses that Joseph persuaded Pharaoh to build to store the grain from the seven plentiful years. And it supports the theory about Yuya being Joseph. Ay was the son of Yuya after all.'

'Holy shit!'

'What?'

'Listen to this: "I pray that one day my bones shall return to the holy mountain of Gerizim".'

'Gerizim?'

'It's a mountain in the West Bank. There's also a valley near there that's believed to be the place where Joseph and his sons were buried.'

'But if Joseph was Yuya, then that can't be, because his mummy is in *Egypt* – the one they found in KV46.'

'Yes, but what about his sons? Do they have the mummy of Ay?'

'No, it was never found. But that's because it was believed to have been removed from the tomb and desecrated by a pharaoh called Horemheb during the counter-revolution that followed the Amarna period, when they restored the cult of Amun.'

'But maybe it didn't happen that way. Maybe the body of Ay was taken when the Israelites gained their freedom. Maybe they didn't succeed in taking the bones of Joseph but managed to take the bones of his sons, or at least one of his sons.'

'That's a lot of maybes! But what *I'm* thinking is maybe we should just make some photocopies and get out of here before we get caught.'

'Okay, you're right, but he hasn't got a photocopier in here.'

They gathered up the papers and left the office furtively. As soon as they left the office, they were spotted by Mansoor's secretary, who was returning to her desk.

'Oh hallo,' she said in Arabic, recognizing the pair of them. 'Is Professor Mansoor back?'

Once again it was Daniel who wanted to stand his ground and try and talk his way out of the situation. And once again, it was Gabrielle who panicked under pressure. Not waiting for Daniel, she dived towards a corridor and ran, leaving Daniel with no alternative but to follow, while the woman who had spotted them was screaming: '*Dsst irt'ra el-erm!*'

Chapter 54

He came through for me, Goliath was thinking as he wandered aimlessly after leaving the hospital. *Once again, he came through.*

Goliath couldn't imagine what strings Senator Morris had pulled to get the police off his back, but whatever it was he had done it. He had known for some time that the senator chaired several powerful committees and that this gave him an enormous amount of influence on Capitol Hill. Some of these committees dealt with foreign affairs so that no doubt gave him a certain amount of clout with foreign governments.

But it was still an awesome feeling, knowing that he had a man with so much power behind him, giving him both guidance and support. It was like having one's own pit bull. Except that this was a pit bull of international proportions.

Yet the intense pleasure of this feeling was dampened by the sobering thought that once again he had failed. Time after time on this sacred mission, he had tried to serve his mentor, and each time he seemed to be failing ever more spectacularly. It was as if God was punishing him for some unspecified sin, instead of rewarding him for his loyalty and devotion. He knew that good works did not in themselves make him one of God's Elect. That was in the gift of God alone.

But God chose his elect by looking into their hearts and choosing them for their sincerity. If God was now spurning his efforts, did that mean that he was not sincere? Did it mean that his motives were tainted by impurity? He had killed the wicked – and those who stood in the way of God's work. That was surely no sin, and even if he had faltered, he had never once thought of personal gain.

And yet now, once again, he had failed. Mansoor and the others were not dead. Daniel Klein and Gabrielle Gusack were not only alive but free and on the run. Their whereabouts were unknown not only to him, but also to the police.

And who was that woman on the road who had thrown the petrol bomb into the jeep? Was she trying to kill him? Or had she thought that he was Daniel or the Egyptian? Was she trying to kill them too?

A thousand questions and no answers. Still he had failed. He hadn't even managed to get a sample of their clothing and that had been his main task. Killing them had been secondary. He didn't even know *why* Morris wanted him to get the clothing. All he knew was that it was God's will. And although they had left their travel bags in the jeep, the jeep had gone up in flames, taking their belongings with it, including the clothes that he had intended to take in accordance with Senator Morris's instructions.

But how could he do it now that Daniel and the others had escaped? Did Senator Morris still want him to? Or had the plan been overtaken by events?

He had just purchased a smartphone with Internet capability, like Daniel's, and thought about contacting the senator to ask him. But that might not be wise. The fact that the senator had intervened on his behalf did not mean that he had done so openly. He might have pulled strings behind the scenes or called in favours from others. The senator had once told him not to mention his name. That probably meant that he operated through third parties and did not like to expose his involvement directly. If Goliath now blew the cover of his patron and mentor might that not be yet another failure? Another breach of his duty? Another mistake?

No, he had to assume that Arthur Morris still wanted him to do what he had told him to do before. And that meant he had to find Daniel Klein and Gabrielle Gusack. As to the other woman – the one who had tried to kill him – he would deal with her later. They had told him her name when they came to warn him that she had escaped: Siobhan Stewart. So at least he had something to work with when the time came. For now, he had to concentrate on finding Klein and Gusack. But how?

He remembered the tracer program that he had planted in Daniel Klein's phone. Was it still working? Easy enough to find out.

He switched on his newly-purchased smartphone and logged on to the search site with his UserID and password. It gave the 'last known location' of Daniel's phone as the Nile Valley, near Luxor. That made perfect sense. If Daniel was trying to avoid being found by the Egyptian authorities, then he would keep his cell phone switched off. Everyone knew that people can be traced by their cell phones. When a man knows that he is wanted by the police then that is the time to switch off his phone or even get rid of it. As long as Daniel didn't know he was being tracked, it was not a problem; but now that he was on the run from the Egyptian police, Daniel was presumably taking elementary precautions. And those precautions would also stop Goliath from doing a live trace.

But then Goliath had another idea. A man on the run wouldn't want to be completely cut off. Of course, he might buy a new cell phone, as Goliath had. But maybe – just maybe – Daniel was switching on his phone temporarily in order to retrieve his messages? That in itself might facilitate tracking by way of giving updated last known locations.

That also afforded another opportunity. It meant that Daniel Klein could be reached. And maybe there was a way of getting through to him. What if that fear could be turned to Goliath's advantage? What if he could prey upon that fear to lure Daniel into a trap?

He knew now what he had to do.

He called Daniel using his new smartphone and heard a standard message for voicemail. He deduced from this that Daniel was one of those people who was too lazy to create a personalized message: the proverbial absent-minded professor.

'Hallo, Professor Klein . . . this is Mr Carter, the man you met on the aeroplane, the rather talkative man as you probably remember me. I've just seen a report about you on television, effectively accusing you of all manner of crimes and misdemeanours; and I have to say, having met you, that it sounds like a load of baloney! I'm sure this is all a misunderstanding and I'd like to help you. I am, as you know, a man who is not without means, and I would like to put those means at your disposal. If you could contact me as soon as possible, I can go about arranging lawyers for you both locally and in Britain. My number is . . .'

When he rang off, he was confident that he had baited the trap. How could a desperate man without a friend in the world, not respond to an offer to help like that one?

Chapter 55

'We can't go by bus,' Gabrielle was saying. 'They'll catch us at the checkpoints.'

'There are checkpoints at the borders too,' Daniel replied. 'Any way you look at it we're going to have to cross a border checkpoint. But I'd've thought that with the buses it wouldn't be as intense as it is at the airports.'

They were in a café by the Nile in a small village outside Cairo, discussing their next move.

'You have to understand, Daniel, that with the bus it isn't just *one* checkpoint. It can be any number. In some ways it's worse than an airport because at an airport you go through passport control and then you're through. They only look at your passport when boarding to match it up to your boarding pass. But with the bus, because it stops at several places on the way, there are several checkpoints. And a checkpoint can be wherever an Egyptian army commander chooses to put one.'

'Well, there's no way we can use the airport. They're bound to be watching that.'

'Okay, so let's say we find a way of getting to one of the borders. Why does it have to be the Israeli border? Wouldn't that be the one they watch most closely?'

'You tell me, Gaby. Do you think the security will be more lax at the Gaza border? Or the Libyan border?'

'We could try and make it to Jordan.'

'We could. But we'd still have to get to Taba in Sinai – even if we wanted to make it across to Aqaba. And besides . . . it's Israel that we need to get to.'

'Why?'

'Because we need to talk to the Samaritans.'

'The Samaritans?'

'Yes.'

'Why in God's name do you want to talk to them?'

'Because I want to show them those copies of the papyri that we took from Mansoor's office. The one that appeared to be written by Ay, whom you think – *we* think – may have been Ephraim, the son of Joseph.'

'Why do you want to show it to them?'

'Because I think they may be able to shed some light on it.'

'Would you care to elaborate?'

'You remember what it said? The author expressed his wish that his bones be returned to Mount Gerizim?'

'Yes, and you said that the valley nearby is the traditional resting place of Joseph and his sons.'

'Yes. But the thing is, although the valley nearby has that tradition, the mountain itself has no major significance to the Jews. *But it is regarded as the most sacred place in the world to the Samaritans.* They even claim that it was the place where Abraham, the Israelite patriarch, was going to sacrifice his son Isaac, until an angel stopped him. And they also claim that it was the site where God told the Israelites to build the temple.'

'But how do you propose to get their co-operation? Are you just going to go up to their leaders, as a complete stranger, and flash this copy of the papyrus and tell them that you've translated it and ask them to share their secrets with you?'

'Basically, yes.'

'Great. So now all we've got to do is *get* there.'

'If we can make it to Taba, I have a plan for getting to Israel. But it's risky.'

'It's also going to be risky getting to Taba, with all those checkpoints in the Sinai Desert.'

'*Daniel!*'

They both spun round at the familiar voice.

'My old friend. How are you?'

It was Walid. He was smiling that constant smile of his. Daniel just wished he hadn't called his name out loud.

'I'm fine,' said Daniel, signalling Walid to join them at the table, preferring to converse with him in muted voices than shouting across a distance of a few feet.

Walid switched to Arabic. 'Have you solved your problems?'

Daniel hesitated. Walid was trustworthy, but Daniel wasn't sure how ongoing the duty of silence was. Technically he was no longer in Walid's 'tent'.

'I need to get to Taba,' Daniel explained.

'You can go by bus across Sinai,' Walid explained. 'Or you can fly to Sharm and then drive north from there. Or you can even drive from here. But it is a long journey.'

Daniel wasn't worried about the length of the trip, only about the prospect of having to show documentation when he hired a car.

'We need to get there quietly . . . without anyone noticing.'

He was about to say that he and Gabrielle had lost their passports, but he didn't want to lie to Walid again. It would be dishonourable, and honour was a very important thing in local culture.

'We can't hire a car, because we daren't identify ourselves.

216

It could lead to problems. But if you know someone who can drive us . . . we are ready to pay good money.'

Walid thought for a few seconds. 'I do not know anyone who can drive you, but I know a group of Bedouin who are going that way on camels.'

Chapter 56

'Passport, please,' said the Egyptian soldier.

The checkpoint was at the entrance to the Ahmed Hamdi Tunnel, just north of Suez. The mile-long, two-lane tunnel would take them under the Suez Canal into Sinai. But first, the pair of soldiers who had boarded the night bus had to earn their keep. Like the threesome who had searched the bus at the earlier checkpoint, they walked up and down, selecting a few people at random for an ID check. This time, however, Sarit just happened to be one of them.

For locals all they had to produce was an ID card, but for tourists it meant a passport. This might have been worrying, but the fact that it was random meant that they were not looking for Sarit in particular. And the fact that they didn't have any computer terminal for checking meant that they could only check the passport against the face, not against background information such as a report about a wanted person or a lost passport. But then again, this was only an *inland* checkpoint, not border control.

She wasn't too worried about getting to Taba. The hard part would be when she had to cross the border into Israel. She knew that the passport would pass a cursory inspection at least. In the old days it used to be easy to tamper with a passport to make it usable by prising open the plastic, taking out the photograph and carefully inserting a new one before resealing it. Even copying the quadra-circle of the ink stamp by hand with the felt tip was relatively straightforward to someone with a steady hand and a good eye for detail.

But now they had holograms, special sealing plastic and a whole host of other technologies designed to prevent tampering. However, Sarit attacked the problem from the other end, *adapting her appearance to the passport*. Most modern women know how to change their appearance in a variety of ways and Sarit's training had augmented this ability considerably. Also, she had selected a target who was in her age range to begin with. Everything else could be changed: hair colour and style, skin tone, even eye colour. In a cosmopolitan city like Cairo, the wherewithal for such a metamorphosis was readily available.

Aside from that, most people don't look anything like their passport picture and are not even expected to. And most of the border officials in Egypt were men – less perspicacious than women at the best of times and brought up in a culture where the very act of looking at women was discouraged!

So as the night bus sped its way across the Sinai Peninsula, Sarit tried to relax as the bus continued on its night-time drive.

When they arrived at Taba, just before dawn, the driver had done the usual trick of offering to take them the extra six hundred yards to the checkpoint into Israel, for a mere five Egyptian pounds. But like the others on the bus, Sarit had refused. She had no particular desire to be first. She was quite happy to be somewhere in the middle, so that the official who inspected her passport would be tired from the ones he had seen already and yet faced with many more in the queue behind her.

But when she got to her turn things did not go as smoothly as she expected.

'Miss Harker?' said the man studying her passport.

'Yes?'

'It says here that your passport was reported stolen yesterday.'

Chapter 57

Mid-April was towards the end of the tourist season, at least for the southern Nile and the Valley of the Kings. Strictly speaking it was the tourist season all year round, but in the Luxor area, until late September, it would simply be too hot for the Western tourists.

Yes, they would still come and they would still take cruises on the Nile, but they would go with the luxury, air-conditioned vessels not the austere *feluccas*. Na'if's father had been lucky to get that job – carrying that Western couple from the Esna Lock to Cairo. Normally the tourists just wanted a two-hour fun trip to get their feet wet, so to speak.

But now with the tourist season nearly over, it would be back to fishing. So now it was Na'if's duty to clean out the boat and get it ready for a fishing voyage. He always hated this time of year. The tourist season was so much more fun. Not just because the money was better, but also because there was more to do. The tourists were always interesting people to talk to. They came from other lands where they did things differently and it was always fun to hear about foreign lands, and especially to meet the Western girls who showed their bodies in the way they dressed.

He wanted one day to go to the West. Maybe to study in one of their universities or colleges. He had heard that in the West you could study to be a reporter for a newspaper or learn how to play football like David Beckham. It would be nice to do that. If only his father had the money to send him.

It was while he was cleaning out the boat that he noticed something that must have fallen out of one of their pockets. It was a mobile phone, one of those big ones with a fancy display. It belonged to the man – Daniel. He remembered that now. He had two phones, but he never used them. And now he had lost one of them.

It was too late to give it back to him because they had left the boat and could be anywhere in Cairo. Besides, Daniel had *two* mobile phones; he had seen that. So why did he need both? It wasn't really stealing because he hadn't taken it, but merely found it. And he couldn't give it back to the owner because the owner wasn't there.

There was no point handing it in to the police. They would never be able to find the owner. So why couldn't he keep it for himself?

He made up his mind in that moment that this was precisely what he *would* do.

Chapter 58

'I didn't actually lose it,' Sarit was explaining. 'I just left it in my hotel room by mistake.'

'But why didn't you tell the police that you found it?'

Sarit was trying to convince the border official in Taba that it was all just a misunderstanding. But the border official was playing hardball.

'I phoned the police and told them. But it was late at night when I discovered it and I couldn't get through to the right person. They said they'd pass on a message.'

'But you don't know the name of the person you spoke to?'

'I'm afraid not.'

'What is the purpose of your visit to Israel?'

'Sightseeing.'

It was normally the Israelis who were more suspicious, but it was understandable that the Egyptians were being cautious under the circumstances.

'You don't think it was a bit careless, leaving the passport in your hotel room and then wasting police time by telling them that it was missing?'

Sarit felt herself blushing. This was good. It would make her seem like an embarrassed, careless tourist.

'I didn't just forget it. It had actually fallen out of my bag in the hotel room and was down by the side of the bed. It was only when I searched really thoroughly that I found it. Look, I'm sorry for all the trouble I've caused. What more can I say?'

The official looked at her coldly. 'We'll have to check with the police in Cairo.'

It was then that Sarit began to worry.

Chapter 59

Daniel had initially assumed that Walid was a local Luxor man, because that was where he had boarded the *felucca*. But in fact he turned out to be a lot more well-connected than Daniel had imagined. He seemed to know everyone in Cairo, or at least everyone in the lower classes, from the waiters to the road-sweepers.

He also seemed to know quite a few of the Bedouin, including this group of five who were making their way across the Sinai Desert. Their original destination had apparently been Sharm el-Sheikh where they were going to ply their trade to the tourists, offering them camel rides.

But Mas'ud, the youngest member of the group, was planning on getting a job as a waiter in the hope of making his fortune or getting lucky with the younger female tourists. In some respects he was a bit like Na'if. When they were asked if they could change their plans and accompany the couple to Taba, he had been the first to point out that there were plenty of tourists there at this time of year, because it wasn't quite as hot as Sharm. And he for his part was quite happy to try his chances there first instead of Sharm.

Of course, with or without a change of plan, escorting the pair to Taba was a service and therefore payment was due. This time Walid bargained on their behalf, promising them he would get them the best possible price. And so, 1,500 Egyptian pounds lighter, they set off on camels, with a five-man escort, from the fringes of Cairo to Taba, travelling when it was cooler, from sunrise till midday and then again from late afternoon till some time after sunset. They slept from late night till sunrise and rested – with or without sleep – from midday until the afternoon sun was low in the sky.

The Bedouin escort rode in formation with two in front of them, several yards ahead, and three a similar distance behind. The three behind were also leading four additional camels that followed by herd instinct without being tied or tethered. As Daniel and Gabrielle were also dressed in Bedouin robes (for an extra 100 Egyptian pounds), anyone in the military manning a checkpoint would have spotted a group of seven Bedouin with eleven camels and thought nothing more about it.

Being positioned in the middle gave Daniel and Gabrielle the opportunity to talk in private.

'The Samaritans are basically concentrated in two communities. There's an Arabic-speaking community in Kiryat Luza in the West Bank, and a Hebrew-speaking community in Holon, inside Israel.'

'And which community are we going to visit? Kiryat Luza or Holon?'

'Ideally Kiryat Luza. It's actually located *on* Mount Gerizim, their sacred mountain, overlooking the town of Nablus. They used to be based in Nablus itself, but they fled to Kiryat Luza in the 1980s during the first intifada because they came under attack.'

'Then wouldn't it be safer to meet the ones in Holon?'

'That's probably what we'll have to do initially. I think that most of their priests are in Kiryat Luza. But if we talk to one of their leaders in Holon, that can get us an introduction until we can meet the high priest and put our appeal to him.'

'And you really think they're going to show you their most sacred documents?'

'If I can show them that I can translate them and reveal the sacred truths, then yes . . . I think they will.'

'But how are we going to get across the border?'

Daniel lowered his voice. 'I have a plan – but it's risky.'

Neither of them noticed that in the group of three bringing up the rear, Mas'ud was taking an unhealthy interest in their conversation.

Chapter 60

Sarit had been sitting in the waiting area on the Egyptian side of the border between Taba and Eilat for the last twenty minutes. They had told her to step aside and wait there so they could process the others more quickly. That did not bode well. Firstly, it meant that they were not letting the queue behind her pressure them into making a snap decision. Secondly it meant that they were taking it a lot more seriously than she had expected. She thought they would simply treat her as a scatterbrained tourist and wave her through. Instead, they were alert to the possibility that she might indeed be a terrorist or at least a passport thief.

The one thing she still had going for her was that it was still early morning and so it was unlikely that the right person would be on duty. Anyone with access to the police computer could confirm that the passport had been reported stolen, but only one or two police officers would be in any position to contradict the claim that the passport had been found or that she was the rightful passport holder.

Sarit didn't even know how long the real Kelly Harker would be staying in Cairo, suspecting that she was on some package tour and that was their 'shopping afternoon' in the bazaar. That meant she had probably by now been given some sort of temporary travel documents by the British

Embassy and then whisked away with the rest of the group. Depending on the itinerary of the group she could be on a cruise boat on the Nile, climbing Jebel Musa (the traditional Mount Sinai), or flying down to Sharm for a few days of swimming and sunbathing.

If so, then it would not be easy for the police to contact her quickly. The most the officer in charge could say would be that he hadn't been updated and the woman had carried on with her tour group. It was extremely unlikely that Sarit would be brought face to face with the woman she was impersonating, but it was touch and go whether she would be allowed through or detained until the matter was fully and finally resolved.

'I have some good news for you, Miss Harker,' said the border official. 'We spoke to the officer in charge, and he said that he was the one who recommended you to look in your hotel room to make sure the passport hadn't fallen out there. He is pleased that you followed his advice, even if you were too embarrassed to tell him.'

A beaming smile broke out across Sarit's face. She couldn't believe her luck. So less than a quarter of an hour later, Sarit was crossing into Israel. On the Israeli side of the border, they started grilling her on the purpose of her visit. She cut it short by telling them in Hebrew that she was not Kelly Harker but Sarit Shalev and asking them to contact Dovi Shamir at a number she gave them.

After a two-minute conversation between officials, she was taken aside to a private room where she was allowed to talk to Dovi herself.

'I've got a lot to tell you,' she said, demonstrating her penchant for understatement.

'You had me worried,' he replied. 'I'll send a chopper.' He hesitated to add that he was *still* worried.

Chapter 61

'Are you awake?' asked Gabrielle.

It was night and the Bedouin were sleeping in what their patriarch had humorously described as a 'thousand-star hotel'.

'Yes,' Daniel replied. 'You?'

'*No*, I'm talking in my sleep!'

Daniel and Gabrielle were supposed to be sleeping. They only had seven hours from their ten p.m stop to their pre-sunrise start. But they both had a lot on their minds, and sleep did not come easily to either of them.

'Sorry, I'm not at my best at midnight.'

He turned in his sleeping bag to catch Gabrielle's face. It was illuminated by the merest sliver of the moon crescent, giving her a strangely vulnerable look.

'I was just wondering what Charlotte would think if she could see you now.'

'What on earth made you think of that?'

'It's just that you . . . you seem to like roughing it. Those outings with your nephews . . . and that time we were on a dig together in Scotland.'

'When you tried to come into my tent . . . yes, I remember. But what's that got to do with Charlotte?'

'Well, she was so spoiled and pampered, with all her creature comforts, and you're the exact opposite. You like the outdoors, you spent six days on a *felucca* without complaining. Now we're camped down here in the desert under the stars. Charlotte wouldn't have lasted an hour doing anything like this.'

'She never really wanted to give it a try. It wasn't her world.'

'So why did you marry the bitch?'

'Oo, miao.'

'No seriously, Daniel. Why would you want to hook up with that scion of Pennsylvania aristocracy with an olive up her ass? Her ancestors would probably have blackballed yours if they'd applied to join the golf club. You're so down-to-earth and family oriented. If you'd had children, you'd probably have fought over whether to keep them at home or send them to boarding school.'

'I guess it's lucky we didn't.'

He felt a stab of regret as he said these words. Gabrielle's probing questions brought back a flood of memories and endless speculations about what could have been.

'Was that what led to the break-up?'

'What?'

'Children – or rather the lack of them. Were you a George and Martha couple?'

'Not by choice.'

'That's what I mean. Neither were the original George and Martha. But the difference is that they *both* wanted children. Not having them was a source of mutual frustration and regret. I don't think it was like that with Charlotte.'

'Maybe *I* was the one who didn't want kids?'

'Are you pulling my leg? I've heard you talking about those camping trips with your nephews and impressing your nieces with magic tricks. I think I can read between the lines. You've got it in you to be a great father. Was that what set you apart? You regretted not having children: she was quite happy that way.'

'That might have been part of it, but the real problem was that I could never fulfil her sense of ambition.'

'That's bullshit. You're *academically* ambitious.'

'Well, thanks for that vote of confidence. But Charlotte thought ambition was something I lacked.'

'What planet was she living on?'

'I guess it's a question of how you *define* success, not how you measure it.'

'Are we talking academic success or social success?'

'Both. Charlotte measured success by how high you rise through the relevant hierarchy.'

'Is there another way?'

'I prefer to live by the motto of my old grammar school: "*Rather use than fame*".'

'*Rather use than fame?* That's kind of clever.'

'It was the quality of my ambition rather than the quantity that set me apart from Charlotte.'

'Now why don't I believe that?' asked Gabrielle, rolling over on to her back and looking up at the stars.

'You tell me . . . Miss Sceptic.'

'The fact that you had virtually *nothing* in common. It wasn't just your ambition. It was everything. You love the academic life. She liked the high life. Your world is the ivory tower. Hers was the salon. You're at your happiest when you're pushing forward the frontiers of knowledge and driving back the boundaries of ignorance. I got the impression that Charlotte was never happy except when she was shopping at Harrods or Bloomingdales.'

'You're making it sound as if she was spend, spend, spend and I'm all work and no play.'

'No, you know how to enjoy yourself. But you find pleasure in doing interesting things. I remember once seeing you teaching your nephews how to make a radio out of household items, using information you downloaded from the Internet.'

Daniel was thinking about this. Gabrielle's assessment had been remarkably incisive. He got his pleasure from the simple things in life and that was something that Charlotte never understood.

'I guess it was the perennial conflict between the two modes of living: the *Having Mode* and the *Doing Mode*. Charlotte found happiness in luxury possessions and the company of well-bred but shallow people.'

There was silence for a while. Then Gabrielle turned back to Daniel and quietly said one word: 'Sorry.'

'For what?'

'I didn't mean to open up an old wound.'

Daniel was silent for a while. Finally he spoke.

'You know what the irony is? It was at a university function that we first met.'

'What sort of function?'

'I think one of her friends had made a big donation and was unveiling a plaque.'

'So it was one of those awkward meeting points between academia and philanthropy, when scholarship and mammon pay mutual homage to one another, with a mixture of envy and guilt.'

'You really are a cynic, aren't you, Gaby?' he said with a smile.

But she didn't answer. Sleep had finally engulfed her.

Gabrielle looked around her. They were closing in on her . . . closing in on all sides. The tracks, the scoop, the rumbling sound.

233

Bulldozers!

The bulldozers were closing in on her: north, south, east and west . . .

They had all points of the compass covered.

There was nowhere to run. It was too late. She was going to die. She was going to die today: crushed by these bulldozers that surrounded her.

'No!' she screamed.

It was dark. She was in a cold sweat. She looked around struggling to gain her bearings.

Daniel too was awake and staring at her.

'Are you all right?' he asked.

'I guess. I think I was having a bad dream.'

Chapter 62

'I'm telling you she's dangerous.'

The professor had asked to meet Senator Morris in private. The senator had been unsure why but had agreed to fit this meeting into his busy schedule.

'Why? She's always supported us in the past.'

'Never without voicing dissent.'

'She's cautious; that's just her nature. But she's always supported us. She just tempers her loyalty with caution – that's what women do.'

'There are too many things going wrong for Goliath. First at the hospital when he didn't get the clothing sample from that boy, and then he botched the attempt to get the clothes from Klein and Gusack and they even got out alive.'

'What are you saying? That she's making things go wrong from thousands of miles away?'

'I think she may have told someone.'

'That's ridiculous,' said the senator. 'The boy from the dig died of the plague and Goliath drew attention to himself at the hospital by talking to a nurse. He might not have got the clothes anyway. They probably had them incinerated as a precaution.'

'And what about the gasoline bomb attack on Goliath in the jeep?'

'Could it be the work of Islamic terrorists?'

'I thought you said the embassy told you that a Western woman had been arrested for the attack?'

'That's right, an Irish woman. And I've since been told that she escaped.'

'Well, that doesn't sound much like an Islamic terrorist to me.'

'The IRA worked with the Libyans. Maybe they're doing the same for the Muslim Brotherhood – possibly in return for being allowed to train in the al-Qaeda camps in Afghanistan and Pakistan.'

'I thought the IRA had given up on terrorism.'

'There's always fringe movements and breakaway factions.'

'Why would they hire a woman from a fringe faction of the IRA to do their dirty work? Instead of using a local who knows the terrain?'

'Perhaps because she'd be less likely to arouse suspicion.'

'But why would they target a foreigner driving peacefully on the road at night?'

'To harm the tourist industry?' the senator suggested. 'To damage the regime perhaps?'

'If they wanted to damage the tourist trade they'd do something more spectacular than attack one man in a car. They'd plant a bomb at a hotel or something.'

The senator realized that the professor's rationale made sense. It *was* suspicious that a young Irish woman had attacked Goliath with a Molotov cocktail on the road in the Nile Valley. But he was a long way from drawing any firm conclusions about the loyalties of Audrey Milne.

'You may have a point. Look, I'll keep her out of the loop for the time being and we'll see how this plays out. Just don't say anything to her to give her the slightest impression that she's under suspicion.'

The professor nodded. The senator was about to say more when his cell phone rang.

'Hallo.'

'Senator Morris.'

'Yes?'

'It's John Pryor here from the embassy in Cairo. Listen, I don't know any easy way to break this to you but I'm afraid I have some bad news about your daughter—'

'*No!*' screamed the senator, before the ambassador could even finish the sentence.

He flung the cell phone across the room and sank to his knees, sobbing into his open hands with grief.

Chapter 63

It had taken three days on camels instead of the eight hours on a bus that it had taken Sarit, but when Daniel and Gabrielle arrived in Taba in the early morning of their fourth day of travel, the dawn was breaking over the Gulf of Aqaba.

Daniel had wanted them to make their way to a hotel right away, but Gabrielle had told him that there was no point. Nothing would be open and in any case, she wanted to watch the sun rise over the sea. So after they took off their Bedouin robes and changed into Western clothes, he indulged her whim and stood there next to her, while she ooed and aahed, gushing like a lovesick schoolgirl. Daniel realized, with some regret, that the love was for the view, not for his presence.

Ahead of them and far to the right was Eilat where construction work seemed to be forever in progress, building new hotels to accommodate the ever growing tourist industry. In some ways it spoiled the view to see cranes and cement mixers and bulldozers in the distance.

The bulldozer kept coming . . . It wouldn't stop . . .
Move! Don't just stand there!
He can't see you!
HE CAN'T SEE YOU.

Get out of the way!
STOP!!!! PLEASE!!!!
She's just a—

'Gaby? Are you okay?'

'Wha . . . what?'

'You're shivering.'

He took off his light jacket and put it round her, noticing as he did so that she was not shivering. She was trembling.

'What's the matter?' he asked gently.

'Nothing . . . I was . . . remembering . . .'

He looked at her, trying to figure out if she wanted to say more.

'Remembering what?' he asked, making sure his tone did not sound too pushy.

'Nothing.'

He took that as his cue to drop the matter, at least for now. In any case, they had more important things to do than reminisce about personal matters.

Realizing that it was still too early to implement his plan, their first port of call was a hotel restaurant, where they had breakfast, explaining that they were not guests there, but didn't like their own hotel's food and wanted to try this one. Sixty Egyptian pounds covered the cost for the two of them and they drew it out for as long as they could, realizing that they had nowhere else to go just yet.

Incredibly, the shops in the hotel arcade were open by eight o'clock, enabling them to buy swimwear, and a snorkel for Gabrielle. She explained to Daniel that it would make her seem more like a tourist, and he approved of her logic, buying a straw hat for himself to add to the camouflage. After changing into their new gear in the beachside toilets, to make sure they looked the part, the third stop was the

239

marina. Hiring a boat meant they had to show their passports. But it was only to verify their ID, there was no attempt to check their names against a list of wanted criminals. The only hair-raising moment was when they were asked for a credit card for a deposit. They were told that they could pay for the boat hire by cash, but a credit or debit card would have to be scanned for a security deposit. No money would be taken off the card, they were assured, unless they failed to return the boat within twenty-four hours.

Gabrielle handed over her card, on the assumption that if the police had tried to set up alerts for tracing them via card transactions, they would have needed the co-operation of the authorities in the countries where they lived. And Austria, which had until recently allowed anonymous passbook accounts at banks, was probably a little bit more bureaucratic than the UK, so it would have been that much harder to set up such a trace in her case. In the event, the scan went through with no obvious alarms being set off, and minutes later they were climbing into the boat and casting off from the jetty.

The boat was a fast little mover, with an inboard motor, and once out of the marina and into the open waters of the Gulf, they lost no time in heading straight for Eilat. The area they were covering was not large. From the shores of Taba it was possible to see Eilat and Aqaba. As they neared Israeli territorial waters, they noticed an Egyptian navy boat speeding out towards them and trying to signal them. It was clear that they were not seen as a threat, merely as careless tourists. But Daniel knew that this would change if he failed to comply. Compliance, however, was the last thing on his mind. Instead, he opened up the throttle and headed full tilt for Israeli waters.

It was at that moment that his actions aroused the

attention of the Israeli navy. This was because he was heading towards them and both countries were more on the lookout for terrorist incursions than for escapees. Neither country had closed borders to the world and criminals trying to escape from one to the other was therefore not a common or everyday threat. But terrorism was something else – both sides had to be constantly on the lookout for that – and a powerboat speeding from one to the territorial waters of the other was a warning sign that something dangerous was about to happen.

So it came as no surprise to Daniel when he saw an Israeli Super Dvora Mk III-class patrol boat in the distance speeding to intercept him, closely followed by a helicopter rising into the sky above Eilat in the distance.

Neither of these things concerned him. What worried him instead was the fact that the machine gun on the Israeli boat was manned and the gun was trained squarely at him. A man on the boat standing next to the gunner was standing with a megaphone, shouting a warning in English. Daniel couldn't hear the words above the sound of his own engine, but he knew perfectly well what he was being told. They wanted him to cut the engine and/or turn back.

But he couldn't be sure that they were yet in Israeli waters. A quick backward glance told him that the Egyptian navy patrol boat was still on his tail. He knew that they wouldn't be safe against being returned to Egypt until they made it to the Israeli side.

He tried calling out, 'We're British!' in the hope that these magic words would calm them down. But before he could say anything more, the shooting started.

Chapter 64

Goliath was beginning to regret leaving the hospital. The burns on his flesh were no longer as painful as they had been, but they still troubled him. He had come so near and yet lost everything when that evil woman – whoever she was – had thrown that gasoline bomb into the jeep.

He had left that message for Daniel Klein, but so far received no reply. Was it because Klein was suspicious? Or was it because he hadn't received the message?

Realizing that Senator Morris didn't have his new number, he phoned the senator, ignoring the time difference.

'Where the fuck have you been?'

'I left the hospital and got a new phone. My old phone got destroyed when the jeep went up in flames.'

'Are you being followed?'

'No. I was careful.'

'Are you *sure*?'

'*Yes!* I was careful.'

'I hope so. You're not the sort of man who can hide in a crowd.'

'You got me out. Thank you.'

'I had to call in a lot of favours when I heard the news about the attack on the road. You did the right thing calling the embassy, but I can't afford to get involved openly.'

'I'm sorry. I just wanted to let you know where I am, and to apologize for screwing up. They got out of the tomb . . . and someone attacked me on the road—'

'I *know* all that! I watch the news.'

'So you know I lost them. I'm sorry.'

'This isn't a time for regret. This is a time for *action*! Those Jewish scumbags have cost me the most precious thing in the world.'

Goliath heard crying on the other end of the line.

'What . . . what happened?'

The senator told him about his daughter. In the past it had been Senator Morris who had comforted Goliath. This time, it was Goliath's turn to play the comforter.

'She will be avenged. I will do anything you ask of me.'

The strength came back to the senator's voice.

'I think it is time I told you my whole plan. If you are going to risk everything, then you must *know* everything.'

Over the next few minutes, the senator told Goliath exactly what he was planning to do and what Goliath had to do to help him achieve it. At the end, Goliath spoke.

'But they will not trust me. Why would they share such precious ancient knowledge with me?'

'They won't. That is why you need to find Daniel Klein. They will trust him. You must use him to get them to show you where to go. Once they have shown you the exact location, you will not need Klein any more. You will not need *any* of them any more.'

'I left a message for Klein, posing as a friend. But he has not answered.'

'Keep trying.'

As soon as they had ended the call, Goliath called Daniel's number again, not sure if it would be worth leaving another message.

'Hallo?'

It was a voice! A human being, not a message. Someone had answered.

'Hallo. Is that Mr Klein?'

There was silence on the other end of the line. Silence? Or hesitation?

'No. This wrong number.'

The English was poor. This was obviously a local who spoke only rudimentary English. But the person did not hang up. Why not? That was normally what people did if someone called them in error. Or maybe the person at the other end was waiting for him to hang up.

'Wait. Is that . . .' He recited the number out loud. Again there was hesitation.

'I don't know.'

'Wait a minute. Is that Daniel Klein's phone?'

Goliath didn't know what mental agonizing was going on at the other end of the phone.

'He left phone in boat. We're waiting for him to come and collect it.'

'Wait . . . look . . . is Mr Klein coming to collect the phone? I need to talk to him.'

'He must come back to get phone.'

'Does he know you've got it? The phone, I mean?'

'We can't call him. But he left it on boat.'

'*We?*'

The man on the other end said nothing.

'What boat?'

'My father and me take him on *felucca*.'

That explained the 'we'. Goliath had pretty much twigged it at this point. This person – probably no more than a boy – wanted to keep the phone. But he wasn't a thief. Then Goliath thought about the local culture and had an idea.

'Look, I'm a friend of his and I need to contact him. I can also help you give the phone back to him. In fact . . .' he paused for effect, 'there's a reward for finding the phone. *Baksheesh*.'

'Yes?'

'If we can meet and you can tell me where you last saw Daniel Klein, I can give you two hundred dollars and make sure that he gets the phone back.'

'Okay. Where you want to meet?'

'I don't know. You know Cairo better than I do.'

'Yes, but where is easy for you to finding?'

Goliath realized how helpful the boy was being. He wanted to choose a place that Goliath could find easily. 'Okay, how about the Sphinx?' Goliath could see Giza from his hotel window. A taxi ride would take no time at all. 'I can be there in half an hour.'

'How I know what you look like?'

'I'm very tall. And I have some bandages on me. I was injured in a fire.'

'Okay. I see you in half hour. I bring the phone.'

'Wait a minute! What's your name?'

'Na'if.'

The boy rang off before he could reply.

Na'if . . . it sounded like naïve. How appropriate.

Chapter 65

A trail of bullets from the Israeli patrol boat raked the water in front of them. Daniel realized that by this stage even turning back would be regarded by the Israelis as aggression, or at least non-compliance. So he cut the engine and let the boat carry on coasting forward. To further indicate his surrender, he raised his hand and stood up slowly.

Gabrielle did likewise, but then looked back, prompting Daniel to follow suit. What he saw was the Egyptian navy boat approaching at speed. At the same time, the Israeli boat had also stopped. Daniel realized what this meant. They had not yet entered Israeli territorial waters and were possibly still inside Egyptian waters. That meant that they could be taken back to Egypt.

No, the Israelis would not have fired into Egyptian waters . . . but might have fired on a vessel in international waters if it was deemed to pose a threat. They might have thought that the boat was packed with explosives and that he was a suicide bomber. Under those circumstances, they would have fired rather than attempt to board.

In fact he was no more than a fugitive from Egypt for trying to leave evading border control, but the Israelis didn't know that. It occurred to him that maybe the Israelis knew who he was. They might have heard those absurd stories about the infectious disease and believed that he and Gabrielle were walking biological weapons.

'What's happening?' asked Gabrielle.

'I think we're still in international waters.'

'So neither of them can take us against our will.'

Daniel was irritated by her legal naivety. 'Actually, they both can.'

'Well, let's hope it's the Israelis.'

Looking at the approaching Egyptian boat and the stationary Israeli one, Daniel realized that her hope was in vain. 'I don't think it's going to be.'

Gabrielle put on her snorkel. 'Do you know what free diving is?' she asked.

'Free diving?'

'It means swimming underwater, holding your breath for as long as you can.'

'You mean we trade in getting shot for drowning?'

Her face hardened. 'This is it, Daniel – our Butch and Sundance moment.'

And with that she dived headlong into the water, disappearing beneath the surface. Taken by surprise, both the Egyptians behind them and the Israelis ahead looked concerned. But when she surfaced again, for less than a second, she was already fifteen yards ahead and clearly swimming towards Israeli waters. The sudden realization that this was an escape attempt prompted the Egyptian coastguard officers to train their guns on Daniel.

He realized what that meant. They were ready to shoot him if he tried the same thing. Drawing deep on his reserves of courage – or desperation, rather – he drew in his breath, dived into the water, and after sinking to a depth of a few feet, began swimming with all his might. He was using the arm movements of the breaststroke, but the leg movements of freestyle and this eclectic mixture of swimming styles seemed to carry him forward faster than he could ever remember swimming.

He wasn't sure how long he could keep it up and as panic and shortness of breath set in, he heard the sharp staccato sound of gunfire above the surface, matched by streaks along the water ahead of him. This time the firing was coming from the Egyptian side.

Painfully aware that one of these bullets could hit him, he came quickly to the surface, alerting both sides to his whereabouts as he took a deep breath and then dived under again. But now, instead of swimming towards the Israeli line, he traversed to his left, putting more emphasis on moving sideways than forwards. Only when he heard more gunfire and saw the bullet trails well to his right, did he change direction and start moving forward towards the Israeli patrol boat. By the time he surfaced, he was well away from the Egyptian gunboat and quite far towards what he thought to be the Israeli territorial line.

Again the Egyptians fired and again he dived and traversed, this time to the right. He realized now that all the firing was coming from behind him. Whether the Israelis had been given new orders or had simply realized that a man wearing nothing but swimming trunks could hardly be a suicide bomber, it was clear that the danger now came from the Egyptian side.

But when he came to the surface, the firing stopped. Daniel realized that he must be in Israeli waters. Ahead of him he could see Gabrielle climbing the ladder on to the patrol boat, being helped by several of the crew, who seemed to be enjoying themselves.

Judging that he was safe from being fired upon, Daniel stayed on the surface and shifted to freestyle as he swam the last few yards to the Israeli vessel. He too climbed the ladder, but found the Israeli navy men somewhat less helpful when it came to helping him clamber aboard. However they were kind enough to give him a towel, before returning their attention to Gabrielle. She seemed flattered by this and even flashed a mocking smile at Daniel, as if noting his jealousy at the male interest she was getting.

They were shown to some quarters, given clothes and told that Captain Ben-Dor wanted to see them in ten minutes. The accommodation seemed quite comfortable and Daniel suspected that this was actually the captain's quarters. They took turns in the shower and when Daniel emerged with a towel around his waist, he was amused to see Gabrielle looking incredibly sexy in a man's white summer uniform that looked a couple of sizes too small for her. His own uniform was a perfect fit.

Exactly ten minutes later, they were taken to the bridge to meet the captain, a slightly paunchy man of the same height as Daniel, with a short grey beard. Anxious to explain as quickly as possible, and lacking any sense of military propriety or protocol, Daniel launched into a mentally rehearsed speech, not waiting to be spoken to.

'I'd like to thank you for rescuing us. My name is Daniel Klein and we—'

'I *know* who you are,' said Captain Ben-Dor. 'You've caused a lot of trouble.'

Chapter 66

It took Goliath somewhat longer to get to the Sphinx than he had expected. Although free to go, discharging himself from hospital had proved to be unusually bureaucratic and at one point he had come close to panic, thinking that the police were going to re-arrest him on some technicality.

He had almost been poised to use force, but he realized that this would merely draw further attention to himself. They had not matched him up to the suspect in the case of the killing of the nurse at the other hospital, but he knew that at any time they might, and he doubted if the senator's influence could get him off a rap like that.

So he kept his head and stayed cool, paid a little *baksheesh* and then took the taxi out to Giza.

Now, as he approached the Sphinx, he found himself looking out for the boy. He didn't really know what to expect other than a young local and there were plenty of those about, offering to sell anything from postcards and tourist trinkets to condoms and private tours.

But there was one, aged about fourteen, who appeared to be doing nothing other than looking around, shielding his eyes from the sun with his hand. In his other hand he was holding a plastic bag which had something small in it. Goliath walked towards him. A look of understanding appeared on the boy's face.

'You must be Na'if,' said Goliath.

'Yes.'

The boy was looking at him with a mixture of curiosity and trepidation. Goliath sensed that this had less to do with his size than with the bandages.

'You said your father brought Daniel Klein and the woman to Cairo, is that right?'

'Yes.'

'On a . . .'

'*Felucca.*'

'That's a boat, yes?'

'Yes.'

'Did they say where they were going in Cairo?'

'My English not very good. But my father see them again.'

'Again?'

'Yes, and they say they want to go to Taba.'

'To Taba?'

'Yes.'

'Did they say why?'

'I don't know. But my father help them.'

'Okay, well, I'll tell you what, I don't really need their phone.'

'But what about *baksheesh*?' He sounded quite anxious.

'Yes, don't worry. I'll give you the money. But not here. There are too many people. Is there somewhere private we can go?'

'The restaurant.'

Goliath was dubious about the restaurant being away from prying eyes, but he nodded anyway. When they arrived, Na'if led Goliath round the back, near the bins. Goliath made a great play of taking out the money – two one-hundred-dollar bills – which he handed over to Na'if.

Na'if accepted the money with watering eyes, put it in his pocket, and then looked at Goliath uncertainly, as if unsure about whether he meant it when he said he didn't need the phone. At that point, Goliath clamped a large hand over Na'if's mouth and a headlock on the boy in preparation to either choke him or snap his neck. He opted for the latter, as it would be quicker, and adjusted the position of his forearm accordingly.

Chapter 67

Captain Ben-Dor had told them very little. Little as in nothing. The only thing he would say was that they were to be taken to Herzliya, just north of Tel Aviv.

The captain smiled when he saw the confused look on their faces. Obviously the boat wasn't going to sail there, as that would mean a somewhat circuitous trip. He pointed to the helicopter hovering above them.

'You'll be winched up there and taken directly.'

Gabrielle smiled at this. It appealed to her sense of adventure. But Daniel had had enough adventure for a whole lifetime and felt somewhat nauseous just thinking about it. However, he was not one to show weakness, especially in the presence of military men, so he gritted his teeth and nodded. When the winch of the AS565 *Panther* lowered the harness to the boat's deck, he even volunteered to go first, but the captain decided that Gabrielle should have that honour.

The helicopter journey was a sombre affair. In any case, conversation would have been difficult above the noise of the rotor blades, but the cold stares from the crew gave Daniel the distinct impression that he and Gabrielle were regarded as enemies, or at least as troublemakers. Nevertheless, they were offered cold drinks at one point, both settling on diet Coke. For the most part they contented themselves with admiring the view as the helicopter sped towards Herzliya.

When the helicopter landed, eighty-five minutes later, it was on the roof of a rather old nondescript building. They were led out and taken to a waiting room. From there, Daniel was called in first.

He found himself sitting in an office in front of a teak desk, opposite a dark-haired Israeli, not unlike himself and about the same age.

'My name is Dov Shamir and I am going to ask you a few questions. I would be much obliged if you didn't try to bullshit me, but just gave me some straight answers.'

Chapter 68

Na'if was struggling frantically for breath. He felt the bandaged man's arm adjust its position and he sensed that something bad was about to happen, but tugging at the man's hand did nothing; the grip was just too tight.

Desperate to escape, Na'if put both his hands on the giant's forearm, intending to use his entire body weight to pull on the arm and break the attacker's grip. But as soon as he put his left hand higher up on the man's forearm, the big man let out a scream and released Na'if.

He didn't know about the burns that Goliath had sustained, all he knew was that the man was in pain and that he had released him. That gave Na'if all the chance he needed. Dropping the bag in the hope that it was what the big man was really interested in, he lurched away, rolled on the ground to get clear and then sprinted as fast as his legs could carry him.

He heard a grunt and looked round to see the big man running after him. He wanted to scream so as to draw the attention of others to what was happening, but that was not a way for a man to act, so he decided against it. Instead he just ran and kept running, making sure to stay in the open as much as possible. He made his way on to a bus leaving the area, constantly looking out the window for any sign of the man who had attacked him. As long as the man didn't get on to the bus, he was safe.

Chapter 69

Daniel wondered if he should ask for a lawyer, but he decided not to push his luck. It wasn't clear if this Dov Shamir was a policeman, an immigration official or something else entirely. He suspected that 'something else entirely' was probably the most accurate guess. So instead he nodded meekly, giving Shamir the go ahead to start the interrogation.

'We know that you were called in to assist Akil Mansoor of the Egyptian Antiquities Authority translate some stone fragments which he believes may be the original tablets of stone from the Bible that Moses smashed.'

Daniel considered correcting Shamir as to the name of the organization that Mansoor headed. However, it would be too pedantic and would not endear him to his interrogator.

'I can confirm that.'

'We also know that you were called in on the recommendation of Gabrielle Gusack, a student of Mansoor's and whose uncle was your professor when you did your PhD at the School of Oriental and African Studies.'

'Yes,' said Daniel. 'Or the School of Anti-Semitism as we sometimes call it.'

'I know. I studied there too. But I presume you're referring to certain sections of the student body, not the school itself.'

'Absolutely.'

'And after examining the stone fragments, you went on a tour with Mansoor, visiting various ancient sites in Egypt.'

'Yes.'

'Could you tell me *which* sites you visited?'

Daniel went through the sites, from memory, stumbling a couple of times.

'Now tell me about the incident at the Tomb of Ay – the one in the western Valley of the Kings. And don't just tell me about the incident itself, I want to know what happened *after* that – right up to you getting picked up by the patrol boat.'

Daniel recounted the story as best he could: from being locked in, the attempts to call for help, the escape, the shooting incident with the police, the message on Mansoor's phone, the journeys to Cairo and Taba and the dramatic escape from Egypt by powerboat. The only thing he left out was what they had found in Mansoor's office and his intention to visit the Samaritans.

Dov Shamir sat there in silence, looking at him. Daniel wasn't sure what to make of this and wondered whether Shamir didn't believe him. *Perhaps he's just trying to give me time to remember more details.*

Eventually, Shamir spoke. 'Who do you think locked you in?'

'I don't know.'

'I never said you *knew*. I asked you who you *think* locked you in.'

'I *can't* think . . . I mean, I can't imagine who would want to.'

'You're not in the least bit curious? Someone tries to kill you and you're not curious as to who that might be . . . or why?'

'I haven't really had time to think about it, to be honest.'

'No? It took you six days on the *felucca* to get to Cairo and four days to get from Cairo to Taba by camel. That's ten days since you were locked in the tomb. And you mean to say that in all that time you haven't thought about who locked you there?'

Daniel was unsure whether to reveal his speculations about the plague or Harrison's cryptic statement that might support those suspicions. At this stage, he didn't know whether to trust Shamir or not. So he took a more cautious line.

'The only thing I could come up with was that someone wanted to stop me from translating the various documents in Proto-Sinaitic script that Mansoor and the Egyptians have accumulated.'

'But you have no idea who that might be?'

'Well, quite frankly, I think even *that* theory is too silly for words. I mean, who would want to suppress such knowledge? A rival academic who's working on it but hasn't got enough to publish yet? Some religious nutter who thinks that we shouldn't tamper with the past, but simply accept the scriptures?'

'I notice that you haven't asked about what happened to Akil Mansoor.'

'We heard on the radio that he was recovering in hospital. Has there been any development since then?'

'Yes. He has since made a full recovery.'

Daniel breathed a sigh of relief. 'And what about that hysteria about me and Gabrielle carrying some disease? I notice that *you* haven't put us in quarantine.'

Shamir smiled. 'We've established that this health scare was a bit of a misunderstanding.'

Daniel was dubious about this. Mansoor had said there was an outbreak of disease at the dig site. Could it have been food poisoning after all? Was the quarantine just a panic response? An unnecessary precaution? If so, what about the curator at the British Museum?

'It was a misunderstanding that very nearly got me and Gaby killed.'

'I know. But then again your somewhat unconventional *solution* to the problem also very nearly got you and Professor Gusack killed.'

'So do we know what our legal status in Egypt is?'

Shamir pursed his lips and thought for a moment.

'You're still technically in breach of Egyptian law because of the manner of your departure. But then again you're not the first Jew to flee from Egypt with the army in hot pursuit.'

They couldn't help but exchange a smile at that one.

'What about *Israeli* law?' Daniel asked with some trepidation. 'Are we in any trouble over our somewhat unorthodox method of entry?'

'Under ordinary circumstances you would be. But I have some discretion in this matter and we have no intention of prosecuting you . . . *or* deporting you.'

In the silence that followed, Daniel realized that Shamir was being helpful and he decided to reciprocate. 'There was another matter . . . I mean, it may very well be related.'

'Yes?'

Daniel explained about his brief return trip to England with Gabrielle and the murder of Harrison Carmichael. Shamir smiled as he spoke, as if he were way ahead of Daniel.

'And you think that the murderer may have been the same person who locked you in the tomb?'

'It's possible.'

Shamir waited a moment before speaking. 'I can tell you that the man who locked you in *is* the same man who killed Harrison Carmichael. But that is *all* I can tell you.'

Daniel leaned forward keenly. 'Who is he?'

Shamir's smile disappeared. 'What part of "that is all I can tell you" didn't you understand?'

'I'm sorry,' said Daniel, realizing that he was lucky that Shamir had told him anything at all. 'But there's more to it than that. Technically I'm still a suspect in the murder of Harrison . . . and because I jumped bail, there's now a warrant out for my arrest.'

'I understand. But perhaps it's better if you leave it to the professionals. We'll liaise with the British authorities and make them aware of your innocence. But leave us to deal with the man who killed your mentor. We're a lot better placed to catch him than you are.'

Daniel realized from these words that the man who had killed Harrison – the man who had locked him and Gaby in the tomb – was still out there. But he wanted to know where he stood.

'So about that problem with the Egyptian authorities . . . I was thinking, not so much about myself . . . but Gaby . . . Professor Gusack . . . is an Egyptologist. It's her career . . . her profession . . .'

Shamir held up his hand to stop Daniel. 'Leave it with me. We'll work something out. In the meantime, you'll both be given three-month tourist visas to stay here. And you're welcome to use that time to pursue your research here.'

'Thank you. Oh, there *is* something else that you might be able to help me with. I was wondering if you could get me an introduction to the high priest of the Samaritans.'

Shamir thought for a moment. 'I may be able to go one better than that. I can try and wangle you an invitation to the Samaritan Passover celebrations.'

Daniel was confused. 'But the *seider* was three weeks ago.'

'It's at a different time to the Jewish *seider* this year, because

261

of different leap years. The Samaritan *seider* is on the twenty-eighth.'

That was in nine days' time. 'And you can get me an invitation? For me *and* Gaby?'

'I have *proteksia*,' said Dov with a smile, using the Israeli slang for connections with people on the inside.

Chapter 70

Back in his cheap hotel room, Goliath was thinking.

Although Na'if had got away, Goliath did not feel the same sensation of failure that had haunted him these past few weeks. Instead, he felt engulfed in a strange feeling of satisfaction, bordering on elation. He had found out that they had gone to Taba and that Daniel didn't have his mobile phone any more. That meant that he probably wouldn't retrieve the message Goliath had left for him.

But why had he gone to Taba? There were surely no antiquities there? It was largely a tourist resort like Sharm el-Sheikh. And the Egyptian authorities were after them. Surely they wouldn't just decide to hang out in a tourist resort?

But there were cheap hotels there, as well as expensive ones. And it was relatively out of the way. Maybe they were planning on hiding out there till the heat died down. Suddenly Goliath had another idea.

He switched on the television and surfed the channels looking for the news, in the hope of hearing anything about the wanted Englishman and Austrian woman. Eventually his eye caught a scrolling text at the bottom of the screen that read: *Shots fired in high-speed boat chase between Egypt and Israel*. Realizing that this might be to do with Daniel, he switched on his smartphone and logged on to the Internet in search of more news.

A few keywords later, he had the report in front of him: the incident at the Supreme Council of Antiquities, Taba, the motorboat chase, the shots . . . Israel.

That made perfect sense. He had been half-expecting something like that when Na'if told him they had gone to Taba. It was close to the Israeli border. Where else would they be going?

But *where* in Israel? There was no point going there unless he could find that out.

Then he had an idea.

Chapter 71

'So what did he tell you?' Daniel asked Gabrielle.

'Nothing. The flow of information was strictly one-way.'

After their debriefing in Herzliya, Daniel and Gabrielle had taken a taxi to Jerusalem. It had been a strange experience getting there. At eleven o'clock, as the taxi was steadily ascending the long and winding road to the city, a siren had sounded. Not a rising and falling siren to warn of an enemy attack, but a flat siren, like the all-clear at the end of an air raid. But in Israel on this day it heralded neither the beginning of an attack nor end of one, but rather the recollection of many battles and their tragic consequences.

When the driver stopped the taxi and stood by the roadside, Daniel followed suit and Gabrielle did likewise. Afterwards, when they got back into the taxi, Daniel explained that it was Remembrance Day and the siren heralded the two-minute silence to honour the war dead, something that Israelis took very seriously.

They had booked into the Leonardo Plaza Hotel, in the centre of town – having to share a room because the hotels were packed for the forthcoming Independence Day celebrations. The hotel stood on the edge of Independence Park and their luxury suite near the top of the tall building had a panoramic view of the whole city. At Daniel's suggestion, they had decided to forgo lunch at the prestigious Cow on the Roof for the 'best little diner in Jerusalem'.

'Far be it from me to endorse any of the age-old stereotypes about women, but I refuse to believe that you didn't pump him for information.'

Gabrielle smiled wickedly. 'Oh, I pumped like a milkmaid. But the udders were dry.'

They were in Pinati, a tiny but packed little diner on the corner of a main road and a side street in the centre of Jerusalem. Clashing elbows at the Formica table they shared with three blue-collar workers, they were tucking into stuffed peppers, moussaka and meatballs with rice and beans, accompanied by pickled cucumbers, onions and chilli peppers. This was after a starter consisting of the best humous they had ever tasted.

'You don't come to Pinati for the décor or the ambience, let alone the comfort,' Daniel had explained. 'You come here for the food.'

And he was right. That's why they had stood outside in a long queue in a city that appeared to be bustling more than usual, with people scurrying to the *souk* to buy *pita* bread, meat, bags of charcoal and disposable barbecues.

'For tomorrow,' their taxi driver had explained cryptically.

'You didn't get anything out of him?'

'All I got was what he told you,' Gabrielle replied defensively.

'They know who locked us in the tomb but won't say who,' Daniel confirmed.

'Did he tell you that the man who locked us in was the man who killed Uncle Harrison?' Gabrielle asked.

'Yes. But he didn't say who it was.'

'I guess that means he doesn't want us interfering.'

'Maybe he's right, Gaby. Maybe we should leave it to the pros.'

'So why is the city so busy today?' she asked.

'Like they told us at the hotel: Independence Day. Actually the celebrations start this evening, because in Israel festive occasions start the night before, running from sunset to sunset. But tomorrow there'll be about a million barbecues. That's the way they celebrate Independence Day over here. So everyone's getting ready for that.'

That evening, Gabrielle decided to sample the true Israeli experience of Independence Day, venturing out into the jam-packed streets and dragging Daniel in tow. Caught in the crush of thousands of happy Israelis, they edged their way along slowly amidst the throngs of mostly young people. Once in a while they emerged into free space, where the people – natives and immigrants – danced and sang to the strains of amplified live bands that filled the air with both modern and traditional songs about Israel. Songs of victory and songs of peace . . . an eclectic mixture of nationalism and optimism.

'What's with the plastic hammers?' Gabrielle had to shout to be heard above the noise of the crowds. She had just been hit over the head for the umpteenth time by a plastic hammer wielded by a child of about four or five, who was seated atop his father's shoulders. It was painless and the father of the child seemed to find it amusing too, even when he in turn was hit by a teenager's plastic mallet in a well-timed counter-strike.

'It's an old-new tradition,' Daniel replied cryptically.

'Isn't that a bit of an oxymoron?'

'It goes back to a merchant who bought them for another celebration. He overestimated the demand and had a few thousand left over, so he sold them off cheaply for Independence Day. That was a few decades ago and it's been an Israeli tradition ever since.'

'I guess I'll get used to it eventually,' said Gabrielle as she succumbed to another couple of sneak attacks. Daniel didn't seem to mind or even notice it when he was the target. But the children – and adolescents *and* adults – seemed to get a perverse pleasure in landing one on Gabrielle's head, as if her height made her an especially distinguished target.

'I'm glad we had a big lunch,' said Gabrielle.

She had a point. Food rather than drink was normally the Israelis' preferred method of celebration. But today there was no one available to serve food.

'What the—'

Gabrielle had just been sprayed with foam by a teenage youth with a cheeky grin on his face. He was clearly being egged on by two of his friends who flanked him and laughed at his antics before moving on to a new target.

'Is that also an Israeli tradition?'

'A more recent one,' said Daniel. 'Albeit a rather annoying one. I think they imported it from Tel Aviv. I thought Jerusalemites had more class though.'

'I guess when you live in a country that has so many wars, it's nice to have one day a year when you can let your hair down.'

Daniel noticed for the first time in the last three weeks that Gabrielle was having a good time. In Egypt, even before the incident in the tomb, she had seemed uptight and tense. Now, for the first time in ages, she seemed to be full of the *joie de vivre* that he hadn't seen in her since she was a teenager.

By two in the morning, fortified by a bottle of Arak that they had managed to obtain in their downtown adventures, Gabrielle had learnt the *hora* – Israel's national dance – and half a dozen Israeli folk songs, or at least the chorus thereof. Her favourite, judging by her constant repetition of it, seemed to be '*Od loh Ahavti Dai*' – 'I Haven't Loved Enough' – an up-tempo song in which the singer laments that they haven't done enough in life, listing all their unachieved ambitions from finding water in the desert to writing their memoirs and building their dream house. But most importantly, not having loved enough.

Daniel realized she was drunk and decided to get her back to the hotel before she embarrassed herself. He had to half-prop, half-carry her to the bedroom as she flirted with everyone from the security man on the door to the night porter. Undressing her on the king-size bed was relatively easy, but he had to remind himself to keep his intentions honourable – or at least his actions.

But when he was undressed himself, she seemed to undergo a revival. 'Come over and kiss me, Danny.'

'You're tired.'

'No I'm not. I'm just drunk.'

'Well *I'm* tired.' He realized that he was drunk too, having consumed a fair amount of Arak himself. 'Goodnight, Gaby.'

He lay down on top of the bed – it was too hot for the covers.

'Now that you've called me Gaby, you've got to make love to me.'

'Goodnight, Professor Gusack,' he said, making his honourable intentions clear.

'If you don't make love to me, I'll have to force you,' she said. And without waiting for his reply, she rolled over on top of him and tried to hold him down with a schoolgirl pin.

It looks like we're going to have that wrestling match after all, he thought, putting up a token show of resistance.

Chapter 72

'So we still haven't got a fix on Goliath,' said Sarit.

She and Dov were in the Mossad's headquarters in Herzliya where Sarit had been debriefed over the events in Egypt and had spent the last week liaising with the Israeli embassy in Egypt to determine the fate of Goliath. They had monitored the press and sent operatives to engage nurses at local hospitals in casual conversations in an effort to extract information. But because of the recent cooling off of relations with Egypt, they had to keep a low profile.

'We managed to trace him to a hospital in Cairo. But by the time we got there, he'd already discharged himself.'

'It feels so silly calling him Goliath. Don't we know his real name?'

'Unfortunately not. Even Audrey Milne doesn't know it. She thinks that the only person who does is Senator Morris and he's keeping his cards close to his chest.'

'You said they operate in cell structure, didn't you?'

'That's right, like all good subversive organizations. Arthur Morris's cell comprises Morris, Milne and Paul Tomlinson, aka "the professor".'

'Plus Goliath.'

'Goliath is more Morris's private asset, essentially his attack dog.'

'But technically part of the cell.'

'Yes, but if we didn't know about them already, the only one he could implicate is Morris.'

'And presumably the others also have their own assets whose identities they don't give away.'

'Exactly. Any member of a cell can have a private asset, known only to him. And an asset of one cell member can be the head of his own cell. If his recruiter wants something done, he may call on his asset and the asset in turn is able to call on other members of his cell who are unknown to the recruiter who owns the asset.'

'So Senator Morris may be an asset of someone in another cell who can call on him to get the kind of results that he specializes in. Morris would either do what he's asked to do or tell them that he can't do it.'

'Exactly. And by the same token, Goliath *could* have his own cell to help him implement the senator's wishes. Although I suspect not.'

'So is it possible that Carmichael was one of Professor Tomlinson's assets?'

Dov gave this a moment's thought. 'It's unlikely. If it were the case, then the professor wouldn't have been so anxious to kill him.'

'Why not? Maybe they saw him as trouble.'

'Well, it was apparently Carmichael's research that alerted them to the possibility of using the plague against us.'

'But doesn't that prove my point?'

'Not really. You see, Carmichael didn't *set out* to work against us. He just made them aware of the fact that the plague could be revived in certain circumstances. He was a senile old man whose occasional lapses into lucidity gave them a heads-up on a plausible strategy to advance their nefarious agenda.'

'And it was those same lapses into lucidity that made him a threat to them. In short, he knew too much for his own good.'

'Exactly. They got some useful info from a paper that he had written and was trying to get published. But at any time he might have realized that he was being played for a sucker and start rocking the boat.'

'And so they got Goliath to kill him.'

'Yes.'

'And they also tried to kill Gusack, Klein and Mansoor.'

'And damn nearly succeeded. But I think we can rule out Mansoor as the main target. It was Klein and Gusack they wanted to silence.'

'And now we're giving them shelter.'

'Well, there's no reason not to.'

'So we're not worried about all that stuff about Joseph and Moses.'

'Why should we be? There's nothing new in it. The theories have been around for ages, and as you said, we can't bump them off just for challenging the Bible.'

'Okay, but what about the plague? Any danger that they brought it with them on their clothes?'

'They arrived in swimsuits that they had just bought in Taba. And before we picked them up, they'd already taken a plunge in the Gulf of Eilat.'

'So they were in water?' she asked, nervously.

'*Salt*water. Trust me on this, Sarit: the worst they can manage is to ruffle the feathers of a few religious fundamentalists. They're *not* going to bring the walls of Jericho tumbling down.'

Chapter 73

Participating in the open-air Samaritan Passover celebrations on Mount Gerizim was a rare privilege. Ordinary members of the public were not allowed into the fenced-off area – for logistical and security reasons – although several thousand came to witness the event from every vantage point they could find. Apart from the seven-hundred-strong Samaritan community and the police and soldiers on security duty, the only people who were allowed in were invited guests – the media, politicians from both Israel and the Palestinian Authority and people with the right connections.

So Daniel and Gabrielle could consider themselves highly honoured just to be there.

Unlike the Jewish *seider* in which any type of kosher meat or fish can be eaten, the Samaritan feast consisted of lamb, recalling the paschal lamb that the Israelites slaughtered and ate on the eve of the slaying of the firstborn son and the Exodus.

The celebration commenced in the afternoon, well before sunset, with the Samaritans clad in white robes and white-turbaned red fezzes making fires in eight-feet-deep concrete-lined pits. Each of the five extended families in the Samaritan community had a fire pit for itself, except the largest family, which had two. The fires were fuelled by branches from olive trees, with the foliage still attached.

Even the children were joining in the fun, with boys as young as five dragging olive branches from a huge pile and throwing them into the flaming pits. The boys were dressed in white trousers and shirts rather than traditional robes and their headgear consisted of baseball caps, some of which were reversed, American-style. Even amidst this ancient and most venerable celebration, there were occasional glimpses of modernity.

Off to one side, a trench was filled with a series of barrels lined with plastic bin liners, ready to catch the blood of the slaughtered lambs. When sunset came, the lambs were slaughtered with razor-sharp knives, the entrails removed, the blood washed away with hoses and the lambs skinned and impaled on huge wooden skewers. It was at this point, or shortly before, that some of the children cried, as the lambs had in many cases come to be thought of as 'companion animals', more like pets than livestock. But this was a rite of passage that prepared them for the concept of sacrifice to God.

After the slaughter, the skin, fat and entrails of the lambs were salted, placed on an altar of a heavy metal mesh over a fire at the end of the trench and offered up to God as a burnt offering, the Passover sacrifice.

Meanwhile, the lamb carcasses on the stakes were salted in preparation for cooking. But as the tradition was to eat the meat at midnight – when, according to biblical tradition, the Angel of Death appeared – the wooden stakes were not actually placed in the pits just yet.

As invited guests, Daniel and Gabrielle were able to wander freely amongst the crowds. Dov had not gone as far as to arrange an introduction for Daniel to the priests, much less the high priest, but Daniel and Gabrielle had been introduced to Aryeh Tsedaka, a Samaritan rabbi based in the Israeli town of Holon. So they took advantage of the quiet time after the stakes were prepared to sidle up to him. Daniel told Tsedaka about their adventures in Egypt, and his translation of Proto-Sinaitic script and the papyrus they had found in Mansoor's office in which Ay had expressed his desire to be buried near Mount Gerizim.

'And you think this man Ay could be the same as Ephraim the son of Joseph?' asked Tsedaka.

'Yes,' Gabrielle cut in. 'And his brother Anen could be Menasha.'

They were sitting a few yards from one of the fires, warming themselves against the slight chill in the evening air. Daniel looked tensely at Gabrielle. He wanted her to take a backseat role in this discussion, but hadn't actually told her that in advance. They'd spent the last few days delicately stepping around the tension that hung between them and they had not talked about the events of the eve of Independence Day. It was as if they agreed, by their mutual silence, to treat it as a big mistake, to be filed away and forgotten.

Aryeh Tsedaka sat in silence for a few seconds, weighing up Gabrielle's speculation. 'And you bring this to me because the Samaritans are descended from the Joseph tribes of Israel?'

'Tribes?' Gabrielle repeated, picking up on the plural.

Daniel stepped in. 'My friend here is an Egyptologist. She is not so familiar with Jewish or Samaritan history.'

'Ah, yes. Let me explain. You see, most Westerners think that there were twelve tribes of Israel – because Jacob had twelve sons. But actually there were thirteen. Joseph was the ancestor of *two* tribes: Ephraim and Menasha, and we are descended from both of those. Except for our priests who are descended from the tribe of Levi.'

275

'Is that why you call yourselves Samaritans, rather than Josephites?'

'We actually prefer to call ourselves Israelites. Samaritans is merely an Anglicization of the Hebrew name *Shomronim*, which simply means "those from Samaria". In fact, a more correct version of our name would be *Shomrim*, which means "the Guardians". Because we are the true guardians of the Torah that God gave to Moses.'

'How do the Jews react to that?' asked Gabrielle.

'That is one of the more sad aspects of our history. The tribes of Ephraim and Menasha were part of the *northern* kingdom – that is, the Kingdom of Israel. This was distinct and separate from the southern kingdom of Judah except for a brief period of unity. We had land on both sides of the River Jordan. When the Assyrians invaded the northern kingdom 721 years before the birth of Jesus, the southern kingdom of Judah was spared because it was a vassal state at the time. But in the northern kingdom, they took 27,290 Israelites back to Assyria as captives.'

'You know the number *that* precisely?' asked Gabrielle.

'History records it,' said Tsedaka. 'However, that was still a minority. Most of the Israelites remained in the land. Then, somewhat later, the southern kingdom of Judah was conquered, this time by the Babylonians, who carried off the Judeans into captivity. But then the Persians defeated the Babylonians and allowed the Judeans to return in the fifth century before Jesus. It was then that our problems began.'

'Why?'

'The Judeans returned in two batches. First a larger group of some 42,360 returned under Zerubbabel, with the intention of rebuilding the temple that the Babylonians had destroyed. But one wise and learned man refused to join them, because he considered the study of the scriptures to be more important than rebuilding the temple. His name was Ezra. Some say his knowledge of the scriptures equalled that of Moses himself. But he returned later, with a smaller group of followers – some 1,500 – all of them men.'

Daniel saw the pain in Tsedaka's eyes as he spoke.

'However, when he returned he was hostile to our ancestors, regarding them as interlopers. Our ancestors tried to befriend the Judeans and even offered to help them rebuild their temple that had been destroyed by the Babylonians. But Ezra rejected their offer. He even refused to believe that our ancestors were Israelites at all. He claimed that they were migrants from a place in what is modern-day Iraq.'

'Why did he do that?'

'He was a determined man who rejected anything that seemed like compromise or weakness. He may well have been sincere. He introduced other reforms, such as forbidding intermarriage between Judeans and others.'

'Oh, so it was the purity of blood thing,' said Gabrielle with a sneer.

Daniel gave her a look to warn her off. The Samaritans too had strict rules about intermarriage, although they were now relaxing them slightly in order to repopulate and reduce the risk of genetic diseases.

'Ever since that time, relations have been strained between us and the Judeans, or Jews as they are now called. If you look at the history of the way we were treated, it parallels the way in which Joseph was treated by his brothers and strangers. But we were also oppressed by Muslims during the Caliphate periods and by Christians during the Crusades. Having said that, things began to improve for us when Israel's second president – Yitzhak ben-Zvi – encouraged the establishment of our community in Holon in 1954. He recognized and acknowledged our connection to ancient Israel.'

A rise in the background volume alerted them to the fact that something important was happening. It was nine-thirty and that meant they were about to start cooking. The men in charge of the operation picked up the wooden stakes with the carcasses, brought them over to the pits – six or seven to each pit – and then when the word went up they quickly impaled them vertically into the dirt floor of the pits. The pits were then sealed by a burlap-covered metal grate, which in turn was covered with mud to trap the heat.

At midnight, in accordance with tradition, the ovens would be opened up and each family would then take its roasted lamb home, where the meat would be devoured quickly. Anything not eaten that night had to be burned, just as in the ancient days of Moses. But that was some two and a half hours away.

The mood relaxed again as people settled in for the long wait. Daniel took advantage of the moment to move things on in his discussions.

'The other thing that caught my attention was a sentence on the papyrus that referred to the "Sibolet stores built by my father".'

'Sibolet?' the rabbi echoed.

'Yes,' said Daniel. 'You see in early Proto-Sinaitic, they didn't have a symbol for "sh". And when they did want to make that sound, they used the same symbol as for the "s" sound.'

'Your point being?'

'That it may have something to do with the war between the Ephraimites and the Gileadites.'

'It was essentially a *civil* war,' said Tsedaka almost defensively. 'Gilead was basically the tribes of Gad and Menasha. It was an internal war between brothers. That too was a very sad episode in Israelite history.'

'I know. But there was a well-known incident in that war

that has left a legacy on the English language. When the Ephraimites were losing, they tried to escape by pretending to be members of other tribes, in the hope of getting across the River Jordan. But if they were intercepted by the Gileadites, they were challenged to say the word *Shi*bolet.'

'I know,' said Tsedaka, meeting Daniel's eyes, but giving little away as to his own thoughts.

'And of course the reason they did that was because the Ephraimites couldn't pronounce the "*sh*" sound. So instead they said "Sibolet". And as soon as they said that, they were identified as members of the tribe of Ephraim and killed on the spot.'

'Pretty harsh,' said Gabrielle with a wry smile.

Again Daniel was irritated at Gabrielle's interruption, but Tsedaka seemed to take it all in his stride.

'That's the way it was in those days.' He turned to Daniel. 'But tell me about this lasting legacy on your language.'

'Well, the word *Shibboleth* has been incorporated into the English language to mean any custom, phrase, collective memory or linguistic peculiarity that acts as a test of membership of a particular religion, social class, nationality, profession or group. And in fact that meaning has now been extended, so it can also refer to any belief, principle, or practice which some people hold in high esteem but others think of as false or at least out of date.'

'I suppose you know that in our prayers we *do* pronounce the "sh" sound. Indeed, we do not pronounce the letter *shin* as anything other than *sh*.'

'Then how can you be descended from the tribe of Ephraim?' asked Gabrielle.

Tsedaka smiled. 'I see we have a sceptic in our midst.'

Daniel seized upon the opportunity. 'Well, maybe between us we can banish her scepticism, Rabbi Tsedaka.'

'How?'

'I was wondering if you have any documents in Proto-Sinaitic script – documents that might be used to prove your origins.'

'We have old documents in Samaritan Hebrew and Aramaic that have been translated. But none of these goes back far enough to conclusively prove our history. But there are other texts that even our priests do not understand. However, to show them to a stranger would be a leap of faith as great as that taken by Nahshon.'

Daniel smiled at the analogy. When the fleeing Israelites reached the Sea of Reeds at the time of the Exodus, with the army of the pharaoh in hot pursuit, they moaned and wailed to Moses that he had brought them out into the desert to die. Then one of the Israelites, a man called Nahshon leapt into the water, thereby showing his faith in God. At that point, the waters parted.

'My motive is both scholarship and friendship,' said Daniel. 'If you have any documents in the ancient script that pre-date the old Hebrew and Aramaic scripts, and if I can translate them, then perhaps I will be able to help you prove your origins.'

Tsedaka seemed to be wrestling with some inner conflict. Daniel remembered that even the *name* 'Israel' meant 'wrestling with God'. He spoke again, desperate to persuade Tsedaka to let him see the manuscripts. 'I know I am asking you to take me on trust. I wish I could prove to you that I have translated those other documents. Unfortunately the circumstances in which we came here makes that impossible. But you can check out my credentials. I am a genuine scholar of Semitic languages.'

Tsedaka smiled. 'I do not have to check out anything. I know who you are well enough. I even knew your teacher, Professor Carmichael.'

Daniel was surprised at this. He looked over at Gabrielle.

'I can tell you that there were two manuscripts older than the Torah that we had in the past, but we now only have one of them. The first – the one that is lost – is called *Sefer Milhamot Hashem*.'

'*The Book of the Wars of the Lord*,' Daniel translated.

'It is actually quoted in the Bible,' Tsedaka continued. 'Numbers 21:14. The quotation contains a reference to the miracles at the Reed Sea and occurs just after the description of Moses and the fiery serpents.'

Daniel remembered his discussion with Carmichael, but said nothing.

'But why is it lost?' asked Gabrielle.

'It was entrusted to the tribe of Menasha,' Tsedaka explained. 'And the tribe of Menasha had land on both sides of the River Jordan. It was to the eastern half of the tribe that the book was entrusted. But you have to understand that over the centuries we have lost many members, not only to wars and massacres but also to enforced conversion. Many of us converted to Islam and many of those converts inter-married. So *The Book of the Wars of the Lord* is now in the hands of the Bedul tribe.'

'Bedul?' Gabrielle echoed.

'A Bedouin tribe living in the Petra area. But we believe that the book has probably been lost or destroyed or buried.'

'You said there was another book,' said Daniel.

'Yes. It is called *Sefer HaYashar*.'

'*The Book of the Straight*,' Daniel translated.

'It is mentioned in the book of Joshua 10:13 and in fact is believed by some to have been written by Joshua himself.'

'And where is this *Book of the Straight* now?' asked Daniel.

'It is kept in the tomb of Joseph in the nearby valley.'

'Is there any chance of us being able to see the manuscript?' asked Daniel. 'So that I can have a go at translating it?'

Tsedaka looked nervous. 'It would involve some delicate negotiation. Just getting access to the site will prove difficult. Religious Jews venerate it and militant Muslims claim that it is actually the tomb of a Muslim scholar called Yusuf.'

'I could try and use my status as an academic to get permission.'

'Yes but there is more, Professor Klein. If *The Book of the Straight* is disinterred, there may then arise some argument as to its ownership. Our high priest might prefer to leave it buried there rather than open up a whole can of worms as to whom it truly belongs.'

Daniel thought about this for almost a minute. 'Okay, well, I won't try to force the issue. What you've told me was in confidence and in any case only you or your priests know exactly where it is. But if you could talk to your high priest I'd be grateful. Tell him that if this document is written in the old script then I can translate and quite possibly validate your claim to be true Israelites.'

Chapter 74

'So you're a veteran?' Goliath said to the brash fifty-something American woman he had got talking to as they hovered around the self-service breakfast tables in the hotel in Taba.

'I wouldn't exactly say a veteran. I mean, three visits doesn't exactly make me a veteran. But I know what to look out for. You have to be careful of some of the men here.'

Goliath didn't think *he* had to be careful of any of the men there, and he suspected that this American woman didn't either. Whilst her ample girth would not necessarily be off-putting to local masculine taste, her age probably would. And if that wasn't enough to put them off, then her loud manner probably would be.

Goliath suspected that what kept this woman coming back was not the sunshine – which she could have got just as easily in Florida – but the prospect of a fling with a local toy boy.

'So what did you think of that Bonnie and Clyde couple?'

He tried various other lines as he mingled with people at other hotels, but the Bonnie and Clyde reference appeared to work best for getting people to open up, even if he hadn't got any useful information yet.

'You mean that British couple who stole that speedboat and went to Israel?'

'Oh, were they British?'

'The man was. I think the woman was German or Swedish or something.'

'Does anyone know why they did it?'

'I think they were just a pair of thrill-seekers.'

Goliath nodded, no longer interested now that it was clear that this woman didn't have any useful information about them.

'Although I did hear a rumour that they were Israeli spies.'

Goliath was still not interested, and was looking for a way to escape from her so that he could pump someone else for information.

'You do know that the Jews run the world, don't you? I mean, no one talks about it, but they run the banks and they were even responsible for 9/11.'

Goliath agreed with her but he didn't have time for a discussion about the evils of the Jewish people.

'You don't believe me, do you?'

'I was just wondering how you knew.'

'I saw something about it on the Internet.'

Goliath suppressed a smile and then adroitly stepped aside to let a couple get between him and the woman. He took the opportunity to get away from her and open a conversation with one of the waiters who were manning the serving tables.

'What do you recommend – the poached eggs or the scrambled eggs?'

'They're both good,' said the young waiter, who couldn't have been more than about eighteen. 'I like the poached myself but . . .' He trailed off.

'Were you here on the day that couple stole that speedboat?'

The young waiter smiled. 'They didn't actually steal it. I think they hired it and then went off to Israeli waters.

The Israelis thought they were terrorists and nearly killed them.'

'You actually saw it?'

Again the waiter smiled. 'Oh no, I didn't see it. I was on duty that day. But my friend Mas'ud came down from Cairo with them. And he overheard them talking.'

Paydirt!

'Oh . . . and where is your friend Mas'ud now?'

'He's working in the kitchen.'

'I wonder if I could speak to him.' Goliath handed over some money and the waiter went to fetch his friend.

Mas'ud was maybe a couple of years younger than the waiter, who seemed curious to listen to their conversation. Goliath gave him a look that told him to get lost. He shrugged and walked off, leaving Goliath to talk to Mas'ud.

'I understand you came down here with that couple who stole that speedboat and went to Israel.'

'Yes. We came down here by camel.'

'And I understand that you overheard them talking?'

'Yes. But my father said I wasn't supposed to talk to anyone else.'

'Why?'

'He said it might be spies. Not the couple, I mean, but people who ask about them.'

Goliath faked a laugh. 'Spies? I think he just doesn't want you talking to journalists.'

'Journalists?'

'Reporters. You know – the press.'

'Oh, yes.'

'But that isn't really fair to you, is it? I mean if you want to talk to a reporter, why shouldn't you?'

He took out some money and held it low, making it obvious to Mas'ud but not to anyone else.

'What do you want to know?'

'Everything you can remember. What were they talking about?'

'Well, they didn't say anything about going to Israel. I mean, I didn't realize that's what they were talking about. But they said something about talking to the Samaritan priests. And they said something about Holon. I didn't think about it at the time, but I think that's in Israel.'

Goliath smiled as he handed over the money. He had everything he needed now.

Chapter 75

'I, Joshua, son of Noon, of the tribe of Neferayim, son of Joseph, give this as my testament.'

Daniel looked at Gabrielle, surprised.

They were sitting in an office in the Conservation Department of the National Library in Jerusalem, together with the Samaritan high priest and two of his colleagues. Outside the office sat an armed guard whose main duty was to lock up when they were finished.

After some robust discussions with the Israeli Antiquities Authority, they had obtained permission to get *The Book of the Straight* from its bolt-hole in Joseph's tomb and bring it to this department where they specialized in restoring manuscripts. It was carefully opened by experts and placed between glass. The process had proceeded smoothly except for one brief hair-raising moment in the tomb when Gabrielle had picked up the clay urn which contained the scroll, in breach of protocol. But she had handed it back immediately and apologized for her over-enthusiasm.

The 'book' was in fact a papyrus scroll. This surprised Daniel somewhat as he had been expecting it to be parchment, in accordance with Jewish law. But then again, that law may well have come later. And the fact that it was papyrus suggested that the document might have some Egyptian provenance. Indeed, the very first line prompted Daniel to ask a question of Gabrielle, drawing on her expert knowledge of ancient Egypt.

'*Neferayim*? Could that be a variant of Ay?'

'I've never heard of him being called Neferayim.'

'Okay, but could it have been *Nefer*-Ay? And then become Neferayim before becoming Ephraim?'

'The word *Nefer* means "beautiful" and is a characteristic of female names in Egypt like Nefertiti and Nefertari.'

'So you're saying it's *only* used for female names?' asked Daniel.

'Well no, there were a few men with "Nefer" in the name, like Neferhotep and Neferkheprure. And of course in those ancient times, they sometimes had several names.'

'So maybe Ay could have had the alternative name of Nefer-Ay, which could then have become Neferayim?'

'It's possible,' she conceded. 'But like I said, in Egyptian writings he's never been referred to as Nefer-Ay, let alone Neferayim.'

The priests sat there in silence throughout this exchange. They, at least, were perfectly happy to be patient. But now, the high priest leaned forward.

'It's consistent with what we know. Joshua *was* of the tribe of Ephraim, so Neferayim could be an alternative name for Ephraim.'

'Okay, well let's put that aside for now and see what else we can find here. You must understand that because I had to leave my notes behind when I made my escape from Egypt, I'm having to rely on my memory for this translation. You'll have to be patient with me.'

He continued to read:

Now one day Pharaoh was visiting the lands he had conquered in Syria and he went to the jail where the prisoners were kept and he saw the prisoner Joseph and he asked—

He broke off and looked at Gabrielle.

'I'm Anglicizing the name. But just tell me one thing, does that fit the historical record?'

'It could be true of several pharaohs. I think I have an idea which one it was, but I don't want to say just yet. Carry on.'

Daniel looked down and continued translating, the words coming not in a flow, but almost in a burst of energy.

He asked Joseph what crime he had committed and Joseph said that he had fought against Pharaoh and was defeated. But he said that he had been betrayed by his brothers who surrendered and offered him as a prisoner that their lives may be spared. He said that they were jealous of him because he wore a coat of many colours and they took his coat away from him when they delivered him into captivity.

Gabrielle was nodding enthusiastically at this. 'A coat of many colours was a sign of leadership. It started with a people called the Hyksos who invaded Egypt 4,000 years ago and were driven out 500 years later.'

'According to the Bible,' said Daniel, 'Jacob gave Joseph a coat of many colours, showing that he was the favoured son.'

'And that made his brothers jealous,' added one of the Samaritan priests.

Daniel carried on reading.

Then Pharaoh told him that he too was in conflict with his brother, for his brother was older and had a greater claim to the throne. And Joseph told him to say to the people that he had had a dream and that in the dream the Sphinx spoke to him and told him to sweep the sand from his feet and that if he did this he would be king.

Daniel broke off, not because he couldn't read any further but because Gabrielle was gripping his arm.

'What is it?' he asked.

'The Dream stele,' she choked.

'What's that?'

'Thutmose the Fourth, the grandfather of Akhenaten, is believed to have visited Syria after conquering it . . . or reconquering it. He had an older brother, but somehow managed to gain power for himself. He then did some restoration work on the Sphinx and had this event commemorated in a small inscribed stone placed between the paws of the Sphinx. On the stone it described how he was out on a hunting trip when he fell asleep and had a dream. And in the dream the Sphinx spoke to him and told him that if he swept the sand away from its feet he would be made king. The stone is called the Dream stele and this passage fits in neatly with it.'

'And I guess it also links up neatly with the idea that Joseph was an interpreter of dreams.'

'Except that according to this account, he wasn't so much the interpreter of dreams as the *inventor*.'

Daniel looked up at the priests to see how they were responding. This was presumably not what they wanted to hear. They were seeking confirmation of the Bible, not a rewriting of it – especially not one that cast their ancestor Joseph in a somewhat more cynical light. They did not look happy, but only one of them looked angry.

Daniel returned his attention to the manuscript before him.

And Pharaoh saw that Joseph was a wise man and he told him that if he agreed to serve him he would give him his freedom and he agreed. And so Pharaoh ordered the jailer to set him free and made him his adviser.

And there was a great harvest that year and Pharaoh and the people were happy. But Joseph advised him that God's will was like the seasons and that God's bounty would not always be with him. And he said to Pharaoh 'Build storehouses for the grain and save some of the grain because the years of plenty will be followed by famine.'

Daniel looked up at the priests. They seemed a lot happier at this. He carried on reading:

And Joseph was saddened by the idolatry of the Egyptians and he said to Pharaoh: 'What use is it to you to have many gods? Do you have many kings? Is it not better to have one god, just as you are one king?' And Pharaoh saw great wisdom in Joseph's words. But he was troubled, for the people were accustomed to many gods.

Daniel looked up again to see the looks on the faces of the Samaritan priests: a mixture of joy and stunned surprise.

Chapter 76

'I'm looking for some friends of mine,' said Goliath, holding up the pictures of Daniel and Gabrielle that he had downloaded from the Internet and printed out.

He was in Holon, randomly accosting people, especially but not exclusively those wearing traditional Samaritan costume. He saw a group of them coming towards him.

'Excuse me, I wonder if you can help me. I'm looking for a couple of friends of mine – a man and a woman. I know they were here yesterday and I am very anxious to find them.'

He held out the pictures. The group looked at them but showed no sign of recognition. Then one of them said, 'I think I saw them. Ask Rabbi Tsedaka.' The young Samaritan pointed. 'He should be in the synagogue.'

Goliath thanked him and walked on. The Samaritan synagogue was in fact just down the road.

'Excuse me,' he said to a man, 'I am looking for Rabbi Tsedaka.'

'He's in the office,' said the man, pointing the way.

Goliath made his way to the office and knocked on the door.

'Come in,' said a voice from inside.

Goliath opened the door and entered. Aryeh Tsedaka was sitting at the desk, writing, his face creased in great thought.

'Sorry, I'll be with you in a moment. I'm just working on my sermon.'

But Goliath was not prepared to wait. 'I'm looking for some friends of mine,' he said, pushing the photo towards Tsedaka.

The look of recognition in the rabbi's eyes was immediate. Which made his answer all the more surprising.

'I'm afraid I don't recognize them.'

Had they told him about the attempt to kill them?

However much or little this man knew, it was obvious that he was protecting them and had no intention of co-operating.

'Could you take another look?' Goliath requested, with an eager look in his eyes.

The rabbi leaned forward as if going through the motions of considering the question again. It was all that Goliath needed. He reached out and grabbed Tsedaka's head and smashed it into the desk. It made a muffled thud, but the cry that followed was loud enough to be heard, and Goliath feared that he would attract attention. He lifted Tsedaka's head with one hand and clamped a hand over his mouth with the other, making it hard for Tsedaka to breathe let alone speak. He could see the terror in the rabbi's eyes.

'I am going to ask you one more time and if you do not tell me the truth I will inflict great pain upon you and then I will go after your family. Do you understand?'

Although barely able to move his head, the rabbi managed what amounted to a nod. Goliath moved his hand away from Tsedaka's mouth. Tsedaka coughed and sputtered, trying to regain his breath. Then in a low, gravelly voice he said, 'They've gone to the Hebrew University . . . National Library . . . Conservation Department . . .'

'What for?'
'To look at the scroll.'
'*Which* scroll?' demanded Goliath.
'*The Book of the Straight.*'

Chapter 77

And Pharaoh died and his son became Pharaoh. And the new pharaoh trusted Joseph for he was his father's loyal servant. And so Joseph became adviser to the new pharaoh.

Daniel looked up from the papyrus at Gabrielle, expectantly. 'It fits what we know about Yuya. He was vizier to two pharaohs.'

The high priest nodded approvingly. They were overjoyed to learn that Joseph – their patriarch – had tried to influence the pharaoh in the direction of monotheism.

Daniel smiled, pleased that his translation was fulfilling everyone's expectations. On the outside he was calm, but on the inside he was in awe of the fact that in his hands was a document that was both changing and reinforcing history. He put his head down and carried on reading.

Now Neferayim took a wife and had a daughter by her and her name was Nefertiti. But his wife died when she gave birth and Neferayim took another wife and she was called Tey and they had a daughter. And Tey also became nurse to Nefertiti. And Nefertiti the daughter of Neferayim married the son of the pharaoh.

After many years Pharaoh died. And his son became

Pharaoh and Neferayim had his right ear as Joseph had the right ear of his father and grandfather. And Neferayim advised Pharaoh that he should cast away Amun, the false god of Thebes and should worship only Aten, the disk of the sun. And he advised Pharaoh that the priests of Amun were wicked and wished him harm. And he caused Pharaoh to believe that it was not he that was advising him but the Aten himself who was commanding him. And Pharaoh saw the wisdom in Neferayim's words and he decreed that Aten, the disk of the daytime sun, was the one true god and Amun and the other gods were false. And he changed his name to Akhenaten . . .

His beloved wife and sister changed her name from Nebetah to Beketaten meaning Handmaid of Aten to show her devotion to the one true god. And in his twelfth year as king she bore him a son, Tutankhaten.

He broke off and looked at Gabrielle.

'Does that fit the record?' he asked.

Gabrielle looked stunned and was almost gasping for breath as she replied. 'Well, we know from DNA evidence that Tutankhamen's parents were brother and sister. There was a tomb in the Valley of the Kings called KV35, which as well as having the mummy of King Tut's grandfather also contained the mummies of two women, known as the Elder Lady and the Younger Lady respectively. The DNA tests established that the Elder Lady was Tutankhamen's grandmother and the Younger Lady was his mother.'

'But this business about the changing of the names – Nebetah and Beketaten?'

'It's been speculated about in the past. Nebetah was never mentioned *after* the Amarna reforms and Beketaten was never mentioned *before* them. So it makes perfect sense.'

But Daniel was confused about something else. 'And why does it say the son was called Tutan*khaten*, not Tutan*khamen*?'

'Tutan*khaten* was his original name. He changed it later to Tutan*khamen* when he reversed the Amarna reforms and got rid of Aten and restored the cult of Amun . . . What?'

'The next bit. If I've read it correctly . . .'

'What does it say?'

He translated.

And Neferayim feared that he would shrink in Pharaoh's eyes because Beketaten had borne Pharaoh a son. So he smote Beketaten and killed her. But he spared the child and Nefertiti became his nurse.

He turned to Gabrielle, ignoring the tension and shock on the faces of the priests. 'Is *that* in the history books? Ay killing Tutankhamen's mother?'

Gabrielle also looked tense, but not unhappy as she drew in her breath before answering.

'Recent CAT scans on the mummy of Tutankhamen's mother showed signs of an unhealed wound from a severe blow to the side of her face. The wound was covered by the embalming process, which means that it occurred before she died. And the latest medical opinion is that *the blow was lethal*. In other words, yes, she was killed by a blow to the head.'

Daniel looked around in response to the intake of breath from the priests. That a queen of Egypt had been killed by a blow to the head didn't bother them, just as it didn't surprise Gabrielle. However, that it was inflicted by the Samaritan patriarch Ephraim in order to maintain his influence over the pharaoh most certainly did. So when Daniel looked down and translated the next sentence in his mind, he was supremely reluctant to say it out loud. But he realized that he had no choice.

Now Neferayim forced Nefertiti to lay with him and they had a daughter, Ankhesenpaaten.

'I don't have to listen to this!' the youngest of the priests interrupted – and it was clear that he couldn't take any more as he stormed out.

'Wait,' said another, following him out.

'I'm sorry,' said Daniel, to the high priest who remained. 'I can only read what is written.'

'Are you sure your translation is correct?'

'I'm sure of the words. I cannot vouch for their truthfulness.'

They both turned to Gabrielle, inquisitively. She shrugged.

'There's nothing in any other written record to support it,' she said tentatively.

'But?' Daniel replied, picking up on the hangnail in her tone.

'It would explain an aberration that was found in the DNA tests. There were two mummified foetuses in Tutankhamen's tomb. But the DNA tests show that they can't both be the children of both Tutankhamen and his wife . . . unless his wife had different parentage to the one the official record shows.'

'So this *is* consistent with the DNA?' Daniel wanted to be sure.

'Yes, but the chronology of the narrative is all wrong. Tutankhamen's wife was born a few years *before* Tutankhamen himself. Yet in this papyrus it is described *afterwards.*'

'The order is irrelevant,' said the priest, his brows furrowing with the weight of the troubles in his heart. 'Ancient narratives often jump around in their order. It is the words themselves that are painful.'

Chapter 78

'Why did we let them get hold of the manuscript?' asked Sarit.

She and Dov Shamir were in the Mossad's headquarters in Herzliya. She was supposed to be going to Eilat for some R&R, but she had asked for permission to stay and keep working on this assignment. She didn't like leaving a job unfinished.

'We couldn't really stop them. They're both prestigious academics and they had the Antiquities Authority behind them.'

'Couldn't we have said it was a matter of national security?'

'The PM *knows* about the security angle. But a three-thousand-year-old manuscript isn't going to threaten national security in itself. Besides, we know that Harrison Carmichael had a copy—'

'Which Goliath destroyed in that fire.'

'The point is he already translated it.'

'Yes, but the New Covenant managed to suppress publication.'

'*Delay* publication,' Dov corrected.

'Well, with Carmichael dead and Professor Tomlinson so well connected, he'll probably be able to block publication.'

'So Daniel Klein'll get the credit when he publishes *his* translation. The point is, Sarit, that we can't stop it.

And there's no reason why we should. The threat to national security is not in the contents, but in what people *do* with the information. And let's face it, *The Book of the Straight* doesn't really tell us the exact location. All we know is that it's somewhere on the other side of the Jordan River. If they knew where to look, they wouldn't have been wasting time trying to get samples of infected clothes.'

'But the infection is still out there. Look at what happened to that curator in England. He had all the symptoms: the fever, the snake-like lesions . . .'

'It doesn't appear to have spread.'

'And what about the Egyptians?'

'They seem to have contained it too.'

'So it's not all that virulent.'

'Not the Egyptian strain certainly. If Carmichael's translation is right, then it mutated into a more virulent strain in the Jordan area.'

'How can we be so sure of that? I mean it's not like Carmichael was an epidemiologist.'

'No, but it's a case of reading between the lines. We got hold of a copy of Carmichael's paper and gave it to our own epidemiologists for an assessment.'

'And how badly should we be worrying?'

'Well, as long as it's in stasis, there should be no problem.'

She was about to say something more when Dov's phone went. She watched as his face went from sombre to grave.

'Has General Security been notified? . . . Okay, keep me posted.'

When he put the phone down, his face drained of blood and Sarit looked at him expectantly.

'That Samaritan rabbi they spoke to, Aryeh Tsedaka . . . he's been found dead in the synagogue in Holon. There were signs of a struggle and his neck was broken.'

Chapter 79

'Shall I wait for them?' Daniel asked Gabrielle when she returned.

She had been outside to find out what was going on. The priest who had stormed out was not merely angry; he was crying at what Daniel had just revealed from the text. The other was trying to comfort him. But Gabrielle did not want to reply until the high priest had spoken.

'It is not our custom to let an outsider read from our scrolls unless at least two priests are present.'

'I don't think they're going to be back anytime soon,' said Gabrielle.

The high priest seemed to be wrestling with his conscience before replying. Daniel knew that this must be hard for him. Ephraim was not just *one of* the patriarchs of the tribes of Israel. He was the patriarch of one of the two tribes from which the Samaritans specifically claim their descent. And this ancient scroll cast him as a cunning schemer, an incestuous adulterer and a murderer.

'Please continue,' the priest said finally through his pain.

In his twelfth year, Pharaoh raised his wife Nefertiti to rule at his right side and she ruled with him, and when his heart was calm he ruled and when his heart was troubled she ruled. And at the end of summer of his seventeenth year, he died and Nefertiti ruled alone. But she feared her father and she feared Horemheb, the chief of the army, and she feared Tutankhaten for he was a troubled boy and both Horemheb and Neferayim tried to be as fathers to him. And he would not listen to her for he was not her son and she did not have a son. So she wrote to the king of the Hittites and offered to marry one of his sons.

Daniel had to break off when he heard Gabrielle's sharp intake of breath. 'Do you know about this?'

'There is a record of such an incident. It's called the Zananza Incident. In the early part of the twentieth century, archaeologists found a huge collection of some 10,000 clay tablets written in cuneiform, at the site of the ancient Hittite capital. And some of the tablets are letters referring to this incident.'

Daniel continued reading.

But the king of the Hittites was suspicious, for the daughters of Egypt did not marry foreign men. So he sent a messenger to Egypt to accuse Nefertiti of deception. So she wrote to the Hittite king again and his messenger brought her words to the king. She told the king of her fears and swore that she spoke true and would give his son the throne of Egypt. And so the Hittite king sent Zananza his son to be her husband, but Horemheb, the chief of the army, heard of this and he sent out his men and they met Zananza on the road and smote him.

Daniel looked up at Gabrielle, waiting for her inevitable comment.

'That's how history records it,' she said. 'But it doesn't tell us what happened to—'

'The next bit does.' He lowered his eyes and continued.

And when this became known in the royal court, there was much anger. And Horemheb accused Neferayim and Nefertiti of plotting with the enemy. And Neferayim swore that he knew not of his daughter's treachery and he had her put to death and Tutankhaten became king.

When Daniel looked up this time, Gabrielle seemed more shocked than the high priest.

Chapter 80

'You have to send me in there,' Sarit told Dovi.

'Send you in where? You think he's hanging around waiting to be arrested? He's got whatever he came for.'

'Let me go to Holon. I can help the police. Give them a description.'

'They've already got descriptions.'

'Well, at least let me work with them.'

'They don't need you. Look, they now know what he looks like and a big man like that is going to find it very hard to hide.'

'He's managed to stay hidden till now.'

'The Egyptians actually had him and then they let him go when Senator Morris intervened.'

'And now he's somehow managed to enter Israel. That makes it personal.'

'That's what I'm worried about, Sarit: you making it personal. He's already survived an attack by you and he knows what you look like.'

'And by the same token, I know what *he* looks like.'

'As long as he's in Israel it's in the hands of the General Security Services.'

'What – that bunch of clowns? If they were doing their job, they'd've arrested Goliath as soon as he crossed the border. How did he even get in?'

'We don't know that yet.'

'And what identity is he using?'

'We don't know that either.'

'So let me get this straight. Some guy who's six foot five tall, who we're looking out for specifically, enters the country undetected, gives the GSS the slip, kills a prominent Samaritan rabbi and then vanishes without leaving a trail?'

'He's evidently a lot smarter than we thought.'

'And what about the senator?'

'What about him?'

'Can't we get anything from the phone intercepts?'

'Goliath must have a new phone and we haven't identified it yet. We're working on it.'

'What about the senator?'

'We can't monitor him with a US-based intercept 'cause it's against Federal law.'

'Do we care? It hasn't been sanctioned by the PM. If we get caught, there could be a whole lot of fallout.'

'It's a matter of life and death!'

'We have to work within our means.'

'So how did we monitor Morris until now?'

'That's why we need assets like Audrey Milne. When he called Egypt, we could monitor locally from Urim. It seems like Goliath is a whole lot more resourceful than we gave him credit for.'

'So all the more reason for me to get in on the act. At least I know what he looks like.'

'But you're no better placed than the security services to track him down. In fact, rather less so.'

Chapter 81

'Look, I know this is painful,' said Daniel. 'If you want me to stop, I will.' He understood how difficult it must be for these serious men of religion to find their sacred truths contradicted by a text more ancient than the Bible; their patriarch exposed as an incestuous adulterer and a murderer who betrayed his own daughter.

The high priest refused to succumb to the pain. 'No . . . please continue.'

Daniel looked down and again struggled with the text as he continued.

And Neferayim had the ear of Tutankhaten and advised him to fulfil his father's wishes and worship the Aten and not to allow the priests of Amun to pray to their false god or to offer sacrifices to him. And the king worshipped the creator of all. And Neferayim persuaded Pharaoh to marry Ankhesenpaaten his favourite granddaughter who was also his daughter. But Horemheb had the other ear of the king and he told him that Neferayim and Nefertiti killed his mother because she wanted to restore the old gods.

'Is that new?' asked Daniel. 'Or more of what we already know?'

'A mixture,' said Gabrielle cautiously.

'But why didn't Horemheb simply tell *Akhenaten* about the murder of King Tut's mother? Why this elaborate, round-about response?'

Gabrielle had to think about this.

'Well, we do know that from the twelfth year of Akhenaten's reign, Egypt was in turmoil. They stopped building in Amarna and Egypt was economically strapped. Their new enemy, the Hittites, were becoming more powerful. And Akhenaten may not have had all his marbles. From what it said earlier in the papyrus, Nefertiti was ruling as co-regent. Although co-regencies were quite common in ancient Egypt at that time, it was rare for it to be with a woman. Not unprecedented, but rare. It was more likely to be with a son, in order to prepare him for leadership. If he ruled with Nefertiti as co-regent, instead of waiting for his son to get older, that could suggest that he was no longer able to rule by himself. Maybe the death of his beloved wife/sister affected his mind in some way.'

'That's logical,' said Daniel.

He looked at the high priest to see if he wanted to add anything. The high priest nodded towards the papyrus, making it clear that all he wanted to do was get this over with. He could have told them to stop, but it was clear that he had no intention of running away from the truth. He would go wherever the truth took him. Daniel continued.

And when Tutankhaten heard this he became bitter and angry and he summoned Neferayim and cursed him and threatened him with death. But Neferayim begged for his life and told the king that it was his daughter and not he who had killed the mother of the king. And so Tutankhaten

*spared his life but ordered him to prove he was true by cutting
out the words that praised the Aten from his tomb.*

Daniel looked at Gabrielle. 'That was at the other tomb,
right? The Amarna tomb, not the one we were locked in.'

'That's right.'

'And *was* it erased? The Great Hymn to Aten, I mean.'

'Parts of it were chiselled out. Let's talk about it later.
Carry on.'

*And Pharaoh restored the old gods and ordered the city of
Akhetaten abandoned and changed his name to Tutankhamen
to show his support for the old gods and their priests. Then
Tutankhamen appointed Horemheb to be his heir.*

'Now we're getting to things that are quite familiar,' said
Daniel.

'Very familiar,' Gabrielle agreed. 'The counter-revolution,
the abandonment of Akhetaten, the restoration of the Amun
priests in Luxor. And that was only the beginning.'

Chapter 82

'Which bus do I need for the Hebrew University?' Goliath asked a random Israeli as he stepped out of the central bus station in Jerusalem.

'What campus you want?' asked the Israeli in broken English. 'Givat Ram or Mount Scopus?'

'I don't know. The one with the library.'

'They both have library.'

'I mean the National Library.'

'Ah, you want Givat Ram. It's near here. You need number nine.'

And with that, Goliath was abandoned and left to wait for the bus. When it arrived at the university it made a sweep round the car park before coming to a stop in a forecourt outside the gates and everyone poured out of the bus.

He had to pass through a cursory security check, but they were only looking for weapons and no one checked his identity. Once inside the campus, he asked the way to the National Library. He was told that it was at the end of the long row of buildings to his right. He walked in the shade, instead of on the grass to the left, and all the while he was thinking about how he was going to do this. How would they react? How good was the security? Was he going to kill them all?

Chapter 83

'Maybe we should wait until they come back,' said Daniel.

He sensed that the high priest was letting him continue, maintaining a stoic bearing even in the face of what must have been the most horrendous revelations in his eyes. But the fact that this old man had to face it on his own somehow made it all the worse. Here was a man who had devoted all his life to a belief system – already having confronted many who denied his people's history and their suffering.

Yet now he was having to face an attack on his ancestral history from a different perspective. Instead of the long-standing Jewish denial that his people were true Israelites, he found himself confronted by evidence that the ancestors of the Israelites were not as good a people as their self-penned history had implied.

And it was the ancestors of the Samaritans in particular who were being singled out. Not Judah, from whom the Jews claim descent, but rather Joseph and Ephraim. Moreover, whilst Joseph was being portrayed as a forerunner to the modern-day political spin doctor, Ephraim was being portrayed as a Machiavellian schemer who resorted to murder to get his way, and who was ready to sacrifice his own daughter to save his own miserable skin.

Strictly speaking, this did not impact directly on the

Samaritan *priests*, because they were a separate branch who officially descended from the tribe of Levi. But this thought gave neither the high priest nor Daniel any comfort. Indeed, what made it worse, in Daniel's eyes, was that he had become the agent of this revelation. Circumstances had caused him to be the one who was inflicting this mental anguish on this kind and gentle man who had agreed to share the innermost secrets of his ancient sect with this outsider. Daniel felt as if he was betraying a sacred trust by revealing these awful secrets.

True, he hadn't known when he set out on this venture what these ancient texts would reveal, and as a man of the ivory tower of academia, his ultimate duty was to the truth. And now he had already told the priest the painful facts, as recorded in this papyrus. He could not take it back. Perhaps if he had translated it in writing first and then had to decide whether or not to reveal it, he would have acted differently. But now it was too late.

'I don't think either of them are ready to hear the rest just yet,' said the elder.

'Then maybe I should just stop.'

'*No!*'

The interruption was Gabrielle's. He could see the look in her eyes: the academic fervour and thirst for knowledge. To him, the ultimate duty to the truth was a painful reality that as a scholar he had to accept. To her it was a passion – a bludgeon to beat down the wishful thinker or a steamroller to drive over the sceptic.

A final glance at the priest . . . a final nod from the priest . . . told Daniel to continue.

Then Tutankhamen died in his illness. But before Horemheb, the chief of the army, claimed the throne, Neferayim married

312

the widow of Tutankhamen, though she was his own grand-
daughter and daughter, and claimed the throne for himself.

Now Neferayim wanted to restore worship of Aten, the
disk of the sun, and forbid the worship of the old gods. But
he was an old man and he was weak and the priests of the
old gods were strong and Horemheb was strong and
Neferayim knew that he could not impose his will upon
them. So he allowed the worship of the old gods. And he
chose his son to be his heir.

But when he died, Horemheb claimed the throne by force
with the aid of his soldiers and killed the son of Neferayim
and he forbade the worship of Aten and he punished those
who had worshipped him. But to those who worshipped the
old god Amun he gave great rewards and he appointed them
to the highest ranks in the land. And he struck the names of
the pharaohs who had worshipped Aten from the names
of kings so that their names were forgotten and their memory
was cursed and their tombs were defiled. But the tomb of
Tutankhamen was spared because he had appointed him to
be his heir and because he was loved by the people.

'That's all pretty much well documented,' said Gabrielle.
'Apart from the actual blood relationships, which has always
been a bone of contention between scholars.'

'Holy shit!'

'What is it?' Gabrielle said, realizing that Daniel was
responding not to what she had said but to what he had just
read.

'The . . . the next bit—'

'What does it *say*?' asked Gabrielle impatiently.

Now Horemheb knew not Joseph . . .

313

It was just five simple words. But they had as devastating an effect on Gabrielle and the priest as they did on Daniel. Because they echoed some of the most ominous words in the Bible:

Now there arose a new king over Egypt which knew not Joseph.

It was a portent to the enslavement of the Israelites in Egypt. They had encouraged and supported monotheism and now that it was completely rejected by the new pharaoh, they were going to pay the price in sweat and toil – as slaves to the Egyptians. They had been loyal to the pharaohs who came before Horemheb, but all of that was forgotten. They were tainted by being associated with the wrong side. Now, with a change of regime and a change of policy, they were to be perceived as the enemy.

Gabrielle looked at Daniel; Daniel and the priest looked at each other.

But before anyone could speak, the door swung open and a tall and powerful man burst into the room. Daniel recognized him immediately. It was the man from the aeroplane.

Chapter 84

Sarit never had been one for following orders. Besides, Dov hadn't actually *ordered* her not to interfere. He simply hadn't authorized specific action. He hadn't told her *not* to go to the Hebrew University in Jerusalem. Indeed, there was no reason at all why she shouldn't go there. It was a public place and the National Library, subject to certain security procedures, was a public building. So she wasn't actually disobeying orders in going there.

She had driven there as soon as her conversation with Dov had ended – she didn't want to waste any time. But she didn't have a university pass, so she would have to park outside the campus and walk in. That would take a little longer.

She wasn't really sure why she was doing this. Presumably they would phone the university to warn them if they thought there was any danger of Goliath turning up. Also Dov had told her that there was an armed guard with them in the lab. But how quickly could an armed guard respond? After all, the corridors of the National Library were full of unarmed civilians. Could an armed guard with a pistol in a holster respond quickly enough to a man like Goliath, and without harming any innocent passers-by?

And what did Goliath and the New Covenant actually

want? If it was what Dov thought it was then it was not to be found at the Hebrew University. It would be somewhere in Jordan. Perhaps he thought that the manuscript would give him the precise location?

No, that doesn't make sense!

If the information he needed was in the translation of *The Book of the Straight* then Senator Morris could have already given it to him based on Carmichael's translation.

But maybe the translation was incomplete? Maybe there were gaps that needed to be filled? Maybe they were waiting for Daniel's translation to put in place the last piece that would help them find the exact location?

Or maybe Goliath was still convinced that he needed a sample of their clothes, unaware that that approach was now obsolete.

Chapter 85

'I assume you know who I am?' Goliath said.

'I remember you,' said Daniel, unsure of how to play it. 'You were the man on the plane. We talked a bit about ancient Egypt and history and all that.'

More than anyone else in the room, Daniel realized that they were in deadly danger, although he sensed that Gabrielle must have at least *some* idea too. It was now clear to Daniel that the pushy man who had spoken to him on the plane was also the man who had tried to kill them at the tomb.

It made perfect sense. The guardian of the tomb's neck was broken and this was clearly a strong man. Daniel knew that Gabrielle had figured it out too. Only the high priest was in blissful ignorance of the fact that standing before them was a deadly assassin.

But what was his cause? And what happened to the armed guard outside? This man was certainly strong enough to have dealt with him. But they hadn't heard a thing. Just as at the tomb, they had only realized when it was too late.

'Let's not beat around the bush, Professor Klein. You know who I am.'

'You're the man who locked us in the tomb.'

'Correct.'

'Did you kill my uncle?' asked Gabrielle.

317

'That too.'

'But *why*?' she asked.

'What is this?' asked the high priest.

'*Shut up!*' yelled Goliath, delivering a vicious blow to the priest with the back of his hand. The blow drew blood.

Daniel took a step towards the big man. He was prepared to fight Goliath, despite his obvious size and strength. But the high priest held up a hand to stay Daniel's advance.

'What do you want?' asked Gabrielle in an even tone.

'I want . . . *that!*'

He pointed to the small papyrus scroll. She moved her hand away nervously, but held his gaze.

'This scroll belongs to the world,' she said quietly, but with a hint of defiance.

'*Enough! I didn't come here to argue!*'

They all fell silent. Daniel eyed the man carefully, wondering whether he stood a chance if he made a move. At the back of his mind was the thought that everyone has a weak spot, but this man had shown that he had speed as well as strength. He realized that any move he might make would endanger not only himself, but also the others.

He wondered if any support might come from outside. An armed guard had been posted at the door. But that was all rather perfunctory; no one had actually expected any trouble. And where was the armed guard now? Had he just gone to take a leak? Or had this man done something to him?

'Give it to me,' said Goliath, pointing to the clay urn that had housed the papyrus. He was staring at Gabrielle. She hesitated for a moment, looking at Daniel.

'*Do it!*' shouted Goliath, grabbing Daniel by the throat to show that they were powerless to resist him. Daniel felt a spasm of agony as the soft tissue of his throat was crushed in Goliath's iron grip. He couldn't kick Goliath, either in the groin or the kneecap because the man's long reach held him too far away, and in any case he was in too much pain.

Then he remembered a self-defence technique he had learnt years before. Reaching over Goliath's left hand he pressed hard on the thumb, forcing his attacker's fingers to open. With Goliath's grip broken, he pulled away, his hands to his throat as he coughed and sputtered.

His eyes met those of the big man, wondering how he would react to being thwarted in this David versus Goliath struggle. He expected to see anger and was fully prepared for an onslaught of rage. But instead he saw a smile, as if his attacker respected him for his effective display of resistance.

Meanwhile, Gabrielle was still hesitating. She looked at Daniel and although he stubbornly refused to nod, it was clear that there was no way they could defy this man. They could shout for help, but who knew how he would react?

So Gabrielle picked up the glass-encased papyrus in two hands and extended it towards Goliath.

'No!' shouted the high priest, diving forward to grab the precious relic before the big man could take it.

Through the haze of pain that still engulfed him, Daniel realized in that split second that the high priest was putting his life on the line. Now was not the time to resist, but Daniel's reactions were not quick enough to restrain the high priest and halt his futile act of opposition. By the time Daniel was able to respond, Goliath had grabbed the high priest by his shirt and pulled him so that the priest was in front of him. With his free hand, Goliath produced a knife and with one swift move he slashed across the high priest's throat, like a ritual slaughterer in a kosher abattoir, cutting through the priest's carotid artery and jugular vein.

Gabrielle stifled a scream. Daniel looked on with horror.

The high priest had trusted them and they had sealed his fate. There was no other interpretation of the facts. Now Daniel suddenly realized that it was him the big man was interested in. That was why he had been on the same plane when Daniel went to Egypt, and he had been following him ever since. In other words – it finally dawned on Daniel – he had effectively led the man here. And this vile man had killed the high priest when he tried to protect his sacred scroll.

But the question that haunted him now was what should he do? Should he dive for the exit and try to raise the alarm? That would merely endanger Gabrielle. Should he throw himself at the man and give Gabrielle a chance to escape? What, indeed, was this man intending? Did he mean to eliminate all witnesses to his actions?

'Give it to me!' Goliath barked at Gabrielle.

This time she did not hesitate. She did as he had told her. The big man put the glass sheets containing the papyrus into the heavy-duty carrier bag he had with him. Daniel's eyes returned to the high priest whose life was slipping away before his eyes. He wanted to help him, but he knew that there was nothing he could do.

'What are you going to do?' asked Gabrielle.

'I spoke to Aryeh Tsedaka. He told me that there is another scroll. *The Book of the Wars of the Lord.*'

Daniel was about to ask why Rabbi Tsedaka would tell him that. Then he realized. And in that moment, he also understood that if the rabbi had been forced to disclose that information then he had probably also been forced to disclose where Daniel and Gabrielle were going. Further, if he had been forced to do that, then he would have wanted to warn them of the danger. He clearly hadn't done so, and that could only mean one thing: Aryeh Tsedaka was dead.

Daniel looked at the man no longer with fear but with

hate. This was an evil man motivated by some sort of religious fanaticism, the nature of which Daniel could barely comprehend.

'He told me that the scroll is in Petra . . .'

'But he said that the book is lost,' said Gabrielle nervously.

'He *thought* it was lost. But he doesn't know. It was entrusted to the Bedouin, and they are very good at preserving the past . . . and you two are going to help me get it.'

And just to make it clear how serious he was, he reached into his pocket and produced a semi-automatic pistol.

He put it back in his pocket as he directed Daniel and Gabrielle to the door. It was late afternoon and there were not many people about so there was little opportunity to resist or to call for help. Besides, it was obvious that the big man was utterly ruthless and ready to kill anyone who got in his way.

What was *not* clear was how strong his instinct for self-preservation was, but now did not seem like a good time to test it. So instead, Gabrielle and Daniel complied as he directed them out of the office. Any residual thoughts of resistance were cut short by the sight of the security guard lying dead by one of the lab machines. There was no sign of a wound, but they knew the killer's strength and his ability to kill with his bare hands.

They walked ahead of him and left the building via the side exit that led to the car park where Daniel and Gabrielle had left their rented car.

He dictated the seating arrangement. Daniel in front, driving. He and Gabrielle in the back, with Gabrielle behind Daniel. That way he could keep an eye on both of them . . . and maintain his threat against both of them.

Chapter 86

There was an eerie silence in the Conservation Department when Sarit gingerly pushed the door open and walked in. She didn't expect to find any work in progress at this time, but the silence was palpable. She looked around and saw no sign of anyone, although the fact that the department was unlocked suggested that there should at least be *some* human presence: a caretaker, a cleaner, a solitary member of staff doing some late-night work.

Where is everybody? Maybe they just popped out for a minute?

No. That didn't make sense.

Then she saw the security guard lying there, unmoving. His eyes were open, but as she studied them for a few seconds she noticed that they didn't blink. She realized that he was beyond help. She studied his body carefully, noting the empty side holster as she pondered her next move.

Sarit looked around to try to get her bearings. At the end of the corridor was a door. It seemed to be beckoning her to enter, but there was something that troubled her. The door was slightly ajar and she felt a strange aura coming from the room.

Stop it! she told herself.

She held her head up, forcing herself to overcome this strange sense of trepidation that had come over her, and walked towards it quickly. Then, instead of opening the door and boldly walking in as she normally would, she simply pushed the door open. It was as if she was waiting for an explosion, as if the door had been booby-trapped.

The room was quiet and eerily still. And lying on the floor, face down with his head turned towards the door, was a man in the traditional robes of the Samaritans. What caught her attention was the trail of blood flowing from his neck. She realized that his throat had been cut, and that he too was dead.

Despite her helplessness, a feeling of solidarity forced her to step forward into the room. Although she was not in fact Jewish, she remembered reading that according to Jewish law one should not leave a dying person, 'lest the soul leave the body bewildered'.

But all of these thoughts were cut short by a rustling sound behind her and a sharp intake of breath. For as she spun round, she found herself confronted by two Samaritan priests, the look of accusation burning in their eyes.

Chapter 87

'Do not give him any sign that you are under duress,' said Goliath. 'I can shoot her before they shoot me and I am not afraid to die.'

Daniel wondered if their abductor was really quite as mad as he sought to portray himself. Did he really have no instinct for self-preservation? There were such people in the world, but was he one of them? But remembering how Goliath had acted at the National Library in Jerusalem, he realized that the man's words were true. He had shown just how ruthless he was when he murdered the Samaritan priest.

So when they showed their passports to the Israeli border officials at the King Hussein Bridge, Daniel neither said nor did anything to alert them to his predicament. He would bide his time and hope for an opportunity. That time was not now.

He wondered idly if the border officials might pick up on the fact that Daniel was sitting alone at the front, while Gabrielle was at the back with the big man. The one thing that worried Daniel was the possibility of one of them being asked to step out of the car. However, the fact that they were from the West and the fact that they were leaving meant that they were not seen as a threat. Their faces were checked against their passports and the passports then stamped to show their exit. Then they were on their way to the Jordanian side, where the process took about the same time. They gave the purpose of their visit as 'to see Petra'.

Then they were through and on the open road.

'Well, that was painless, wasn't it?' said Goliath sarcastically.

Daniel forced himself to put his thoughts on hold as he drove. But every so often he glanced in the rear-view mirror to assure himself that Gabrielle was all right.

'When we get there, we'll buy one-day tickets,' said their kidnapper.

The drive to Petra along the desert road took about three hours and Daniel's mind was reeling, desperately trying to think of an opportunity to disarm their abductor and get away. Sitting in the front as he drove along this naked stretch of road with very little traffic, there was not much he could do.

When they arrived at the visitor centre, local Bedouin – mostly children – swarmed around their car, offering them local souvenirs. A snarl from Goliath chased most of them off and the remainder drifted away when they saw that these tourists were not interested.

They went into the centre and Daniel bought one-day tickets for all three of them, as Goliath had instructed him. He wondered if the tension in his face had caught the attention of any of the staff, but there was no sign in their eyes that it had.

'We wanted to ask you about guides,' said Goliath, keeping the gun concealed in his pocket.

'We have guides who offer tours in English as well as many other languages—' The woman behind the counter broke off in response to Goliath's raised palm.

'I have a rather unusual request. What we'd really like is someone who truly knows about the ancient history of Petra, including the period before the Nabateans.'

'Ah . . . okay. The man you want is Talal Ibrahim. He's a member of the Bedul community – a sheikh in fact.'

'Bedul?' Goliath echoed.

'A local Bedouin tribe.'

'Are they the ones who claimed to be descended from the ancient Israelites?'

The woman at the counter looked surprised. 'Oh, yes. They did claim that at one time. In fact the second President of Israel – Isaac ben-Zvi – even went as far as to claim that the Bedul had retained aspects of Israelite culture and language.'

Daniel smiled, remembering what Aryeh Tsedaka had told him about the Samaritan community in Holon.

'But that view isn't supported by serious historians,' the woman continued. 'There certainly isn't any *written* record to suggest it.'

'So they came . . . when?' asked Goliath. 'The time of the Muslim conquest? The seventh century AD?'

'Oh no, they pre-date the Islamic era, but probably not by all that much. Of course, their ancestors converted to Islam many centuries ago.'

'So when did they arrive in this area?'

'Well, their main claim is that they're descended from the Nabateans who built Petra.'

'Is there any possibility that we could persuade this Talal Ibrahim to give us a tour?' asked Goliath. 'We're only here for one day and—'

'Wait a minute – are you asking about Sheikh Ibrahim?' asked another woman behind the counter.

'Yes.'

'He is here today. He actually had a group booked for a tour, but their coach broke down and they had to cancel. I think he's still here. I can page him.'

Half an hour later they were walking along the *Bab as Siq* – sometimes called the 'outer *siq*' – a road bordered by slopes that ran by the side of Wadi Musa between the visitor centre and the entrance to the inner *siq* that most tourists took to get into Petra City.

'The inner *siq*,' Ibrahim explained, literally "the shaft", is a long, narrow passage through the red rock leading into the actual city of Petra. It was created not by man, but by nature and it stretches for two kilometres, bending and twisting this way and that along the way. It is barely three metres wide, sometimes less than that.'

Two things had struck Daniel within a few minutes of each other: the advanced age of the sheikh – it was hard to tell exactly how old he was – and the magnificent mountains and steep hills that surrounded them.

'I thought the rock was red,' said Daniel in his naivety.

'That's further in,' said Ibrahim. 'Out here it is white.'

The valley began to narrow.

'What's that?' asked Daniel, pointing to three square towers carved into the rock.

'In Arabic we call them *sahreej*, which means cistern. However, the name is misleading because they have nothing to do with channelling or storing water. Most English speakers call them *djinn* blocks, using the Arabic word for an evil spirit, which I believe you sometimes call a genie.'

'Were they carved by the Nabateans?' Daniel asked.

'So it is believed. This is a theory that they represent the Nabatean god Dushara. They are also believed to be tombs. And these are not the only ones. More than twenty of these *djinn* blocks have been found in Petra.'

A little further down, Sheikh Ibrahim stopped and pointed to a small entrance cut into the rock on the other side of the road from the *djinn* blocks.

'That is the entrance to the Snake Tomb.'

It was so unobtrusive that they could have gone right past it without noticing it. He walked in, followed by the others, who formed a nervous huddle just behind him.

'There are twelve graves here,' the sheikh began.

'Why is it called the Snake Tomb?' asked Daniel, thinking about Moses and the fiery snakes.

Sheikh Ibrahim switched on a torch and aimed it at the floor. He moved the torch and directed its beam on to the wall where a carved relief image of a pair of snakes attacking a dog or jackal was illuminated. Above it and to the left was a relief of a horse mounted by some indeterminate figure.

'Not many people know about this place. It isn't considered important, but I presumed that as you wanted someone with deeper knowledge than usual, you might like to see this. A little tomb that most tourists don't bother with.'

They went outside and drank some water to cool off.

'There is something I wanted to ask you,' Goliath said to the sheikh.

Daniel tensed up, wondering if Goliath was about to show his true colours and produce the gun. It would be risky; there were other people about. And no matter how ruthless Goliath was, it would do him no good to find himself surrounded by armed guards ready to shoot to kill before he had accomplished his goal. Moreover there was no reason to assume that Sheikh Ibrahim would yield to a threat.

In the event, Goliath kept his hand in his pocket.

'You see that man?' He nodded at Daniel.

'Yes,' said the sheikh, puzzled by the question.

'He is the world's foremost expert on ancient Semitic

languages, and he has deciphered the ancient script. He is so wise and so trusted, that the Samaritans have given him their most precious manuscript. Let me show you.'

He produced the glass sheets containing *The Book of the Straight* from the bag he was carrying with him.

'Well, go on, take a look,' said Goliath encouragingly.

The Bedul sheikh looked at the glass-encased papyrus and his eyes welled up with tears.

'They *gave* you this?'

'Only temporarily,' said Goliath. 'We will give it back to them, of course. But they gave it to us to show it to you, so you would see that they trust us . . . in the hope that you will trust us too.'

'T . . . trust you?' Ibrahim could barely trust his own voice. 'I assume you know what that is?'

'I think so.'

'It is *The Book of the Straight* written by Joshua the Hebrew prophet. You can tell this from the ancient script in which it is written.' With trembling hands, he gave it back to Goliath. 'If they let you have this in your hands – even for a minute – then they must trust you like a brother.'

'Yes,' agreed Goliath, putting it away. 'And that man over there . . .' he pointed to Daniel, 'has translated that scroll. He can translate *your* scroll too.'

'*My* scroll?'

'The scroll that is guarded by your people.'

'What scroll?'

'The sacred scroll that was entrusted to your people. The scroll that your ancestors have protected all these years. The scroll that was written by Moses himself. *The Book of the Wars of the Lord.*'

Daniel saw no fear in the sheikh's eyes, just a hint of lingering suspicion. He wanted to warn him, but dared not.

He hoped that he would say that he didn't know what the man was talking about, or alternatively claim that the ancient scroll was lost.

'And if *The Book of the Wars of the Lord* still exists?'

'Then . . .' again Goliath pointed to Daniel, 'that man can reveal the sacred truths that have remained hidden – even from your own ancestors – for over three thousand years.'

The sheikh leaned towards Goliath. Goliath had to move forward and crouch down to hear him. Ibrahim spoke, almost in a whisper.

'It is not a scroll.'

'Then what is it?'

The sheikh smiled, a bewitching smile, as if mocking the naivety of the big man. 'Very few have set eyes upon it.'

'And are you one of those few?'

'Only once, when my father handed over to me the task of guarding it.'

'Then let us see it,' said Goliath, feigning the pleading voice of a man with good intentions. 'And let my friend translate it.'

'All right. I will show it to you.'

Chapter 88

'I'm telling you – I didn't *do* it!' Sarit explained for the umpteenth time. 'Look at his neck! You can see his throat's been cut. Can you see any knife on me? Can you see any knife in the room?'

The two priests who had returned to find her standing there over the body, and the half dozen or so other people who had crowded into the room looked around. They could indeed see nothing resembling the type of weapon that had inflicted these wounds. But they *had* found her with blood on her clothes.

She knew that it was only a matter of time before the police got there, probably only a few minutes. But she saw the anger in the eyes of the younger priest, and she feared that she might have to resort to her *krav maga* fighting skills to defend herself. In fact, her fears were unfounded. He did not lift a finger against her.

'Look,' she said quietly, 'there is something I need to know. Did either of you see a very tall man outside?'

They shook their heads.

'I know that your high priest was here with two people to hear a translation of an ancient manuscript. Were you here when it happened?'

The two priests exchanged a glance. Finally the older one spoke.

'We were listening to the translation, but my young colleague found it a bit stressful so he had to go outside. I followed him to see if he was all right and we stayed outside for a while. When we came back we found you standing over the body.'

'But you didn't see the man and the woman leaving?'

'No.'

'And you didn't see a big man with them?'

Again they exchanged a glance. The younger priest shrugged.

'No.'

Now Sarit understood. She remembered the empty holster of the dead guard outside and that said it all. They were being taken somewhere under duress. But where? She also realized that time was of the essence. With the police on their way, the shit was about to hit the fan.

She took out her mobile phone and called a number. 'Hallo Dovi. I've got a bit of a problem.'

The Samaritan priests and the others who were congregating in the tiny space heard shouting from the other end of the phone, while Sarit tried to answer calmly. Meanwhile, the university's own security guards had entered and were trying to keep people back.

The last words those who were in close proximity heard the man at the other end of the phone say were: '*Ahni baderech.*' Those of them who spoke Hebrew knew that this meant: *I'm on my way.*

It was evident when Sarit put the phone away that she was far from relieved. If anything, she looked more tense now than she did before the phone call.

She looked down at the body once again, not really knowing why. Was it a sense of regret, knowing that she hadn't got here soon enough? Was it a sense of guilt that she hadn't confided her suspicions to Dov as to where the person

332

who killed Aryeh Tsedaka was likely to be going? Or was it a sense of anger at the waste of life and the obvious viciousness of the killer?

She was not supposed to let her emotions get the better of her. In her line of work one had to develop a stomach for blood and suppress one's emotions if there was even the slightest chance that they would interfere with the job. But still she looked at the body, lying there face down in that pool of blood. She noticed the crooked finger of his extended right arm that reached beyond the pool of blood. And she noticed something else. The finger had blood on it – just the end of the finger, above the last articulation – as if he had been writing with his own blood.

She knew that she shouldn't interfere with the body until it had been pronounced dead by the coroner and then photographed in situ by the investigating officers. She also knew that to approach the body and touch it would contaminate the crime scene, making it harder for the forensic scientists to obtain useful evidence and making it easier for any defence lawyer to undermine that evidence. But right now the immediate priority was not preserving evidence: it was preserving something infinitely more valuable.

She went up to the body, clambered over to the other side and crouched down, peering at it, as if trying to see what was underneath it. But she couldn't see clearly and she knew now that time was of the essence. So she inserted both her hands on the underside of the body, palms upward. Then she lifted one side of the body, twisted her hands round and gave an almighty push, rolling the body over on to its back.

Some members of the crowd gasped in surprise but Sarit had no interest in their reaction, nor indeed any in the state of the body. She was only interested in what was *underneath* the body, and that appeared to be a very specific bloodstain on the floor – too purposeful to be random or accidental. It was an arrow drawn in blood. And the arrow pointed to four Hebrew letters.

She realized now what had happened. In his dying seconds, even as the life drained out of him, he had drawn the arrow and written the letters in the only thing he had available: his own blood. But then, in order to ensure that it wasn't drowned out by the blood that was gushing from his throat, he covered it with his body and was, in the words of the Bible, gathered to his people.

But it was the letters that interested Sarit now. There were just four of them, and interestingly they were in Hebrew – possibly an indication of who they were intended for. They were the letters *Pay, Tet, Reish* and *Hay*. The equivalent of the consonants P-T-R-H.

There was no doubt in her mind what this man was trying to say in his final message. The arrow was an indication that someone was going somewhere. And the letters stood for the name Petra.

Chapter 89

'There's something I don't understand,' said Goliath as they clambered up the steep slopes and over craggy rocks on their long trek. 'The Nabateans were in the sixth century BC, but the ancient Israelites were a lot older than that. I think they entered the land of Canaan in something like the *twelfth* century BC. So why would *The Book of the Wars of the Lord* be here?'

Sheikh Ibrahim smiled. 'We're not actually going to the *city* of Petra. That's why we didn't go through the *siq*. You have to understand that people lived in this area as nomads as far back as 7,000 years before Jesus. The first people to actually settle here did so around 3,200 years ago.'

'That was just after the Amarna period,' Gabrielle proffered. 'Although I think this place is even mentioned in the Amarna letters.'

'Exactly,' said Ibrahim. 'And this is reflected in some of the names. For example, that is Pharaoh's Column.'

He pointed to a cylindrical column of red rock in the distance. They looked briefly, but stopping and admiring the scenery was almost as tiring as walking, not physically but psychologically, because it kept them further from their goal. So they trudged on, not fully appreciating the explosion of colour – running the entire gamut of the rainbow – that was written across the landscape in solid rock.

'We are actually taking the old caravan route that Bedouin and other nomads used to take between Sinai, the Araba valley and Petra itself. There are many shrines and tombs in this area which may be associated with the Israelites. Stations 19 to 26 of the Exodus are in or around the area of Petra. This is also reflected in some of the names of the places here. For example, Wadi Musa means the Valley of Moses. The wind that roars through the valley is sometimes called Aaron's Trumpet. And of course there is also Jebel Haroun, which means Mount Aaron, where the brother of Moses is believed to be buried.'

'Is that where we're going?' asked Goliath.

'No, but where we are going is on the road to Aaron's tomb. It is called the Snake Monument.'

'But I thought we'd already seen . . .' The big man trailed off in a state of confusion.

'No, that was the Snake *Tomb*. What you're going to see soon is the Snake *Monument* – something very different.'

As they carried on in silence, Daniel wondered what was going on in Gabrielle's mind. Outwardly she was calm, but he was worried about her. Their abductor had made it clear that she would be the first one to be killed if there was any show of resistance. But would he let them live if they offered *no* resistance? Could he afford to? He had already shown his true colours; the man was ruthless. Was doing nothing really an option?

As they gained altitude, the colours converged on a kind of pale yellow.

'There it is!'

From the mountain ridge on which they stood, they found themselves looking across a gulch at a massive square-cut rock upon which stood the lower extremities of a stone snake.

Gabrielle wanted to ask a question, but she found herself struggling to find her voice. 'That's not . . . a natural feature?'

'Of course not,' said Sheikh Ibrahim. 'The base has been cut by the hand of man into a shape resembling a cube. The snake too was carved out of the stone.'

'It doesn't look much like a snake,' said Goliath.

'That is all that remains. It is believed that it was once a full snake, but it was worn away by the passage of time. Come this way.'

Without waiting for anyone to respond, Ibrahim began scrambling along the rock, using his hands as well as his feet to traverse the difficult terrain. Daniel followed automatically, but Gabrielle only went when Goliath gave her a shove. He followed close behind her.

They arrived at a cave which Ibrahim had already entered.

'Come on,' said the sheikh. 'There's nothing to be scared of.'

Daniel knew that in fact there was a great deal to be scared of. Once Goliath got his hands on *The Book of the Wars of the Lord*, then what would he do? At that point he would have no further use for any of them. Would he kill them? Would he simply destroy both documents? Or would he take them and let them live?

The more he thought about it, the more Daniel realized how perilous their situation was. He wished he had offered some resistance before now. The trouble was it was so much easier being an armchair hero than a real one.

Daniel entered, his trepidation notwithstanding. Gabrielle and Goliath followed. The cave in fact was quite small, more like an average-size living room. Relying on nothing but the light entering from outside, Ibrahim went to a wall of the cave and removed a number of stones to reveal a crevice in the rock. He reached deep inside and seconds later his arm emerged holding something the size of four bricks, two on

337

top of the other two, wrapped in a fragile, almost decaying white linen.

'This isn't the only thing that was found here,' Ibrahim said in a conspiratorial tone. 'A few years ago, they found some old bones.'

'Bones?' asked Gabrielle.

'They had been buried here but an animal had apparently dug them out – or partially dug them out.'

'And what were they? Animal bones?'

'No . . . human.'

'What, like . . . recent? I mean . . . new bones?'

'No . . . they said they were old. Very old.'

'And what happened to them?' asked Goliath.

'They were taken to the University of Jordan to do some tests on them.'

'And?' asked Gabrielle.

'That was the funny thing. I asked the professor from the university afterwards and he didn't want to talk about it. He told me not to ask about it ever again. I think he was afraid of something.'

'Who was he?' asked Gabrielle.

'The professor? His name was Fikri – Hakim Fikri.'

He put the linen-wrapped package on the floor of the cave and carefully unwrapped it, putting the linen to one side, to reveal a set of tablets made from the red clay of Petra.

'I think I'll take that,' said Goliath, reaching out and grabbing the linen shroud in which the tablets had been wrapped.

'What are you doing?' Ibrahim demanded indignantly.

'I'm going to make the evil usurpers drink the water of death!'

'You cannot!' said the Bedouin.

Daniel didn't understand what Goliath was doing. He had left the tablets and grabbed a torn and ragged piece of cloth.

It made no sense. But it made even less sense that Ibrahim was challenging a man nearly twice his size to stop him. He tried to warn the sheikh not to resist, but before he could get more than the first syllable out of his mouth, Goliath had produced the semi-automatic and shot the sheikh, once, twice, three times, a vicious smile on his face, as if he took pleasure in the excess of force.

I should have acted before, Daniel's mind screamed, cursing himself for his previous indecisiveness. There was no reasoning with this man. He was mentally deranged beyond all logic. But regrets served no purpose. If Daniel was to redeem himself, the time to act was now when his and Gabrielle's life hung in the balance.

He hurled himself at Goliath, clamping his left arm around him in a headlock and hooking his left leg around Goliath's right in an effort to wrestle him to the ground. He lacked the strength to bring down the bigger man, but as they twisted this way and that, Goliath's mobile phone fell from his pocket with a sharp, staccato thud.

Goliath swung the semi-automatic towards Daniel and Daniel intercepted it with his right hand, clamping his fingers across the top and his thumb at the base of the slider that reloads the chamber. The gun discharged a round that rico-cheted off the walls of the cave producing a moment of panic before the bullet found a resting place somewhere in the sand outside. But the vice-like grip of Daniel's hand and the desperate pressure of his thumb prevented the slider from coming back to discharge the empty cartridge and reload the chamber.

With a violent twisting motion, Goliath managed to wrench the gun free from Daniel's grip; but when he swung it back, aimed at Daniel's head and squeezed the trigger again, he was greeted by a soft click as the firing pin landed not on a live round but on the empty cartridge of the previous round.

Daniel and Gabrielle were not safe yet. Their deranged enemy could still pull the slider back manually with his right hand. But Goliath wasn't thinking rationally and he assumed that the gun had jammed or malfunctioned in some way. Besides, he was ultimately reliant on superior strength and brute force to prevail. To this end, he dropped the gun and delivered a vicious punch to Daniel's face, sending him reeling to the ground, landing next to Gabrielle.

However, before Daniel could think which way to roll or jump, Gabrielle had scooped up a large rock and smashed it into Goliath's face. A cry of pain rang out from the big man's throat as he reached out to grab Gabrielle's wrist. But she pulled back as quickly as she had closed in, retaining possession of the rock. He lunged at her trying to grab the improvised weapon, but Daniel stuck his leg out tripping Goliath so that he landed on the rock floor of the cave with a terrific thud.

Without a trace of hesitation, Gabrielle rolled clear. Goliath, for his part, pushed himself up on to his hands and then stood up, turning around in the process.

For a second, Daniel and Goliath eyeballed each other and Daniel wondered if he was dead. Then Goliath smiled at him, turned abruptly and left the cave, still holding the linen shroud.

Daniel watched with puzzlement as the giant disappeared from view. Meanwhile, Gabrielle rolled back into a seated posture gasping for breath.

'What the hell was that all about?' she asked.

'I don't know. I thought he wanted the *Book of the Wars of the Lord*, not some stupid piece of cloth.'

He looked round at the supine form of the Bedul sheikh, but there was no trace of movement or even breathing.

'We need to get out of here,' said Gabrielle, helping Daniel to his feet.

'What are you talking about? We need to report this.'

'And we will, only not now.'

'What do you mean?'

'We don't know how the authorities will react. Two people from Israel and a dead Bedouin sheikh. What do *you* think they'll make of it?'

'But we can't just run – not again.'

'We don't have any choice. Look, at least let's get out of here for now. That'll give us time to think. We have to get back to the visitor centre anyway, and the only way back is on foot. It's too late for him. Let's get back there and then decide.'

Daniel nodded reluctantly. As they were about to leave the cave, he noticed that Gabrielle had gone over to where Sheikh Ibrahim had put the red clay tablets.

He saw immediately the writing on the first tablet. It was Proto-Sinaitic.

'*The Book of the Wars of the Lord*,' said Daniel.

Gabrielle nodded and carefully put them into Goliath's carrier bag.

'This is what *we* came for,' she said.

'I'm not sure if that's the most important thing right now,' said Daniel.

'Why do you say that?' asked Gabrielle.

'That man killed your uncle and several other people and tried to kill us for something. If it *wasn't* for those tablets or the *Book of the Straight*, then what on earth *was* it for?'

Chapter 90

'What the hell do you think you were playing at?'

Dov Shamir had flown in from Herzliya by helicopter and asked Sarit to join him there so that he could talk with her in private. It wasn't every day that someone was murdered in the National Library or that a helicopter landed in the grounds of the Hebrew University, so the whole scene had already attracted a certain amount of attention.

When he had first arrived in the lab, he had found Sarit looking remarkably calm considering what she had just been through. She had been about to throw her arms around him, but he gave her a look that warned her off; he didn't want their romance becoming any more public than it was already. There was a certain amount of whispering about it in Mossad – that was in the nature of things where female officers were concerned and even non-existent romances assumed the aura of reality in the tight-knit world of intelligence – but he wanted to keep a lid on it as far as possible.

'I'd like to speak to her alone,' Dov had said to the senior police officer at the scene, flashing his ID in time with the request.

'Of course.' The officer signalled the other police there to let them leave unhindered. Only once they were inside the

342

helicopter, where they had complete privacy, did Dov give vent to the full force of his anger . . . and his concern.

'After you told me about Aryeh Tsedaka, I figured he'd come here.'

'*Who*, Sarit? Figured *who'd* come here?'

'Whoever killed Tsedaka.'

'And I told you that was the business of the General Security Services, not Mossad.'

'Not any more it isn't. They've gone to Petra.'

'What are you talking about?'

She explained about the body and the message that the high priest had left for them, written in his own blood.

'That still doesn't explain why you came here in the first place.'

'I was worried that we were going to lose them. I guess I feel bad because I cocked up in Egypt. I wanted to make up for it.'

'And it didn't occur to you that stepping on the toes of GSS out here might cock it up even more?'

'If I'd seen any sign of GSS I'd've backed off, but I didn't. Look, it seems to me that GSS aren't exactly on top of the situation.'

He didn't like the way she had turned the tables on him like that. But what she had said was true.

'The fact is, now that we've got ourselves involved, it gives them leverage for blaming us.'

'Is that what this is about, Dovi? Inter-service fucking rivalry?'

'It's politics, Sarit. Something you have the luxury of not having to deal with!'

'All right. Look, I'm sorry I jumped the gun and didn't tell you what I was doing. But the fact is it's a whole different ball game now. He's gone to Petra and he's got two hostages with him.'

'I know that. I'll get on to our contacts in Amman.'

'Why don't you send me out there? To work with them?'

'Look, Sarit, I'm not going to send you to Jordan, okay? That's final! We've got a liaison office out there to deal with that. I can't send unauthorized officers without clearance from the Jordanian government – not after some of the other cock-ups we've had in that area.'

'So get authorization. Tell them it's an emergency – for them as well as us.'

'I can't do that, Sarit,' he said, his tone almost apologetic.

'Why not?'

'Because you're suspended.'

'Suspended?'

'Yes, suspended. I don't even want to see you in the office! God knows how I'm going to clear up this mess.'

He looked at her, wondering what her reaction was going to be.

'So what am I supposed to do? Just sit around doing nothing?'

'You're due for some leave anyway. Why don't you spend some time at that kibbutz in the Galilee? The one where they have that great fish restaurant you're always going on about?'

'I can't just sit around. I need some excitement.'

'I'd've thought you've had enough of that for a lifetime.'

'I guess it's like what we call the hair of the dog. The only cure for too much excitement is *more* excitement.'

'Then have an adventure holiday. Do some paragliding in Tel Aviv.'

'It's too humid on the Med.'

'Well, stay in Jerusalem.'

'I just said I wanted some excitement and you want me to sit out my vacation in the most boring city in Israel?'

344

He looked at her with a brotherly smile. 'Are you trying to be difficult?'

'Not really. I'm just trying to say I feel like doing some scuba diving in Eilat.'

'Well, at least we've found something to occupy your time,' he said with a sense of relief.

'Not to mention all the excitement of driving through Palestinian territory and army checkpoints.'

Something in the way she said this alerted Dov.

'You know . . . I'm not sure if I can trust you.'

'What – to go to Eilat? You can if you fly me there in that chopper.'

'I think I might just do that.'

An hour and a quarter later, the helicopter landed in Eilat at the north end of the airport. Dov saw Sarit into a waiting taxi which would take her to the hotels that were all grouped around the lagoon and the beach. Then he had the helicopter refuelled and took off for Herzliya.

From inside the taxi, Sarit watched the helicopter vanish into the distance before jumping out, apologizing to the taxi driver and dashing to the main building to hire a car with four-wheel drive.

Then she drove to the Yitzhak Rabin terminal on the Israeli side of the border, presented her Irish passport and passed through the Wadi Araba, crossing into Jordan as Siobhan Stewart.

From there, she proceeded north to Petra.

Chapter 91

'We shouldn't be doing this,' said Daniel, still in a daze from what had happened as he sat in the driver's seat of the car outside the visitor centre.

'Doing what?'

'Running away. If they find Sheikh Ibrahim's body back in that cave—'

'They *won't* find it. At least not for a long time.'

'We can't just leave him there. His family has a right to know . . . to give him a decent burial—'

'Okay, but we need to buy some time.'

'For what? At the moment we're just wasting time.'

His heart was still pounding, after both the events at the cave and the long trek back.

'Well, I for one would like to know what's in *The Book of the Wars of the Lord.*'

And with that she took the tablets out of the carrier bag and put them on the space between the seats.

'We can hardly go through it here.'

'Why not?'

'Well, how long is it?'

'There are five tablets.'

She picked up the first of them.

'What's the hurry?' he asked irritably. 'Why don't we just take it back to Israel?'

'And what if we're searched and they catch us trying to smuggle historical artefacts out of Jordan? I don't know how this is going to pan out, but if we're arrested now, there's a chance that we may never see these tablets again. Now I don't know about you, but if these tablets were written by the hand of the biblical Moses, then I want to see them translated.'

'Then maybe we should just turn it in to the authorities here.'

'And never see it again? Remember what Ibrahim said about those bones. They took them to the university and wouldn't talk about them after that.'

Daniel realized she was right. This was a piece of ancient history they held in their hands. And there was no guarantee that they would get another chance like this.

'Okay.'

Gabrielle breathed a sigh of relief as Daniel put a large, illustrated guidebook on his lap and then placed the first of the tablets on it. He raised one knee to tilt the tablet slightly to catch the light better and then studied the script.

'Can you read it?' she asked.

'Barely.'

I was fed milk from the breast of an Israeli woman and her son was like a brother to me, more than my brother Sethi, the son of Mernepteh, my King, my Lord whom I served with loyalty despite his wickedness to Israel.

'Wait a minute,' he said, breaking off. 'Can you work out from that who the author might have been?'

Gabrielle gave this a few moments' thought.

'Let's see. He refers to Sethi as his *brother*. Now there were a number of people called Sethi,' she said ponderously. 'But he *also* calls him the son of Mernepteh! That's the one who wrote the famous Mernepteh stele that we saw at the museum back in Cairo. So that would make his son Sethi the *Second*. And that means that this was written by someone called Amenmesse who may or may not have been Sethi the Second's brother but who was certainly involved in a power struggle with Sethi the Second.'

'Is there any evidence that this Amenmesse had a Jewish wet nurse?'

'There's no record of it. But then again, not much is known about him at all. It certainly wouldn't have been impossible by any means.'

'I was just thinking about the story of Moses,' said Daniel. 'After his mother hid him in the bulrushes and he was found by Pharaoh's daughter, his real mother came forward and offered to be his wet nurse.'

'Then this reference to her other son being more like a brother than Sethi . . .' She trailed off.

'Could be a reference to Moses' brother Aaron.'

'Go on,' she prompted.

The wife of Mernepteh bore a son without the spirit of life and he asked the priests of Amun what sin he had committed that he be punished in this way and they told him that it was not his sin but that of Shifra the woman who brought the baby out of its mother for she was an Israelite woman and she worshipped false gods. And he had her put to death and he decreed that for one year all the male children of Israel shall be put to death.

They looked at each other, astonished.

'The slaying of the firstborn son,' she said. 'Just like on that papyrus that was found at the same site as the Mernepteh stele.'

'Not quite,' said Daniel. 'The slaying of the firstborn *Egyptian* son was the last of the ten plagues. However, this refers to Pharaoh's decree that all the male *Israelite* babies be put to death – hence the incident with Moses being hidden in the bulrushes. But of course there is an approximate symmetry between the two events and also, I guess, a certain poetic irony.'

'So it could be that this one event was the *source material* for both those biblical legends?'

'I suppose. But does this fit the *Egyptian* record?'

'Only that papyrus Mansoor showed us, which was written in Proto-Sinaitic. There's nothing specific in the annals to confirm it, but that doesn't rule it out. If you take the line in the Mernepteh stele about "Israel is laid waste, nought of seed" and combine it with the papyrus and now this, then I suppose it counts as a record. How does it continue?'

Daniel read aloud.

An Israelite man had been adopted into the household of the chief of works in the Place of Truth and he was brought before the judge for punishment and the judge decreed that he shall be beaten. And so he begged to put his plea to me. And I heard his plea and I remembered the pain that my brother had inflicted upon his people. So I spared him and I dismissed the judge.

'Papyrus Salt 124!' Gabrielle blurted out, letting the excitement get the better of her academic reserve.

'What's that?'

'Remember what we talked about when you were released on bail after my visit to the British Museum? The Place of Truth is the village where the artisans and craftsmen who worked in the necropolis lived.'

'I remember, but what has—'

'Wait! Let me explain. Henry Salt was a contemporary of William John Bankes. He was one of that whole crowd of Victorian British explorers and adventurers from the great age of Empire who travelled to Egypt and the Middle East in search of the treasures of the ancient world. He was a wealthy man and during the course of his travels he acquired a papyrus now known as Papyrus Salt 124. It was one of a number of papyri that he donated to the British Museum.'

'And what made you think of that just now?'

'Because that's what this is about! It refers to the same events.'

'How do you mean?'

'The papyrus consists of a complaint by the brother of someone called Neferhotep. Neferhotep was the works foreman for the necropolis. And the complaint is mainly against someone called Paneb, but also partly against someone called Mossy or Mussi.'

'And who were they?'

'Paneb was Neferhotep's adopted son. Mossy or Mussi was someone in a position of authority who took Paneb's side when the case against Paneb was brought to judgement. And Mossy or Mussi also appears to be the author of this text.'

'But I thought you said that the man who wrote this text was called Amenmesse.'

'Yes, but there has long been speculation and debate as to whether Amenmesse and Mossy were one and the same. And the problem is compounded by the almost biblical use of ambiguous pronouns.'

'So wait a minute – what exactly happened? I mean, who judged who and what was the outcome?'

'That's what I'm trying to explain. The complaint makes all manner of accusations, some of them quite possibly exaggerated. It starts off by saying that Neferhotep, the complainant's brother, was killed by some unspecified "enemy" – a term usually reserved for a traitor to Egypt. Then it says that Paneb usurped his role as works foreman by bribing a corrupt vizier with five of the late Neferhotep's own slaves. But the complaint also goes on to list all manner of other crimes allegedly committed by Paneb *during Neferhotep's lifetime*, including stealing from the necropolis, threatening to kill Neferhotep, beating up nine guards that Neferhotep set to guard him by night and various rapes of both women and boys.'

Daniel was puzzled by this account. 'So why didn't Neferhotep bring the complaint himself? Before he was killed by this "enemy", I mean?'

'Well, first of all, like I said, there may be an element of exaggeration in the complaint itself. But secondly, Neferhotep *did* bring a complaint against Paneb to the vizier – not the corrupt vizier, but his honest predecessor. According to the papyrus, the vizier who heard the complaint *upheld* the claims and ordered that Paneb be flogged for his crimes. But Paneb then appealed the ruling and the appeal came before this Mossy or Mussi.'

'And who was this Mossy or Mussi?' asked Daniel.

'We don't know who he was. But one thing we can be sure of is that he must have been someone of high enough rank to veto the local vizier. One suggestion is that it was Amenmesse who ruled part of Egypt during his power struggle with Sethi the Second. Another is that it was someone called Messuwy, who had previously been the pharaoh's viceroy in Nubia. Yet another theory is that they were one and the same – although there is some vigorous debate about this.'

'Well, from what you've said, Gaby, this text suggests that it was Amenmesse.'

'Yes, but the name Mossy sounds like Messuwy. So taken as a whole it could also be interpreted as meaning that they *were* one and the same. Anyway, go on!'

Daniel turned to the second tablet, which lay between

them on top of the remaining two. He switched on the car light to illuminate it better and continued reading.

When my brother Sethi heard of this he was angry with me and wanted to kill me. So I fled to a place nearby where I came face to face with the one true God, whose face cannot be seen. He appeared to me in fire on this sacred ground and revealed his true name to me and it was Jehovah. And he commanded me to end the cruelty against Israel. So awed was I by this wondrous place that I engraved words in the writing style of Israel upon the stones nearby.

'Wadi el-hol!' said Gabrielle.

The name sounded familiar to Daniel. 'The place where they found an early sample of the ancient script?'

'Yes! Remember . . . it's only twenty miles from the workers' village. He must have run away when he realized that the pharaoh was after him.'

Suddenly Daniel found himself gripped by the excitement of a profound realization. 'Then this phrase "appeared to me in fire" must be a reference to the burning bush . . . the burning bush which *Moses* saw after he ran away from . . .'

'What?' asked Gabrielle.

'After he *killed the Egyptian taskmaster who was beating an Israelite slave!*'

'Holy shit!' said Gabrielle. 'It really happened . . . maybe not quite the way the Bible described it, but it really happened.'

There were tears in Daniel's eyes.

'And Mossy must have been . . .'

'Moses,' Gabrielle muttered, barely able to raise her voice above a whisper.

Chapter 92

'Excuse me, I know this is going to sound awfully silly, but I was looking for some friends of mine. I was supposed to meet them here, but I got a bit delayed.'

Sarit was talking to a woman behind the counter at the Petra visitor centre.

'We get so many people passing through here.'

She had been about to tell the woman the names of her 'friends' – but the initial response made it clear that this would serve no useful purpose.

'One of them is quite tall.' She made a gesture with a raised arm and right-angled hand to indicate height.

'Oh, wait a minute, yes, I remember them. They went with Sheikh Ibrahim.'

'Sheikh Ibrahim?'

'Yes. They wanted a special tour with someone who really knows the history.'

'You mean like a private tour?'

'Yes.'

'Well, do you know where they went?'

'Not really. I mean, knowing Sheikh Ibrahim it'll be well off the beaten track.'

'But you don't know where.'

'I'm afraid not. But I can give you his mobile phone number.'

'Oh, er . . . thank you.'

She hadn't expected that. Less than a minute later she was outside trying to get a signal. She had to move a few yards away from the building, but eventually she got one. She called the number. It rang for such a long time that she expected it to cut out and transfer to voicemail. But eventually a man answered.

'Hallo.'

The voice sounded rasping, like he was in some place where he couldn't speak freely, like a church or a library.

'Sheikh Ibrahim?'

'Who is this?'

'My name is Siobhan. You don't know me but I'm—'

'Help me,' the voice croaked.

Sarit froze. The pain in the voice sounded real.

'Help me,' the voice said again, in a muted rasp. It sounded like he was struggling to speak.

'Who is this?'

'Ib . . . Ibrahim.'

'Where are you?'

'Snake Monument.'

She tried to ask him more questions, but was greeted by silence. She realized that she would have to go there, with or without a guide.

Chapter 93

Daniel had recovered his composure and was reading out loud.

I returned to the city and claimed the throne of Egypt and fought against my brother Sethi. And the Jehovah-ites helped me against the might of Egypt.

'Jehovah-ites?' Gabrielle repeated.

'It says *Yahowa da'im*. That could be translated as the ones who knew Jehovah. But it could also be *Yehudim*: the Judah-ites, which in English is translated as *Jews*.'

'What else does it say?'

He carried on translating.

But my brother's army was too strong and so we fled into the desert: Israel and the Jehovah-ites.

'So you've got two peoples joining forces: the Jehovah-ites or Judah-ites . . . *and* Israel.'

'That's what it appears to be saying.'

And we celebrated our freedom like the sed of Pharaoh.

He broke off. 'I don't know if I pronounced that right.'

'You did,' said Gabrielle. 'The *sed* festival was a great feast that the pharaohs had to celebrate their thirtieth anniversary – those that *had* such an anniversary, that is. Then they had other *sed* festivals every three or four years thereafter. Ramesses the Second, who ruled for sixty-six years, had fourteen *sed* festivals.'

'And what were they? I mean, how did they celebrate?'

'The *sed* festivals were essentially great banquets for the royal court with sumptuous food and singing by choirs consisting of the royal wives. They also had singers from the temples and performing acrobats and the whole thing was officiated over by the daughters of Asian princes whose main job was to pour drinks for the pharaoh four times into his royal goblet . . . Daniel?'

He realized that the look on his face had arrested her exposition midstream. 'Say that again.'

'I said, the festival of *sed* was a—'

'No, the bit about the drinks.'

She blinked, uncertain of what he was getting at. 'They were poured by Asian princesses who—'

'No, I mean how many times?'

'What – how many times did they pour the drinks? Four, according to the descriptions in the ancient texts.'

'*Four* drinks.'

'Yes,' Gabrielle replied, still unsure of what Daniel was getting at.

'And it's called the festival of *sed*?'

'*Yes!* Look, what's all this about? What's so special about four drinks? As opposed to three . . . or any other number.'

'The Jews celebrate the Exodus at Passover—'

'Yes, I know that!'

'No, what I mean is that Passover starts with a festive

356

family dinner accompanied by a religious service at the dining table called a *seider*. That means *order*, in both biblical and modern Hebrew, because things have to be done in a particular order.'

'Mm . . . I never thought of that.'

'But there's more. It's a tradition at the *seider* service that we drink *four glasses or cups of wine!*'

'Good God!'

'*That's* what I was getting at. Specifically *four!*'

'And you think that this *seider* service could originate with the festival of *sed* that the Egyptian kings used to celebrate?'

'That's what I'm beginning to think.'

Gabrielle was unable to contain her curiosity. 'Does it say any more?'

'I was translating from the bottom of the second tablet.'

'Then let's go on to the next one.'

The Jehovah-ites were a warrior people and did not wish to stay outside Canaan as we did. So they entered Canaan in battle with their leader Judah.

'Did the Israelites have a leader called Judah at the time?' asked Gabrielle.

Daniel's eyes lit up. 'No, but there was a *tribe* called Judah! And for much of history Judah was a separate kingdom from Israel. And of course Judah can also mean the One Who Knew Jehovah.'

'That would explain the fragmented history of your people,' she said with a smile.

'Absolutely. It explains quite a lot of things such as the varying linguistic styles of the early parts of the Bible and some of the apparent contradictions . . .'

Again his train of thought had been arrested. This time by the words that he had just read and translated in his mind.

'Daniel?'

But the people complained against me and against Jehovah because there was no water. And so I built an idol to the Snake God that was the god of the place where we settled, to appease its anger and we prayed to it for food. But Jehovah was jealous and he sent a plague against the people. And we were afflicted with boils on our skin that looked like fiery snakes. And the people came to me and begged me to take the snakes away. But I knew that the snakes on our flesh were a punishment from Jehovah so I told the people to destroy the snake idol and repent to Jehovah . . .

He couldn't continue.

'So that's what the Snake Monument was,' said Gabrielle.

'It's mentioned in the Bible, in the book of Numbers, albeit in somewhat different form – just before the reference to *The Book of the Wars of the Lord* in fact. Remember what I told you about the fiery serpents and Moses putting a snake on a pole so that when they looked up at it, they were cured.'

'But that stone base was hardly what you could call a pole.'

'I know,' Daniel replied. 'But *pole* is just a modern translation. It could be a pedestal or base. Aside from that, in order for the Israelites to see it, it must have been something *big*. A small serpent on a pole would hardly be visible to such a numerous band of people. But a huge stone monument on a huge base is something else.'

'But didn't you say it was a bronze or copper snake? Not a stone one.'

'Yes, but that was just other people's interpretation. Later parts of the Bible describe how the bronze snake head of Moses' staff was used to burn incense in the temple – until it was destroyed by one of the kings of Israel. He said it was being used for idolatry. He called it the Nehustan, which is a corruption of the Hebrew for snake.'

'Let's go on with the translation,' Gabrielle suggested.

It was Jehovah's will that we leave the accursed place and go into Canaan as the Jehovah-ites had done. So I sent men to spy out the land and they returned and one of them whose name was Caleb told me that it is the will of Jehovah that we enter the land of Canaan and fight for its holy soil and its fruits and its trees. But the other spies said that the men of Canaan are giants and we are like grasshoppers in their eyes.

'What about Joshua?'

Daniel's eyes widened.

'Oh, come on now, Danny, I may not be a Bible scholar like you, but I *know* the story of the twelve spies that Moses sent to spy out the land. Ten came back with negative reports but Joshua and Caleb said it was a land flowing with milk and honey and they could beat the natives and conquer the land.'

'Well, in this narrative there's no Joshua, just Caleb. Oh, hold on . . . wait a minute . . .'

'Yes?' she said, desperate to know.

'This next bit . . .'

'What?'

The man at my right hand Joshua said to me that Caleb was a righteous man. But I am old and I know that I cannot lead the people in battle. And when I told Joshua that he must lead the people, he said that he did not wish to leave my side. He said that if I was too weak to lead the people in battle, then they would stay here with me. But now I too am stricken by the plague and I know I will soon see God face to face. So I told him to leave this place and lead the people into the land of Canaan.

He looked up at Gabrielle, unable to continue. It was Gabrielle who spoke. 'The plague?'

'I know.' His tone was solemn.

'Does that mean . . .'

'You remember what Sheikh Ibrahim said about those bones in the cave?'

'Yes.'

'How the bones were taken to the University of Jordan and then they gave Ibrahim the silent treatment when he asked about the results?'

'Yes,' said Gabrielle, realizing where this was heading.

'I think we have to go to Amman. We need to talk to that professor.'

Chapter 94

Finding the Snake Monument and the path leading to it was easy enough using the map that they had provided at the visitor centre. But finding the specific cave was another matter. They had suggested she take a guide, especially as she didn't have a travelling companion. But Sarit knew that the danger of taking trails without guides was somewhat exaggerated and she couldn't afford to have anyone else around right now. She had a problem to deal with.

Fortunately there was no one else around, no local Bedul families with screaming kids, and no one making any noise that might prevent her fine-tuned ear from finding what she was looking for.

'Sheikh Ibrahim?' she called out tentatively. 'Sheikh Ibrahim!'

She heard her own voice echoing back to her; but no response, even as she strained her ear to detect the slightest sound. She trudged on a bit more.

'Sheikh Ibrahim!' she shouted a little louder than before. She didn't want to alert others, but she had to find him.

A faint trace of a voice rippled towards her from the distance, but it was hard to gauge its location.

'Where are you?' she called out, plugging one ear with her finger and straining to hear.

'Over here.' The voice was still weak, but at least she

could determine its direction. It appeared to be coming from a ridge above her and to the left. She made her way to it and as she got nearer, she could make out the entrance to a cave.

'Sheikh Ibrahim,' she repeated.

'In here.'

The weak voice confirmed that she was in the right location. Rather than venturing directly into the lion's den, she peered in to assess the situation. It was hard to see, because her pupils were contracted against the bright light outside the cave. Eventually they adjusted sufficiently to make out some semblance of what was inside.

And what she saw was a bloody mess.

On the far side of the cave a man lay covered in blood. That, she realized, was Sheikh Ibrahim. She approached him cautiously.

'What happened?'

'He shot me.' The voice was still weak. This was no act. The man was clinging on to life by a precarious thread.

'*Who* shot you?'

'The big man.'

'What happened to the others?' she asked. 'The other man and the woman? Did he take them with him?'

'No.'

She was nervous when she asked the next question.

'Did he kill them?'

'No. He took the shroud and left.'

'The shroud?'

'The shroud that the tablets were wrapped in.'

She realized what this meant.

'And where are the man and the woman? Did they go to get help?'

'No . . . they thought I was dead.'

Looking down at him, she realized how close to death he was.

'Listen, I'll go and get help.'

'No. You must stop him.'

He grabbed her arm, as if to emphasize the seriousness of the situation. 'He has taken the shroud!'

'I'll go for help,' she said.

But as she looked down at him now, she saw that he was beyond help. She knew that she had to find Goliath and stop him. But how? And where were Daniel and Gabrielle?

It was then that she saw the gun.

Was that the gun that he used to kill Sheikh Ibrahim?

She noticed that it was jammed. But firearms had been part of her Mossad training and she had learnt several methods of clearing a jammed cartridge from the chamber of a semi-automatic. The quickest method was known as tap-rack-bang.

Running on adrenalin as she followed her training to the letter, she tapped the base of the magazine with the palm of her left hand, to make sure it was firmly in place, then racked the slider back in a fast snapping motion to discharge the empty cartridge. There was no need for the bang as she had no reason to fire. But she felt safer having a weapon.

'Goliath! Are you there?'

Sarit froze. It was a man's voice, but there was a strange paradox in the sound. It sounded like the man was shouting, and yet the volume was muted. It was tinny and muffled. And it was coming from inside the cave.

'Goliath!'

No! It was coming from inside Ibrahim's body.

She looked at him in the dim light of the cave, trying to understand. Then she noticed the strange glow coming from beneath his body.

That was when she realized.

She reached under his torso, forcing her hand in deeper against the weight of his body. She had to use her other hand to lift him slightly before she was able to extricate the mobile phone that he had fallen on.

She raised the phone to her ear.

'Goliath!' the voice said again.

'Hallo,' she replied.

'Who is this?'

'My name is Siobhan. Who are you?'

The line went silent. She looked at the phone and saw that the battery was down to 3% – too little to make a call. Any minute it would die completely. But before it did, she checked the number: +1 202 . . .

She didn't know all the US regional phone codes, but there were a few that stuck in her memory. 212 – New York City, or at least Manhattan. 213 – Los Angeles. And 202 – *Washington DC*.

Senator Morris. It had to be.

She would have liked to follow it up, but right now she didn't have time to find out. She had urgent business to attend to.

Chapter 95

'Now then,' said Professor Fikri, 'what is this fascinating academic matter that you wanted to talk about?'

They were in the office of Hakim Fikri at the University of Jordan, sitting opposite the man who had been entrusted with the task of examining the bones found in the cave at the Snake Monument. A man of average height and build in his forties with a dark, neatly trimmed beard, he had agreed to see them at short notice because of their academic credentials: the world's foremost expert on Semitic languages and a leading Egyptologist who worked closely with Akil Mansoor. They had only revealed this when they arrived at the reception desk, not before. But they had not told him what they wanted to talk about.

'We met a man called Talal Ibrahim,' said Daniel. 'Sheikh Ibrahim.'

Daniel was studying Professor Fikri's face for signs of recognition. There was a slight flicker, but no more than that.

'Oh, yes, Talal. How is he?'

Daniel felt his face flushing. He didn't know what to say.

'He's fine,' said Gabrielle, stepping in to fill the silence. 'He sends his regards.'

'I'll come straight to the point, Professor,' said Daniel.

365

'The reason we're here is because we wanted to ask about the bones.'

This time it was Fikri's face that flushed. 'Bones?'

'We understand that some bones found in Petra were brought here for you to study.'

'Well, quite a number of bones and skeletal remains have been brought here for study,' said Fikri, 'especially from Petra.'

Daniel nodded. 'I know. It's a site of great archaeological importance, and there's a considerable necropolis there. But the bones we're thinking of were found at one particular cave, overlooking the Snake Monument.'

Fikri swallowed nervously and appeared to be looking around the room, almost as if he wanted to run out.

'There are so many cases I deal with. I'd have to look it up. I can't remember that one. I'm sure it can't have been anything special otherwise I would have done.'

Daniel knew that he was lying. Even apart from his manner it made no sense. An academic would *love* to make a big find and publish a major paper on the subject. And Sheikh Ibrahim had told them of how cagey Fikri had become.

But what was he afraid of?

Daniel decided to help the professor to open up by asking a few leading questions.

'Presumably you were going to conduct radiocarbon tests to date the bones, DNA tests to determine the ethnicity and maybe a magnetic imaging scan to determine possible causes of death?'

'I think you've been reading too many thrillers,' said Fikri with a forced smile. 'An NMR scan can only reveal physical and anatomical characteristics. Unless the cause of death was violence or injury such tests are pretty much useless.'

'And *was* the cause of death violence or injury?' asked Daniel.

'No.'

'Were there any other tests you could do to determine cause of death?'

'We took a couple of tooth and gum samples for toxicology and came up negative. But that doesn't rule out poisoning, of course. Not all poisons would show.'

'I was wondering why nothing has been published about those bones?'

'It wasn't all that interesting.'

'But Sheikh Ibrahim told us that last time he asked you about it you didn't even want to *discuss* the subject.'

'Come on now, Professor Klein. You know how cagey we academics can be before we publish our results.'

'Yes, but you *didn't* publish your results. I could understand if that was the silence before publication of a paper discussing the subject, but you said yourself it wasn't that interesting.'

'Look . . .' he was *very* nervous, 'there are some things that are better not to talk about.'

Gabrielle stepped in. 'Could I ask you point-blank, Professor Fikri: is there any chance that these are the bones of the biblical figure Moses?'

'I think you may be getting a little carried away, Miss Gusack.'

Daniel expected her to quibble over her title. But this time she ignored it completely.

'We were told that there are local traditions linking Petra to the encampment of the Israelites before they entered the land of Canaan. Pharaoh's Column, the Valley of Moses, Mount Aaron.'

'I know that,' he said stiffly, 'but you're serious scholars. Those local legends are based on a somewhat literalistic inter-pretation of the Bible – not to mention a desire to pander to Western tourists.'

Daniel was hoping that Gabrielle would resist the temptation to mention *The Book of the Wars of the Lord*.

'But even if you *don't* take it literally,' said Gabrielle, 'there still must have been a kernel of truth in it. In the ancient times people made up stories as stylized accounts of real events. And that includes the possibility of a biblical character called Moses, or with some similar name.'

Fikri squirmed. 'Well, I suppose they *could* be the bones of the biblical Moses, but the only way we could know for sure is by doing a DNA comparison between them and a known relative of Moses. And when I last checked there weren't any.'

It was a crude attempt to use sarcasm to brush off their probing questions. But Daniel wasn't convinced. And he knew that neither was Gabrielle. He decided to leave it to her.

'No, but you could have compared the DNA to various ethnic groups – including Jews.'

Fikri seemed to grow bolder at this. 'As a matter of fact, we did. And the DNA didn't match the genetic types that we normally associate with Jews. It was actually more like the genotype we associate with Egyptians. Maybe it was a refugee from Egypt.'

Fikri was smiling at his own sarcasm. Daniel was not. Gabrielle however *was* smiling, because of the full implications of what Fikri had intended as a brush-off.

'And what about the age?' asked Daniel.

'It was an old man,' Fikri responded. 'Surprisingly old, considering that human lifespan was shorter in those days. But that still doesn't make it Moses.'

'Sorry, that wasn't what I meant. I was asking about the age of the bones. How long ago are they from?'

'Well, we—'

Fikri broke off, realizing that he was doing the very thing that he had tried so hard *not* to do: talk about it. But the looks on their faces made it clear that he had passed the point of no return. He had already implied that the bones were old by using the phrase 'in those days'.

'We carbon dated them to around 1200 BC.'

Daniel decided to summarize. 'So let me get this straight. You found the bones of someone of probable Egyptian origin—'

'*Possible* Egyptian origin. Probable is too strong a word.'

'*Possible* Egyptian origin . . . in a cave in Petra in an area associated with the Israelites. And the bones date back to the late Bronze Age – exactly the time associated with the biblical Exodus and the Israelite conquest of Canaan.'

'Yes. But I wasn't going to make an ass of myself by publishing a paper saying we've found Moses.'

Daniel decided to back off slightly. He was in a foreign country, sitting in the office of a leading professor of medical pathology who had been kind enough to give him time at very short notice. It was not Daniel's place to question the probity or veracity of his host, but he hadn't come all this way just to draw a blank. Over the last few weeks, he had been locked in a cave, shot at, threatened by an oversized lunatic and now he was on the verge of making a major discovery. He *had* to find out the rest – especially considering how high the stakes were.

'Could I ask you about the cause of death?'

'As I said, we conducted various tests, but there are no guarantees that one can find the cause of death in three-thousand-year-old bones.'

Daniel's alertness was highly tuned by now and he picked up on a curious omission in Fikri's statement: he hadn't actually said that he had *failed* to establish the cause of death. He had merely alluded to the *difficulty* of the task.

But Daniel also remembered something he had read from the clay tablets . . . *we were afflicted with boils on our skin that looked like fiery snakes.*

He decided to take the bull by the horns. 'We believe that he may have died of some disease . . . possibly a disease that produced red elongated lesions.'

Fikri froze. 'How could you possibly know that?'

Daniel knew that he had him. Now he had to press home his advantage. 'Suffice it to say that we do.'

'Then you'll also know that the last thing we need is to encourage tourists to start swarming over the area.'

'I don't quite follow your logic, Professor.'

'We found spores in the linen shroud that the bones were wrapped in. We studied them under the microscope and they were in stasis – but we know that spores can remain in stasis for tens or even hundreds of years.'

Daniel was not a doctor, but as a bit of a renaissance man he had some medical knowledge and he knew that stasis was a kind of state of suspended animation that spores and certain other biological matter could stay in for a long time.

'We'd already carbon dated the bones and we've never seen cases of spores remaining in stasis for three thousand years. But we couldn't rule out the possibility. So we tested them in controlled conditions and discovered that there were two factors that kept them in stasis: heat and dryness. The hot, dry conditions of Petra made it ideal for keeping the spores in stasis. But if their temperature was lowered and they were exposed to water – fresh water, that is, or even just humidity – they could be reactivated and turned into the pathogenic bacilli.'

'The disease-causing bacteria,' Daniel said to Gabrielle, much to her annoyance. He had to know more. 'How virulent was it?'

'Well, we could hardly test it on people. But we did some toxicity tests on rhesus monkeys and it was fatal in the cases of the old, the young and the frail.'

'So it wasn't fatal in healthy adults,' said Gabrielle.

'In some cases them too.'

'And how contagious was it?'

'We didn't do any epidemiology trials. But any disease spread by spores is going to be highly contagious. We knew enough and so we froze a few samples and then destroyed the shroud.'

'And the bones?'

'What about them?'

'Did you destroy them?'

'We considered them important enough to preserve . . . so we irradiated them.'

'And where are they now?'

'I've said all I can say.'

He got up from his desk and made it clear that he meant not only with regard to that last question but with regard to this entire conversation. Daniel sensed that Gabrielle wanted to press on further, but he also sensed that this was not a good idea. They had gone as far as they could and would not get any more useful information from this man. If they pushed their luck, there was a danger of them outstaying their welcome and possibly getting themselves into trouble.

'Well, thank you, Professor Fikri,' said Daniel, standing up and seizing the initiative back from Gabrielle. 'You've been most helpful.'

Gabrielle, who had remained seated, looked daggers at Daniel. Finally, she stood up and muttered a polite thank you.

Chapter 96

Goliath had taken the bus from Petra back to Amman, knowing that if he took the car, Klein and Gusack could report it to the police and they would be on the lookout for the vehicle. It wouldn't be so easy to catch him on a tourist bus packed with other people.

His plan had been to hire a car to drive back across the King Hussein Bridge and then to Israel's main Ayalon Highway. However, he was told that because today was Friday, the King Hussein Bridge was closed from midday and would not reopen till Sunday. That left him with a problem. The longer he waited around, the greater the likelihood that he would be stopped.

And he had no intention of being stopped.

Then someone told him that there was another way of getting into Israel – if he hurried.

Chapter 97

'The spores must have got reactivated at Petra and become even more virulent,' said Daniel. 'And the so-called fiery snakes in the Bible that bit the Israelites were actually snake-like boils that infested their skin.'

They were driving from Amman to the King Hussein Bridge, Gabrielle at the wheel.

'But *why* would the spores come out of stasis? Petra's a pretty hot dry place—'

'Wait a minute, I have an idea.'

He opened the glove compartment and took out a compact book. It was a copy of the Bible that Daniel had bought in Israel and had been keeping with him for reference. He started thumbing through it.

'Are you looking for anything in particular?'

'Numbers 21. Oh, yes. Here it is. The Israelites are complaining about not having any water.'

'Was there ever a time when the Israelites *didn't* complain?'

This brought a laugh from Daniel. 'Not then and not now!'

Gabrielle remained surprisingly straight-faced at his levity. 'As if *they're* the ones who have something to complain about,' she responded, under her breath. 'Anyway, what was it about that passage that interested you so much?'

'Let me read it to you.'

And Moses and Aaron gathered the people before the rock and he said to them 'Hear me rebels, are we to bring forth water from this rock for you?' And Moses lifted up his hand and smote the rock with his rod twice and water flowed forth in abundance and the congregation and their cattle drank.

'So they may have had the spores on their clothing,' said Gabrielle. 'And all it took was exposure to fresh water and the plague came back.'

'That explains what must have happened at the dig. Presumably there were traces of the spores at the dig site.'

'I must have had some spores on my clothes that infected the curator.'

'Oh my God!'

'What?'

'I've been racking my brains wondering why Goliath wanted the shroud!'

Gabrielle's jaw dropped.

'You mean . . .'

'But who is he planning on using it against?'

'Wait a minute, Daniel. What did he say?'

Daniel searched his memory.

'"I'm going to make the evil usurpers drink the water of death"'.

Suddenly, the car behind started to overtake them. Then Daniel noticed that the woman who was driving it was pointing, and appeared to be mouthing the words 'Pull over.'

Gabrielle wasn't having it, however. She was getting increasingly angry, and the fact that the woman in the other car appeared to be trying to communicate with her only made her angrier.

The other car continued veering right to push them off

the road, and Gabrielle finally snapped. She spun the steering wheel of their much bigger vehicle sharply to the left, side-swiping the smaller car. The trouble was that Gabrielle hadn't given her own vehicle enough time to recover and it ended up skidding to the side of the road.

Gabrielle screamed, but it was Daniel who was flung against the side as the vehicle rolled. By the time it was inverted, the front airbags had inflated, protecting the occupants from any further damage but forcing Gabrielle to stop. All three of them got out aggressively and in the ensuing confrontation Daniel noticed that the woman from the other car was quite attractive.

'What the bloody hell were you trying to do?' he asked.

'I'm sorry,' she said. 'My name is Sarit Shalev. I work with Dov Shamir.'

'You nearly got us *all* killed,' said Gabrielle.

'Like I said, I'm sorry. But I think we have an emergency on our hands.'

Chapter 98

There was a look of solemnity on the faces of Senator Morris and the professor as Audrey entered the library of Morris's house in north-west Washington DC. For some reason, the senator had called this meeting in his home, instead of the Capitol Building, and Audrey had no wish to rock the boat by questioning him on it.

The professor did not even look up from the cherrywood table, let alone rise to greet her as she approached them. Morris did, but there was a look of sadness in his eyes, as if he had some bad news to tell her.

'Has someone died?' she asked, using the old gambit of humour to divert or soften the tension that confronted her.

'You don't know?' said Professor Tomlinson.

Audrey looked at him with shock and confusion written across her face and then at Morris, hoping for an explanation.

'Sit down,' said Morris softly, indicating the chair that he had pulled out for her.

She sat, as did Morris.

'I tried to call Goliath. He was supposed to be going to Petra.'

'Petra?'

'To get the shroud that *The Book of the Wars of the Lord* was wrapped in.'

'And?' asked Audrey.

'There was someone else there.'

'So?'

'Using his *cell phone!*'

'I . . . I don't understand.'

'He would never give his cell phone away unless he was killed or captured!'

'You mean . . . '

'He means that you *betrayed* us, you bitch!' shouted Professor Tomlinson.

For a second or two, Audrey was afraid. But then she overcame her fear.

'Whatever you think about the Jews, or the Israelis or the Zionists or whatever you call them, you have no right to play God.'

'I *didn't* play God. I am a *servant* of God.'

'And Goliath? Is he a servant of God too? Killing Professor Carmichael who had done us no wrong?'

'Goliath is God's avenging angel.'

'An avenging angel who knows no bounds! Just like *you* know no bounds. Do you really think you have the right to commit genocide?'

'It isn't genocide, it's pest control,' said Morris. 'You could call it de-lousing.'

'You're sick,' said Audrey.

'*At least he isn't a traitor!*' shouted the professor, almost rising out of his seat towards Audrey.

Morris stayed the older man with a gesture of his palm, a feeble sign of his ailing authority. Audrey wasn't afraid of the professor's anger, but she wanted to know more. She wanted to understand what Morris was telling her.

'What did they offer you?' asked the senator. 'Thirty pieces of silver?'

'Oh, I didn't do it for money. I did it because I didn't like what you were doing – didn't like what my husband was doing.'

'I never trusted you!'

'And you were right. I *was* against you the whole time. Only it took me a while to realize how right I was.'

'You prefer to sit back while those pasty-faced mongrels take over the world.'

'Oh, not *that* old chestnut again.'

'You think it's just a myth? The World Trade Center, the Kennedy assassination—'

Audrey burst out laughing. 'My God! You really believe your own bullshit! I thought you just sold it to the rednecks. I didn't think you actually bought it yourself.'

'And what about all the things you can't deny? Bernie Madoff, Ivan Boesky, Michael Milken—'

'Albert Einstein, Ernst Boris Chain, Yehudi Menuhin, Kirk Douglas—'

'What's *that* got to do with it?' shouted Tomlinson angrily.

'You think you're the only one who can memorize a string of names and spit them out on demand? Save the demagoguery for the men in white sheets!'

'Well, what does *your* list prove? It's easy enough to achieve success when you run the world!'

'Oh yeah! And what does *your* list prove? That a few Jews have broken the rules? I could just as easily throw *other* names at you . . . like Charles Manson, Sirhan Sirhan, Timothy McVeigh. But what does it prove? That you can use a handful of facts to sell a conspiracy theory? I'm in the newspaper business, buddy! I could write the book on that!'

'*You're one of them!*' said the professor.

'One of whom, for God's sake? There is no *them*. It's just a paranoid myth that power-hungry demagogues feed the people when they're outside of government.'

'Next you're gonna say there's no *us*? But that's the myth that the people on the *inside* like to spread when they've got their snouts in the public trough.'

'So what's the story, Paul? You wanna fight corruption? Then go fight corruption! But don't use it as an excuse for hate-mongering.'

Paul Tomlinson was looking at her as if seeing her for the first time. He had always doubted the strength of her commitment to the cause. He knew that she could never be quite as committed as her husband. He'd put that down to her being a woman. He thought that she was merely a bit wishy-washy. But now he realized that it was not a case of her being too soft. She was simply an enemy of their cause. She had never been one of them.

And she had just admitted that it had been she who told the Israelis about Goliath. *She* had betrayed them and got Goliath killed, and now she was sitting here taunting them with her treachery . . . mocking them for their credulity . . . gloating over her betrayal of their righteous cause. It was all too much for Professor Tomlinson to take. He stood up and moved towards her menacingly, with hatred in his eyes.

Chapter 99

'What do you mean "an emergency"? Daniel asked, although he already had some idea.

Sarit was looking at them intently, like she had a lot to say and very little time in which to say it. The sinking sun made her shadow look ridiculously long.

'The man who locked you in the tomb – the man who forced you to go to the cave in Petra. He was working for an organization that hates Israel and the Jewish people.'

'Look, there's no point beating about the bush,' said Daniel. 'We know about the spores.'

'Then you know what Goliath is planning to do.'

'Goliath?' Gabrielle echoed, unable to suppress the smile.

'That was his code name. The people he's working for wanted to use the spores for a terrorist attack on Israel. You may not know this, but they sent Goliath to get a sample of that boy, Joel's clothes from the hospital. He failed. And he also wanted to get a sample of *your* clothes when he stole the jeep after locking you in the tomb. I put a stop to that, but I understand that he's got the shroud now.'

'How do you know?' Gabrielle challenged.

'Sheikh Ibrahim told me.'

'He's still alive?'

'Not any more. But he told me that Goliath took the linen

shroud that the tablets were wrapped in and that means he intends to use it. We need to warn the Israeli authorities. The battery on my mobile phone died. I found the one Goliath dropped in the cave, but the battery's run out on that one too.'

Daniel took out his mobile and was frantically trying to get it to work.

'Damn,' he said. 'Mine's out of juice as well.'

They looked over at Gabrielle. She shook her head.

'If we drive fast we might be able to make it to the King Hussein Bridge just after him,' said Daniel. 'Then we can warn the authorities.'

Sarit was shaking her head.

'It's Friday. The bridge closes at lunchtime.'

'Then he must be stuck on this side too,' Daniel replied with relief.

'Not necessarily,' Sarit contradicted. 'There are two other crossings that are open until eight: the Yitzhak Rabin Crossing in the south and the Nahar Yarden Crossing in the north.'

'He left us in Petra,' said Gabrielle. 'So he probably took the one in the south.'

'Damn!' shouted Sarit. 'That means he's probably in Israel already. We have to get to a phone! We have to warn them!'

Then Daniel remembered something.

'I don't know if this helps, but there was something he said when he took the shroud.'

'What?' asked Sarit.

'He said: "I'm going to make the evil usurpers drink the water of death".'

Sarit thought about this for about half a minute. Then it suddenly hit her.

'Of course!'

'What?' asked Daniel and Gabrielle in unison.

'You know what the main reservoir for the State of Israel is?'

'No,' said Daniel.

'The Sea of Galilee.'

Chapter 100

Recognizing the encroaching danger in the professor's approach, Audrey stood up too.

'No, Paul,' cried Senator Morris. 'Not here!'

Tomlinson pushed Audrey against the wall. But he hadn't noticed the lamp with the heavy bronze base on the side table. Even in the agony of Tomlinson's stranglehold, Audrey had the presence of mind to grab the lamp with one hand and smash it down on the professor's head.

She only had to do it once and her attacker fell to the ground in a lifeless heap. As the lifeblood returned to her head, her arm dropped to her side and she let the lamp slip from her hand. It landed on the floor with a thud.

Realizing what she had done – what she had been obliged to do – she turned to the senator.

'You killed him.'

'It was self-defence.'

'What are you going to do?' he asked weakly.

'What I should have done from the beginning: tell the truth.'

'You're going to tell them about the New Covenant?'

'Yes . . . both the police and my readers.'

'But that'll destroy us.'

'I certainly hope so, Arthur. I certainly hope so.'

For a moment, she wasn't sure she had said the right thing. Senator Morris was capable of anger himself. She had seen that in the past. But as she saw the faraway look in his eyes, she realized that his anger had spent itself.

Barely a couple of seconds later, he broke down in tears.

'My daughter,' he sobbed.

'Jane? What about her?'

'She died . . . of the plague.'

Finally Audrey mellowed slightly.

'I'm sorry.'

She was tempted to remind the senator that it was he who had sent his daughter on the dig. It was he who had used her for his own means. He had told her to get a sample of Joel's clothes and if he thought that they contained the spores then it meant he was ready to risk her life for his evil cause. Like Agamemnon sacrificing Iphigenia to get wind for the sails of his ships in the war against Troy.

There was no reason to sympathize with him. With Jane perhaps – but not with Morris.

But in an instant, all that was swept into irrelevance as the senator clutched his chest and fell to the floor, writhing in agony.

Chapter 101

'So what is this organization that hates Israel and the Jews so much?' asked Gabrielle.

Abandoning the car that Gabrielle had been driving, they had piled into Sarit's and were heading north, with the sun low in the sky to their left.

'They're called the New Covenant and it isn't only Israel and the Jews. It's the West in general. They hate the United States. They hate Britain. They hate blacks. They hate liberals.'

'So it's not Islamic extremists then?' asked Daniel.

'No, nothing like that. More like those racist rednecks that support the Ku Klux Klan and think there's a Jewish conspiracy running the world. But their leaders aren't stupid. They're smart people who pander to gullible followers.'

'So why hasn't anything been done about them?' asked Daniel. 'I mean if you know who they are.'

'Well, we don't know who *all* of them are. They operate within a cell structure. But we've built up a pretty good picture and we're keeping tabs on them – along with the FBI and various other law enforcement agencies.'

'But I mean why haven't they been prosecuted on terrorism charges?'

'Well, up until now they've been mostly a talkshop. Big on rhetoric but nothing else. They spread stories over the

Internet and in newspapers when they can. They talk the talk but they seldom walk the walk. Only now it's different. They decided to try and get their hands on the spores that caused an ancient plague and use them to destroy Israel.'

'But how did they *know* about the spores?' asked Daniel. 'I mean the people that this . . . Goliath was working for?'

'One of the members of the New Covenant is a professor of Linguistics or something like that. He was asked to peer review a paper by Harrison Carmichael in which he essentially deciphered Proto-Sinaitic script.'

'He told me about it . . . sort of . . . but I didn't take him seriously at first.'

'That's understandable. He was suffering from the early stages of Alzheimer's disease. But that didn't detract from his intellectual powers. He had, in fact, translated *The Book of the Straight*.'

'That's *impossible*!' said Gabrielle. 'How could he even have got hold of a copy? They only took it out of its hiding place when we persuaded the Samaritans and the Israel Antiquities Authority to let us. And they said it had been kept there for a couple of centuries.'

'It may have been at that particular hiding place for a couple of centuries, but it had been taken out some time in the last couple of hundred years and copied on to parchment. We know that because your uncle *had* that parchment copy. We believe that he'd had it for a few decades and that he'd been working on it ever since. But he didn't have what you and Professor Klein here had to help you.'

'What do you mean?' asked Gabrielle.

'I understand from what you told my colleague in Herzliya that you had the benefit of other texts that you could compare to their biblical equivalent. Your uncle didn't have that. So it obviously took him a lot longer. But he got there first.'

'Then why didn't he publish?' asked Gabrielle.

'Because of that professor – the one who peer reviewed it. He used his prestige to delay publication.'

'But if they were anti-Israel why did they want to stop the paper being published?'

'Because they wanted to draw on the information inside it. The paper revealed the disease that afflicted the Israelites. They figured out from the contents that it was a spore-borne disease. They saw the possibility of getting the spores and using them against Israel, so they bided their time.'

Now Daniel was even more confused. 'But the information about the plague was in *The Book of the Wars of the Lord*, not *The Book of the Straight*. And it was pretty minimalistic information.'

Sarit was shaking her head. 'It was in *The Book of the Straight* too – and in far greater detail.'

An uneasy silence settled over them, as Daniel had a deeply discomforting thought.

Chapter 102

'It says that the crossing is open till eight!' Goliath was shouting, pointing at the sign.

He was at what the Jordanians call the 'Sheikh Hussein Crossing' between Jordan and the north of Israel.

'You have to arrive an hour before,' the middle-aged Jordanian official was explaining.

'But this is an emergency!' Goliath pleaded, not sure of what he would say if they asked him what he meant. 'And it's not like there's a whole long queue. The hour before is presumably to give you time to do the paperwork.'

Friday is the Islamic day of rest and in Israel everything stops early on Friday in order to enable Jews to prepare for the Jewish day of rest which commences half an hour before sunset on Friday night and carries on until sunset the next day. It was now half past seven and the sun had just set.

'I could let you through on this side, but the Israelis won't let you through.'

'Can't you at least ask them? My sister is sick. I just had a call from my brother-in-law. I was visiting Petra and I was due back in a few days, but I got a call and he told me to come back. The other bridge was closed so I thought it was better to come this way. I am not even sure if she is in a hospital now because I lost my phone. All I know is—'

'Wait a minute,' said the Jordanian official.

He walked off and spoke to a colleague. Then he walked over to the Israeli side and spoke to several of their officials. The talk seemed to last for ages. When the official finally came back he was smiling.

'Okay. You can go through.'

Chapter 103

'How far are we?' asked Daniel.

'We're nearly there. When we get to the crossing, let me do the talking.'

'Is there likely to be a problem?' asked Daniel.

'Strictly speaking we're too late. But leave it to me.'

Daniel noticed that Gabrielle had been strangely silent for most of the journey. It was as if Sarit's very presence bothered her. And because they were in Sarit's car, it meant that Sarit was in control.

'There's something I don't understand,' said Daniel. 'You said that they knew about the spores from Harrison Carmichael's translation of the *Book of the Straight*.'

'Yes.'

'Well, I could understand if you said, *The Book of the Wars of the Lord*. I found some references to it there. But we've just translated the *Book of the Straight* and it didn't have anything about that. It didn't even mention the plagues at all. It described a power struggle in Egypt covering the period of Joseph and his son, when the Israelites were first enslaved.'

'Look, I'm not an expert in biblical history or anything like that,' said Sarit. 'I can only tell you what I know from my briefing. Carmichael obtained a parchment copy, translated it after many years of effort and it was sent for peer review. The professor delayed publication and passed on the information to the rest of his cell and they've been sitting on it because they didn't know where to look for traces of the spores.'

'What do you mean sitting on it?'

'Well, the manuscript described how the plague swept through the Israelites, prompting their decision to abandon the place where they were staying and cross into the land of Canaan. But it didn't say where exactly they'd been staying on the other side of the Jordan River, so the New Covenant didn't know where to look and couldn't make much use of the information. But once that dig started in Sinai, they saw a possibility. They figured that the Israelites must have been carrying the spores on their clothes even before the outbreak, because of the sixth plague that affected the Egyptians.'

'And that's why the volunteers and the curator got ill,' said Daniel.

'Exactly,' Sarit replied. 'They were monitoring the dig and they got all excited when the stones were found. That implied that it was a site where the Israelites had been. Then when the kid Joel got ill, that confirmed it. From then on, they've been trying to get a sample of the spores and we've been trying to stop them. When he locked you in the cave, it wasn't you he was after, it was your spare clothes in your bags. You were merely expendable.'

Daniel was looking at Gabrielle inquisitively.

'Gaby?'

'*What?*'

Daniel couldn't tell if the tone was aggressive or defensive – maybe the former to cover the latter. But he noticed a single tear on one of her cheeks.

'You kept feeding me clues.'

'What?' Gabrielle replied.

'When we were trying to identify the papyrus from the museum in Cairo, you suggested that if it wasn't the Aswan High Dam then it might be another public works project. That's what pointed me in the direction of the Suez Canal.'

'But it was *you* who suggested Aswan in the first place and *you* who came up with the idea that it was the Song of the Sea.'

'But whenever I faltered, it was always you guiding back to the right path. Before I translated *The Book of the Straight*, there was a brief moment when you handled the clay jar container and I remember it very briefly disappeared from view.'

He had been hoping – *praying* – that he was wrong. But the fleeting look of fear on Gabrielle's face was enough to tell him that he was right.

'What are you saying, Daniel?'

'I used to be an amateur magician when I was younger, and you also had an interest in the subject for a while.'

'So what are you suggesting? That I magically changed the content of the papyrus?'

'No, Gabrielle. I'm suggesting that you substituted it for a forgery.'

'That's ridiculous! Oh, Danny, you can't possibly believe that!'

Her tone had changed. She didn't sound like a confident woman any more. That gushing, eager 'Oh, Danny' was the way she used to talk as an overenthusiastic teenager.

'Can't I? It wouldn't have been so difficult for someone skilled in sleight of hand to make that substitution.'

'No, but first they'd've needed something to substitute. In order to slip in a forgery, there first has to be a forgery to substitute.'

'After I deciphered the script, after we came to Israel, we had enough time for you to create a forgery.'

'On an ancient papyrus?'

'I've heard of cases where they found unused or blank ancient papyri in Egypt. With your knowledge and prestige it wouldn't have been hard for you to get hold of one. In fact, that would have given you even longer to work on the forgery.'

'You're forgetting, Daniel, that we jumped off the boat and arrived on that Israeli gunboat wearing nothing but swimsuits. That means I'd've had to get the ancient papyrus here in Israel. And as far as I know, you don't have ancient papyri in Israel. Parchment, yes. Papyrus, no.'

Daniel thought about this for quite some time. Then he remembered. 'The snorkel! I wondered why you needed it. And then when we jumped into the water, you had it but didn't use it. You're a competitive swimmer and if anything *I* would have needed it. I reckon it has a one-way valve and a stopper. You must have rolled up the papyrus and put it in there.'

Gabrielle smiled. 'You're very clever, Daniel. You've got it all figured out.'

'Look, I don't care about your seedy little academic secrets,' said Sarit. 'What you professors get up to in your ivory towers is the least of my concerns. But that's the border crossing ahead and I need to stay focused, so I'd be grateful if you two would cool it.'

Chapter 104

Goliath had made it into Israel and the Sea of Galilee lay ahead of him, illuminated by the light of the three-quarter moon.

Senator Morris had told him that it was the main national reservoir for the State of Israel. It had been greatly depleted over the past ten years due to drought and this was evident from the low water level and the marks around it. But that was no concern of Goliath's. The suffering of Israel meant nothing to him. Indeed he was now going to put them out of their misery.

He knew that any place in the lake was as good as any other. It was fresh water and it would bring the spores to life, producing the bacteria that would reproduce and multiply and be drunk by the Israeli population until they were all infected.

He wasn't sure if the purification process for the water would kill the bacteria but even if it did that was no matter. Fish from the lake, including the famous 'St Peter's fish' – unique to the Sea of Galilee – were a staple to many Israelis, especially in the north.

Once in the food chain, it would spread.

So he drove to the lake. He wondered where St Peter had operated from. That would have some symbolism, he thought. But he didn't know where that was and in any case it would be hard to find in the dark. Finally he set his sights on a point ahead where the road came closest to the lake itself.

That was where he would do it.

Chapter 105

While Daniel and Gabrielle remained in the car, Sarit had gone into the terminal on the Jordanian side and there had been some frantic talking and gesticulating. They had signalled some people over from the Israeli side and a whole group of them were engaged in earnest conversation, dominated by Mediterranean-style gesticulation which could variously be a sign of anger, concern or just a desire to be heard.

Gabrielle sat there in tense silence. But Daniel felt betrayed. He wanted answers.

'The only thing I don't understand is why.'

'I'm surprised you haven't figured it out. I like the idea of cutting your ethno-religious tribe down to size.'

'Ethno-religious tribe?' asked Daniel, aghast.

'Your snobbish little closed shop whose members think they're the bee's knees and that you can only join by maternal inheritance. Only it's all built on myth. The descendants of a smooth-talking Syrian soldier who helped a usurper steal the Egyptian throne from his brother. His son, a murderer, adulterer and incestuous pervert who slept with his daughter and then married his granddaughter to steal the throne? So much for your holier than thou, ethno-religious club.'

'Except that your version is an even bigger fake, isn't it?'

'Maybe, but it fits the character of your people. I should

have known even as a kid that you'd never be interested in a *shiksa*.'

Daniel noticed the tears welling up in Gabrielle's eyes and he realized that there were things in her heart and mind that had been buried there for a long time.

'Is that what it's all about? Some unrequited schoolgirl crush?'

'Don't flatter yourself, Danny! Any feelings I had for you died a long time ago.'

He was tempted to remind her about her drunken behaviour a few weeks ago. But that would have been twisting the knife – something he was loath to do.

'You were fifteen when we met. It wasn't my religion that stood in the way. Hell, I don't even *have* a religion, except in name. It was my sense of responsibility.'

'Oh, you have such a great sense of propriety, don't you? But only on personal matters. Not on the issues that really count!'

'What are you talking about?'

'Do you remember when we worked together on a dig in Jerusalem two years ago?'

He looked at her, confused. 'Yes. What about it?'

'We didn't dig on Friday or Saturday. One Friday morning I was in an expanding Jewish suburb where building work was taking place, and there was this bulldozer and it was knocking down some olive trees that belonged to the nearby Arab village. The bulldozer was being driven by a soldier. I asked why they were doing it and someone told me that the olive trees were being used as cover for children to throw stones at cars driven by people from the Jewish neighbourhood. And there was this kid – she couldn't have been more than four or five – standing in front of the bulldozer . . .' The tears were welling up in her eyes again. 'And the

397

bulldozer . . . it wouldn't stop . . . and I just stood there frozen . . . too frozen to speak . . . it wouldn't stop . . . and the girl's mother was screaming . . . and *I* was screaming in my mind . . . and it wouldn't stop . . .'

She broke down in hysterical tears.

Daniel moved towards her and tried to put a comforting arm around her, but she brushed him off.

'Don't touch me! If you want to make a moral stand, make it over injustices like that instead of remaining silent!'

There were a thousand things he could say. About the injustices on the other side too. About not judging a nation by individual instances, even if they could be strung together to present a negative picture. But none of that was a valid answer to her criticism. If that child was killed in the way she said and if the driver of the bulldozer was not held to account, then a grievous wrong had been done.

Sarit returned. Ignoring Gabrielle's tearful hysterics – or at least pretending to – she got back into the car and drove it across the border into Israel.

'I've notified the authorities in Israel and they'll be sending up flares and soldiers to look out for him. But I'd like us to keep driving around the lake in case we see him. We're the only ones who know what he looks like.'

Chapter 106

Goliath pulled up and got out of the car. He was at the spot. He took the white linen shroud and began walking to the water's edge. There were people about, but what did it matter? They were hardly going to stop him throwing a piece of white linen into the lake.

He felt gripped by that sensation of the power that he had whenever he killed someone: that feeling of being in control. That feeling that he was doing God's work for which he would be richly rewarded, if not in this life then in the next.

He was at the water's edge. Now all he had to do was throw it.

About fifty yards away, Sarit had seen him. Although she couldn't make out the facial features from this distance, the height made him unmistakable. She slammed on the brakes, causing the car to skid to a halt.

She regretted this because the noise caused Goliath to turn his head and see them. But in the distance – and in the darkness – all he could see was the car, not its occupants. Her Mossad training had included shooting *through* a car window from the inside – a skill that is learned by only the most elite of fighting forces.

She had aimed for the torso, the broadest part of the body – and Goliath was a big target. So she knew she had hit him with her 'double tap' even before he clutched his chest and staggered backwards. But Goliath was a strong man, and he was down but not out. She leapt out of the car intending to finish him off with a second shot. Gabrielle and Daniel followed her out and as she levelled the gun for the coup de grâce, Gabrielle jumped on her and tried to grab the gun, both women crashing to the ground.

Unsure of what was happening or why, Sarit threw the gun clear, giving her attacker a choice of whether to go for the gun or fight her.

Daniel saw what was happening in horror and unlike Sarit he had at least some idea of the reason.

But could Gabrielle be that mad? That far gone?

The question was answered as Sarit staggered to her feet and tried to run towards the gun. Gabrielle got up and jumped on Sarit again, this time sending the pair of them tumbling into the water where Gabrielle's advantage in size was compounded by her strength built up through competitive swimming.

Less than a second later, Gabrielle's powerful arms forced Sarit into a kneeling position and began thrusting her face under the water, choking the life out of her.

Daniel was about to intervene, but then he saw something that filled him with terror.

Less than fifty yards away, Goliath had rallied his strength and was now limping slowly forward once again towards the water's edge a few yards away. In a matter of seconds, he would be in a position to drop the shroud into the water and it would be the end of the State of Israel and its people: Jews and Arabs.

Daniel knew that the danger to Israel outweighed the danger to Sarit and he did the only thing he could do. He sprinted towards Goliath.

The giant turned round just in time to see Daniel closing the last few yards and although he could have thrown the shroud in the water quite easily, a sense of anger and pride prompted him to turn to Daniel instead to fight him.

Daniel threw himself on to Goliath and tried to wrestle him to the ground, but even though Goliath was wounded, he was still too strong. The giant tried to get him in one of his infamous headlocks but the one thing Daniel had going for him was that he had the inside position. This made it harder for Goliath to work his set piece.

More importantly, Daniel noticed that Goliath had dropped the shroud.

Realizing that his own life too was less important than that of a nation, he put his foot on the shroud and with a scraping motion kicked it backwards so that it was behind both of them.

Sarit's lungs were filling up with water and she could feel her consciousness slipping away. Her head was thrashing this way and that as she struggled to come to the surface. Somehow she managed to force her head above water long enough to take a breath, but first she had to expel the water from her lungs. She coughed and choked and sputtered, spurting out some of the water, but not all of it.

And as she drew in her breath, the strong hands and arms of Gabrielle forced her under the water yet again. This time, she managed to hold her breath and not take in any more water. But she didn't know how long she could hold out. She had been well aware, throughout this assignment, that Goliath was a dangerous adversary. But now as she felt herself slipping into unconsciousness, she remembered that Gabrielle was a former competitive swimmer.

Think, Sarit, think!

Sarit was half a head shorter and not nearly as strong. But she *was* trained. Suddenly, all her training came back to her. Instead of her futile, feeble efforts to pull Gabrielle's hands away, she realized she needed to do an inside sweep. The problem was that she was practically kneeling and couldn't get the leverage.

Nevertheless, she clenched her fists, inserted her arms inside Gabrielle's grip and swept upward and outward with an almighty thrust. Despite the power of the move, it failed to break Gabrielle's grip, accomplishing at most a slight loosening of the assailant's fingers. But that was enough. It made Sarit realize that she had a second line of attack.

Lightning fast, she delivered a vicious punch between Gabrielle's legs. A cry of pain went up from the Austrian woman and at the same time her grip slackened. That was all the opportunity Sarit needed. In a split second, she grabbed Gabrielle's hair and pulled her head forward and downward. At the same time, forcing herself against the pressure of Gabrielle's mighty hands, she managed to lift her own head to deliver a vicious head butt, breaking the blonde's nose.

Gabrielle screamed in pain and anger, for a second time releasing her grip to clutch her broken nose. Sarit leapt to her feet and they stood there eyeball to eyeball in the shallow water. But Sarit realized that she was now in even greater danger.

Wounded animals are the most vicious.

Despite his best efforts Goliath was slowly gaining the upper hand. Daniel realized that any minute now, Goliath would have him in a hold that would enable him to snap his neck.

Desperate to get free, he smashed his elbow into Goliath's ribcage four or five times in rapid succession.

Already in pain from his gunshot wounds, Goliath's grip slackened and Daniel was able to push Goliath's left arm away long enough to duck out of the headlock without breaking his neck. He twisted away sharply and took a stride towards the shroud in the hope of throwing it clear even further, but Goliath twisted round too and dived at him, catching his leg and bringing him down.

Daniel twisted on to his back to free his leg, scooping up the shroud in one hand. But as he retracted his legs and tried to push himself on to his feet, Goliath rose up again and was now poised to dive on top of him, pinning him to the ground.

Meanwhile, Sarit had kept her cool. With Gabrielle clutching her bloody nose, she was momentarily defenceless. Sarit seized upon the opportunity by forming a double-handed grip and delivering a vicious chop to the side of Gabrielle's head, sending her reeling.

Quick as a flash, Sarit took two awkward strides through the shallow water and jumped on Gabrielle from behind. Her plan was to get the blonde into some kind of full nelson and hold her face down on the ground. Unfortunately Gabrielle was too quick and managed to twist away, tearing her shirt in the process.

Gabrielle had only been momentarily dazed by Sarit's unexpectedly effective resistance and now, with renewed strength, she charged at Sarit sending the pair of them reeling and tumbling on to the riverbank where they tore and clawed at each other. Eventually superior strength won out and Gabrielle ended up straddling the hapless Sarit.

Then lights appeared to shine at them out of nowhere.

Gabrielle looked up to see a jeep filled with soldiers. They seemed to be amused by the sight of these two women fighting. Then Sarit took the opportunity to reach up and claw at Gabrielle's eyes. The bigger woman let out a scream and staggered backwards as Sarit leapt to her feet with the last of her strength and pointed to Gabrielle.

'*Hee mehabelet!*' she shouted, meaning, she's a terrorist. Unsure of what to do, but hearing no words of dispute from the bigger woman, the soldiers ran towards them to separate them. Sarit, struggling to regain her breath and composure, half-turned and pointed to Daniel and Goliath.

A malicious smile graced Goliath's lips as he prepared to dive on to Daniel, crushing him beneath his weight. But Daniel had one last trick up his sleeve. His hand groped on the ground for the rock that he had seen nearby. Finally he found it and just as Goliath realized what was happening, Daniel's hand shot out sending the rock smashing into Goliath's face with a velocity that Daniel did not think possible.

The big man let out a cry of pain that sounded like thunder in the night and then fell backward, unconscious.

Seconds later, Daniel got to his feet, holding the shroud and praying that it had not got damp during the incident. Sarit and two of the soldiers came running over.

Ignoring the potential danger from the shroud, Sarit approached him.

'You got it wrong, Daniel. It's supposed to be *David* who uses a stone to defeat Goliath, not Daniel.'

He smiled.

'I guess we'll have to rewrite the Bible.'

Epilogue

A couple of weeks later, on the morning of 19 May, Daniel was in the Old City of Jerusalem at the Western Wall, celebrating *Shavuot*, the Jewish festival that commemorates Moses receiving the Torah.

There were several congregations there, each with their own rabbi. The Wall was not a synagogue, but a place where individuals or groups could pray. Anyone can visit the Wall, but once he had put a *kippa* on his head and a *talis* round his shoulders, he had effectively identified himself as a Jew and was promptly invited to complete a *minyan* or quorum of ten men required by Jewish religious law for group prayers.

Sixty feet above them, on what Jews call the Temple Mount and Muslims call *Haram ash-Sharif*, devout Muslims were praying in the Dome of the Rock and al-Aksa Mosque as well as kneeling on their prayer mats in collective worship all over the site. And in other parts of the Old City, Catholic and Eastern Orthodox Christians were going to church for the matins. The churches were not quite as busy as they had been six days ago on Ascension Thursday, but they would be busy again next Sunday for Whitsun.

But Daniel – ever the academic – had other things on his mind, such as his forthcoming paper on *The Book of the Wars of the Lord* as well as his efforts to secure publication of Harrison Carmichael's paper on *The Book of the Straight*, a copy of which Audrey Milne had managed to find in Senator Morris's home. He had been careful in his own paper to acknowledge Carmichael's prior claim to the decipherment of Proto-Sinaitic script.

The Israelis were still engaged in some delicate negotiations with the Jordanians over ownership of the *Book of the Wars of the Lord*. There had been threats of official diplomatic complaints and there was even a possibility that the Israelis would return the tablets to Jordan. In a way that would be better for Daniel as he might otherwise find himself persona non grata in a number of Arab countries, not to mention a target for arrest on an international warrant for stealing historical artefacts.

One of the things that pleased him was that Akil Mansoor still wanted to work with him on the paper about the finding of the Mosaic tablets. The self-styled 'crusty old Egyptian' had explained to the authorities in his own country how Daniel had tried to help him and nearly got killed because of a big misunderstanding. He knew that he would be going back to Egypt soon, but he felt a tinge of regret about Gabrielle who was now in an Israeli jail.

The health scare had finally abated as Israeli doctors had been able to use the shroud to breed the bacteria *en masse* from the spores and then irradiate them to produce a vaccine.

Goliath had survived, but Daniel was unable to give them much information other than what they already knew about Senator Morris. All Dov Shamir would tell him was that the conspiracy reached all the way up to the 'top of the administration.'

Daniel was snapped out of these thoughts by the sound of revelry as a man he didn't know, but with whom he shared a common bond, raised an open Torah scroll high into the air showing three columns of text. The singing of the congregation had a familiar ring to it.

'And this is the Torah that Moses placed before the Children of Israel . . .'

All of a sudden, Daniel's childhood memories came flooding back to him as he remembered the Hebrew words and added his voice to those of his brothers.

'From the mouth of the Lord and the hand of Moses.'

Killer Reads.com

The one-stop shop for the best in crime and thriller fiction

Be the first to get your hands on the **latest releases, exclusive interviews** and **sneak previews** from your favourite authors.

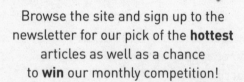

Browse the site and sign up to the newsletter for our pick of the **hottest** articles as well as a chance to **win** our monthly competition!

Writing so good it's criminal